SCORE

Troublemakers & Heartbreakers
book three

mary cain

SCORE

ISBN-13: 979-8-9921606-2-8

First Edition: November 2025

For my friend who's writing a book she's afraid she'll never finish:

I know you will and I know it will be worth the wait.

1

No Mama's Boys

Taylor

TAYLOR SNUCK OUTSIDE, WELCOMING the brisk air and the snowflakes that landed on her face like tiny frozen kisses.

Of all the weddings she'd hosted at the inn, this cozy, fireside ceremony, followed by a quaint reception, ranked as her favorite. It didn't hurt that she adored Brody and Morgan. As a longtime family friend of Brody's, she'd had to juggle being a guest with being a host. Maybe it was that balancing act that had her feeling like if she didn't get a couple of minutes to herself, this tightness in her chest would increase, taking her ability to breathe from difficult to *never gonna happen*.

She sat in a patio chair close to the house, blocking most of the wind so she could light her joint.

Five minutes.

That's all she needed.

Five minutes to recharge with fresh air, quiet, and medicinal marijuana.

The back door creaked. Apparently, it was a no-go on the quiet

She attempted to shrink into the chair, tucking herself into the shadows of the dark corner of the patio.

"Taylor." Nick dragged her name out in a sing-song tone, like he'd done when they'd played hide and seek as kids. His dress shoes crunched against the snow-covered slate.

Shit. He'd been engrossed in a game of pool in the billiards room when she'd decided to slip out. She tried to discreetly stub out her joint against the brick exterior of the house, but what did she do with the smoke in her lungs?

It was cold enough that his breath came out in a white puff as he walked closer, giving her the idea to subtly release the smoke slowly, so it resembled the cloud of air he'd breathed out.

She did not pull it off. Between the marijuana-scented plume surrounding her and the racket of her lungs throwing a tantrum, her chances of fooling Nick dropped to zero.

"Always sneaking off to do bad girl things." He *tsk*ed. His gaze swept over her, lingering on her black opaque tights, red mini skirt, and black four-inch, platform heels. "Risked life and limb for it too, huh?"

The patio had been cleared earlier, but an inch of snow blanketed it now. The snow wasn't the problem. The icy slate under it was. She should have changed into her winter boots, but she'd been in a hurry to get outside, needing the quiet to ebb away her overstimulation.

He pulled up the collar on his gray dress coat. It tapered in at his narrow waist and ended mid-thigh. The appreciation that came with seeing Nick dressed like a grown up didn't sit right with her. She'd seen him in everything from Oshkosh overalls to a Major League Baseball uniform and never felt any type of way about it. Well…the uniform hadn't left her totally unaffected.

Nor had the thirst trap videos he'd been posting online.

But this was *Nick*. Her bestie since she was four. She'd never say he was like a brother to her. Maybe because she was an only child, and she didn't know what that would be like. What they had was deeper than friendship. It was like life had assigned them to each other. Soulmates, maybe, in a platonic way.

Maybe what she needed wasn't a joint and a few minutes of quiet. Maybe it was Nick. She never had to pretend with him. Neither of them did. Being around him felt the same as wearing her favorite hoodie, the one she'd had since high school that'd been washed so many times it was soft, but still cozy.

"Don't be jealous." Teasing him might be her favorite thing in the entire world.

"Me? Jealous?" He scoffed. "Of what?"

"Of me being able to do whatever I want." The flare of his nostrils and tight set of his lips fueled her drive to dent his ego.

He tilted his head. "What can't I do?"

"Eat a greasy cheeseburger and fries and wash it down with a butterscotch shake."

The narrowing of his eyes had her biting the inside of her lip to keep from laughing outright. "I can but choose not to because I feel better and perform better when I eat right."

"Lame," she coughed the word into her fist.

He chuckled, then crouched in front of her, forearms braced across his thighs. With how much he'd had to drink tonight, that level of balance was impressive, but she supposed a major league catcher could hold that position for hours. "It's seventeen degrees and you came outside in a mini skirt and stilettos. Why?"

She pressed her knees tighter together. "I'm catching a buzz. Obviously."

"I know you get overstimulated and need to isolate. I'm drunk, not braindead."

"Well, if you know why I'm out here, then why did you ask?"

He ran his hands up and down the backs of her calves. The warmth against her chilled skin caused prickles. "Because there's more going on. I can always feel it when you're bottling something up."

There *was* something bothering her beyond simple overstimulation, but the only way she could explain it was that she was bothered that she wasn't bothered. Her indifference to her future concerned her. Every one of her friends looked forward to something—a career, traveling, getting married, having babies. Taylor wasn't against those things, but she also didn't crave them. She'd wanted to turn her great aunt's mansion into an inn. Now that she'd done that, she was coasting, no destination in mind, no rush to get anywhere.

She closed her eyes and sighed. "Do you think there's something wrong with someone if they neither look forward to or dread the future? If they just sort of…exist?"

"Yes. Sounds sociopathic."

Her eyes flew open.

He grinned, and the moonlight, reflected by the snow-covered ground, highlighted the angles of his face. Even in the dark, his blue eyes shone brightly as he stared at her. He trailed his big hands up, wrapping his fingers around the top of her calves and sweeping his thumbs across the spot below her knees. "Want to know what I really think? I think more people should be like that. Content. Living in the present. Having gratitude for what they've achieved instead of onto the next bigger and better thing."

"But what if life leaves them behind? What if they end up alone because of it?"

"You're not going to be alone," he said, his voice huffy.

"I wasn't talking about me."

He pulled a flask from inside his coat, but his other hand remained on her leg. He offered the flask to her, and when she declined, he twisted off the cap with his thumb and took a swig, then slipped it back inside his coat. "Maybe this person you're talking about *who definitely isn't you* doesn't want more right now because whatever they're meant for isn't a possibility yet."

Taylor pressed her brows together. "You think I'm meant for something? Like a destiny? I didn't know you believed in that kind of thing."

"We're not talking about *you*, Taylor." He sighed loudly, like his patience was slipping, but the amusement in his eyes couldn't be missed, even with only moonlight illuminating his face. "But yeah, I think the universe has designs for each of us."

"I don't." Her declaration came out flat and coated in pessimism. Sure, she could get down with the idea that she and Nick were soulmates... soulfriends? But she had freewill and didn't think her whole life had been mapped out ahead of time.

Every trace of merriment left his expression. "Jeez, Taylor. When did you get so jaded?"

That was probably a rhetorical question, but either way, she didn't have an answer—no, not true. She had no control over the disillusionment that had changed everything for her. She could, however, spare Nick. Sometimes, she fantasized about what she'd be like had she been left in the dark. Maybe that'd be better than enduring this chronic disappointment. Maybe not. All she knew was that she loved Nick too much to weigh him down with something he couldn't do anything about.

"Are you"—he skimmed his hands over her knees, palms flat on her thighs, fingers outstretched, gaze cast down like he wasn't comfortable with what he was about to ask—"lonely?"

The pain in his voice was difficult to examine while he touched her like this. It was not their norm. They hugged. He kissed her on the forehead when they said goodbye. Occasionally, they snuggled up together to watch a movie. This touch felt innocent, but also sensual, and she didn't understand how that could be possible.

His gaze slowly rose, his expression a rare shade of somber.

She'd always had to kick him under the table for being goofy when it wasn't appropriate. Before attending funerals, she would make him vow to behave, threatening to not sit with him at the next one if he didn't, but neither of them ever followed through. Of course, *she* was the one to receive the dirty looks for laughing. Every time.

"If I say yes, are you going to hook me up with one of your teammates?"

She wiggled her eyebrows and grinned.

His grip on her thighs tightened. Speaking of dirty looks…*damn*. "I asked if you were lonely, not horny."

"I can't be both?"

He held his scowl.

So much for trying to lighten the mood. "What's the problem? I've dated your teammates before."

"In high school," he nearly shouted. "Those were guys I'd known since elementary school. I trusted them, and they knew I'd fuck them up if they hurt you. Not to mention your dad was the coach, Taylor."

"You're right. It's best if you get to know them and screen them. I'm not opposed to trainers, medics, or coaches, but no conservatives or mama's boys."

His eyebrows shooting up made her snicker. Nick was a mama's boy through and through. His dad had been needed at the farm, so his mom took him to all his practices and games, even when he'd played travel ball and they'd had to drive or fly around the country. "You're rude."

"Sorry." She tried to calm her laughter, hoping her shaking shoulders weren't too obvious. "I adore your mother. Your relationship with her is lovely."

He rolled his eyes. "You wouldn't date someone who's close to their mom?"

Taylor wrapped her arms around herself. "Nah, it wouldn't bother me, but I'd never date a professional athlete." That life wasn't for her. She was a homebody. The idea of even standing next to someone in the spotlight made her tense up.

His nod and the protrusion in his cheek where his tongue stuck in it didn't make sense. First, he'd acted like he'd be pissed if she slept with one of his teammates, but he didn't seem any happier with her claim that she had no interest in getting involved with an athlete.

She shivered and put her hands in her pockets.

"Want to go in?" The deep tone of his voice and his slowing drawl meant that flask he'd tucked into his jacket was probably nearing empty. He slid his hands to her ankles and back up.

Taylor shook her head and smiled. "Not yet."

She wanted him to herself for just a little longer. "Remember when we got snowed in here with Aunt Penny and you gave me rug burn on my face?"

He winced. "Explaining that to your dad sucked. 'You wanna play ball or you wanna wrestle, boy?'"

She laughed. "Didn't he threaten to kick you off the team?"

"Yeah, but I mean, he did that on a weekly basis, so it wasn't that big of a deal. Though, it did scare the shit out of me when he said that we were too old to be wrestling and if you ended up with any more marks of any kind on your body from me, that he'd take it up with *my* dad and let *him* talk to me about it."

Taylor pressed her teeth into her lip. They'd been thirteen. Her parents were younger and a little bit more relaxed about certain things. If Mr. Lewis thought Nick had been rough with her, though, she wouldn't have seen him for a week while he spent every waking minute that he wasn't in school or playing ball doing extra farm chores.

"Why do you want to know if I remember that?"

She shrugged. "That's always what I think of when it snows."

"Looking for a rematch?"

"We're a little old for that now, Nick." Once upon a time, she'd been able to hold her own against him. Then he'd hit puberty and started lifting weights. Most of their roughhousing stopped at that point.

"No, we're not." His hands warmed her thighs as they crept under her skirt.

She put her brainpower into her argument for why the two of them wrestling was an idiotic idea instead of letting it run in the direction of what the fuck Nick's hands were doing under her skirt. "It wouldn't exactly be fair. Your job is literally to work out and get stronger and faster. I weigh a lot less than you do, and the most strenuous thing I do at my job is bake pies."

Nick tilted his head to the side. "I'll go easy on you."

"Why are you touching me?" She pressed her lips together, despite it being too late to take the words back. Her heart slammed in her chest hard enough to bruise a rib.

Instead of removing his hands, he slid them higher, fingers curling over the outsides of her thighs. His thumbs brushed the edge of her skirt. "Why are you letting me?"

Because she liked it. Because it felt good. Because she trusted him.

Because all she had to do was say the word and he'd stop.

"Because you're you."

He crooked his eyebrow. "Meaning?"

Neither of them had ever attempted to cross that line. Sure, they'd touched plenty of times, but not like this. It still didn't feel like he was crossing any lines, though.

She shrugged. "I don't know."

"What else can I get away with because I'm me?"

"I don't know the answer to that, either, but don't try to talk me into anything. It's been a long day, and I am not up for your shenanigans."

"Crazy like…going back inside and seeing if I can give you rug burn again?"

"I'm not wrestling you. Shut up about it."

"There's other ways to get rug burn, Tay."

She gasped and shoved his hands away. "You're so drunk. I should be recording this so I can show it to you when you're sober and make fun of you."

He sucked in his bottom lip for a second. "What am I doing that I should be embarrassed of?"

"For one thing, you just had your hands up my skirt." She narrowed

her eyes, astounded that she had to answer that question.

"And you let them stay there."

Her face burned. Luckily, her rosy cheeks could be blamed on the cold. "For thirty seconds."

"It was longer," he said. "Come visit me next weekend."

The abrupt change in subject threw her for a loop. She shook her head, as though the action would magically help her make sense of the conversation. "I work weekends. My only days off are during the week."

"Come during the week, then."

"Maybe. For a day."

He put his hands on the arms of her chair and leaned forward, bringing his face close to hers. "Three days."

"One." She leaned back, creating more space between them.

"Two." Nick took her hands between his and rubbed like he was trying to warm them.

"None." What the hell was going on with him? He wasn't usually touchy and flirty like this. Not with her.

"It used to be that you didn't come visit me because it was too far, or you were busy getting the inn off the ground." His voice came out soft and warm, the acceptance and lack of resentment radiating through her body as though she stood near a glowing fire. "Now, I'm two hours away and I still don't see you unless I come home. I'm starting to think it's not the distance."

She shifted, uncrossing and recrossing her ankles. "What do you think it is, then?"

"I don't know, but I know that I don't like it."

Taylor sighed. "You're being dramatic. You only moved back in state a few weeks ago. I'm busy. It's hard to get away, especially overnight."

"I moved back to Maryland three months ago."

She counted the months in her head. *Oops.* "It doesn't seem like that long."

"When the season starts, I'm going to be traveling a ton. I won't be able to come home much. I want you to see where I live and work."

"I'll think about it." Taylor placed her hands on his chest and pushed as she rose from her chair. It probably made her the world's worst best friend, but she didn't want to meet the new people in Nick's life or tour the stadium. Not because she didn't love Nick. Not because she wasn't ecstatic that his dream came true. She loved baseball almost as much as he did and couldn't wait to go to every one of his home games.

She wanted to stay separate from that part of his life, though, and she didn't have a good reason for why that was.

He stepped—well, *staggered*—backward. "I don't get it, Tay. This is a huge deal for me. Why don't you want to share it with me?"

"I'm over-the-moon happy for you and it means a lot that you want to include me, but it's your thing. I can't really share it with you."

"If it's my thing, I can share it with whoever I damn well please."

The rawness in his voice brought forth a surge of guilt.

This was supposed to be a happy occasion. Time to turn things around before it was too late. A little humor should do the trick. "I know you're very proud of it, and I'm sure someday some woman is going to be very into your *thing*, but we've made it over two decades without discussing our private parts. Let's not make this weird."

He tilted his head to the side and shot her a look that said he was two seconds from tickling her until she hyperventilated.

"Come on," she said, heading toward the door. "I'm putting you to work."

Nick followed her inside but grabbed her hand as soon as he shut the door. He dragged her into the laundry room that branched off the kitchen and reached for the top button on her coat. "You can't go back to the party yet. You smell like pot."

She stared at his head as he bent his neck, seeing to her buttons. He always had her back. "Thanks."

His lips pulled into a slight smile as he ran his hands inside her coat, over her shoulders, pushing it off. He grabbed it before it hit the ground, then slung it behind him on the laundry-folding table.

Taylor lifted the lapel of the blazer she'd worn over her black bodysuit and sniffed. "Do I still smell?"

He stepped even closer and lowered his face, sniffing near her shoulder. "Yeah, but it's not your clothes." He pulled the fuzzy pom-pom-topped hat off her head and ran his fingers through the curls she'd spent a good forty minutes creating. "It's your hair."

There wasn't time to wash and dry her hair, and she didn't want any of the remaining guests to get a whiff of her and think she was a pothead. She shrugged out of her blazer and gave it to Nick, who took it but stood there, staring.

He draped her blazer over his arm and put the hat on top, then put his hand on her waist. His gaze dropped, intently sweeping from the mock neck of her bodysuit down to her red skirt. He wet his lips and dug his fingers into her waist, pulling her closer.

She put her arms up between them and flattened her palms on his chest, keeping herself from crashing into him. Weirdness that wasn't necessarily bad, but definitely unfamiliar and hard to decipher, wrapped around her like a ribbon. Her breath caught and she blinked at him, eye level thanks to her platform heels. His strange behavior tonight made her heartbeat quicken and her nerves simmer like liquid about to boil over.

His gaze lifted to hers and he tilted his head. "I'm drunk enough to admit I like how you look in this outfit so much I'm starting to think about taking it off you."

She gasped and slapped his shoulder. "Nick!"

He stepped back, chuckling. "I'm not *going to*. Be a lot easier to not have those thoughts if you didn't keep getting hotter."

No. Nick was not allowed to be attracted to her. That wasn't how things were between them. He couldn't go changing that after all these years.

She was being a hypocrite and she knew it. Just a little while ago, she'd been appreciating how well his clothes fit. But the difference was, she kept it to herself. Because she didn't want to make it weird.

How would he feel if she said the same thing to him? If she told him he was hot, would he…like it? Maybe he wouldn't even care. His looks got him so much attention, he had to be immune.

"Don't look at me like that, Taylor." He reached out and grabbed two dryer sheets from a box on a shelf. "I'm a guy. You can't dress sexy like this and expect me not to notice."

Yes, she could.

He rubbed the dryer sheets lightly over her hair, mussing it a little.

"What are you doing?"

"Trying to make it so your hair doesn't smell like a dispensary *and* take care of the static from your hat."

She swallowed, her desire to berate him for making things awkward drowned by the sweetness of him taking care of her—so typical of the Nick she knew and loved.

But if someone found them in here, they'd jump to the conclusion that he *was* taking her clothes off, so she did her best to help him eliminate any suspicious odors and return to the party as fast as possible.

Everyone was saying goodnight when they returned to the gathering room where the small ceremony and reception had taken place. No one had to go far. Taylor had made rooms available for everyone. Nick's family would stay in the main house and Morgan's family in the cottages.

Once the leftover food had been stored and the dishwashers loaded, she showed Nick to his room. They'd taken shots while cleaning up and he was so wasted he stumbled down the hall.

The room she'd reserved for him was the one closest to hers, as well as the one most in need of redecorating. For now, she wasn't sure if she wanted to keep it as a bedroom or find another purpose for the space.

"This room gives me the creeps. Sleep in here with me." He kicked off his shoes, then pulled his white T-shirt over his head. He'd ditched his tie and dress shirt before they'd cleared all the used glasses and cake plates.

"No." She forced her attention to turning down the bed.

Nick had never been shy, but learning he found her attractive stirred her curiosity. Panic sizzled in every nerve because if that curiosity got the better of her, and she took a good look at her best friend's half-naked body—which was very likely the most beautiful male body she'd see in her lifetime—she'd be powerless against an involuntary lust-driven reaction.

Sharing a bed with him? Hell to the no.

"Let me sleep in your room. I'm scared."

She whipped her head in his direction and shot him a *stop fucking around* glare.

He stuck out his bottom lip. His pouting might've been more effective if his abs weren't so distracting. The steely muscles of his torso tapered in at his pelvis and the elastic of his underwear peeked over the waistband of his dress pants.

Taylor shook her head and fluffed his pillow. "Stop being a baby."

He grumbled and stretched out across the end of the bed. "Morgan and Brody are having a baby. We should do that."

"Do what?" she asked, her voice so high it hit the ceiling. "Have a baby?"

"I've thought about it—you, having my baby."

He was so drunk. This was nuts.

And she wasn't buzzed enough to seriously entertain such a ridiculous proposal. Actually, no amount of alcohol could get her to that level of insanity.

"That's just because your brother is having a baby and it got you wondering when you'll start a family." Blaming his boldness on his intoxication was unnecessary. Nick's middle name was Ridiculous. It was like he was born with a mere fraction of the fucks everyone else had to give.

"Maybe, but you're the only woman I can imagine getting pregnant. That's weird, right?"

Yep. All his fucks were long gone.

Did he understand what had to take place for a man to impregnate a woman? They'd never done that. They'd never done anything even close to that. Oh, shit. Had he thought about doing *that* with her?

"Sounds like something you should talk about with a licensed therapist," Taylor said, surprised she could get out any coherent words at all the way her heart raced, and her throat contracted.

They were friends. If he could imagine having a baby with her, it probably had to do with some subconscious comfort or familiarity thing. And as far as she knew, he wasn't seeing anyone, and it'd be odd for him to fantasize about a stranger having his baby. Either way, she hoped this was the last time they talked about it. He probably wouldn't even remember tomorrow. She wasn't going to bring it up, that was for sure.

"I get so confused around you, Taylor." He angled his head to the side and stared at her with drooping eyelids. "It's like the wires get crossed and my body doesn't know, or maybe doesn't care, that you've been my best friend since preschool. But it's not just my body that wants your body. My mind is turned on by you too. I dream about you, and sometimes when I'm in the gym, I catch myself zoning out, thinking about what you're doing, or remembering something cute you said or how your eyes turn deeper brown when I tease you. But you're my best friend and I don't wanna fuck that up, especially since I know you don't feel that way about me."

Taylor tried to quell her rising anxiety and form a response.

He didn't mean it. This was Nick being extra because that was his only frequency.

Before she said anything, he gave up the struggle against keeping his eyes open.

She stood frozen. As far as confessions went, that one was a little clumsy, but he tended to ramble when he was being vulnerable. Damn it.

How could this man—a man with five million social media followers, all thirsting for his shirtless videos, a man who'd basically made a career out of flirting, a man about to start his Major League Baseball career—be as obsessed with her as he claimed? And how long had he kept it to himself?

This had to be an emotional reaction to his brother getting married and expecting a baby. Maybe it had something to do with his dad's health too. And the stress and excitement of his dream becoming a reality. With all that, it'd be understandable if his attachment to her got twisted into something he interpreted as romantic feelings. Totally understandable.

And booze. Booze never helped anyone be rational.

Any number of things, or a combination of many, could have skewed his perspective. The possibilities really were endless.

Nick didn't like her that way.

And he better not remember any of this.

2

Bad News for the Bad Ass

Taylor

WITH A SIX-PACK OF beer and an inflated ego from scoring the winning home run on her rec league baseball team, Taylor waltzed into Morgan and Brody's house.

She set her beer on the coffee table. "Did I miss anything?"

They were curled up in an oversized chair watching Nick's game.

"It's the bottom of the first." Brody reached for the beer Taylor held out to him. "In the top, they had two strikeouts and a pop-fly. He didn't get to bat."

That wasn't a good start, but at least she hadn't missed him batting. She'd known it was pushing it stopping for beer on the way, but it was June and hot and she'd earned it with that home run. If Nick didn't score a run, she was going to tease him mercilessly. Who cared if he was up against other professional athletes and her opponents had dad bods and drove mini vans? Not her. She'd rub it in his face and love every second of it.

The morning after Nick got drunk and said all that nonsense, he'd acted normal. No mention of his whack comments about having a baby with her, or him being attracted to her. No embarrassment. No indication he remembered any of it. What a fucking relief. They'd gone back to how they'd always been, and everything made sense again.

She'd been to five of his home games and watched the away games on TV. Seeing him playing live on the top sports network was weird. Not as weird as watching a thirty-second video of him in all his catcher's gear, minus the shirt and chest protector, though. The algorithms had decided his thirst traps were the very first thing she needed to see whenever she checked social media.

Okay, so maybe she'd lingered on his page for a little longer than she should have. Keeping up her *I don't think my best friend is hot* front proved more difficult while watching the videos where his face was obscured by his catcher's mask, or a baseball hat pulled down over his eyes. That sculpted body could belong to anyone.

It didn't, though.

It belonged to Nick. And feeling flushed while watching him flaunt it was not okay.

Watching him play ball was different. It was comfortable. It was exciting. It was the best feeling seeing him do something he'd wanted to do since he was a kid.

Besides, Nick really was a badass catcher.

"Is your dad watching?" Brody asked.

Who cared? Not her. She hated even thinking about her dad cheering for Nick. If she could wave a magic wand and erase the relationship he had with Nick, she'd do it in a heartbeat. Maybe that was selfish of her. That relationship was one of the most important ones in Nick's life. It had been one of the most important ones in her life too—until it wasn't. She'd been a daddy's girl since birth. It wasn't a loss she took lightly, but there was no undoing it.

"I'm sure he is." She took a pull from her beer bottle and kept her gaze glued to the screen. Her dad never missed Nick's games. Even when he'd played college ball, her dad had driven several hours to watch him— which made it extra tense between her and Nick that she didn't come. But she didn't want to tell Nick that she couldn't bear to spend that much time alone in a car with her own father. He'd have questions.

Taylor took off her baseball hat and set it on the coffee table. She'd chosen stopping to grab beer over going home to change out of her uniform—a white jersey with blue trim and white pants. "I want to run invitation designs for your baby shower by you."

Morgan's due date was still months away, but with her friends and family having to travel to get here, Taylor wanted to give plenty of notice. Out of the corner of her eye, she caught Brody rubbing Morgan's belly and smiled. He was a good guy. She liked seeing him happy, especially with someone as awesome as Morgan.

The other team's first batter got on base. The second batter got a double.

Taylor shook her head. "What do you think Nick's muttering under that mask?"

"Words he wouldn't say in front of our mother."

Morgan laughed and tried to get up from the chair, but Brody had to give her a boost. "I made a veggie tray. I'm going to get it."

"Baby," Brody said in a tone that expressed he found her equally adorable and naïve, "that's not baseball food. Back me up, Taylor."

Taylor shrugged. "I could go for a celery stick."

"Yeah, with wings and blue cheese dressing," he muttered.

She waited until Morgan had disappeared into the kitchen before grinning at him. "Wings sound good."

Brody pointed the mouth of his bottle at her. "The next time you need someone to take your side against my brother, don't look at me."

Her grin stayed in place as she turned back to the game.

Nick stood on home plate, mitt held out, waiting to catch the ball as a runner barreled toward him.

She leaned forward and set down her beer, sucked into the play. The instant the ball hit the center of his mitt, she opened her mouth to cheer, but as the runner slid down the baseline, his momentum triggered panic in her.

His legs disappeared between Nick's wide stance, but they somehow got tangled, and Nick's left leg shot out to the slide. He landed hard, but the cloud of dust that surrounded him prevented her from seeing anything.

Except for the runner. He pushed himself up from the ground and stood.

Nick stayed down.

The smile fell from Taylor's face. She wet her very dry lips. "He's hurt."

As if they'd heard her, coaches and medics appeared, huddling around him.

She'd never seen him get injured on the field and not walk off, even if he collapsed when he got to the bench. He was hurt bad. The kind of hurt that a professional athlete couldn't afford to be.

Taylor had come to Brody and Morgan's to watch Nick's game, jumping at the chance for an excuse not to watch it with her parents. But right now, the only place she wanted to be was Texas, even though, if she had been, she'd never get on the field to be close to him. But at least she'd be there, not sitting helplessly on a couch a thousand miles away.

Brody got to his feet. "He'll be okay."

She stared straight ahead at the television screen, unable to see it past the tears welling in her eyes.

Brody sat next to her. "It looks bad, but Nick is—"

"Fucked," she said.

3
Logic-Challenged
Nick

Of all the things Nick Lewis should be thinking about, how to make an entrance into a baby shower should be the last.

He had two weeks. Two weeks to break the news to his family that his professional baseball career was over. Two weeks to decide whether he would accept a position as one of the team's social media experts. Two weeks to make a choice he wouldn't spend the rest of his life regretting.

Up until he'd gotten behind the wheel of his car, his mind had been consumed with how to salvage his future now that baseball was off the table. But since he'd turned onto the interstate, his pride had not shut up about limping into the party with a cane.

Showing up a little late meant he could slip in subtly. If he didn't take too many steps at once, his limp wouldn't be that noticeable. Hopefully, everyone would be focused on the mommy-to-be, but if anyone asked questions he didn't want to answer, he'd redirect the subject to Morgan, his brother, and their future little bundle of joy.

No one from home had seen him walk with a cane yet. They knew about his injury. It was fucking televised. His doctor said after some physical therapy, he'd be able to play again. Then he'd met with a specialist. She'd disagreed. So did the next three doctors.

That was the part his family didn't know. He'd played down the severity of his pain and the extent of the injury. His dad's condition was enough for them to deal with. They didn't need to feel obligated to come rushing to his side.

He turned into the Van Belle Mansion. Fields of lavender flanked the long driveway, swaying in the dusk breeze. Nick rolled down his windows and let the warm summer air wash over him as he remembered catching lightning bugs with Taylor on the edge of those same fields. Hard to believe she owned this now.

Her eccentric aunt's mansion didn't look like it had when they were kids, though. Taylor had it painted white, and the landscaping had never been this elaborate.

In all his deliberating about how he'd arrive at the baby shower with as little wake as possible, he'd overlooked the parking lot situation. As the last to arrive, he had to park the farthest away. His knee throbbed just thinking about it. Okay, so his knee constantly throbbed, but it got *worse* when he thought about walking that far.

He grabbed his cane and gift off the passenger side, then got out of his car, wincing when he put his weight on his left leg. Taylor had a golf cart to get around the property. He could call her and ask her to give him a lift. But he wasn't gonna.

He didn't want to miss the chance to see her before she saw him. He loved doing that, and with how shitty things had been for him lately, he needed it. Although, when she did see him and he told her what he wanted to tell her, she'd probably knee him in the nuts.

Not fun.

But necessary.

Whether or not he accepted the position he'd been offered was contingent on how she reacted when he told her he wanted to date her.

No. Date her wasn't exactly the right way to phrase it. He would date her. He'd take her on all kinds of dates. But it was more than that. And if she was even the slightest bit interested, he'd turn down the job and move home.

If she wasn't into it, he couldn't hang around this small town and watch her end up with someone else. Once, Brody had asked him what he'd do if down the road, he got invited to Taylor's wedding. Having that thought put into his head had wrecked him for days. Watch her marry another man? He couldn't. But it didn't matter because Nick refused to live his life waiting for the worst-case scenario. If he wanted a certain outcome, he manifested that shit. And worked hard as hell to obtain it. Sometimes, he'd been to known to get creative, if the situation called for it. He didn't mind getting creative with Taylor if he had to.

He would definitely have to.

Once he was within spitting distance of the front door, he spotted a sign with an arrow pointing to the backyard. "Party this way," he muttered. "Why the fuck not?"

Halfway around the house the sound of laughter and chatter reached him. He stopped for a second and tried to prepare. It'd been weeks since he'd seen anyone other than his mom, who'd find a way through a SWAT barricade if one of her kids was on the other side. Facing his family wasn't bothering him, though. *That* conversation would happen later. Where no one would see his mom bawl her eyes out. He wasn't looking forward to it, but his mind had other problems to occupy itself with. Like if limping into the party with a cane was going to make him less attractive to Taylor.

Although, *less* implied that she found him attractive at all and that's where he got hung up. He had enough followers strictly interested in his looks that he knew he wasn't unattractive. But Taylor? She always seemed so unaffected. Immune to his charms and looks. Oblivious.

There were people who'd say he only wanted her because he couldn't have her.

Fuck them.

Like he'd risk ruining his relationship with his best friend because of his ego.

He tilted his head back and breathed deep. He couldn't strut in like he would have before. He couldn't scoop up Taylor, making her squeal and beg to be put down. He couldn't be the Nick she'd always known.

Get it together, man.

Rejection wasn't something he'd feared too much in the past. It never slowed him down. Didn't shake his confidence.

Letting it get the better of him when it mattered most?

Fuck that.

Nick shook off his self-doubt and headed to the patio. The party was everything he'd expect from Taylor—flowers, string lights everywhere, artfully displayed gourmet food on elaborately decorated tables. According to the invitation he'd gotten in the mail, the theme was *Twinkle, Twinkle, Little Star*, which explained the giant illuminated moon and glowing stars suspended from an arbor over an upholstered bench that was flanked by stacks of gifts.

He scanned the scene, staying in the shadows of the trees in the backyard. When his gaze landed on her, his chest got tight.

In a teal dress that evoked a fantasy of spinning her on a dance floor— something he'd never be able to do thanks to his knee—she sat across from his dad at a small round table. Her hair spilled across her face as she dipped her head, giggling at something his dad said to her. She pushed her long, light brown hair out of her face and the curled ends settled over her shoulder.

As if she sensed someone staring at her, her gaze lifted, immediately connecting with his. Her mouth turned up at the corner and that right there, *that's* why he wanted to see her when she spotted him. The sparkle in her eyes was the prettiest thing on this earth.

Slowly, she shifted her gaze to his dad and pointed in Nick's direction. Maybe he loved too many things about Taylor, but how she *always* took time to visit with his dad made him happiest.

His dad glanced over his shoulder, then turned halfway in his chair. Thanks to an experimental treatment, he didn't need constant oxygen anymore and could get by with keeping a portable tank with him to use if he needed. It wasn't a cure, but it had vastly improved his quality of life.

He couldn't delay any longer. He headed for Morgan's baby shower throne to add his gift to the mix. After balancing it on top of one of the towers of wrapped boxes, he turned, holding his breath, hoping that seeing him limping across the patio hadn't changed Taylor's expression.

Brody blocked his line of sight. "I was worried you weren't going to show."

Nick lifted a shoulder. "I'm here."

His brother's gaze shifted to the cane. "It's good to have you home."

He tilted his head, trying to see around Brody.

"Who are you looking for?" he asked, his tone bursting with amusement.

Nick glared at him.

"I don't know how she hasn't realized you have those kinds of feelings for her," Brody said. "It's so fucking obvious."

"You done?"

"For now."

Thank fuck. His brother had been riding his ass about making a move on Taylor for the past year. Nick didn't need to be told that he should let her know how he felt. He knew that. But this wasn't a normal situation. Asking her on a date would be out of left field. And up until recently, he couldn't give Taylor the future she wanted. He didn't even know what she wanted, but he knew it wasn't a long-distance relationship with a professional athlete.

His ball playing days had been numbered, but he'd believed he had a few years left. He'd been sure in that time Taylor would wind up with someone else. He couldn't walk away from everything he'd worked for his whole life to have a relationship with Taylor any more than he could ask her to give up the inn.

But now…

His career wasn't an obstacle.

And nothing else was a big enough one for him to dwell on. As of right now, he was on the injured list and racking up even more views than usual on his socials. He'd started posting videos while in the minor leagues. One thirst trap led to another and suddenly, he had five million followers and a major league baseball contract.

Thanks to his ongoing online popularity, which saw a spike when he'd gotten injured and steadily continued to climb, the team wanted to stay affiliated. They had offered him a position in the social media marketing department. He'd get to be involved in the game despite not being able to play.

It wasn't a bad offer. But it wasn't his first choice.

By the time Brody walked away, Taylor was gone. He didn't see her anywhere.

He pulled up a chair by his dad, and immediately got swept up in a tornado of his mom, sister, and sister-in-law giving him hugs and asking him questions.

Taylor came out of the house carrying trays of food.

He pushed up from his chair, but his dad cleared his throat. He sat back down. "Yes?"

"I want to have a talk with you about the future."

"Now? Dad—"

"Not now. Tomorrow morning first thing, but I'm telling you now because it's important and I don't want you to be hungover."

Nick stretched his neck. "I won't be."

It used to be standard for him and Taylor to get smashed the first night he was back in town after being away for a while. But he didn't care to have his reflexes dulled or his balance impaired when he already struggled to walk. He also didn't want to get drunk around Taylor and say anything that'd be better said while sober.

Nick kept his gaze on Taylor as she walked to the opposite end of the patio and lit the four fire tables with cushioned seating surrounding them.

"She wouldn't even look at you when she walked by," his dad said. "Did you do something stupid?"

Not yet. "I haven't seen her in four months. What could I have possibly done?"

His dad relaxed in his chair, squinting like what his son had told him didn't make a lick of sense. "She didn't come to see you after you got hurt?"

Nick shook his head. That had been her plan, but… "I told her not to come."

"You didn't let her come see you?" The astonishment in his dad's voice made him feel five years old.

"There was nothing she could do."

"Son, you can't push a woman away for months, then show up and expect everything to be peachy."

Nick crossed his arms, miffed that his dad thought *now* was the ideal time to give unsolicited advice. "Did she say something to you?"

"No. We talked about Hope working here. She pointed you out to me when you got here, then excused herself."

"We're good. I've talked to her plenty of times since then." They were good, right? Damn it. His dad had him questioning it, replaying phone calls and text messages, combing them for any piece of hostility or resentment.

Taylor glanced their way but quickly averted her gaze and headed into the house.

His dad laughed so hard he wheezed.

"She's busy."

"Busy avoiding you," his dad shot back.

Fuck. It looked like that may be the case.

"She made time to talk to me."

"Wow, Dad. Aren't you special?"

"No, but Taylor is. You better go find a way back into her good graces."

"I haven't fallen out of her good graces," he said through clenched teeth. He wished his dad would stop saying shit like that.

"Go find out."

He would have five minutes ago if his dad hadn't stopped him. Christ. He pushed out of his chair and steadied himself before walking to the house.

The view of the backdoor was concealed by tall landscaping and a trellis. When Nick got around the barrier and started up the slate path, the door opened.

Taylor had her head down, looking at the huge rectangular basket in her arms as she kept the door wedged open with her hip.

A brown blur slipped past her and bounded down the steps. The Leonberger puppy he'd gotten her was now 150 pounds—which was good because his purpose was to protect Taylor, but bad because he got excited whenever he saw Nick and was surely going to knock his pathetic ass down.

A second after Cal's paws landed on his chest, a twinge of pain tore through his knee and stole his breath.

"Fuck," he muttered. His knee gave out and he landed on his hip and elbow, scraping the hell out of it on the rough edges of the pavers.

"Nick," Taylor said on a whoosh of air. She knelt and set down the basket, then loomed over him.

His pain no longer existed. Fuck, why did Taylor always make everything better? The wrinkle between her eyebrows was so damn cute.

"Nick?"

"Hmm?"

"I asked if you're okay." She grunted while shoving Cal out of the way.

Nick groaned and pushed himself to sit up, but Taylor stayed close, practically on top of him. And he didn't hate it. "Yeah. Nothing hurt but my pride."

She grabbed his wrist and looked his arm over. Where the rolled-up sleeves of his button down exposed his forearm, the skin was raw. Blood dotted the shallow abrasions.

"Did Taylor beat you up?" Brody asked from somewhere behind him.

Nick glanced over his shoulder as his brother made his way around the trellis that hid the back entrance of the house from the rest of the patio. "Yeah."

She rolled her eyes. "I'm happy to make that true."

Brody stood over him and held out his hand.

Nick grabbed his cane, then took his brother's hand and got to his feet.

Taylor stood with her basket, then shoved it into Brody's stomach. "Take this s'mores stuff to the fire tables so I can torture your brother."

"Done and done," Brody said too chipperly and practically skipped off.

"What are you going to do to me?"

She gestured toward the door. "Go inside."

"Just because I'm pretty, doesn't mean I'm stupid. I'm not letting you get me alone after you just admitted you're going to torture me."

"Yeah, you are." She winked and walked to the door, then threw a glance over her shoulder. "Come on."

Follow the beautiful woman into the house where no one would hear him scream? Yeah, he was that stupid. If Taylor was part of the equation, his brain cells weren't.

He glanced at Cal who stood by his side, tail wagging. "Don't judge me."

Moving slower than molasses, he made it inside and over to the plush armchair next to the window in the sunroom off Taylor's kitchen. With his bad leg elevated on the ottoman, he slumped back, resting his head against the cushion.

Taylor stopped rummaging around in the kitchen and sat on the edge of the ottoman with a first aid kit on her lap. "You never mentioned the cane."

"I was hoping it wouldn't be permanent and when I saw you, I'd no longer need it."

She sighed so heavily her cheeks puffed out. "Why are you so dumb?"

"I prefer the term 'logic challenged.'"

She grabbed his wrist and tugged his arm closer, then swiped an antiseptic wipe over his scrapes. "What other secrets are you keeping?"

The sting of the antiseptic barely fazed him. The burn in his chest from knowing he had hurt her by delaying telling her the whole truth was more painful.

He breathed deep, then slowly released it.

Her gaze rose to his and locked on. This wasn't the sparkly-eyed, *I'm so glad to see you* expression he'd looked forward to. Yeah…maybe his dad was right, and he had fucked up.

4
Fluttery Stuff
Taylor

"I'M DONE PLAYING BALL."

Her lips parted, but she couldn't form words. She glanced away.

That news struck her, stunning her, the same as being hit with a Louisville Slugger. She'd known in her gut that she'd witnessed a career-ending injury. She rifled through the first aid kit for gauze, blinking back tears.

"Taylor, don't fucking cry." Nick pulled her into a hug that would have been awkward if he hadn't pushed the first aid kit to the side and lifted her into the chair with him. He tucked her head under his chin and wrapped his arms tightly around her. "I'm sorry."

She sniffed and pulled back to look at him. "Why are you apologizing?"

"Because I let you down. I let everybody down. So many people were invested in my career, and it was all for nothing."

"It wasn't for nothing." She wiped at her face with the back of her hand. "You played college ball, and you played in the minors, and the majors. It's not your fault you got hurt."

"I know it's not my fault, but the guilt remains."

"Who have you told?"

"You."

"Just me?" It wasn't unusual for her to be the first person—sometimes, the only person—Nick told things. But this was big. He should have told his family first. "Your mom said your injury wasn't career-ending."

"That's what they told us initially. But then I got a second opinion, and that doctor didn't agree with the first. I didn't want to worry her until I consulted more doctors."

"How many more opinions did you get?"

"Enough."

Wrapping her head around this major shift in his future was like trying to wrap her head around learning there wasn't going to be a tomorrow.

She moved back to the ottoman and cleaned his scrapes with antiseptic and cotton balls. "When are you going to tell everyone else?"

"Probably not at Brody and Morgan's baby shower."

"Good call." The news would be upsetting for his family, and while Nick was known for being a ham, he would never rain on anyone's parade.

"I'm going to miss talking to you after games," he said in a near-whisper.

She met his stare, her stomach doing weird fluttery stuff that she didn't understand. "Not as much as you're going to miss playing."

"I'll miss those talks more."

A croak built in her throat. The way he looked at her and spoke to her was next-level awkward. His tone was so freaking sincere that it tickled her flight response. And if her knees hadn't felt so weak, she might have fled. "Don't get all sappy."

"I'm not too down about it, to be honest. Not when it means I'll get to talk to you face to face every day."

Her spine tensed. "You're moving home?"

"Considering it."

Nick moving home would be...

She didn't know what it would be.

As adults, Taylor had decided on a future rooted in their hometown. Nick hadn't. Naturally, a future in playing professional baseball wasn't a forever thing, but it'd been the only thing on his horizon, and she'd never once considered he'd move home and live out an average existence.

"You look really pretty."

Taylor froze. What the fuck was going on? He'd told her she looked pretty before. But it'd never made her feel anything than more slightly flattered. It was sort of his obligation as her best friend to toss her a compliment her when she dressed up.

No woman minded hearing that or being looked at like he was looking at her—like he couldn't look anywhere else if he tried—but it didn't deliver the goosebumps it would have if someone else had said it. Or…it never had *before*.

"I look like I always do," she said, trying her best to pretend none of this was happening.

Nick scooted forward. "I know."

She released the tiniest gasp, then started putting things back in her first aid kit. "So, you're going to come back and help Brody run the farm?"

Nick sagged into the chair. "I don't know. In two weeks, I'm doing a press conference to announce that I'm done playing. I hope to have it figured out by then."

"If you don't take care of the farm, what would you do?"

"Long term? I have no idea. I'd like to finish my master's, though."

He might not admit it to everyone, but his education had been as important to him as baseball. He'd walked away from a full athletic scholarship to a big school and accepted a partial athletic / partial academic scholarship so they could go to school together. The only problem was, she'd inherited the inn, and had no way to pay the property taxes.

"I thought you'd be happier about the possibility of me moving home. I'm sorry I didn't let you come see me, okay?"

His insistence that she shouldn't come hadn't felt good, but she'd known she'd be in the way and that him seeing how upset she was would make things worse. For both of them. She couldn't hide her emotions from Nick. It was like he could see into her mind. Which was happening now, except that he'd gotten it *a little* twisted.

"It wasn't because I didn't want you there," he said. "I didn't want you to see me like that, Taylor. I was freaking out not knowing if my injury was going to ruin my career. I could barely walk or do anything for myself. I was in pain. I was miserable to be around."

"Do you think I can't handle you at your worst?"

"No, I know you can." He ran his hand through his hair. "I didn't want you to be in that position, though. Besides, you can't leave the inn for long, and you'd be stressed the entire time you were away."

Even when his world was falling apart, he was considerate of her. Nick always put her first. She didn't have anyone else in her life that she could depend on like she did him. Learning her parents weren't who they pretended to be took them out of the running.

"I don't hold it against you that you wouldn't let me visit, and I'd love it if you moved home."

Or she would have before his drunk confession had seeped into her mind, causing her to feel flustered when he was around. She didn't like it, and she wished she could unknow what she knew. Losing Nick as her friend because they made the dumb mistake of trying to be more would crush her.

5
Ten Extra Hot Points

Taylor

THE POSSIBILITY OF NICK moving home birthed inexplicable chaos in Taylor's brain. Last night, their conversation hadn't gone any further than him apologizing for not letting her come see him before his mom had come in and interrupted that fun little chat.

They'd rejoined the party and between the fireworks, his family. and her role as the host, they hadn't interacted much.

But she hadn't been able to stop thinking about him telling her she looked pretty. It was the first thought in her head when she'd woken up. The words weren't the part tripping her up. Nick had told her she was pretty before. Not like that, though. That tone. That body language—him leaning in close enough that the smell of leather and soap surrounded her like a blanket of pure masculine goodness. Mostly, though, it was the heat in his gaze when he'd said, "I know," after she'd claimed to look how she always looked.

Taylor wanted it to be all in her head. Made up. A trick of her imagination. That'd be so much easier. Whatever this weird crap going on with her was, it was minimal. She could shove it down and forget about it.

Nick was the problem.

Especially if he was moving home.

The back door cracked open. Drew Miller popped her head inside. "I heard you have the good stuff in here."

Taylor raised an eyebrow at Morgan's brother's fiancée.

She entered the house in a high-waisted, white mini skirt with gold buttons at the hips, like sailor pants, and a cropped white summer sweater. Her auburn hair was pulled into a high ponytail that swished back and forth as she bounced into the house. Her impressive gold high-heeled sandals clicked on the hardwood floor. "Coffee? Real coffee. Not that single-serve crap."

"Not just real coffee. I have fresh fruit, banana bread, bagels, lox, capers, and cream cheese." Taylor waved her hand over the spread she'd put out on the kitchen island, then checked to make sure Cal hadn't moved from his doggy bed. He was used to guests, and she'd trained him to not approach them unless paid attention to him first, but with certain people, he failed to comply.

Drew snagged a stool on the other side of the island and as soon as Taylor set a full cup of coffee in front of her, she took a sip, then moaned. "How are you single?"

"It's a small community. Slim pickin's." No lie. Most of the bachelors in the area were guys she'd gone to school with. They weren't all duds, but none of them made her heart flutter, either.

"Oh! Let me set you up with my brother. I think you and Aubrey would really hit it off."

Taylor wrinkled her nose. "Does he live in Savannah?"

"Sort of. His job takes him all over the world, but—" Drew wrinkled her nose. "Why are you making that face?"

"The face where I'm imagining dating someone who not only lives several states away, but is often in another country? Thanks, but no thanks."

"What about Brody's brother?" She picked up the little glass creamer pitcher and poured a splash into her mug. "Am I the only one who thinks the cane gives him ten extra hot points?"

Taylor choked on her coffee. "I have so much to say right now. I don't even know where to start."

"Start with the cane. Hot or not?"

Hot. But why? The cane should have no effect on his attractiveness. It certainly shouldn't enhance it. But it did. Maybe it was because for the first time in his life, Nick wasn't in constant motion, joking with everyone, or sneaking up on her so she'd squeal. Suddenly, he seemed more mature. With him sitting or standing still, she'd noticed things she'd never noticed before, like his thick forearms and how his muscles flexed when he reached for his drink. She really shouldn't have picked up on the way he ran his tongue across his bottom lip after taking a sip of said drink.

Even though it was due to his injury, he kept most of his weight on his right leg when leaning on his cane, and for some reason that drew her gaze to his ass if he had his back to her.

So, yeah, the cane did add something to his attractiveness. At least she wasn't the only one who'd noticed. But absolutely no one was ever going to know that.

"We've been friends since we were little. I don't see him that way."

Drew's jaw dropped. She scrambled to pull her phone from her pocket. "That's not possible." She swiped and tapped, then held up a video of Nick without his shirt. "Watch this and then tell me you haven't thought about licking his abs."

Taylor opened her mouth to defend herself, but the door opened, and Morgan entered with Lucy, the woman who'd helped her uncle raise her and her brother.

Morgan's curls were pulled up on top of her head and her face was flushed. She looked cute in black shorts and a white ribbed tank top that stretched over her belly, but this god-awful temperature and humidity was clearly getting to her.

The heat didn't seem to have bothered Lucy. She wore an olive-green dress with an empire waist. The stretchy fabric would have been wet with sweat in multiple places if Taylor had been the one wearing it. Lucy's blond bangs curled over her forehead perfectly and the rest of her hair curled under her ears in a sleek bob. It was so immaculate that she looked like she'd just walked out of a salon.

"What's going on in here?" Lucy asked, sidling up to Drew.

"We're looking at Brody's brother's thirst traps," Drew said with zero shame.

"What's a thirst trap?"

"It's this." Drew turned her phone screen to face Lucy.

Her eyes widened. "Oh my."

Morgan walked around the island, shaking her head. "Drew, does my brother know that you follow Nick?"

"I'm supporting family."

Morgan facepalmed. "You're not related."

"Yes, we are," she practically sang. "His brother is married to my fiancé's sister."

"That's not—"

"Look at this one." Lucy's focus was glued to the phone screen. "I've never seen anyone do push-ups like that. That's one lucky floor. If he can do that, can you imagine what—"

"Stop sexualizing my brother-in-law." Morgan ripped the phone out of her hand and placed it face down.

"He's sexualizing himself." Taylor snickered. "That's the entire premise of his account."

"Exactly. Five million followers lust after him, so don't tell me you don't." Drew punctuated her accusation with a finger pointed in Taylor's direction.

"He's my best friend."

Morgan turned to Lucy. "Got any advice for her?"

"Me? Why would I have advice for her?"

"Because you became more than friends with your best friend."

"No, I became best friends with my ex-boyfriend. That's different. And it was messy and painful and now we barely talk." Lucy looked at

Taylor. "You're the one who has to live with the choice. Do what feels best to you."

Everyone needed to slow the fuck down. Or just stop. She and Nick were not a thing that was happening. Ever. "There's nothing to decide. Nick and I aren't like that."

Morgan pulled a *yeah, okay* face.

"Oh! What was that?" Drew pointed at Morgan. "She knows something. He's into her, isn't he?"

She tilted her head and frowned at Taylor. "This cannot be news to you."

Knowing her face was well on its way into tomato territory, she took the carafe back to the machine and busied herself making a fresh pot. Typically, guests had their breakfast in one of the common dining areas of the inn, but since Morgan's family were her only guests, they'd insisted on keeping it simple and easiest for Taylor by having breakfast in the kitchen each morning. If she'd known it was going to come with a side of interrogation about Nick, she'd have gladly passed on the convenience

"If she didn't know, I think we should give her some space to digest it," Lucy said.

"Did you know?" Drew asked, most of her silliness from earlier fading.

Taylor turned back to them, wishing she could ignore the tightness in her throat. "The night of Morgan and Brody's wedding, he was drunk and said some stuff, but he didn't remember he'd said it the next day, and I thought it would be best for our friendship if I—" She wasn't sure how to finish that sentence. Pretended like it didn't happen?

"If you never brought it up?" Morgan's eyebrow winged upward. "What did he say?"

She shook her head and waved it off. "It was crazy, drunken Nick talk. It didn't mean anything."

"Drunk people words are a sober person's truth," Lucy said as she poured cream into her cup. "Everybody knows that."

"He doesn't even drink often, but it was his brother's wedding, and he was riding the high of starting his first major league season. Nick can be very…enthusiastic under normal circumstances. It's not unusual for him to buy the entire bar drinks or tell everyone he loves them."

Drew gasped. "He told you he loved you?"

If she'd produced a bucket of popcorn and started eating it as she waited for a response, Taylor wouldn't have been surprised.

"No," she shouted.

"So, what did he say?" Morgan asked, narrowing her eyes.

"Good morning." Coming from the foyer, Jaci lugged a camera bag and lighting equipment into the kitchen. She had on a loose-fitting denim overall with a teal tank underneath that complimented her brown skin. Her black curls bounced as she bent to set her things on the floor. "He who?"

"No one. It's nothing." She ushered her into the kitchen. "Everyone, this is Jaci. She's doing boudoir photos for a guest. You already know Morgan. This is Lucy, Morgan's mom, and Drew, her brother's finance. They came for her baby shower."

Jaci had moved to the area a few months ago and despite having little in common, they got along great. With a new friend, she hadn't been bored enough to go out with Pace in weeks, further cementing her acceptance that she didn't, and never would, have those kinds of feelings for him. The feeling, or lack of feelings, must be mutual because he hadn't asked her to go out with him in that time, either. She'd been friends with him almost as long as she'd been friends with Nick. That probably had a lot to do with it because when it came to looks, Pace had it going on. He was tall, blessed with dark curls, and spoke in a deep and silky voice she could listen to for hours. But that was the only thing she was compelled to do with Pace.

Jaci set down her equipment and extended her hand to each of the guests. "I'm early and I've got time if anyone else wants to do a min-shoot. Boudoir—I don't do maternity. Unless you want boudoir maternity photos."

"I don't think so," Morgan said, her cringe comical.

"You should do it," Lucy said to Drew, elbowing her.

"I'll do it."

Everyone whipped their head in Taylor's direction.

"Enjoy your breakfast. There's plenty of coffee. Don't worry about cleaning up." Taylor grabbed Jaci's bag and headed for her bedroom.

"That's called avoidance, Taylor," Morgan called after her, but she kept going, walking into the small corridor off her personal living room that led to her bedroom.

Jaci closed the door. "Is this where we're doing the other session?"

"No. Shit. Sorry. I wasn't thinking. Could we just hang out in here and pretend to take the photos?"

"Why?"

Taylor flopped onto the bed and stared up at the ceiling. "I wanted to escape."

"You can escape them, but not this shoot. Now, where's your lingerie stash?"

"Jaci, I'm not doing a boudoir shoot."

"Uh, yeah, you are." She walked to the tall dresser on one side of the bedroom and opened the top drawer. "I have never seen you so wound up. What gives?"

"They were trying to talk to me about Nick."

"What about him?" Jaci had yet to meet Nick, as she and Taylor hadn't met until after Nick's injury and he hadn't been home in that time. All she knew was that he was her bestie and played baseball.

"He came home for the shower, and his knee is worse than he let on. He'll never play again. And so, he walks with a cane, which Drew thinks is hot for some reason, and she thinks my coffee should have earned me at least a boyfriend by now, and—"

"Rate your anxiety on a scale of one to ten." Jaci walked to the side of the bed and crossed her arms.

Taylor closed her eyes briefly, then peeked at her with one. "A solid seven."

"Because Nick is home?"

"Because they were encouraging me to hook up with him."

"As someone who has watched his videos with you while our jaws rest on the floor, if it's a possibility, as your friend, it's my duty to tell you passing that up would be a horrendous mistake."

"Jaci, knock it off. I can't hook up with Nick." Her new friend was full of jokes. It made hanging out with her a blast, but sometimes it was hard to tell if she was truly being serious.

"Why? He's…" Jaci held up her hands then flipped them forward dismissively. "Look, you've seen him. Hell, you get to see him in person, up close. Does he smell good?"

"Jaci, I don't want to talk about this." But yes, Nick always smelled amazing.

"That's not a no. And as we've already established, he's attractive. He's fairly intelligent?"

"*Highly* intelligent."

"Okay, so, no problem there. He respects you?"

Taylor pushed up onto her elbows and nodded.

Jaci walked back to her dresser, pulled out a black bustier, and examined it. "Taylor, this man is fine as hell, super smart, respects you… Does he make you laugh?"

She groaned. "Yes. Of course, he does. He's my friend."

"Exactly. You know everything about him and like him anyway. You could have that, or you can meet some strange dude that will probably lie to you, or you'll realize you don't like his friends, or that he's dumb as a rock. Trust me, girl, you do not want to venture into the world of dating apps when you have that right in front of you."

"Nick and I have never done anything. I wouldn't know how to be that way with him." It'd be so awkward. She couldn't even imagine it without getting weirded out and shutting down that part of her mind.

"Let him kiss you. I bet you'll figure it out *real* quick."

Taylor glared at her. "I don't want to figure it out. I value our friendship. I don't want to mess that up."

Jaci held up a long, yellow satin gown with slits high up each side and lace details on the bodice and the back. "This one."

"I have no need for boudoir photos."

"First off, you have the best lingerie collection I've ever seen. If for no other reason, do it for yourself to commemorate it and that smokin' body of yours. But...if something does go down with Mr. Abs, you'll have these in your back pocket to use as a special gift."

"I'm not giving Nick photos of me in lingerie," Taylor said, her voice squeaky. "And my body is not smokin'. It used to be, but I eat too many baked goods for that these days." Which is also a reason why she wouldn't want someone who worked on keeping their body in top condition to see her naked.

"You wanna make a bet?"

"No."

"Come on," Jaci said. "I bet I can make you fall in love with your body with one photo. If I don't, then I won't take any more. You don't even need to wear lingerie."

That was a tall order, no matter how talented Jaci was. This was a bet Taylor could win.

"I promise you, it'll be a photo you'll *want* Nick to see."

Taylor's face heated. "I don't care about that."

"Fine. Maybe not Nick. Whoever you want to give them to if you're ever in that situation."

"One photo and you'll stop hassling me?"

"One."

"Go ahead."

Jaci shook her head and wagged her finger. "I said you didn't have to wear lingerie, but I am going to make some adjustments to your outfit."

She had on a white sleeveless button-down shirt and a knee length pencil skirt in navy blue with a skinny tan belt.

"Unbutton your top and slide it off your shoulders a little bit."

By the time Jaci got everything how she wanted it, Taylor was sitting on her heels in the center of her bed, her skirt bunched around her thighs and one hand spread across her pelvis and the other braced behind her as she leaned back and looked over her shoulder.

"This is awkward," she said.

"Just one photo."

"Hurry up."

"Tilt your head all the way back and close your eyes."

Jaci stood on the bed, moving around while looking through her lens. Finally, she snapped a shot. "Okay, that's one." She sat on the bed next to her. "Are you ready to see this?"

"No."

She laughed and held the camera so Taylor could view the screen. "You'd be embarrassed to show this to someone you wanted to attract?"

Taylor blew out a breath. "I don't even know the answer to that. There's never been anyone that I wanted to be sexy for."

"Then why the fuck do you have so much lingerie?"

She shrugged. "Online shopping addiction?"

Jaci narrowed her eyes. "So, no one has ever seen you wear any of that?"

She shook her head. "I'm allergic to latex, which most bras and panties have. I don't enjoy having welts in those areas, so I shop higher end for my lingerie. It makes me feel feminine and classier than I actually am, so it's become my guilty pleasure."

"Then, we're definitely doing a shoot. Because you are super feminine and classy and after you see these photos, you'll never doubt that again."

"No."

"If you do it, I'll give you my nana's apple cake recipe."

"Don't do that to me." She'd been asking for that recipe since the night they met. They'd been at a party where everyone brought a dish, and that cake was the best thing to ever grace her tastebuds.

Jaci grinned like an evil genius with a plan.

6

Cactus Everdeen

Nick

THE MEN IN NICK'S and Morgan's families got up at dawn to go on a crabbing boat and get a first-hand experience of what it was like to be a waterman on the Chesapeake Bay—except Nick. Even on a good day, he wouldn't be able to get from the dock onto the boat without assistance and his pride wasn't having that. His dad had forgotten all about the trip until the shower ended and Morgan's uncle said he'd see him bright and early, so Nick had gotten off the hook for having that little chat his dad requested they have.

With nothing better to do, he'd gotten roped into giving his little sister a ride to her new job, which was A-okay with him because he'd thought of nothing but her employer the entire morning.

Hope called out for Taylor as they entered the inn and headed toward the kitchen.

No answer. The kitchen and living room in this wing of the mansion that she utilized as her own living space, separate from the rest of the inn, were vacant. The island wasn't, though. It was covered in fruit and baked goods.

He helped himself to a melon ball, but froze, the ball suspended in front of his lips, as Taylor came around the corner from her bedroom.

She stopped abruptly when she spotted him.

But she wasn't alone. A woman who'd been following behind her bumped into her. After a moment, Taylor rushed into the kitchen and began cleaning up breakfast. "Nick and Hope, this is Jaci. She moved here a few weeks ago."

"We met at a wine tasting—what, five, or is it six, weeks ago? And we became instant besties." Jaci smirked in a way that made every muscle in Nick's back stiffen.

First of all, fuck that. *He* was Taylor's best friend. Secondly, what was going on here? What had they been doing in her bedroom? They both looked flushed, and Taylor's shirt was buttoned wrong. What. The. Fuck.

Were they in her bedroom doing…

…each other?

Was Taylor—

No. Not cool at all. If she liked women instead of men, he was going to lose the will to live. She'd dated boys in high school, though, and he was aware of at least one, albeit brief, relationship she'd had with a man. Maybe she was bi? Wouldn't she have told him?

"What do you want me to do?" Hope asked. "I can clean this up."

"Sure," Taylor said. "There are containers in that cabinet."

"I'm going to go get the rest of my stuff from the car." Jaci dipped out of the kitchen.

If Hope hadn't been present, he'd grill Taylor about her new friend. It took every bit of control he possessed not to blurt out the thoughts circling in his mind like a tornado of paranoia, frustration, despair, and torment.

She pulled a watering can from the cabinet under the sink and put it under the tap. With her back to him, he let his gaze drift from her long, free-flowing hair to her ass. Lust squeezed itself between the frustration and despair. Mentally, he'd gotten her skirt worked up her long legs to her hips when she turned.

Their eyes locked momentarily, and he swore he saw a flash of something that mirrored his exact cocktail of feelings. She lowered her head and scurried off to water a big potted plant by the window.

"What's that one's name?" he asked, grinning over how Taylor had more plants in her house than anyone he knew and every last one had a name.

"Lord of the Leaves."

He snorted. "What happened to Cactus Everdeen?"

"She got sent to District Eight, AKA my bedroom."

Apparently, everyone had gotten an invite to her bedroom but him.

"Don't you have things to do?" Hope asked as she wrapped half a loaf of poppy seed bread in plastic wrap.

"No." He furrowed his brow. "I'm going to stay and help." Like he always did when he came home once he did whatever needed to be done at the farm.

Hope glared. "This is my first day at my first job."

"A job you got because I'm your brother."

"Okay, you two," Taylor said and moved to the next plant. "Yes, knowing Hope since she was a baby did get her in the door, but her work ethic, skills, and positive attitude got her the job. Nick, it's check-in day and I have a new employee to train. I appreciate your willingness to help, but you'll just be in the way."

In the way. Great. As if he didn't already feel inadequate with his hindered mobility.

"Bye now," Hope said in a cheery tone and fluttered her fingers.

"I'm not going to be in the way. I might not be able to run, but I can walk. You think I can't put sheets on a bed? Maybe not as fast as you, but that's nothing new."

Taylor sighed. "It's got nothing to do with you being injured, Nick. It's going to be a hectic day and I don't have time to explain what needs to be done."

"Isn't that what you're going to do with Hope?"

"She's going to shadow me, so no. And before you say anything, I can only handle one shadow, and as your sister has already clearly communicated, this is her first day and she doesn't want her big brother hanging around."

He frowned and pushed away from the counter he'd been leaning on. "What a warm homecoming this is."

"We can hang out later." Taylor returned to the sink and refilled her watering can. "Things should slow down around four or five."

"We have cornhole at six," Jaci said, hands on her hips in the doorway.

Taylor's shoulders fell and she angled her head back. "Shit. I forgot."

"Nick could come with us," she said.

How fucking generous.

"Screw it," he muttered and passed by Jaci heading for the front door.

"Nick," Taylor called after him, but he kept going.

Be a third wheel? Nah. Not him.

7
Boudoir Nerves

Taylor

"This woman is freaking out, and I don't think offering her Nana's apple cake recipe is going to help in this situation."

Taylor rubbed her forehead and stared at the door to the room Jaci had set up for the boudoir shoot booked by a guest who wanted to give her husband a priceless gift. "Should I talk to her?"

"That's up to you," Jaci said. "I've pulled out all my tricks. I've got nothing left. I feel bad because she said it's something she's always wanted to do, but she's super self-conscious about her scars."

Sabrina's scars covered fifty percent of her body. The resulting trauma from a plane crash. Her brother flew small planes and it'd been the first time he'd taken her up. Unfortunately, there'd been a mechanical failure. She'd survived—barely—but her brother had not.

"Damn," Taylor said under her breath. "I'll talk to her."

Although, she had no idea what to say. Sabrina and her husband, Gavin, had booked a cottage at the recommendation of a friend who'd stayed at the inn previously. The couple were in the public eye—they had half as many followers as Nick on the same platform, but that was still a lot. Sabrina claimed they couldn't go anywhere without being recognized, and when looking to have a romantic weekend away, they'd wanted to be left alone.

The photos were to be a gift for Sabrina's husband for their three-year wedding anniversary and she had even paid an upcharge to Jaci to edit them and gets prints overnight. If she'd changed her mind, that was okay, but Taylor was going to at least try to help her work up the nerve.

"Give me a few minutes. I need to grab something from downstairs first."

"Okay. I'll try to get her to relax a little."

Taylor rushed downstairs and told Hope to finish putting cut flowers in all the vases throughout the common areas, then stock the supply closet with the new shipment of shampoo, conditioner, and soap that had come in. She grabbed what she'd come for, then headed back up the stairs.

"Hi, Sabrina." She set a basket full of miniature bottles of liquor on the vanity. This room was one of the most recently renovated rooms at the inn. Her aunt had originally used the space as a guest room. Like most of the rooms, it had huge windows that stretched almost all the way from floor to ceiling, letting in an abundance of natural light. The ornate iron bed frame and vanity were the only pieces of furniture Taylor hadn't replaced.

"I'm so sorry, Taylor." Sabrina dabbed at her eyes with a tissue. "You went to all this trouble to set this up and I'm too lame to go through with it. I'm still going to pay Jaci."

She grabbed two bottles in each hand and held them out so Sabrina could note the selection. "Vodka, rum, whiskey, or tequila?"

Sabrina blinked at her. "It's not even eleven a.m."

"So?" She set down the bottles and twisted the cap off the whiskey and knocked it back. She hissed as it traveled down her throat. "You're about to take off your clothes and let a stranger take photos of you. Trust me, booze is essential."

Sabrina released a soft, uncertain laugh. "I could drink all of those and still not have the courage."

"I get it." She sat on the chaise next to her. "Jaci had to bribe me to pose for mine."

"You had them done?"

She nodded. "I promise it's not as scary as you're imagining, and you're going to feel confident and beautiful and sexy by the time Jaci is done." None of that was anything other than utterly true. Jaci *knew* what she was doing. During the shoot, she'd been patient, encouraging, and she'd known exactly when to provide comic relief.

"I can strategically position you and use props to hide your scars," Jaci said. "Or I can edit them out."

"Your husband sees you naked regularly, doesn't he?" Taylor asked.

She stared at her hands in her lap. "Yes."

"Had he seen you naked before you were married?"

"Yes."

"Do you doubt that he's attracted to you?"

"No." Sabrina picked up the mini bottle of tequila and opened it.

"I bet he doesn't think you're beautiful in spite of your scars. I bet he sees them as part of what makes you beautiful. They're a testament of your strength. I saw a video where he was telling the story of how you had to learn to walk again and how your jaw was wired shut, so you couldn't chew food and could barely talk. He's proud of you, Sabrina. There's no denying that. When he looks at these photos, all he's going to see is his gorgeous wife who he's attracted to just the way she is. Don't hide your scars or have them edited out of the photos."

A tear slipped down Sabrina's face. She swiped at it. "That's what he'd say too."

Jaci squeezed Taylor's arm.

She slipped out of the bedroom, quietly shutting the door. She went down to her bedroom and out to her private patio and dropped into a chair. It might only be eleven, but it had been one hell of a morning.

The patio was small and surrounded on three sides by trees, bushes, and grasses that hid it so that her guests never even knew it was there. She stared at the open space in the center. She didn't know what to do with it.

"This is what I have to do, sweetheart. I'm doing it for us. If Sabrina finds out and leaves me, I'll be cancelled."

Taylor recognized that voice. There was only one person staying at the inn who had a Boston accent. Gavin's tone sent a sick feeling through her before she had time to process his words. But when she did, that sick feeling turned to fury. That woman was upstairs, overcoming her anxiety and stepping outside of her comfort zone for *him*. She'd almost died. She didn't deserve this. No woman deserved this.

"It's not forever. Just until we have enough money saved up to start over. Then I'll give it all up—her, the channel, the fame. We can move to the mountains where we won't have to see anyone else for days. Maybe weeks."

What a scumbag. What was all that bullshit about him being so proud of her for how hard she'd work to regain functionality after her accident? Just him using her tragedy to get more views and likes, probably.

Her stomach twisted and bile crept up her throat. Spending a romantic weekend with your wife but dipping out to call your mistress was trash behavior.

The volume of his voice grew fainter and fainter until she could no longer hear him.

Taylor went back inside and rushed upstairs. She knocked on the door to the bedroom being used for the photoshoot and waited, wringing her hands.

Jaci popped her head out. "Yes?"

"I need to talk to you."

"We're mid-shoot." Jaci turned her head. "Sabrina, give me a minute."

In the hallway, Jaci softly closed the door, then turned to Taylor. "What's going on? You look like you're mid-anxiety attack. For the second time this morning, I might add. Is this about Nick too?"

"No." She lowered her voice to whisper. "I overheard Sabrina's husband talking on the phone to another woman."

"Like…as in you think he's cheating on her?" she whispered back.

"He said he's only staying with her because he'll be cancelled if anyone finds out his whole devoted husband spiel is a lie."

Jaci blew out a breath. "Are you going to tell her?"

"I don't know. What kind of person does it make me if I let her spend a romantic weekend here and give him these photos that she pushed herself way out of her comfort zone to have taken when the whole time it's all a sham because he's just trying to keep her happy, so he doesn't lose his platform?"

"It makes you the kind of person who minds their own business. But…"

"But what?"

"What kind of person does it make me if I go back in there and keep photographing her knowing she's going to be presenting them to her cheating husband?"

Taylor squeezed her forehead. "That's not the type of women we are. We don't look the other way when someone is being wronged."

"Agreed. But what if she doesn't believe us?"

Good point. Sabrina didn't know them. Most likely, she'd confront Gavin and he'd deny it. Would she believe him or two women she'd met today?

"You should have recorded him. Then we'd have proof."

"I didn't think about it. It happened so quick."

Jaci twisted her lips to one side and huffed through her nose. "This could get really ugly. He said he doesn't want Sabrina to leave him because everyone would think he's a fraud and his little social media stardom would be down the tubes?"

Taylor nodded. "When she booked their stay, she told me how important privacy was to them because they get recognized a lot, and they wanted a weekend without that type of attention. So, I looked them up online. He gives advice to other men on how to be a wonderful husband. She appears in a lot of the videos, but he's definitely the star."

"What a sick fuck. He's not going to come clean, Taylor. It's going to be your word against his. Are you sure you want to do this?"

"What if I could get proof?"

"Like hope you overhear another conversation with his mistress and record it?"

"No, like…I don't know. Anything that proves he's got a side piece. Maybe he's got a credit card statement showing he bought flowers or lingerie that wasn't for Sabrina."

Jaci's eyebrows drew down. "How would you get access to his credit card statements?"

"I know someone who I think could do that. Or at least, she might know someone who can."

"How long is that going to take? You can't let her go back to their cottage and bang while you're waiting for someone to hack his financial records."

"Go finish the shoot. Drag it out as much as you can. I'll pay for the extra time."

Jaci glared at her. "I'm not going to take your money."

"We'll discuss that later. You stall while I make a call."

Jaci nodded, then went back into the room.

Taylor went back down to her personal living space and sat on the couch. She pulled up Morgan's number on her phone and hit send.

"What's wrong?" Morgan answered instead of a greeting.

"How do you know something is wrong?"

"Sixth sense."

"I need to get in contact with that friend of yours who is a cyber sleuth. Also, I need this information fast. Like today."

"Um, okay. I'll give her a call. What's this about?"

Taylor gave her the rundown.

"If he's internet famous, I imagine it won't be all that hard for her to at least breach his privacy. Maybe he's got messages from his mistress."

"I'll take anything. I just need something to back up my claim so he can't deny it."

"Okay. Look, text me whatever info you have on him, and I'll pass it along. Hopefully, Nova can get to work it on it right away. I'll tell her it's urgent."

"Thank you."

Now, all she had to do was waylay Sabrina from seeing Gavin until she heard from Nova.

8
An Unwanted Title
Nick

"NICK, YOU'RE DRIVING ME mad," his mom said after stepping out onto the porch.

He launched the rubber baseball in his hand at the porch post again, but she intercepted it on the bounce back. He frowned and slouched, leaning back against the exterior wall of the house from his spot on the bench.

"What's bothering you?"

"Nothing," he muttered and tugged down his ball cap, which probably was childish behavior, but the only person around was his mom and technically, he was her child.

"I know you're devastated that you can't play baseball anymore, but everything will work out as it's supposed to."

"I've made peace with my career ending."

"What are you out here ruminating on then?" She sat on the bench next to him.

He sighed and leaned forward, bracing his arms on his thighs. "While I'm home, I planned to confess my feelings for Taylor and see if she'd give us a shot. *But* it seems she's into someone else."

His mom's silence was more profound than anything she could have said.

He glanced at her. "Well? Don't you have anything to say to that?"

"What were you expecting? Me to be shocked that you have feelings for Taylor?"

"Did Brody tell you?"

"No, Nicholas. I've known it since you were four years old. I always believed you would wake up and realize your feelings went deeper than friendship, but I didn't think it would take this long."

He scrunched his face. "You knew when I was four?"

"You've always had big feelings for her, even if they weren't romantic. Her parents couldn't set her down without you hugging her so fiercely you'd knock her over." She rubbed his back. "Why do you think she's interested in someone else?"

Out of respect for Taylor's privacy, he wouldn't tell his mom about her coming out of her bedroom looking freshly fucked with Jaci on her heels. "An educated guess."

"I'm sorry. I'm sure that's very painful."

"I don't want pity. Can't you tell me she'd be better off with me or something?"

She laughed and tossed the ball at the post, then caught it on the ricochet. "Would that really make you feel better?"

He shrugged. "Probably not. The possibility of having a relationship with Taylor took a lot of the sting out of my career ending. I guess I was naïve thinking that I'd even stand a chance."

"Why don't you ask her if she's interested in this other man?"

For one, because it wasn't a man. He could compete with another man, but if she wasn't interested in men at all, any chance he'd hoped he had never existed. "Maybe I'm afraid of the answer."

"The way I see it, you've got two options. Ask her and if she says yes, tell her how you feel before it gets serious"—she handed him the ball, stood, and smoothed her apron— "or hold your tongue and have a zero percent chance."

He hung his head, gripping the ball so tightly his knuckles burned. He sat there staring at the porch boards long after she'd gone into the house. His mom's logic couldn't be argued with. Accepting that didn't make the tight feeling in his chest any less painful.

His memory played a scene where Taylor came up to him after his first major league game and jumped into his arms. He'd wanted to kiss her. Maybe he should've. Even though he'd acknowledged he had romantic feelings for her, acting on them hadn't seemed fair. He wouldn't give Taylor less than she deserved, and at that time, he'd been unable to put her first.

He grabbed his cane and stood. Not knowing would eat at him. With only two weeks to convince her no one would ever love her like he loved her, he didn't have time to waste wondering if her preferences took him out of the running.

He got in his car and made it to the inn quicker than he ever had before. Nick was no stranger to speeding tickets, so that really said something. Half a second after shutting off the ignition, he got out. If he let himself hesitate even for a minute, he'd start second-guessing his decision.

Taylor had an open-door policy. It said so right above her doorbell. Guests and visitors need not knock. She locked the doors at nine p.m. and the security system activated. Anyone who'd booked a stay there received a temporary code to enter after that. Like he always did, he walked in and headed straight for the kitchen.

She looked up from her phone from where she sat at the island on a barstool.

"I need to talk to you about something."

Footsteps on the stairs caught her attention. She slid from her stool and headed in his direction. As she passed, she linked her arm through his and tugged him toward the foyer. "I am a thousand percent looking forward to having that conversation with you, but first, I need you to do me a favor."

He let her drag him along, not sure what to do with the gumption he'd worked up to ask Taylor if she was sleeping with Jaci. It'd been eating at him for hours and he wanted an answer to put him out of this misery.

Although, if the answer was yes, his misery was going to be far worse. "What're you getting me into?"

"I need you to entertain a guest for a little while."

"Why?" he asked.

"Because I don't want her to go back to her cottage yet."

He scrunched his face. "Is there something wrong with her cottage?"

"No. It's a long story," she said. "Just please do this for me and I'll fill you in on everything later."

Like he could say no to that face.

She stopped in the foyer at the base of the stairs.

Jaci and another woman came down.

"How did it go?" Taylor asked.

What the fuck was with Jaci and being with other women in bedrooms? Assuming that's where they'd been as the second floor was nothing but bedrooms.

"Great. We finished, but I have to run. My nana's caretaker called. She's refusing to take her medicine."

Taylor nodded and turned to the other woman.

She was short and curvy. She tucked her shoulder-length hair behind her ear and waved goodbye to Jaci. "Thank you."

"Sabrina, this is my friend, Nick. You mentioned wanting to see Aunt Penny's library. I'm expecting an important phone call, so I'm going to have Nick take you on a tour of the east wing. He spent a lot of time here with me when we were kids. He'll make the perfect tour guide."

"Oh, okay." Sabrina fidgeted with her necklace. "I'll call Gavin so he can join us."

"No," Taylor blurted out. "I think I saw him launching one of the kayaks. You can show him around yourself later."

Sabrina's nodded. "Alright."

"Oh, and you two have something in common. Nick also has a big following online. Although, his content is very different from yours."

Taylor turned to him, and he knew exactly what she was communicating without her saying a word. *What would I do without you?*

Her fingers brushed his as she moved past him and through the corridor to the kitchen.

"I hope that's what my husband's face looks like when I'm walking away from him."

Nick snapped his attention to Sabrina. He raised his finger to his lips, then winked.

Her eyes went wide. "She doesn't know?"

He shook his head, unable to suppress a grin because it *was* funny how everyone else picked up on it but her, even someone who didn't know them at all. If he didn't find the humor in his situation with Taylor, he'd turn into a whiny little bitch. "Hi. I'm Nick. Taylor's best friend since we were four."

She smiled big and shook his hand. "That's an impressive title."

"I'm kind of tired of it, to be honest."

Her smile grew bigger. "I'm Sabrina. My husband and I are here for the weekend. A friend recommended Taylor's inn because we wanted to go somewhere no one would recognize us, or at least if they did, they'd have the decency to leave us be."

"Well, it is pretty secluded here and Taylor works hard to keep the vibe lowkey." He nodded in the direction of the east wing of the house. As they walked down the hall, Nick asked, "What type of content do you make?"

"It's really my husband's account. Gavin is a licensed marriage counselor and posts about how to be a good partner. He has a book coming out."

Yeah, that was entirely different from the content he posted. His audience wasn't married men, for sure.

"And before you ask, no, our marriage is not perfect, and neither is he, but we keep trying."

"Is creating content your full-time job?" he asked, leading her into the library. Aunt Penny loved to read, and she'd often had boxes of books she'd rescued from the trash. Taylor and he had spent hours organizing the shelves with them.

"No. I'm a flight attendant." Sabrina's head swiveled as she took in the floor to ceiling shelves filled with books.

"That's cool. Where do you fly to?"

"O'Hare, mostly. What do you do?"

"Until recently, I played baseball."

Sabrina glanced at his cane. "I'm sorry."

Nick shrugged. "Life must have other plans for me."

She plopped down on an oversized reading chair. "Do you think Taylor's a part of that plan?"

"She *is* the plan."

They spent the next twenty minutes chatting about flying. She'd come from a family of aviators, and she'd been in a plane crash with her brother, who'd been the pilot. He hadn't survived, and for a while she never wanted to leave the ground again, but her brother had been fearless, and she wanted to honor his memory by being the same.

Taylor joined them in the library, shoulders slumped and face devoid of any joy. "Nick, could I talk to Sabrina alone?"

9
Who's Blushing Now?

Taylor

TAYLOR WALKED INTO THE kitchen, taking deep breaths, and trying not to puke. It wasn't the first time she'd told a woman her husband was a cheating asshole, but she imagined it wasn't something a person got used to.

Morgan's friend had cyber stalked him, or hacked him, or whatever, and apparently, it hadn't taken much effort to find the account of a woman who Gavin consistently liked posts of on a different platform than the one he posted on. She'd been able to get into her account and sure enough, found several months' worth of messages between the two of them. Nova had sent the screenshots of every message to Taylor's phone, but Taylor had been selective in what she showed Sabrina. The one with a selfie of the woman kissing Gavin's cheek was the one that had made Sabrina burst into tears.

After Sabrina went back to her cottage, she found Nick in her living room, folding towels from a basket she'd left on her giant ottoman. He glanced over his shoulder. "Do you have a minute?"

"Not really, no." She grabbed a glass and filled it with water.

"Can you make one for me? I did what you asked."

Taylor chugged down her water, then pulled her hair out of its ponytail and massaged her scalp. A tension headache was brewing. "What is it, Nick?"

He joined her in the kitchen and leaned his cane against the island. "Do you like women?"

"That's what you came here to talk to me about?" She closed her eyes and pinched the bridge of her nose.

"When I was here earlier, you came out of your bedroom with Jaci."

"And? You've been in my bedroom, and we haven't—" Taylor pressed her lips together and her face heated. Pointing out that she and Nick had never had sex wouldn't have made her blush until recently.

"So, you come out of your bedroom with her, and when you see me, you blush like you're doing now, and you want me to believe you weren't fucking?"

"Nick, it is none of your business what I do in my bedroom, but for the record, I like dick."

He drew back, like she'd hit him with something he hadn't seen coming. Okay, so, he probably hadn't seen that coming.

"Who's blushing now?" she asked.

The shock faded from his face, and the dimple in his cheek appeared. "You don't have to be so crass about it."

Taylor grabbed an orange from the fruit bowl and threw it at him.

Nick caught it like it was nothing, looked at it, then glanced back at her.

Oh, right. Professional baseball player.

She glared. "It would be nice if sometime when I throw something, it actually hit you."

"Or you could just not throw things at me." He took a step closer. Then another and another, until she backed into the sink.

He stopped in front of her. "Remember how I said I was thinking of moving back?"

She gave a barely perceptible nod.

"I was thinking we could try to...be more than what we are right now." He winced. "I butchered that. What I meant was—"

She put her hand up. "I know what you meant."

And this was not the time to discuss it. There really wasn't a time she'd ever want to talk about it, but this for sure wasn't it.

"I have feelings for you, Tay. I want to explore them."

She stared at him, paralyzed. It'd taken a lot to convince herself that Nick would never do this sober. It had kept her up at night for the first few weeks after he'd made his drunken confession. As time went on, and he never brought it up, she'd chalked it up to nonsense because he'd had too many drinks.

"Well?" he asked.

She raised her shoulders. "I don't know what you expect me to say."

"Yeah, I don't, either." Nick raked his hand through his hair.

"You don't like me like that." Maybe he thought he did, but he didn't really.

"Yeah, I do."

Her mouth went dry and her heart beat double-time. This was going down as one of the worst days of her life. "Well, you should've kept it to yourself until it went away."

"I tried that."

"Try harder."

"Really, Taylor?" He shook his head. "Look, I didn't think you were going to say you feel the same way, but it's pretty fucked up for you to think I'd bring it up on a whim."

"It's pretty fucked for you to spring this on me when I'm working, and if you can't tell I'm having a bad day, then you don't know me as well as you think you do." She pushed his chest.

He didn't budge. "I've felt this way for over a year, and I've only got two weeks to decide if I should move home or take an off-field job with the team. I don't have time to waste. I want to spend as much time with you as possible so I can prove this would be good between us."

"You can't show up and expect me to drop everything. I have a business. And a personal life."

"Does that mean you're dating someone?"

"Yes." Why did that lie come out so easily? Probably because right now she was scared to death and looking for an easy out.

"Who? Do I know him?"

"Yes." It wasn't entirely false that she was seeing someone. She'd been on a few dates with Pace Bloom. It hadn't gone anywhere. No chemistry existed between them, although she did enjoy his company.

"Who?"

"Pace."

Nick threw his hands up in the air. "The fuck? You're not serious."

"Why not?" He didn't get the right to judge her dating life. She'd never voiced her opinions about the bimbos he'd gotten involved with.

"Because…he's…"

"A decent guy? Someone we've both been friends for since first grade? Hot?"

"He's not gonna be after I smash his face in."

Her jaw dropped. "Nick, that's one of your oldest friends you're talking about."

"Who's hotter? Me or him?" He crossed his arms and waited.

He was insane. One hundred percent psychotic. "What does that have to do with anything?"

"It's just a question. Who do you find more attractive, Pace or me?"

"Well, I'm dating Pace, so…" This lie was growing. It was like her brain and her mouth had divorced and her mouth was wilding out. Pace was very good looking, but he didn't have Nick's swagger, or his piercing blue eyes. He was fit, but he didn't have Nick's chiseled abs or biceps the size of a football.

"That's not an answer."

"I'm not attracted to you. We've been friends since we were four."

"You've been friends with Pace almost as long."

"I'm trying to avoid hurting your feelings."

He scoffed. "No, you're not. You're trying to avoid admitting you find me attractive at all, let alone more attractive than Pace."

"Your ego is absurd. Honestly. All those viral videos really did a number on your grasp on reality, huh?" She tried to get around him, but he put his hands on the sink's edge, trapping her.

He shook his head slowly. "It's got nothing to do with that. I can feel it the second I walk into a room you're in—I don't know where it came from, or how, but something changed between us. I know it's not one sided. You don't act the same around me. You're fidgety, and you look away when I catch you looking at me. Learning that I can make you squirm, and blush, inflates my ego way more than social media ever could."

"Please stop," she said in a calm but verging on furious voice. "Don't do this to our friendship."

"I'm not asking you for anything right now, except maybe to acknowledge to yourself that you're attracted to me and agree to spend time with me while I'm home."

"Don't you think it's kind of shitty that you're trying to talk your oldest friend's girlfriend into spending time with you?"

He lowered his face closer to hers. "I've known him a long time, but I'd burn our friendship to the ground for you. You're more important. You always have been, and always will be, even if you do something stupid like marry Pace. I will always be in your life. There's no getting rid of me."

"You sound like a fucking stalker."

He grinned. "The way you have me twisted might turn me into one."

"This isn't funny." Nick was her safe space. The most important relationship in her life. She'd be lost without him. Trying to navigate a romantic relationship could ruin what they had now.

"Has *he* been in your bedroom?"

"That's none of your business."

The back door opened, and Hope came in.

Nick let go of the counter and put space between them, limping to do so. "I know you're busy, so I'm gonna go, but I'm coming back tonight. We're not done talking about this."

"I'm going out with Pace tonight." Apparently, panic made her into a liar. She didn't want to talk about this ever again, and she'd say anything to get out of it.

His eyebrow shot up. "Thought you were playing corn hole with Jaci?"

Shit. "I am. Pace is on the league too. We're going out afterward." Not all lies. Pace really was on the league. And as soon as Nick left, she was going to text him and see if he wanted to go out with her after corn hole.

"Taylor," Hope said. "I filled all the bird feeders. What do you want me to do next?"

"Check the pool. It was vacuumed a few days ago, but there might be some leaves. Do you know how to test the pH?"

"No."

"Don't worry about it, then," she told her. "I'll show you later. Use the net to get out any leaves, straighten the chairs if needed, and put up the umbrellas."

"Okay." Hope shrugged, then bounced out the door.

Nick stepped into her personal space. "I want to spend time with you regardless of whether it leads to more. If you've got plans tonight, fine. Give me tomorrow night."

Telling him she had plans then too was on the tip of her tongue, but she resisted the urge to lie again. "I'll think about it."

He pressed his lips firmly together and shook his head. After one last scorching look, he walked out.

10
A Chance to Slide In
Nick

Taylor had a boyfriend.

And it was Pace.

What. The. Fuck.

Damn it. That was almost worse than her being a lesbian. Almost. He could compete with Pace. Not so much with Jaci if Taylor had been with her.

He thought about showing up at corn hole, but that'd piss her off. His quota for that had already been met today. Physical therapy and editing videos took up his afternoon. He had enough footage to get him through the next two weeks without having to shoot more.

After dinner with his family, he went for a drive to get out of the house and find a way to blow off steam. He ended up driving by Colby's house. Spotting him sitting on his front steps, he pulled into the driveway. They'd played ball together from tee ball to high school. Nick didn't consider him as close of a friend as that mother fucker Pace, but they'd always gotten along and had fun together.

"What's good, man?" Colby asked as Nick walked up to the porch.

Colby had a little girl and an even littler boy, who were using chalk on the sidewalk.

"Don't ask me that right now." Nick couldn't think of one good piece of news to share.

Colby lifted his chin. "What's up with the cane?"

"My injury is worse than I was ready to admit at first."

"That sucks. Want a beer?"

"I want many beers." Getting drunk wouldn't solve his problems, but it's not like he had anything better to do.

Colby nodded at the two kids on the sidewalk. "Keep an eye on them."

Nick eased himself onto the second step and stretched his legs out. "That's a pretty good dolphin," he said to the girl. Colby's son was scribbling like a maniac. "I like those colors, bud."

They both smiled at him, then returned their focus to their artwork.

Colby came back, sat next to him, and handed him a longneck. "Moving home for good?"

"Thought about it, but nah, probably not." Nick twisted the cap off his beer.

"What're you gonna do?"

"I got offered a position on the team's social media team, and there's been some talk about being an assistant coach too."

"That's pretty sweet."

"Yeah, I guess. The best possible outcome if I can't play, right?"

Colby swirled the beer in his bottle. "Unless you got somethin' else you'd rather do."

"Ideally, I'd move home, help run the farm, and I don't know, I thought about settling down and doing the family thing."

"Got a baby mama picked out?"

Nick shot him a pointed look.

"Taylor?" Colby's eyebrows shot up. "Damn. Does she know that?"

"I told her today. Not the settling down part. Just that I had feelings for her and wanted to pursue them."

He whistled. "How'd she react?"

"Told me I shoulda kept it to myself until I got over it. She's dating Pace. Did you know?"

"Uh"—he scratched his chin— "I've seen 'em out together. It didn't

seem like they were hot and heavy, though. Just hanging out as friends."

"She's going out with him tonight."

"You talk to him yet?"

"No." He'd driven in the direction of his house. But Nick didn't trust himself not to fly off the handle. A few days to digest this turn of events and cool down would be wise.

"Know where they're going?"

"She said out to dinner but didn't say where." He shoulda fucking asked, though. The news had scrambled his brain.

"There's not that many restaurants in town."

Nick squinted at him. "Are you saying I should track them down and interrupt their date?"

Colby shrugged, then took a swig of his beer. "I think you should judge for yourself if she's all starry eyed, or if there's a chance you can slide in there."

"She'll kill me."

"Don't let her see you."

"I don't trust myself not to cause a scene if I don't like what I see, and then she's really gonna be pissed. Probably kill me, and then resuscitate me so she can kill me all over again."

"I'll go with you and hold you back."

"You're gonna be the voice of reason?" Nick laughed at the absurdity. Colby's impulsiveness rivaled his. He was the kind of guy who got into bar fights, not the kind who broke them up.

"Might be the blind leading the blind. We should still do it."

"Is Bree gonna be cool with it?" Nick asked.

"If I tell her I need to be your moral support while you endeavor to win Taylor's heart? Hell, yeah. Especially, if I handle bedtime first. '

"I don't wanna go to bed," Colby's son said, staring up at his dad with round eyes.

"Not right now, little man." He glanced at Nick after the boy had gone back to his sidewalk art. "I swear he's a sleeper agent and his trigger word is bedtime."

Nick walked into Mallard Point, Colby on his heels. He shouldn't be here. He should've stayed home...losing his mind while Taylor laughed and blushed and failed to see that she didn't belong with Pace.

Nick's jealousy was making him into one of those people. The kind who pulled stupid shit because he couldn't stand to even think about her with anyone else. The kind who would do something rash and unhinged if anyone breathed too close to her. The one who people whispered about because he acted like a goddamn fool.

Yeah, that was definitely him. Twenty-three years of being smooth, and not getting attached to any one girl went out the window. Forget it. That Nick was dead. The new Nick was a headcase. The reason they made straitjackets and built padded cells.

He didn't care. His awareness that he was acting irrationally didn't change a thing.

His gaze tracked around the bar, landing on two people standing at the jukebox looking awfully cozy. Pace placed his hand on her lower back, on the bare skin between Taylor's skirt and her shirt.

Nick gritted his teeth.

Colby slapped a hand on his shoulder and nudged him toward the bar. "Be cool, man. Don't talk to her until your head stops threatening to explode from seeing his hands on her."

"Is that what you do when someone touches Bree?"

"Nobody fucking touches Bree. Because she's my *wife*. Taylor isn't even your girlfriend. Trust me on this, if you want her to be, you need to settle the hell down and be smart about how you handle it."

He wanted to punch Pace in the nuts for asking Taylor out, but he'd feel shitty if this ruined their friendship, so he slid onto a bar stool. Maybe Nick's attraction to Taylor was beyond his control, but he'd set this in motion. He'd chosen to make a move on her, just like he'd chose to show up here. If he lost his two oldest friends, he'd have no one to blame but himself.

He ordered beer for him and Colby and had the bottle to his lips when he felt it—her glare. Slowly, he turned on his stool.

She sat at a table near the jukebox and...yep. Meanest glare in history.

Pace took the chair across from her. His attention stayed locked on Taylor and his brow furrowed.

Nick kept his face neutral—or at least hoped he pulled it off. He didn't want her to think this was amusing for him.

Pace tapped her arm, said something, then stood.

"Pace is coming over here," Colby said. "He's gonna fuck you up."

"Nah."

"What are you guys doing here?" Pace shoved his hands in his pockets.

"Getting drunk." Colby sucked down the rest of his beer.

Pace pinned Nick with a stare. "You here for that too?"

Nick shook his head. "Nope."

"What'd you do to Taylor?" he asked in a *what did you do this time* tone.

Anyone who'd known them for more than a second knew Nick was the last person Taylor needed protecting from. No one had ever messed with her without regretting it.

Nick shifted his gaze from Taylor to Pace. "Why do you think I did something to her?"

"I dunno. Maybe because she's looking at you like she wants to strangle you."

"She's a keeper." Colby winked at Nick. "I'm gonna go say hi."

Pace took Colby's spot, facing the bar, while Nick kept his back to it, never taking his eyes off Taylor.

Her gaze left his and flicked up to Colby as he approached.

"She's been in a mood all night," Pace said.

Nick sucked back his smile. He shouldn't be happy she was feeling even a fraction of the misery he did. But it meant that she'd been unable to stop thinking about him even while out with another man.

He liked that.

"Not my fault you can't keep your date happy, Pace."

Actually, it was. He grinned.

But that grin fell away when she stood and pushed by Colby, her sightline on Nick as intense as a laser.

She stopped in front of him and crossed her arms. "I can't believe you showed up here."

"You thought I was joking when I said you could turn me into a stalker?"

"Leave."

"No."

"What's going on?" Pace asked.

"Fine, then, if you won't leave, we will." Taylor grabbed Pace's arm and tugged.

After a weighty sigh, Pace stood. "Can't you two compromise on whatever it is you're fighting about?"

"You wouldn't be suggesting that if you knew what he wants," Taylor said.

"Tell him, Taylor. Tell Pace what I want to do to you."

Her face turned as red as a cherry. She tugged Pace again. "Come on."

"What's he talking about?" he asked, rooted to the floor.

Nick smirked against the rim of his beer bottle.

"We can talk about it on the way home." She pulled him again.

Pace followed her this time.

"I wouldn't exactly call either of them starry eyed, would you?" Colby asked once they'd gone out the door.

Nick shook his head. Pace seemed mildly interested, but his effort was minimal. The way he touched her was awkward, not familiar or possessive.

"What now? You gonna let them leave together?"

He rolled his shoulders and got up from his stool. "Nah."

Colby grinned and shook his head. "Fight fair. No using that cane as a weapon."

He rolled his eyes. "It's more likely that Taylor's gonna be the one throwing punches."

"You're probably right about that. I'm right behind you. Gonna get another beer first."

Nick left his half-drank beer on the bar and headed for the exit.

Taylor and Pace hadn't gotten far. They stood facing each other in the parking lot, and judging from her body language, he'd say their conversation was nothing if not tense.

She glanced Nick's way, arms crossed. "Can you leave us alone?"

He slowly shook his head. "Clearly, I can't."

"Let's go," she said to Pace.

"I wanna talk to Nick."

She glared at him. "Before you talk to me?"

"He'll tell me what's going on," Pace said. "You'll try to protect my feelings. I want the truth, so, yeah, I want to hear what he has to say first."

"You know what?" Taylor held her hands up in front of her. "You two have a nice chat. I'm going to get smashed with Colby."

Pace tipped his head back and groaned, but it did nothing to stop Taylor.

She passed by Nick, giving him the dirtiest look he'd ever received.

"What happened, Nick?" Pace asked, once Taylor was back inside the restaurant. "Didn't realize you wanted her until you couldn't have her?"

"I wanted her long before you started seeing her. How come neither of you told me there was something going on between you two?"

Pace knit his eyebrows together. "I thought you told each other everything. I assumed she'd have filled you in. I don't know why she didn't."

"I want you to bow out."

Pace bristled. "What?"

"I'm asking you to stop seeing her. This shit between me and her is complicated enough without adding you into the mix."

"We're not exclusive."

Nick took a step toward him and got in his face. "I'm not sharing her, Pace."

"That's not what I meant. Taylor can see whoever she wants." The calmness Pace always seemed to exude didn't make sense. He had a chance with a beautiful, smart, funny woman, and another man was getting in his way. If Nick had been in his shoes, he'd have already thrown punches. "If you want exclusivity, then you should ask her."

"She's not ready for that, so I'm asking you to back off. I've known you most of my life and I wouldn't think twice about taking a bullet for you, but I swear to God, Pace, if you come between me and her, I will rip you apart piece by piece."

"Christ, Nick. Settle the hell down." He shook his head. "I'll stay out of your way. This thing between me and Taylor isn't going anywhere—hasn't gone anywhere."

"You haven't had sex with her?" He held his breath waiting for the answer.

"Why haven't you asked her that?"

"I did."

"What did she say?"

"That it was none of my business."

Pace barked a laugh. "Good for her."

"She's mine."

His friend raised his eyebrows.

Nick's shoulders slumped. "I don't want to spend the rest of my life not knowing if my friend fucked my girl."

"The problem with that is, she's not your girl." Pace pulled his keys from his pocket. "Sounds like you're getting ahead of yourself."

"Something has changed between me and Taylor. It's not like it used to be. There's this electricity when I'm near her and I know she feels it too. I've never felt anything like it and I'm not going to let it slip through my fingers. I can see my future with Taylor. But I need a fair shot at getting her to see it."

"I didn't fuck her, Nick." Pace squinted at him for a minute. "I haven't gotten past a peck on the lips."

"Why do you keep asking her out if you know she's not into you?" It didn't make sense to him. Pace was laidback, but he wasn't a pussy. He'd never been shy with women.

"She's good company. We never run out of things to talk about. She always says yes, not to mention, she probably calls me more often than I call her to ask me out."

Nick narrowed his eyes. "Did she ask you out tonight?"

Pace nodded and jangled his keys. "To get at you, apparently. I feel so cheap and used."

"Well, it certainly fucked me up." Taylor was avoiding, and deflecting, and refusing to give in to something that had the possibility to be *everything*.

"Good."

11
Just Nick
Taylor

TAYLOR NEEDED OUT OF here. She'd been having a good time until Nick's idiotic ass had ruined it.

Or at least she'd been trying to have a good time. She'd been off at cornhole and had her first loss in the longest time. Yeah, Nick had ruined it before he'd even showed up.

For some stupid reason, she'd started comparing Nick and Pace. Then, she'd done something even stupider—tried to imagine what a date with Nick would be like.

She picked up one of the shots the bartender set in front of her and Colby. "Cheers."

She didn't wait for him to clink glasses, just tossed it back, then hissed and wiped her mouth with the back of her hand.

She sensed Nick behind her before she heard him.

"Come on. I'll take you both home."

"We're not ready," Taylor said without turning around. She didn't know why she had to disagree with him all the time. She wanted to go home, but she felt irrationally oppositional whenever he opened his mouth.

"Taylor." The flatness of his tone had her swiveling on her stool. He stood in a pissed off stance, white knuckling his cane.

She involuntarily gulped, then vehemently hoped he didn't notice. "It's still early."

"Today has felt like an eternity. I'm exhausted. Mentally. Physically.

Emotionally. My knee hurts like a bitch. I need to get off it."

A heaviness landed on her shoulders. What was she even doing? She loved Nick. Not romantically, but he was the most important person in her life. She didn't want to cause him pain, whether it be emotionally or physically. The problem was she didn't know what to do with any of this. He'd put her in a lose/lose situation.

"I'll find a ride home," she said, not meeting his gaze.

"Do you really think I'm going to get any rest not knowing how you get home from the bar?"

Her gaze jumped to his. The answer was a solid no. Even before he'd admitted his feelings, when everything was still one hundred percent platonic, he'd never have been okay with that arrangement.

"Taylor, give in this one time. It's not going to kill you."

Her stomach fluttered. The defeat in his tone and posture sent waves of shame through her. "Fine." She put cash on the bar and slid off the stool.

"I'm gonna stay. I'll get a ride home with somebody else," Colby said. "Don't kill each other."

On the way home, Nick's silence unnerved her. He didn't even turn on the stereo. His eyes stayed on the road, the veins in his forearm bulging from his grip on the wheel.

"How did this get turned around where you're mad at me?" she asked. "You're the one who crashed my date."

"A date that you set up to make me jealous." He still wouldn't even spare her a glance.

"That's not why I asked Pace out."

"Then why did you ask him out?"

"Because I thought it'd be easier to get past this if you thought I was unavailable."

"I don't want to play games, Tay. I get that you're struggling with this, but if that had been anyone other than Pace, I would be in the back of a cop car right now with bloody knuckles."

Taylor sucked in a breath and pressed her knees together. Oh, no. That was not the response her body should be having to that admission. "You're right. I'm sorry."

He sighed, and neither of them said anything until he pulled into the drive that led up to the inn and idled by the front door.

"You aren't coming in?"

The look he pinned her with made her feel even worse than she already did. "I think it's best if I go home."

"I don't." She unlatched her seatbelt. "You can ice your knee here."

"And then what? Are we going to hash this out? You wanna tell me again how you're not attracted to me and I'm selfish for admitting my feelings to you?"

"I never said you were selfish, Nick." She huffed. "Do you really need me to tell you that you're good looking?"

"Yes!" He slapped the steering wheel with both palms. "Is it really that hard to comprehend that I want the person I'm attracted to to think I'm attractive too?"

"You are attractive. But my feelings for you aren't those types of feelings."

"Goodnight, Taylor." He stared out the driver's side window, elbow on the door, fist to cheek.

"Come in. I said I'm sorry." Oddly, when they'd first gotten into his car, she didn't want him to come in when they got to the inn. She'd been panicky and desperate to get away from him. But now...

Him coming inside was the only thing she cared about.

Nick sighed and straightened his posture. "I'm not mad at you. Just... disappointed at how this all went down. And tired."

Her heart ached. Nick really hadn't done anything wrong. All he'd done was be honest, and she'd allowed her anxiety to convince her to treat him like his feelings didn't matter. But he was the only thing that mattered. She couldn't see herself with him that way, but she should have been more considerate of his feelings. Damn it.

She turned in her seat, facing him, tucking her leg underneath her. "Nick, please come in. Let me take care of you." That degree she'd planned to get in sports medicine would've come in handy right about now. She'd been all set to go to college—with Nick. Her first property tax bill for the estate she'd inherited from her aunt changed all of that. She couldn't keep the inn if she didn't have a fulltime income. It wasn't a decision she'd made lightly, and years later, she didn't regret it, but she'd always carry guilt for how that decision had impacted Nick.

He slowly turned his head. "Get out."

Taylor jerked her head, banging the back of it against the window. She put her hand over the throbbing spot and breathed through the pain. "You don't have to be rude."

"Get out, so I can park and come inside."

"Just leave it here. It's not in the way." She didn't want him walking that far with his knee already bothering him.

Nick killed the engine and unlatched his seatbelt.

She got out and waited for him by the front steps. His limp was more pronounced, and his pain and exhaustion showed in his slumped shoulders.

Inside, he made it to the small settee in the foyer and collapsed on it. He closed his eyes and leaned his head back.

Cal came into the room, tongue wagging. He snubbed her and went right to Nick who scratched behind his ears.

"Taylor," her mother whispered from the kitchen. She mouthed the words, "Do you want me to go out the back?"

She rolled her eyes. "Mom, come say hi to Nick."

She rushed into the foyer. "Oh, it's just Nick. I thought you had brought home a man."

"I'm not a man?" He darted his gaze darted to Taylor, then mouthed, "Just Nick."

Taylor bit into her lip. Her mom filled in as caretaker when there were

guests and she had plans that took her out of the house.

"You Van Belle women really know how to dent a man's ego."

"I didn't mean it like that," her mom said. "I thought it was someone she was more than friends with."

Nick scowled. "Nope. Just me, Miss Vi."

"If I'd known you were home, I'd have made you a white potato pie," her mom said. "Taylor, I bought you some new latex-free cleaning gloves and an aloe plant."

"Thanks, Mom." Her mother had lost a lot of her respect over the past few years, but she was a good mom. She catered to her latex-allergy and remembered all her likes and preferences. She turned to Nick. "I'll get you an ice pack. Do you want something for the pain?"

He gave a slight shake of his head.

"I'm going to get out of here. I just took Cal out about fifteen minutes ago."

As if he needed to prove he'd been properly cared for and was content, Cal laid next to Nick's feet.

With her mom gone, Taylor went about the kitchen hastily, snagging an ice pack from her freezer and wrapping it in a tea towel as she walked back to the foyer. She dragged an armchair closer to Nick and laid a throw pillow on the seat. "Put your leg up."

Without lifting his head or opening his eyes, he propped his leg up on the chair.

She knelt on the settee with one leg and put the ice pack on his knee. The lump in her throat made it hard to gain a decent breath. Crazy how someone she'd felt so comfortable around for her entire life suddenly had her flustered.

"Taylor, I'm getting second-hand stress. Stop thinking about it so hard. It's not that complicated."

"It's very complicated."

Nick rested his interlocked hands on his stomach, eyes still closed.

"No, you're making it complicated."

She took the deepest of deep breaths. "No, Nick, you made it complicated when you got drunk and spilled your guts. Now, I'm walking around with the knowledge that you've thought about…about getting me pregnant."

"What? I didn't say—" His mouth snapped shut. He opened his eyes and looked at her as solemn as she'd ever seen him. He swallowed. Hard. "When?"

"After Brody and Morgan's wedding, not long before you passed out."

"Fucking hell." He rubbed his forehead. "What exactly did I say?"

"That I'm the only one you can imagine having a baby with."

Cal lifted his head and whimpered.

Nick glanced at the dog. "Don't worry, bud, you don't have to share your mom with a sibling. She'd have to be attracted to me for that to even be a possibility."

The air around them was thick and charged with tension.

But suddenly, that feeling, that lump in her throat that made her unable to verbalize her feelings, disappeared. "We're not on the same page. You've already thought about all of this and decided you want things that I haven't even considered. I feel like I have five seconds to make the biggest decision of my life when you've had months to think it over."

He wiped a hand down his face. "I'm sorry. I don't want you to feel that way. You're right, I know what I want. It's you. And now I'm impatient to have you—not like that. I mean, yeah, I'm looking forward to that part, but I just want you to be mine, Taylor. And the last thing I want is to pressure you. I'll back off. I'll give you time." Nick grabbed his cane and used it to help him stand.

"My brain doesn't work like yours." She got to her feet. "I don't consider every angle, make a choice based on that data, then go for it. I wade in and figure things out as I go. I course correct all the time. Figuring out what I want isn't an instantaneous process for me."

"Taylor, you don't have to explain that shit to me. *I know*."

"Where are you going?"

"Home. I need to rethink what the fuck I'm doing."

12
The Van Belle Slugger
Taylor

"Leave me alone, Gavin."

Taylor glanced up from where she'd knelt to pull weeds from a flower bed next to the back steps.

Sabrina stomped up the path from the cottages to the inn.

"Let's go home and work this out in private," Gavin called as he followed her.

She stopped in her tracks and swiveled. "Don't talk to me about privacy. You had no problem telling the entire internet all the horrific details of my accident and my brother's death. You used my pain for your social gain. And you let everyone think you're the model husband, all the while you fucked your side piece. Get out of my face!"

"Go get in the car, Sabrina," he hissed. "*Now*."

Uh-uh. Taylor quickly grabbed her baseball bat from where it leaned next to the coat tree inside the back door. She came back out twirling the bat through the air like she was warming up to hit a homerun as she walked to stand next to Sabrina. She didn't say a word, but she did stare Gavin down. Hard.

He narrowed his eyes at her and crossed his arms. "What are you going to do with that?"

"Probably beat your ass with it if you don't get off my property right the fuck now."

His eye roll got under her skin. "This is between me and my wife."

She grinned and perched the bat on her shoulder. "Not anymore."

"I should report you to the business bureau for what you've done. I'm a guest and you violated my privacy. I'll tell them all about your trashy little bed and breakfast where you arrange for women to get sleazy nude photos taken and sell them sex toys like some back alley adult novelty store."

Not all were scum men. But this one for sure was.

Sabrina and Gavin weren't just any guests. They were pearl card guests. That meant they'd been referred to the inn by another pearl card guest. These were couples who sought discretion. Sometimes, that's all it was—a weekend away out of the public eye. But many of the guests took advantage of the additional services on her à la carte menu. Sabrina had requested the boudoir shoot, but it was Gavin who'd wanted to browse her "inventory."

And now that he'd got caught being a disgusting piece of shit, he wanted to have a tantrum and try to break Taylor down.

Well, good luck, ya ass.

She brought the bat down from her shoulder and slapped it against her palm. "The thing you don't realize about me, Gavin, is that I'm really good at getting stains out. For instance, blood from patio pavers."

His gaze tracked to Sabrina. "We have a life together. You can't just throw it all away."

"Me?" she shouted. "You cheated on me."

"We can work through this."

"I don't want to."

Taylor smirked. Good for Sabrina.

He huffed. "You're not coming home with me?"

Sabrina shook her head. "I'd rather be homeless."

"Well, you will be!" He raised his hands in the air. "Baby, come on. You're not thinking clearly. We'll go back and I'll sleep on the couch while we work through this."

"Don't gaslight me, Gavin. You've already spent an entire night trying to convince me to stay and you failed. How delusional do you have to be to think that I'd go back to that house where you screwed your mistress every time I was out of town?"

"That's not what happened."

Sabrina crossed her arms and glared. "Look me in the eye and tell me you never had her in our house while I was gone."

His mouth opened, then closed. He raked his hand through his hair.

"Goodbye, Gavin."

"Sabrina—"

"I didn't hear her stutter when she said goodbye." Taylor took a step toward him. "Leave. Do not make me tell you a third time."

He glared. "You're not going to do a damn thing."

Her eyebrow winged up. Challenging her was not a wise move on his part. Playing sports with boys since she was young had taught her that if she made a threat, she'd better follow through and show she meant business. She glanced at the bat, then back up at him for a half a second before she swung. The blow to his stomach sent him staggering, gasping for air like he'd swallowed a baseball.

"Oh, my god." Sabrina's hands pressed against her cheeks.

"Don't worry. I didn't hit him hard enough to do any damage, just enough to prove that I wasn't bluffing."

"Crazy bitch."

"You're right about that," she muttered. "If you've got any brains at all, you'll go to your car right now before I take another swing. Next time, I'll do a lot more than knock the wind out of you."

Taylor and Sabrina stood side by side as Gavin hobbled toward the parking lot.

"You can stay as long as you want," Taylor said once he'd gotten in his car and started down the driveway. "Either in the cottage, or I've got plenty of rooms in the house."

"I just need a day or two to figure out where I'm going to go." Sabrina brushed away a tear that streaked down her face. "I've had to start my life over before. I can do it again. At least I found out before we had kids."

Taylor's stomach knotted and she blew out a breath. "A few years ago, I found out that my dad cheated on my mom. A lot. It felt like he betrayed me too. I had to work up so much nerve to tell my mom, only to learn she already knew. And stayed. It was like losing both my parents—or at least the versions of them I'd believed they were. You did the right thing."

"I'm sorry. This must have opened those old wounds."

She ushered her into the house. "First off, you're not responsible for what happened with Gavin, so don't apologize. Secondly, those wounds have been infected and oozing puss since it happened. But, in a way, it is healing to see a woman I admire respecting herself enough to leave a bad situation."

"I wish that it were as simple as walking away, but we just finished renovating the house we bought. We've lived there less than six months. The worst part is that thousands of people are going to know. I won't be able to wallow in private. It's going to get out and everyone who follows him is going to have an opinion about it."

"Well, fuck them. Stay offline and protect your peace. They'll forget about it soon enough."

"I don't feel very peaceful. I'm so pissed, I want to break something."

"How about hitting something?"

"What do you mean?"

"I'm all worked up—not about this. I've got my own troubles. I was gonna go to the batting cages and take my feelings out on a bucket of balls."

"I never played baseball or softball."

Taylor shrugged. "I'm sure you'll do fine. Come on."

After letting off steam at the cages, Taylor and Sabrina came back to the inn. Sabrina went to her cottage to shower and rest.

Jaci was waiting for Taylor in the kitchen, bouncing right out of her skin.

"What?" she asked, mentally exhausted and glad she didn't have to pretend to be polite with Jaci.

She held up an iPad and squealed. "I have your boudoir photos."

Great…

"I don't want to look at them right now." Or maybe ever.

Jaci stuck out her bottom lip.

"Trust me, they'll be better received after I've eaten, had several alcoholic beverages, and gotten out of this bra."

"I'm insulted. This is my art and I'm proud of it and anxious to show you."

She pulled two bottles of beer from the fridge. "I'm sorry. I just… everything is so wrong right now. The whole debacle with Sabrina and her cheating scumbag of a husband. Not to mention, Nick told me he has feelings for me, and then he crashed my date."

"Nick told you he has feelings for you? And you didn't lead with that? Was he sober this time?"

"Yes." Taylor handed her a bottle and walked to the back door. She went to grab Cal's leash off the hook, but it wasn't there. "Cal?" When he didn't come bounding around the corner, she looked at Jaci. "Have you seen him?"

She shook her head. "No, but I'm sure he's somewhere in this big ass house. He probably found a sunny spot to take a nap in."

"He's not here." Taylor set down her beer and pulled her phone from her back pocket. She pulled up Nick in her contacts. As soon as he answered, she asked, "Where's my dog?"

"Having a blast running around the farm with Reece."

It wasn't uncommon for Nick to take Cal to his family's farm to run around with his brother's dog, but he'd never done it without her. "You couldn't have let me know?"

"Who else is this big mutt gonna willingly go with? I didn't think it'd take much for you to figure it out. Do you want me to bring him back?"

"No."

"Ever?"

She rolled her eyes and suppressed a laugh. "You may not steal my dog, Nick."

"I can't steal something that's already mine."

"You gave him to me. You do realize that means he's mine, don't you?"

"I realize that, but he doesn't, so…" It was too easy to picture the big, dopey grin he probably wore. Cal had been bonded with Nick since he was a puppy, and the dog's affection for him inflated his ego.

"Give him a bath before you bring him home."

"Yes, ma'am."

"Bye, Nick."

"Bye, Taylor," he said, drawing her name out. She'd always liked the way her name rolled off his tongue, but this time there was an undertone to it that made her stomach do weird flippy-dippy things.

She caught Jaci grinning after she ended the call. "You know you get all smiley when you talk to him? I've never seen anything like it."

"I smile all the time."

"Not like that you don't."

Taylor set her phone on the coffee table, twisted the cap off her beer, and plopped onto the sofa. "Don't give me a hard time about this or I won't look at your pictures."

Jaci set the iPad on the coffee table. "The photos can wait. But my curiosity about what went down between you and Nick can't. I want the tea."

"Well, it started with him asking me if I'm a lesbian."

"What?" Jaci laughed and dropped into an armchair. "Why would he think that?"

"Because he's an idiot. When he saw us coming out of my bedroom together, he jumped to that conclusion."

Her eyes went wide. "And he was jealous?"

She nodded.

"That's too funny."

"I probably should have just let him think that. Instead, I exaggerated about my relationship with Pace."

"Taylor!"

"I panicked. And once the lies started rolling, I couldn't seem to make them stop."

"He thinks Pace is your boyfriend?"

"No. We got that cleared up."

"So, now what?"

"I don't know. I told him I needed time to process."

"Are you considering—What is it exactly that he wants?"

"He wants…" She took a deep breath, then slowly released it. "He wants it all."

"All? You mean like all of you…forever?"

"I think so."

Jaci's mouth formed a perfect O. "That's intense. How do you feel about that?"

Taylor chugged down her entire beer.

"That good, huh?"

"What if I turn him down? Am I going to regret it one day? And what if I do and it's too late because he finds someone else?"

"You're having Nick FOMO?" Jaci tilted her head side to side. "I mean this in the most loving, supportive way possible, but Taylor, you are really good at not knowing what you want."

"I know," she whined, then hung her head.

"Do you really think there's a possibility that you'll change your mind?"

She gave a slight shrug. "I can't see myself with Nick, but the idea of him with someone else…yeah, I don't like that at all."

"When you try to picture yourself with him, is it on a date or…?"

"Not exactly. It's not like I'm trying to imagine us in bed together, but just different than we are now."

"Do you think he's going to treat you differently?"

"Well, yeah." She went to grab another beer.

"How so?"

"I assume he'll want to kiss me and shit."

Jaci laughed. "Yeah, probably."

"What if kissing him is like kissing Pace and there's no spark?"

"When you're around Pace, you're calm. When you're around Nick, you get flustered. You wouldn't be like that if you didn't have a crush on him."

"A crush on Nick? Please."

"Taylor." Jaci gave her a stern look. "You were flirting with him on the phone."

"No, I wasn't. That's just how we interact."

"Exactly. You already have chemistry in spades, but you don't recognize it for what it is because it's always been there."

Taylor chewed her bottom lip while she considered whether that was an accurate statement. She couldn't argue that they didn't have a bond. But she didn't know about chemistry. What she felt for Nick was not what she'd always assumed being enamored with someone would be like.

"Look, I think you just need to retrain how your mind sees Nick."

"And how am I supposed to do that?"

"Remind yourself that he's a potential candidate for a trip to Pound Town."

Taylor flicked her bottle cap at her.

Jaci giggled. "No, but for real, Taylor, don't lose sight of the fact that that man is every woman's fantasy, but the reality is he wants *you*. If you want to, you can go from being one of the many who stalk his profile for new videos every day to the one who gets to see him all the way naked. You can be the one who gets to touch him. You can be the one he presses up against a wall and goes feral on."

"He wouldn't do that."

"See, that's the problem. You're confusing what he won't do and what he wants to do."

"You don't know what he wants."

"Trust me when I say he is holding back out of respect for you. There's zero chance he doesn't think about all the ways he wants to get his hands on you."

13

Lego, a Leonberger, and a Longshot

Nick

"How do I get her to give me a chance?" Nick glanced over at his passenger.

Cal stared at him for a moment, then went back to looking out the window at the fields of wheat they passed.

"I could spend a lot more time with you if me and your mom were in a relationship."

The dog rested his head on the door, snout out the open window.

"Fine. Don't help me. I'll figure it out on my own." He turned onto Taylor's driveway. Once the house was in sight, he spotted her out front, cutting roses from a bush. He parked in the main lot and walked around to the passenger side, opening the door for Cal like he would for a date. When the dog didn't immediately exit, he whistled and gestured with his cane in the direction of the house. "Let's go."

Cal whined, but complied, trotting next to him.

Taylor waited for him on the front step with one hand on her hip, and a basket with the roses looped over her other arm. The sleeves of her black button-down shirt were rolled above her elbows. Her cream-colored skirt clung to her hips and tapered in at her knees where it ended. Her long hair in loose curls pushed back over one shoulder. She looked super sophisticated, aside from being barefoot. When Cal reached her, she crouched and rubbed his head. "Did you have fun?"

His tail wagged wildly.

Her gaze traveled up to Nick. She slowly rose. Without a word, she walked inside, then turned to him, her back against the door.

He made it up the steps and into the house without too much struggle.

Neither of them said a word until she'd filled Cal's food bowl.

She dropped onto her couch and shifted around some tiny pieces of plastic on the coffee table.

"What are you doing?" he asked, amused to see her assembling LEGO.

She tapped a box with a depiction of a little house with a bunch of balloons attached to the top. An old man figure, a little boy, and a dog were positioned in the yard. "Wanna help?"

He raised an eyebrow, but her gaze stayed trained on the instruction book in front of her. His thigh brushed hers when he sat next to her, but she didn't scoot away, so he stayed glued to her side. "Since when are you into LEGO sets?"

"It gives me something to focus on so I don't dwell on things that make my anxiety spiral out of control."

"You could've called me. I'm a pro at distraction."

She snapped together two small pieces and without looking up said, "How's that supposed to work when you're the thing I'm dwelling on?"

He flinched. Being reminded that she'd known how he felt for six months and hadn't breathed a word about it was a sucker punch every damn time. "I'm the reason you have anxiety?"

She flipped a page in the instruction book. "Not exclusively. Definitely top three, though."

"What are the other two?"

She sighed and brushed her hair out of her face. "I'm on the verge of losing my shit. I just want to put together some LEGOs and let my emotions take a nap."

Shit. He wanted to be the one to put her mind at ease, not stress her the fuck out. He'd always been that for her in the past and it absolutely sucked that after all this time, he'd ruined that.

Maybe he could turn it around.

It's not as though he had anything even close to a plan to win her over and hell if he was going to wing it. Right now, he didn't even care about convincing her they'd be good together. Because being with Taylor was good. It was always good. That's all he wanted—to be with her. Next to her. If she wanted to build LEGOs, then they'd build LEGOs and not talk about relationships or feelings.

"How am I supposed to help when you have the only instruction book?" he asked.

She pushed two cellophane bags to the side, directly in front of him. "Put together the balloons. I'm sure you can figure that out without instructions."

"Your faith in me is impressive."

Her gaze cut to him, and she squinted, her lips pursing in that way that perfectly translated what a dumbass she thought he was. But a dumbass she had a soft spot for.

He winked, then bumped his shoulder to hers.

Her elbow connected with his stomach.

"Ow," he said in a flat voice.

"You're not tough." She snapped another plastic brick into place.

He chuckled and reached for a bag. "Is that a challenge?"

"No. Just a fact."

He snorted. "You think you could take me?"

"I took my bat to someone today. Don't think I won't do it again."

"I'm sorry. You did what?"

"Sabrina's soon-to-be ex-husband was hassling her into leaving with him. I warned him to back off, but he didn't comply fast enough."

What the—"You for real hit him with a bat?"

She nodded.

"Did he leave after that?" That fucker better have.

"If some crazy chick hit you with a bat, would you hang around?"

"If that crazy chick was you?" he asked. "Yeah."

"Well, he's smarter than you, I guess."

"Is Sabrina okay?"

"Probably not. She's going to stay here for a while."

"So, you're having a fun week, huh?"

"Mmhmm."

Kinda scary that Taylor had hit some dude with a bat. It had nothing to do with the violence she'd directed at him—that fuckhead deserved it—and everything to do with the uncertainty of other people's behavior. The guy could have retaliated instead of leaving. Nick worried about her being here with a bunch of strangers less since he'd given her Cal, and Taylor could take care of herself for the most part, but no one was immune to bullets.

On top of her physical safety, her emotional wellbeing also had him concerned. It wasn't enough that she had a business to run all by herself, she belonged to all sorts of committees and social groups and regularly hosted cocktail hours and brunches. And she didn't even like being around groups of people. Since she'd chosen to run an inn, she'd put her all into it, and she wanted the community to take her seriously, especially since she'd been so young when she'd taken it on.

Brody and Morgan's wedding had been a small affair, but that didn't stop Taylor from going all out. The baby shower was a little more lowkey. It still wasn't an easy task to organize and host, though. Then, he'd showed up and dropped his news—both the announcement about his career ending that'd made her cry *and* his feelings for her. To make matters worse, he'd stalked her and ruined her date with Pace. Although, honestly, he was having trouble feeling bad about that.

Taylor's happiness was everything to him. He didn't want her sad or stressed, and moreover, he didn't want to be even a small part of what caused it.

"Do those look like balloons to you?" she asked.

He glanced at the pieces he'd been putting together while he'd been lost in thought. Instead of connecting the straight pieces meant to be strings to the colorful sphere-shaped ones, he'd absentmindedly linked them one after another. It looked more like one of those dividers with small buoys every few feet that mark off the lanes in swimming pools.

"You didn't even let me glance at the directions," he muttered.

She tapped the box. "It's only three pieces."

"I'm doing my best." He flopped back against the couch cushions. "Guess my back-up plan of starting a construction business needs some rethinking."

Her laugh spread over him like an unexpected breeze on a sweltering hot day—rejuvenating, blissful, and reminding him how divine life could be. "You could have a bright future in dog-sitting."

As if he'd been listening, Cal came over and got up on the couch, sitting in Nick's lap like he was a two-pound Pomeranian and not a 150-pound Leonberger.

"Cal," Taylor shrieked like a mother whose child had unexpectedly been disobedient.

Nick scratched behind his ears. "He's okay."

She shifted, turning her body toward them. "He's not allowed on the furniture."

Cal whimpered and shrank down, like he could merge his body with Nick's.

"Stop being such a meanie."

"Stop being such a softie. Make him get down."

Nick sighed and pushed Cal. "Come on, boy, you know the rules. Your mom won't let us hang out anymore if she thinks I'm a bad influence on you."

Cal didn't budge.

"Oh, my god. You've ruined my dog."

That might not be entirely inaccurate. Taylor had been firm with him since he was a puppy, and he always followed her commands. But when it was just the boys, Nick let him get away with things she'd never allow. She didn't lie when she said he was a softie—a softie for the dog, and an even bigger softie for her.

If they ever had kids together, he'd have to get his act together or she'd be pulling out her hair trying to keep them in line while he played the fun parent. That's not how he wanted to be, though. Nick was on a mission to be more than her comedic relief. He wanted to be her partner. The one who she leaned on and unloaded on. The one she could fall apart on because she knew he'd put her back together. He wanted to be the one she *needed*—in every way.

"Cal, *get down*," she said forcefully.

He whimpered again but laid on the floor next to Nick's feet with his head rested on his paws.

"You're going to be the uncle who takes Brody and Morgan's kid for a day and brings them back filled up on sugar, missing a shoe, and so wound-up it takes them a week to get them settled down, aren't you?"

"No," he blurted out, his tone filled with offense. "They'll be missing both shoes."

She glanced at the ceiling and shook her head, but her bright smile let on that she didn't think he was one-hundred percent terrible.

"Maybe Aunt Taylor can keep us in check."

Her smile fell and she tensed.

"I didn't mean it like that." He really hadn't. Did he want to marry Taylor? Fuck yeah, he did. But even if they stayed just friends, she'd be Aunt Taylor to Brody and Morgan's baby. Even if she hadn't known him and Brody most of their lives, the bond she'd developed with Morgan made her family. "There's no doubt in my mind you're going to be super involved in that kid's life. And I was just joking anyway. I want to be the fun uncle, but I don't want to create headaches for the parents."

"I know you've got the best intentions, Nick. You have to admit,

though, that child is going to learn as quickly as Cal did that their uncle is a big goofball who can be swayed with *pity me* eyes.

He frowned and pushed up off the couch. He might be fun, but he was trustworthy. Brody and Morgan could depend on him to be responsible when looking after their kid. "I returned Cal in one piece, and gave him a bath, which I would have done whether you ordered me to or not. Being fun doesn't mean I'm negligent."

"Nick…" She sighed. "You're taking what I say the wrong way."

No, he wasn't. It was just that the way she saw him and the way he wanted her to see him were two vastly different things. He couldn't hold it against her though because how she saw him was what he'd spent the last twenty years proving he was.

14
Taking Notes
Nick

"She doesn't take me seriously," Nick said.

"To be fair, you're a fucking clown ninety percent of the time." Brody swung a leg over the bench of the picnic table in his backyard and sat.

"That's an exaggeration."

He squinted against the sun. "Is it?"

"You tease Morgan all the time."

Brody nodded slowly. "What do I tease her about?"

"I don't know." Lots of things. Nick didn't take notes on his brother's relationship with his wife. Maybe he should, though. She and Taylor didn't have much in common, but he wanted what Brody had with Morgan. Or at least something close to it. They weren't lovey-dovey all the time, but no one could be around them for five minutes without picking up on how crazy they were about each other.

"Banging her, Nick. I tease her about banging her. And then—get this—I bang her. Is that your dynamic with Taylor?"

His shoulders slumped. "No."

"Morgan takes me seriously because I do what I say I'm going to do, even when I'm clowning around with her."

"Good for you, I guess." Coming to Brody for relationship advice might not have been the best idea. So far, all it was doing was making him bitter.

Last night, he'd stayed up thinking about why Taylor had tried to make it work with Pace. He'd narrowed it down to the one thing Pace had that he didn't—tranquility. Brody had the same steady confidence Taylor seemed to seek, so here Nick was.

"Look, man, you've treated Taylor like your friend for twenty years. If you want her to see you differently, maybe you should treat her differently. You know, like a woman."

Nick blinked at him.

"Fucking hell, Nick." Brody shook his head. "Let her know you want her."

"I already told her I want her."

He shook his head. "Show her."

"How? Kiss her?"

"No. Get her so twisted up that she *wants* you to kiss her."

Nick had always been kind of a ladies' man. He knew how to flirt— some might even say exceptionally well. But he couldn't say what he said to other woman to Taylor. Not because it was scandalous or disrespectful. Just because it didn't feel right to. "I don't know how to do that with her. She's immune to my charm."

"She's watched you flirt your way through how many girls over the years? Do you think she wants to be wooed the same way you wooed them, or maybe, just maybe, she wants to feel special?"

"Oh."

Brody steepled his hands on the table and tilted his head. "What's the longest Taylor's been in a relationship?"

"I don't know. Three or four months? Unless she hid it from me like she did with Pace."

"Pace?"

"Yeah, they've gone out a few times. Maybe a lot of times. I don't know. He said nothing ever happened." Pace wouldn't lie to him, so he believed it, but he still didn't like it that he'd have taken the opportunity if Taylor had been down for it.

"Is he going to take her out again?"

"Not unless he wants to end up in the morgue."

Brody shook his head. "I can't wait until she finds out what a psycho she turns you into."

Nick groaned.

"Actually, maybe that'd help."

"What?" He raised an eyebrow. If his brother had any ideas at all, at this point, he'd try anything.

"She likes that you make her laugh. If she didn't, she wouldn't have put up with you for this long. So, I don't think you being a clown is turning her off. And I could be wrong about this but...I think Taylor's lack of concern over finding Mr. Right is because she knows she's already found him. Subconsciously. If she witnesses how intense you get at the mere mention of her with another man, maybe it'll trigger something."

"You think me acting jealous will make her realize we're meant to be together?"

Brody laughed in his face. "No, dumbass. I think seeing that possessiveness might turn her on."

"Oh." He scratched the back of his neck and squinted. "Really?"

"You're fucking hopeless."

"How am I supposed to know that me dismembering some prick for eye-fucking her will make her hot for me? Not a situation I've ever been in, ya fuckin' jerk."

Brody grinned. "Maybe it won't. Don't know if you don't try. But don't take her out and purposely get into a fight. All you gotta do is let her know she doesn't have to be with you, but no one else is going to be with her."

"Fuck. That's good." He pulled his phone out and started typing in his notes app.

"What are you doing?"

"Writing that down so I don't forget," he said without looking up.

"Dude, when did you get to be this pathetic?"

Nick shrugged and kept typing. "It's not cool being hung up on someone you might not ever get to be with."

"I know," Brody said flatly.

He pinned his brother with a *don't expect me to feel sorry for you* glare. "You got the girl."

"I spent five weeks believing that even though I'd never love anyone as much as I loved her, I was going to have to live without her. I get how you feel."

Yeah, that had sucked. Brody had been a miserable SOB during those five weeks. Nick had tried over and over again to get him to go after her, but he'd been stubborn, wanting Morgan to meet him halfway. He supposed groveling wasn't his brother's style.

It might be Nick's, though. He couldn't say he wouldn't do some pathetic shit if it meant he'd end up with Taylor.

"You're gonna get the girl too, Nick. But I wouldn't expect it to happen overnight."

15

Fuck This Slow Shit

Nick

NICK WHISTLED AS HE walked through Taylor's foyer. A new day, a new plan. A solid one. Taking things slow with Taylor might be the most mature thing he'd ever decided to do.

No making moves on her until she invited him to do so. Until they figured this out. At her pace. It'd be fine. He could do that.

He froze in the threshold between the foyer and the kitchen, stopping mid-whistle. Kinda hard to whistle when he was choking on his tongue.

Taylor slid across the slick floor in her socks.

And not much else.

She caught her balance, then made a pathetic attempt at tugging her white T-shirt farther down her thighs, but it sprung up the second she let go, not quite covering her ass. "I wasn't expecting company," she blurted out.

Nick stayed in the threshold between the foyer and the kitchen. His gaze shifted up and down her body a few times. Her white cotton panties showed when she moved the smallest bit.

"This really isn't fair," he muttered and tugged his hat down, blocking his view, but the image of her hard nipples peeking through her shirt was burned into his memory. Apparently, the universe wanted to test his newfound patience.

"I'm going to go change."

He popped his hat up and gave her another up-and-down pursual.

Taylor shifted her weight from side to side and wet her lips.

Fuck this slow shit. He couldn't do it. Not if he was going to walk in on her looking like a wet dream on steroids.

And if a little part of her didn't want him to see her like this, she'd be in her bedroom changing, not standing there looking like the sexual tension radiating between them was so sweltering hot and thick she couldn't move.

Nick set his cane behind her on the island, then tugged one of the tendrils that had fallen out of her sloppy bun. "You have no idea what it does to me that I'm the only one who gets to see this Taylor—*my Taylor*." He trailed his fingers down her neck, across her shoulder, over to her arm, coasting the length of it.

"I don't belong to you." Her words caught in her throat, barely audible.

Nick grabbed his hat by the brim and tossed it on the island. He leaned his face closer to hers, using one hand on her back to press her tightly against him. "Are you sure?"

Her sucked-in breath made him ache to kiss her.

Their faces were close enough if either of them moved, their noses would touch. He wasn't going to make her beg him to kiss her like Brody suggested. He was going to make her come to him, so she couldn't say later that it'd been one-sided.

"We shouldn't be doing this."

"Let's stop, then. Go put on some clothes."

She wasn't going anywhere. He knew it. She knew it. She wasn't going to own up to it, though. Her chest rose and fell but her feet stayed put and her gaze stayed locked to his. Her lips parted, but no words came out.

Then, those lips brushed over his.

Nick wanted to pull her in even tighter. He wanted to crush his mouth to hers and touch every inch of her—see how wet he could get those panties. Instead, he took it nice and easy. The last thing he wanted was to get pushed away because he'd come on too strong.

She slid her palms up his chest and draped her arms over his shoulders. The movement did two of the best things that had happened in the history of ever—raised her shirt higher so that it no longer covered her underwear and pressed her tits to his chest.

Heat flashed through his body as he slid his hand under the fabric covering her hip, hooking it with his thumb. He spread his fingers and moved his palm to cover her ass.

Taylor's lips were soft, silky clouds he could spend all day kissing. She ran her hand up the back of his neck, her fingertips at the base of his skull.

He slanted his mouth across hers again and again until her hips started moving. He ended the best first kiss of his life, then stared at the backsplash. "Go get dressed."

Her stare was heavy enough he could feel the weight of it without looking. Probably wondering why he was giving her mixed signals.

"Do you for real think I'd let our first kiss turn into sex on the kitchen floor?"

"No, Nick," she said dryly. "You're the least impulsive person I know."

He let his jaw drop. *Rude*

"Don't even act offended."

He grinned and let go of her ass. "Keep me humble."

"Someone's got to. It's not a job for the weak or easily frustrated."

"I think this should be the official uniform for that position."

She tried to get out from where he had her caged in against the island, but he kept his grip on the edge with both hands. "I don't get your fascination."

"I guess because it's a plain shirt and panties, but you make it look like the sexiest thing to ever grace a woman's body. It's also *just* see-through enough to get my imagination running."

She stared at the letters on his T-shirt. "What now?"

"I'm in—into you. If I've got a shot, I'm going to take it. So, do I?"

"I don't want to make this decision."

Nick pressed his forehead to hers. "It kills me that you even have to think about it."

She might as well have ripped his heart out and poured acid on it. Not that she'd ever intentionally hurt him. Acknowledging that made it worse. It didn't matter how much he'd steeled himself against the possibility that she'd reject him, it crushed his soul that it wasn't an instant yes.

She looked to the side and pushed at his chest. "I have to consider the consequences."

Nick put his finger on her jaw and guided her gaze back to his. "What consequences, Taylor? If it's not what you want, I'll respect that"—while slowly dying inside— "but being worried it won't work out? I don't get that. Think about it. We're compatible. There's no one else I'd rather spend my time with. Hell, there's no one I'd rather fight with."

"Exactly. We have all of that. Can't it be enough?"

"No," he said hoarsely. "It's not enough for me. I don't want to feel guilty for how much I think about you or wonder what's so wrong with me that you don't want me like I want you."

Her chin dropped to her chest. "Nothing is wrong with you, Nick."

"Did you like kissing me?" If she said no, he was going to demand a redo.

"Yes," she whispered.

"Good. Now, get your ass in the bedroom. Fix your hair and put on your respectable inn keeper costume."

Her gaze lifted. "Costume? It's not an act. I grew up, Nick."

"You definitely grew up." He grabbed the back of her shirt, pulling it until it tightened over her tits. The fabric was thin enough to show the color of her nipples. He was so unbelievably hard right now he could barely see straight. "But this Miss Americana Inn Keeper persona? That's all it is—a persona."

"So, I'm fake? That's what you're saying?"

"Not at all. I'm telling you that I get it. It's your brand. I only show my audience a small part of me too."

"You don't have one single video with a shirt on. You show them plenty."

"Of my body. They don't see who I am when I'm with my friends and family, who I am when it's just you and me."

Taylor crossed her arms, taking away his view. "I don't have an audience."

"You do. Your guests. The community. The business association." He grabbed his cane and took two steps back. "But I don't fit into the image you want to portray, do I? It's one thing to be friends, but you don't want people to think you're dating a guy who is known for taking videos of himself in his underwear."

16

Her Plaything

Taylor

TAYLOR STAYED PUT, ARMS crossed and glare hardening. How dare he accuse her of being afraid of what others thought or putting on airs?

"The only image I'm trying to maintain is that I'm a capable business owner. You don't know what it's like trying to be taken seriously by a bunch of people who've run businesses or multiple businesses for years, or people who've got an MBA when all you've got is a high school diploma. But my personal life is none of their concern. I'll date whoever I damn well please."

"Prove it."

"No." She stormed past him, heading for her bedroom.

"Taylor, don't get all pissy." He tried to follow her into the room, but she shut the door in his face.

Whatever he thought, he was wrong. She'd never be embarrassed to have any type of relationship with Nick. He was so stupid. Her head spun as she selected clothes from her closet. Then, it hit her all over again. She'd made out with Nick in her kitchen. He'd had his hand in her underwear, grabbing her ass.

She sat on the side of her bed and took deep breaths.

A knock came from the other side of the door. "Can I come in? I know you're in there having an anxiety attack."

"No." She stripped out of her shirt and pulled the blue seersucker sundress she'd taken out over her head, then stood and tried to pull up the zipper. Her hands were too shaky to succeed. She'd had Nick zip up her dresses before, but she'd never wondered if doing so had affected him. Now, it was all her mind would focus on. She stood in front of the closed door, wringing her hands.

After a few minutes of pure panic, she reached for the door and flung it open.

Nick was leaning against the wall across from the doorway with Cal at his side. A wicked smile crept to his lips.

"Stop looking at me like that." She half-turned and motioned to her back. "I need you to zip me."

He pushed away from the wall and turned her completely around. His fingers brushed her spine as he slid the zipper up, sending her stomach into a tumble. "Is it really that terrible that I'm attracted to you?"

"It makes me uncomfortable." She headed for the bathroom.

"Why?"

She glanced at him, where he stood just outside of her bathroom. How didn't he understand this? "We've been best friends for so long. It's an adjustment realizing you think about me...sexually."

"You know it's more than that, don't you?"

She shook her head and wet her dry lips.

"Taylor, you're gorgeous. You're also funny and smart and creative. You get me. You're my person. You've always been my person. But now, I want to be more than just your friend. I want to be your man. I don't want there to be anyone else for either of us."

She turned on the water while he leaned his cane against the sink vanity and hopped up on the counter. After she'd washed and dried her face, she said, "I'm the same person I've always been. I don't know what happened to change the way you felt about me."

He blew out a breath and rested the back of his head against the mirror. "Maturity? Mine, not yours."

Hair freed from her scrunchie, she grabbed her hairbrush. "What do you mean?"

"When I started posting videos, the girls that were sliding into my DMs were all the same. Obsessed with their looks. Obsessed with mine. But that's about it. They lacked substance. Then, I realized whenever I was with you, I wanted to impress you a lot more than I wanted to impress them."

She pulled half of her hair back and secured it with a barrette. "Have you considered this is just you wanting what you can't have?"

"For a minute, but then, I realized that you'd started looking at me differently too, so maybe I could have what I wanted."

"I only started looking at you differently because you started posting those videos. Ironic, huh?"

Nick slid off the counter. "Are you saying it's only about my looks for you?"

"Are you going to cry if I say yes?" She grinned.

"Probably."

"You know that I enjoy spending time with you. But how we do that is going to change and I have to get used to that."

He pulled her into his arms and rubbed her back. "It's not going to change. Let's just hang out. I won't kiss you unless you ask me to."

She was going to have to ask him? The tightness in her chest increased and the back of her neck got clammy. That did not put her mind at ease. "I can't hang out. I have to go to an open house at the Slack Tide Inn."

"Play hooky."

"The owner texted me this morning to make sure I'd be there, and I said I would."

"Can I come?"

She froze. "If I say yes, are you okay with being introduced as my best friend?"

"Nope. Tell them I'm your plaything or I'll cause a scene."

"Stop being dumb."

He laughed. "How else would you introduce me if not as your best friend?"

"I don't know what you expect. That's why I asked."

"Tay, I'm the same easygoing guy I've always been. You need to get it out of your head that I'm going to pressure you into anything you're not comfortable with—whether that's how you introduce me to people or me touching you. Honestly, at this point, I'd probably make you beg a little just to make sure your consent is enthusiastic."

"Nick!" She smacked his biceps with the flat back of her brush and tried to curb her smile. He was ridiculous.

17

The Legend of the Lingerie Drawer
Nick

AT THE OPEN HOUSE, Nick got separated from Taylor. People recognized their hometown's pro ball player and wanted to chat, and the owner of the inn whisked her away to introduce her to his son—a bachelor with a perfect smile and perfectly pressed clothes. It made sense now why the man had been so eager to make sure Taylor attended this boujee party.

At the first opportunity, he excused himself from the small group of people asking him questions about his ball career and pretended to be casually getting a glass of lemonade from the refreshment table which happened to be a few feet away from where Taylor stood with the owner, the owner's husband, and his son.

"I gave Taylor a copy of your book, Pete," the owner, a graying man with peach Bermuda shorts and a white polo said.

"Oh," Pete said, lighting up. "Have you read it yet?"

Taylor lowered the wine glass she'd been taking a drink from and swallowed. "Mmhmm. Just finished it the other day, actually. I loved it."

He grinned. She was lying through her teeth. No one other than Nick could tell, but there was no way in hell she had read this dude's book. That was the same look she got in her eye when her mom asked if she'd been drinking the kombucha she kept buying for her. She hated the stuff and instead of telling her mom the truth, she loaded Nick up with her supply whenever he visited since he didn't mind drinking it.

"What was your favorite part?"

Nick fought off a laugh. He couldn't wait to see how she got out of this one.

"Oh, gosh. It's hard to choose just one. It's so well done that each part just seamlessly flowed into the next. There wasn't any fluff, which I appreciated. Every chapter had purpose, but that ending?" Taylor waved her hand in the air. "Perfection."

Pete beamed and leaned closer. "I'm flattered."

Of course, he fucking was. He had no idea it was all bullshit.

Nick walked over and stood next to her, so close that half his thigh disappeared in the folds of her swishy dress. His hand itched to reach around and settle on her waist.

"This is Nick Lewis," she told the group of men as she put her hand on his shoulder. "He plays for the Chesapeake Hustlers."

Pete's gaze shifted to his cane.

"*Played*," Nick corrected.

"Rough break." He reached out to shake his hand. "I'm Pete. Have you met my father, Bert? And this is his partner, Giles."

"I don't know how rough it truly is." Nick shook hands with them. "Getting injured sucked, but the silver lining is standing right here." He dipped his head in Taylor's direction.

She blushed and pressed herself up against his side.

Huh. Maybe Brody was onto something with the possessive strategy. He took her PDA as permission to throw out some of his own and wrapped his arm around her.

"Well, I guess we have two celebrities in attendance today." Bert patted his son on the back.

"Oh. Who else?" Nick glanced around the room.

Taylor's body convulsed slightly. She pinched his arm.

"Pete is an author. Obviously, his face isn't well known, but I'm sure you've heard of him. Pete Hencham."

Nick shook his head. "Doesn't ring any bells."

"Not a reader?" Pete asked.

"I read, but up until my injury, mostly non-fiction. Since I couldn't do much else, I read about thirty novels in six months."

"Any particular genre?"

"Nah. A little bit of everything. What genre do you write?"

"Postapocalyptic fiction."

"Interesting." Nick wasn't interested at all. Fuck this guy. "What's the title of your book?"

"Letters to the Last Light."

"Oh, I think I've seen that on Taylor's nightstand."

She cut her eyes at him, then turned back to the other men with a polite smile. "Is it okay if I show Nick your new outdoor shower? You've inspired me to put one in and Nick's planning on going into construction as his next career, so I thought I could give him his first job."

"Absolutely," Bert said. "Right this way."

"Oh, you don't have to leave the party. You're the host. I know where it's at and can show him—if that's okay?"

"Of course."

Taylor looped her arm through Nick's and tugged him toward the back door.

They went out onto a deck that overlooked the bay.

"You're bad," she muttered.

"Me? You're the one in there lying about reading his book and luring me away to the shower."

"You don't know that I didn't read his book."

"Did you?"

"No."

He grinned.

"And I'm not luring you to the shower for anything kinky, jackass." She let go of him and descended the stairs that led to the yard. "It was an excuse to get you out of there before you started telling them about my lingerie drawer."

He went after her as fast as he could manage. "You have a lingerie drawer?"

"Nick."

"What?" he asked once he'd reached the bottom where she waited for him. "You can't say shit like that to me and expect me not to get curious."

"I have no interest in Pete. There was no reason for you to imply you've been in my bedroom."

"Whether anything happens between you and me in that bedroom is entirely up to you, but I can promise you that you won't be having any other man in there."

She crossed her arms. "I never agreed to date you, let alone be exclusive with you."

His jaw about snapped from clenching it. "Show me the shower," he managed to grit out.

She rolled her eyes, then huffed and walked toward a small pergola with huge, lush plants growing around it, shielding the interior from view. Bamboo blinds hung from the roof, providing more privacy. Taylor pushed aside a thin, white curtain and stepped inside.

A stone bench was to one side, next to a teak table with an assortment of shampoos and body products. He counted a total of nine spray heads and a rainfall head. The floor looked like sand with shells and sea glass, but it was solid and not gritty. Powered-off twinkly lights were strung around each beam of the pergola roof.

He could never dream up something as cool as this. Forget about building something like it. "Very funny about my construction career, by the way," he said as he took a seat on the stone bench.

She stood to the side, a few feet out of reach.

"So, you wanna give this a go but you're not ready to stop playing the field?" He stretched his legs out. Taylor the player. What a riot.

"You said you weren't going to tell people we're more than friends while we were here."

"And I didn't. You were the one who cozied up to me. All I did was follow your lead."

She raised her hands and mimicked strangling him.

He lost the battle against keeping his smile off his face. "Relax, Taylor. All that happened was that Pete guy thinks you're spoken for. If you have no interest in him, what's the problem?"

"Because you took it too far, like you always do. Or you would have if I hadn't interfered."

"All I said was I saw his book on your nightstand."

"Implying that we've..." She trailed off and held her hand out as if he should be able to fill in the blank.

"That freaks you out, doesn't it? The idea of you and me having sex?"

"Yes. And I can't go five minutes without being reminded that you expect that to happen."

He narrowed his eyes. "That's bullshit. I've barely mentioned it, and when I have, it wasn't in any way that would have made you feel pressured. I told you that it's up to you. But that's not what's bothering you."

"Oh, really? What's bothering me then?"

"You're freaked out, but you also can't stop thinking about it. That's on you, not me. You can't blame me for it, which is really what's got you so pissed off."

She gasped.

He shrugged. "Tell me I'm wrong."

"I haven't been thinking about it that much."

That wasn't a denial. He raised an eyebrow.

She dragged her fingers through her hair.

"Taylor, come here."

She shook her head.

He nodded and crooked his finger at her.

When she was within reach, he grabbed her hand and gently tugged her to him, guiding her to straddle him.

"What are we doing?" she asked, tense and not fully lowering herself, her hands on his shoulders.

"I'm centering you."

"What?"

He cupped her face and forced her to look at him and nowhere else. "Listen to me. There's no catastrophe. Everything is fine. We're good. If it doesn't work out, I'm not going anywhere. You can't lose me."

She wilted, pressing her forehead to his. "Promise?"

"Promise."

He rubbed his thumb against her bottom lip. "You get to set the pace. All the control belongs to you."

"I don't think I want that," she whispered.

"No?"

She leaned back and shook her head. "I don't want to call all the shots. Thinking about it adds to my anxiety."

He grinned. "I'm still not gonna kiss you unless you ask."

She shoved his chest. "Then I guess there will be no more kissing."

"Up to you, babe."

18
No one's Plan B
Taylor

TAYLOR HOPPED OUT OF her Jeep and strode in the direction of the glowing campfire in Colby and Bree's backyard. After they'd left Bert's, Nick got a text from Colby inviting him over later, and Nick made her promise to meet him there after she ran errands, and he did physical therapy and spent time with his family.

A lot of promises were getting made today. She didn't know how to feel about that.

A pickup truck was parked on the grass, alongside a swing-set. The tailgate was down and Colby and Nick had perched on it.

Nick's gaze landed on her and the slow hint of a smile emerged before he lowered his head, his ball cap concealing his face.

"Cuz!"

Arms circled her middle and her feet left the ground.

"Spat, put me down," she squealed. Spat was her first cousin on her mom's side, tall as hell, and loved to toss her around like a rag doll. He set her back on her feet, and she smacked his shoulder. "Don't do that!"

He tilted his head and chuckled. "I'm never gonna stop doing that. It's my duty as your favorite cousin."

"Oh, man, I'm about to break your heart. Tig is my favorite cousin." She didn't really prefer Spat's brother over him, but she couldn't resist the opportunity to tease him.

"Liar," he muttered.

If he hadn't been a foot and half taller, she'd have patted him on the head. He was a good guy but his taste in women was shit. His worse half was probably around here somewhere. Maybe Taylor would get lucky and be able to avoid Olivia.

"You wanna do a shot?" he asked.

"Maybe in a bit."

Spat's gaze slid over to the truck. He flipped the bird at Colby and Nick. "Better be on our best behavior. He's watchin'." Okay, so maybe the fuck you was aimed at Nick solely.

"He's probably worried you're going to get me wasted and he'll have to deal with getting me home."

"He'd be right." He slung his arm around her neck and pulled her along to the house. "Did you two finally fuck?"

She pushed him away. "No. Why would you even ask that?"

"He's putting out vibes. I mean, he's always been protective of you, but something about how he was watching us felt different. I don't know, Tay. Maybe at the end of the night, he'd rather be pulling your hair than holding it back while you puke."

"You don't know what you're talking about."

They walked in through the back door and into the kitchen. Bree stood by the sink, blending something pink in a blender. Silver, Pace's younger sister, stood next to her, and smiled at Taylor.

"Let's get Taylor drunk so she doesn't have to do the dirty with Nick later." Spat grabbed a bottle of rum off the counter.

The blender stopped and Bree's head whipped around. "What?"

"You're an awful human being," Taylor muttered before turning to the women. "Disregard that. He's just talking out his ass."

"What woman would want to get out of that?" Silver asked. "I'll gladly bear the burden."

How much she wanted to knock Silver's teeth out must have been written all over her face because Bree raised an eyebrow at her.

"Nick would never touch you." Spat pointed at Silver. "He knows Pace would murder him."

"She's got a point, though," Trina said as she walked into the kitchen from the living room. Jeez, Taylor hadn't seen her since graduation. "His thirst traps have made me question how gay I really am. Besides being hot, I've never known him to be an asshole to anyone. I've never understood you two being just friends."

Bree handed Taylor a strawberry daiquiri. "Can y'all back off Taylor? She didn't come here for an interrogation about her relationship with Nick."

"My bad," Trina said, hands up. "I'm gonna go roast a marshmallow."

"I'll come with you," Silver said.

Spat lined up three shot glasses and filled them.

After they'd downed them, Bree crossed her arms. "I know I told them to leave you alone about Nick, but it's just me and Spat. What's this about Colby going with Nick to Mallard Point to be moral support while he crashed your date with Pace?"

"Exactly that." There weren't a lot of people who Taylor would feel comfortable discussing this with, but they'd all known each other since before they could walk. Besides, Colby had probably already given his best friend and wife his version of the story. She wanted to give hers.

Spat choked on his second shot of rum. "Say what?"

She took a sip of her drink. "He flipped out when I told him I was going out with Pace."

Bree's eyes widened. "Did you really end up going home with Nick instead of Pace?"

"Yes, but nothing happened. Until this morning."

"I fucking knew it," Spat muttered.

"So...how was it?" Bree asked.

"We didn't have sex. He kissed me. That's all."

"Is he a good kisser?"

Taylor nodded, her face heating.

Spat refilled her shot glass. "So, are you gonna be a baseball wifey?"

"I'm not gonna be any kind of wifey." She threw back the shot. "But Nick's done playing ball. He's not going to recover from his injury enough to continue his career."

"Um…" Bree pulled a face. "So, he never brought up wanting to have a relationship with you before he knew his career was over?"

Taylor's throat constricted. "No."

"That doesn't bother you?"

"Well, it does *now*."

"Good job, Bree," Spat said and slapped her on the back. "Colby's knack for saying the exact wrong thing has rubbed off on you."

"I'm sorry." She cringed. "I love Taylor. She deserves to be more than Nick's backup plan."

Taylor sunk onto a chair at the table. "He said he felt this way before he got hurt."

"Then why didn't he say anything?"

"Stop talking. You're making it worse." Spat pushed Bree behind him, then gave Taylor a look as serious as she'd ever given her. "If there's one thing I know about Nick, it's that he's always put you before himself. If he waited to tell you, it's probably because he didn't think he was worthy and couldn't handle it if you rejected him."

"I need to get drunk." She picked up her daiquiri, but before she got it to her lips, Spat poured rum on the top of the icy slush.

"You came to the right place."

Two hours had passed since Taylor had arrived at Colby and Bree's house and Nick had yet to say a word to her, or even come within ten feet of her. But he'd winked at her from across the yard, and his lips had twitched into a grin whenever he'd caught her watching him.

She'd spent the first hour alternating between taking shots with Spat and listening to Bree and Silver psychoanalyze Silver's ex, and theories about what Olivia was doing. No one other than Spat was buying her story that she'd gone to take care of her boss's dogs while she was in the hospital.

To prevent feeling like shit tomorrow, Taylor had stopped drinking an hour ago. She had too much to do at the inn to nurse a hangover. The party had grown larger, more and more friends stopping by. Peopled-out, she walked to the swing-set and dropped onto one of the swings and rested the side of her head against the chain.

She wished she'd stayed home, but even though she wasn't trashed, she was still too tipsy to drive. She pulled her phone out to text Jaci to see if she could come get her, but her feet left the ground as she was pushed backward. Her phone fell as she grappled for something to keep her from falling.

"Nick," she shrieked, looking at him from where he held her suspended off the ground. Her butt started to slide off the swing, but he pulled the chains toward him and wedged himself between her thighs, keeping her from falling. "Oh, my god. Let me down."

"No."

"I will kick your ass if you don't."

His expression said, *can't you see you're in no position to make threats?* Unfortunately, he had a point. He had her trapped.

"Should you be doing this with your knee?"

"I've got two of 'em. But don't worry, I can still do plenty of stuff from my knees."

"Like beg?" Her eyes widened. Where had that come from?

"If you want me to."

Her face flashed with heat. She didn't know what to say, so she stared at him and said nothing.

He slackened his hold on the chains, allowing gravity to bring them even closer, her chest pressed to his and their lips inches apart.

"Why did you stay away from me all night?" she asked, the words hushed.

The moment stretched on and on. But then he said something that made her heart pound. "I was waiting for you to come to me."

"Why?"

"I meant it when I said you're going to have to ask me to kiss you. I keep second guessing whether I've pressured you into this or if it's something you want. And if it is something you want, I don't want to rush you."

Taylor closed her eyes to ward off her tears. Her tears were a response to his consideration. Of the patience she knew he'd had to dig deep for. Patience and Nick were not well acquainted. But she didn't want him thinking she was an emotional mess and that he was to blame.

"Do I get to ask why *you've* been avoiding *me*?"

Because she was avoiding asking him the question she needed to ask before this went any further. "I need to ask you something and I'm afraid I won't like the answer."

"Yes, I'll stop posting videos and I'll shut down my account."

"What?" She shook her head. "That's not what I was going to ask."

She'd never ask him to do that. Good to know he would, though.

"Would this be happening if you were going to keep playing ball?"

"No."

Her eyes stung and she blinked a few times to ward off her tears. "So, I'm your plan B?"

"Not at all. If I'd have thought you'd be happy being the girlfriend of a professional athlete, I'd have told you how I felt before now."

"How do you know that I wouldn't be?"

"You hate crowds. You hate car trips. You get sick on planes. And you deserve someone who is around more than I would've been."

She stared at him, speechless.

Taylor needed to find a way to blend the comfortableness she felt with him, and this newfound anticipation for what might happen between them.

She reached for his hat and turned it backwards.

The dimple in his cheek became visible.

She softly pressed her lips to his as her pulse raced so hard, it thumped in her ears.

He let go of one of the chains and cupped her jaw.

She pulled back. "I don't know how to do this."

"You're doing just fine." He let go of the other chain and snaked his arm around her waist. Slowly, he let her to her feet, her body sliding against his on the way down. "Let's get out of here."

"Are you embarrassed to kiss me in front of our friends?"

"Taylor, I wouldn't be embarrassed to strip you and lick you head to toe in front of our friends. The only reason I wouldn't do it is I don't want to have to kill all the guys because they saw you naked."

Her eyebrows shot up. "What is wrong with you?"

He shifted ninety-degrees, moving her with him, and perched on the cross bar of the swing-set with her standing between his legs. "I don't know but it's probably your fault."

Her mouth fell open.

He smirked, then put his hand on the back of her neck and pulled her in for a kiss.

This kiss—just like their first kiss—went beyond her expectations.

How could it be like this with someone she'd known forever? Had it always been there, and she'd been oblivious, or was it entirely new?

His mouth slanted across hers again and again until she was so needy that she arched into him, desperate for friction. And when that friction hit—in just the right spot—she moaned against his lips.

He growled, then pulled back. "Come on. I'll take you home."

"Take me home? Why does it sound like you don't plan on coming in?"

"Because I don't."

"Why not?"

"You were right. I shouldn't have strained my knee. I still have a flight of stairs to make it up when I get home, and I'd like to get ice on it before it swells up too much."

"I have ice."

His eyebrow winged up.

"Do you want to stay over? Maybe watch a movie?"

"Taylor Van Belle," he gasped, clutching imaginary pearls. "Are you asking me to Netflix and chill?"

"No!" Heat spread over her cheeks, ears, and neck.

He chuckled. "If I spend the night, are you going to put me in the creepy room?"

"I hadn't planned on it, but now that you've brought it up…"

He pressed his forehead to her shoulder and pretended to cry.

She rubbed his back. "Poor baby. I'll give you a nightlight."

"I'll sleep on the floor in your bedroom next to Cal before I sleep in that room of horrors."

She laughed and tried to push away from him, but he held tight. "Sleeping on the floor isn't necessary. I have over twenty beds in my house. I also have a very comfortable sofa."

Nick released a breath and wiped his forehead dramatically. "For a second there I thought you were going to offer to share your bed."

Taylor knocked the bill of his hat upward, sending it to the ground. "Yeah, you dodged a bullet."

"Right? I have an image of purity to protect. If anyone found out, I'd be ruined."

She rolled her eyes, something she did exponentially more when in Nick's presence. "I'll ruin you, alright."

He squeezed her waist. "Please do."

19
Fuck, She's Pretty
Nick

NICK SAT ON TAYLOR'S couch with an ice pack while she went to change out of those devastating short shorts and the tight T-shirt she'd worn to the party. He should have worn shorts because if he iced his knee through his jeans, they were going to end up with a big wet spot on them.

He couldn't wait, though. The swelling was already bad enough. Fuck it. A good portion of the population, Taylor included, had seen him in his underwear. He unfastened his pants and slid them off, then sat back down in his boxer briefs and put the pack on his knee.

Their taste in movies was the same, so he picked up the remote and searched for something he hadn't seen yet. It really didn't matter all that much because he planned on doing more chilling than watching, although he wouldn't let things go further than heavy kissing. Not only were they not ready for more than that, but she wasn't entirely sober.

She came out wearing a tank top and a pair of boxers—yellow, girly ones with flowers on them, not men's, thank God. He didn't wear boxers and he'd have had trouble keeping his mouth shut about who they belonged to.

"What are you doing?" she asked, her voice hoarse.

"Icing my knee. What are you doing coming out here in those skimpy shorts and no bra? Kinda seems like a double standard for you to be aghast about me like this when you've got more skin showing."

A blush dotted her cheeks and spread to her chest, but her gaze stayed glued to his body and her jaw slack.

"Taylor, you've seen me in my underwear before."

She nodded.

He grinned. "Your eyes are more glazed than a donut."

She made a soft grunt of agreement.

"You're going to have to get used to it."

Taylor made her way over and sat sideways with one leg tucked under her. More than a foot of space remained between them, but Cal must have taken that as an invitation because he came over and jumped up, half on top of her and half on top of him.

"Cal!" She glared at Nick. "He never does this when you're not here. Make him get down and be firm. No scratching his head or talking to him in your *good boy* voice."

"Cal, get the fuck down so I can put the moves on your mom."

He slinked off the couch and went to lie on his bed over by the hallway to her bedroom.

"Like that?" Nick asked.

She rolled her eyes. "Have I told you what a jackass you are yet today?"

"Yep." He rested the side of his face on top cushion and stared at her. Fuck, she was pretty. Even when she was glaring at him like she wanted to put him in the timeout corner. Joke was on her, though, because he *needed* someone who'd not cut him any slack. He should've realized that if he was going to fall in love with anyone, it'd be her. It was going to be tough not saying it until he knew she was ready to hear it. It was killing him to not blurt it out right now.

"You should be elevating your leg." She stood and pulled an ottoman over. Bent over like that, he got a nice view of her cleavage. Which was not what he needed while he was sitting here in his underwear.

Think about that time Hope's cat got an infection after having kittens and mites got to her tail and ate at it so bad it had to be amputated.

"You look nauseous."

He snorted. "I am."

"Do you want something? Mint tea?"

"No. Just sit down and watch this movie with me. I'll be fine."

She eased onto the cushion next to him.

He put his arm around her shoulders and pulled her into his side.

After stretching her legs out across the length of the couch, she laid her head against his chest. He wanted to think that she was starting to adjust to having physical intimacy with him, but they'd cuddled while watching movies before, so it wasn't that big of a deal. He hit play on the remote and tried to concentrate on the screen.

Five minutes in, she took a shaky breath and he realized he'd been trailing his fingers under the hem of her tank top.

"Sorry."

She lifted her head and leaned in to kiss him.

Nick cupped her neck and groaned into her mouth. He turned his body, lifting his good leg next to hers on the couch and urged her to rest more on top of him. Once she'd melted into him, he tossed his ice pack on the coffee table and flipped her, settling between her thighs, almost forgetting the pain in his knee.

He moved his mouth to her neck and kissed there, working his way to her shoulder, where he pulled the strap of her tank top off to give him better access to her soft skin.

She tugged at his shirt, so he lifted up, and pulled it over his head.

He didn't hate it that she took a long appraisal of his chest while running her hands over it.

"Every woman on the internet hates me right now. Or they would if they knew I had my hands on you like this."

He laughed. "To hell with them."

Her arms moved up his chest and around his neck.

He lowered his mouth to hers. He kissed her until she started rubbing against him. After a solid minute of that, he couldn't take anymore.

"What's wrong?" she asked when he sat up.

"If we keep going, I'm going to come in my pants."

"You're not wearing pants."

"You know what I mean."

She bit her lip.

"Don't laugh at me. Now, who's being a jackass?"

"We don't have to stop."

"The fuck we don't." He got up and pulled his pants on. "I'm not doing it like this, Taylor."

"Like what? On the couch?"

He picked up his shirt. "No. Like...like *this*. Watching a movie in your living room after you've been out drinking. I wanna do it right."

"I'm sober enough."

"Not enough for my liking. Besides, an hour ago you were nervous about kissing me. You're not ready."

She sat up and tugged her shirt over her stomach. "That's fair."

He pulled his shirt on and dropped down on the opposite end of the couch. "You deserve romance, but I keep making a damn mess of things."

She shifted onto all fours and prowled closer. "You wanting to make it special for me *is* romantic."

He frowned. "You're just trying to make me feel better."

She sat sideways on his lap and draped her arms over his shoulders. "What's wrong with that? I care about making you happy too."

Damn it. He didn't need to fall for her any harder than he already had.

He pecked her on the lips. "Let's watch the movie."

"Can we cuddle?"

"Obviously."

20

Rested and Ruined

Taylor

TAYLOR BLINKED HER EYES open, wondering why she was so warm.

Oh.

Because Nick was spooning her, holding her tight, his breath warm against her neck. The movie had ended, and the menu filled the screen.

She tried to peel his arm off, but he tightened his hold. "Nick."

He grumbled and nuzzled the soft spot beneath her ear.

"The movie is over."

"What time is it?" he asked, voice groggy.

"I don't know. Let me up."

He released her and once she'd stood, she turned to see him up on one elbow, rubbing his eyes.

"Come on, sleepyhead." She grabbed his arm and tugged.

"I'm fine here." He yawned and his eyes drifted closed.

"You'd be better in bed next to me."

He peeked one eye open.

"Unless that's not where you want to be."

He pushed to his feet, grabbed his cane, and followed along to her bedroom.

She pulled the covers back and crawled onto the bed and turned on her hip to face him. Hopefully, it wasn't obvious that seeing him stripping down to his underwear affected her ability to breath normally.

If he noticed, he didn't seem to care. He simply slid into bed with her.

"Roll over."

Once she'd followed his command, he snuggled up to her as he'd been on the couch, pulling the covers over them. "You're actively ruining me, Taylor." He yawned again.

Her cheeks hurt from how big she smiled. She closed her eyes and listened to his breathing grow heavy.

Resting in Nick's arms was oddly the freest and lightest and most relaxed she'd felt in the longest time. The hundreds of sleepovers they'd had contributed to it, but that wasn't all. She trusted Nick inside and out, through and through. There was no worrying about whether she'd wake up to him trying to put his hand down her pants or if he'd even be there when she woke up. There weren't any unknowns. At least, not ones that gave her anxiety.

A loud crash of thunder startled her. Enough light filled the room to indicate it was morning and she'd drifted off to sleep, even though it didn't seem like it could have been more than a few minutes.

Rain pelted the windows. Lightning cracked in the distance.

She rolled over to face Nick.

He was wide awake and stared at her with an unreadable expression.

She stared back.

Time didn't exist. Not moving slower or frozen, but it wasn't even a thing. No forward or backward. Their connection pulsed, radiating around them, blooming and fading simultaneously.

Whatever he was feeling, she felt too, and no words were needed to confirm that. She didn't even know what the words to define the feeling were, nor did she care to search for them.

He slowly lifted his hand and tucked her hair behind her ear.

Her heart beat fluttered. They'd slept in the same bed before. They'd woken up together before. But she'd never laid in bed with him like this, wishing he'd kiss her.

His gaze lowered, focusing on her mouth.

Great. He could read her mind.

She leaned over, propping herself up with her palms pressed into the pillow next to his head.

He grinned up at her and cupped the back of her head, pulling her face closer to his.

She pressed her mouth to his softly.

He matched that softness, their kiss slow and sweet.

Her lips left his and she gazed at him, no idea how they'd found this place, but wanting to stay in it forever.

Lightning cracked and a spark of light flashed through the room.

He angled his head and kissed her again, just as sweet, if not sweeter.

The unhurriedness of it left her in awe. No one had ever been so tender with her. Well, no one besides Nick—just not like this. That caring and gentleness had come in other ways. Forehead kisses. Icing her thigh when she'd gotten a giant bruise from sliding. Rubbing her back while he hugged her when she'd really needed it during tough times, holding her until all her tears had been shed. Tucking her into bed when she'd been hospitalized with pneumonia and telling her his absurd versions of bedtime stories.

This lazy, rainy morning in bed was everything she didn't know she needed. It healed the cynical side of her that accepted life was hard and messy and that beautiful moments like this only existed in the movies or fantasies. It planted a little seed of hope in her starved heart.

She wanted her cynicism proven to be unfounded. If she could have this with Nick, she wanted it. She wanted his hands roaming her body. She wanted to feel his heart beating beneath her palm. She wanted her heart to race, wondering how far they'd take things. She wanted to forget about everything and everyone and it just be the two of them. She wasn't going to share him with anyone. She was going to keep him all to herself for an hour or two.

With a hand on her hip, he guided her overtop his body. His mouth moved to her throat, causing a shiver as his lips skimmed her skin on the way to her chest. His hand was wonderfully warm as he slid it under her tank top, and so big that with his fingers spread, it nearly covered the width of her back. He gazed at her with parted lips and trailed his knuckles down her cheek.

He rubbed his nose against hers, then delivered the sweetest of all kisses.

For once, she didn't have sixteen different thoughts dancing in her head, depriving her of the ability to enjoy the moment. It was bliss.

She skated her fingertips over the shell of his ear, down the column on his neck. His body intrigued her. Not just his muscles, but the smooth, silkiness of his shoulder, so different from the rougher texture of his unshaven face against the smoothness of her face. She reveled in the size of his hand as it moved from her back to her stomach, his palm spread, wandering upward. His thumb outlined the swell of her breast, then swept over her nipple.

A gasp escaped her throat. Her breasts ached. The sensations coursing through her turned her needy. The way he was unraveling her was not okay. Crumbling for him after something as simple as his gaze dropping to her mouth was pathetic. Keeping her attraction to him locked up so tight that she wasn't even conscious of it to *this*? Crazy. Absolutely wild. Apparently, once those binds were released, it spilled out with the force of a tsunami.

Maybe it was a good thing they'd never considered a romantic relationship before now because a younger version of herself wouldn't have been able to handle this intensity.

Another thing even more pathetic…her whimper when his work-roughened hands squeezed her breast. He found her lips with his and gently pulled at them.

Nick wedged his thigh between hers, the friction of the movement not helping this whole desperate and needy situation she had going on. He grew hard, his length pressing into her.

She sat up, straddling him, and gripped the hem of her tank top. She dragged it up and over her head.

Nick's gaze intensified, shifting from her face to her chest and back. He grasped her hips, lifting her while rolling to the side, laying her on her back, and kissed a path from her jaw to her chest. Heat ignited inside her, pleasure consuming her.

He lowered his head to her chest and swirled his tongue around her nipple.

She arched into him and moaned.

He took his time working his way to her waistband, tracing the skin just above the fabric.

There was no holding back from writhing under his touch, silently begging for more. Her body knew how to ask for what she wanted, even if she didn't.

He braced his weight on his elbow, intently staring at her face as he crept his fingers into her shorts. His fingers passed over her smooth skin and he groaned and froze for a second before lifting his gaze.

Her eyelids fluttered closed, but she forced her focus back on him.

That hungry, panty-melting look made the awkwardness and pain of a full wax worth it. Luckily, her last appointment was a week ago, so it was prime time for showing it off. She'd been getting waxed long before she'd cared about Nick seeing her naked, but his reaction ensured she'd continue to keep her appointments.

He worked her shorts and panties down her legs, then ran his hands from her ankles to her inner thighs and spread them as he covered her body with his. The tips of his fingers against the crease of her thighs kicked her lust up so many notches that she could feel herself getting wet.

He made a noise that matched her desperation. He brushed his thumb across her slit.

"Nick."

"Don't do that," he whispered, his nose rubbing against the soft space under her ear.

"Do what?"

"Say my name." He swept his fingers through her wetness.

She moaned. The ache building inside her grew and grew until she was desperate to appease it. She needed it to end, so she reached for the waistband of his boxer briefs, but he caught her hand and laced his fingers between hers.

He pressed his forehead to hers and took a deep breath, like he was bracing himself to face a challenge. "I don't want to stop."

Stop? Who said anything about that? No. Why? "I'm not asking you to. Please, don't."

He groaned. "Do you have a condom?"

Taylor stared at him, waiting for him to think about what he'd said and why it was not a problem. And it had nothing to do with her being excessively prepared for any eventuality or having a closet full of sex-essories.

"What?"

She rolled her eyes. "Nick, do I have any allergies?"

"Yeah, latex—Oh. I never thought about that. Aren't there latex-free options?"

She nodded. "I can get one if you want to use it."

"If I want to? You don't want to?"

She slowly shook her head. "Not with you."

"Taylor." His voice cracked and he closed his eyes.

"If we're doing this, I don't want anything between us. I want to be as close to you as possible. That's the only way I know how to be with you." She ran her fingers down his chest. "I've been tested and I'm on birth control. You get tested regularly, don't you?"

Nick valued and took care of his body. Not only that, but she could say for almost certain that he'd never have sex with her if he hadn't been tested, regardless of whether they used a condom.

He ran his hand down her arm. "You're sure about this? Not just the protection. Are you sure you want to do this?"

"Nick, for once, I'm not overthinking something. I want this with you."

"Well, since you asked so nicely…" He ran his hand down her torso and between her legs. He stroked her until she couldn't think straight. His touch set her on fire.

Then he stopped and glanced over his shoulder. "Don't move."

He lifted himself from her and grabbed his cane.

Taylor grabbed the sheet and used it to cover her naked body, as he walked to the door.

Nick whistled and Cal rose from the floor next to the bed and trotted over. He gestured for him to get out, and once he had, he closed the door and came back to bed.

He shed his boxer briefs, then loomed over her, his hips between her thighs. He lowered his head and kissed her.

Taylor raised her hips and Nick slid his cock against her, but not inside yet.

She turned her head toward him, ducking under his chin, too flooded with pleasure to maintain eye contact. She moaned against his neck, but he shifted back, exposing her, then dipped his head and crushed his mouth to hers.

With one arm braced on the pillow next to her head, he slid his hand from her hip to her knee, guiding her leg to wrap around him. Instead of feeling trapped by the weight of his body, it soothed her, maybe because she was exactly where she wanted to be.

She shifted her hips, succeeding in taking the tip of his cock inside her.

They gasped simultaneously.

Nick slid deeper, then paused and cupped the side of her face. He kissed her deeply, intensely.

She put her hands on his lower back, then slid them up, splaying her fingers across his muscles.

His movements were slow and sure. The slack pace made it seem as though he was unraveling her, removing the binds that kept her in opposition to everything, even herself. She wasn't a virgin by any stretch, but she'd never done *this* before. Every sensation was heightened, whether emotional or physical.

His warm skin against hers and his hands wandering her body felt incredible. She tried to voice how beautiful she found everything he was doing to her, but her brain blanked and all she could do was hold onto him.

He brought her hand to his mouth and kissed it, then laced his fingers through hers and held it to the pillow, squeezing as he thrust deep.

His kiss muffled her moan.

He answered with a growl, then slid his hand between her lower back and the mattress. Holding her tightly against him, he rolled, putting her back on top.

Without missing a beat, he pushed himself up, reclining against the headboard, his hands on her hips, and lifted her until his cock was almost out, then thrust back in.

Taylor held onto his shoulders, rolling her hips against him.

His hand moved from her hip to her breast, cupping it and brushing his thumb across her nipple.

She arched toward him, her head tilting back.

Nick pressed hot kisses along her neck.

Pleasure flooded her, robbing her of any thought other than wishing this would never end. Ever.

He trailed his hand from her breast to her belly, then lower, circling her clit with his finger with a touch so light it made her ache for more. Slowly, he increased the speed and pressure, sending her spiraling toward release.

Her thighs shook as tremors rippled through her and noises she couldn't control escaped her throat.

He kept stroking her clit until she became overly sensitive and had to push his hand away. He pulled her in for a kiss, thrusting slowly but forcefully.

When he came, his cock pulsed inside her and his fingers dug into her hips.

She wilted against him, her chest rising and falling heavily.

He kissed her temple while running his hand up and down her back. They stayed connected until their breathing slowed to a less frenzied rhythm. Nick placed a kiss on her shoulder, then put his finger under her chin and directed her face toward his. His lips moved lazily against hers while they rode out the afterglow.

Out of nowhere, a wave of uncertainty rolled over her and the undertow dragged away the glow.

21
The After-No
Nick

H E TRIED TO TALK himself out of the stirring in his mind whispering that Taylor wasn't okay. Her silence meant nothing. Neither of them had said much since they'd woken up. She'd untangled herself from him so she could go clean herself up.

Her change in demeanor was all in his head. His intuition was off. She'd come out of the bathroom in a minute and climb back in bed. She'd curl up against him and put her head on his chest. She'd spend the rest of the morning in his arms. She'd spend the rest of all her mornings from here on out in his arms.

"Fuck this," he muttered and got out of bed. He pulled on his boxer briefs, then rapped his knuckles against the bathroom door. "Taylor."

"It's open." The unsteady cadence of her voice left no question that she'd been crying.

He turned the knob and pushed the door open, sweeping his gaze around the bathroom.

She sat on the floor, her back against the sink cabinet, knees pulled to her chest. A white fluffy robe surrounded her body. She wiped at her cheeks and sniffled.

His chest locked up, her pain spreading to his heart. Coming down— no, being slammed down—from where he'd been floating was a kind of hurt that he wanted to end immediately and never feel again.

He stepped inside the threshold but went no farther. He couldn't trust himself. Every move he made with Taylor turned out to not only be wrong, but damaging in ways he doubted he'd ever be able to repair.

"I didn't know it was going to be like that." She hugged her knees and kept her stare on the tile floor.

He might not know anything else, but he was positive she'd enjoyed him touching her. He'd never put so much care into anything as he had that. And he'd still failed. "Like what?"

"Like—like something I'm not ready for."

Nick's stomach sank. He hadn't planned on things going that far. It'd naturally progressed, and he had waited for the green light on every move he'd made. "You seemed ready. You said you were sure."

She shook her head, then wiped a fresh tear track with the sleeve of her robe. "I was ready for the sex, but—"

Had he been too intense for her? Shit. How did he keep fucking everything up so bad?

"I don't know why I thought—No, I didn't think at all. I never considered that how safe I feel with you and how much I trust you would translate to—" She waved her hand around in the air.

The devastation gripping his heart released. He walked closer. "To what?"

"You unraveled my soul and now, I'm...overwhelmed with the finality of it."

"Finality?"

"Like someone told me how the story ends before I've even read the first chapter. I've been trying to figure out what I'm doing with my life, and now, it feels like this part just fell into place, but it's too advanced for me and I can't find the instruction manual."

"Okay," he said slowly and sat beside her. "I hear you. I don't think there is an instruction manual, though. There's no right or wrong way to do this. It's our story and it's not the end that matters. It's *this*, Taylor. It's us sitting on the bathroom floor, figuring it out together that matters.

It's that we've always figured it out together and if my future is made of moments of us sitting on the floor lost, wondering how to do this, I'm good with that. I'd rather be lost with you, than on a smooth course with someone else."

She dipped her head to the side, resting it on his shoulder.

He wrapped his arm around her and tilted his head back against the cabinet, staring at the ceiling.

"I love you, Nick."

Those words brought a smile to his lips, even though she didn't mean it in the way he wanted her to. As long as she wasn't running away from this, he could wait for that admission to come with the certainty that she'd given him the piece of her heart she'd been saving for someone that made it flutter. "I know, Taylor. I love you too."

22
Make Her Fall
Nick

NICK HAD STAYED FOR a cup of coffee and helped Taylor finish the LEGO house. He'd even kissed her goodbye without her clamming up. He'd offered to take her to get her car from Bree and Colby's, but Jaci and she had plans to go to lunch, so she was going to have her pick her up and drop her off at her car afterward. Just as well, because he had a call scheduled with his team's manager and he needed to talk to his parents beforehand.

His mom raised her eyebrows when he walked into the kitchen but said nothing as she took a sip from her coffee mug and scrawled a list on a notepad.

He walked over and kissed her on the cheek. "Is Dad awake?"

"He's doing his breathing treatment."

That meant he wouldn't be able to talk, so he grabbed a box of cereal from a cupboard and set it on the island. Some days, he needed his cane less than others, but today, he depended on it more than usual. The price of having sex with Taylor cost him both emotionally and physically. Worth it, though.

Only able to carry one thing at a time, it took him longer to get set up to eat a bowl of cereal. When he took a stool at the kitchen island, his mom set down her pen.

"How's Taylor?"

He kept his gaze on the Cheerios floating in his bowl. "She's alright."

"I'm assuming you spent the night there, so I take it everything is okay between you two?"

He nodded. "She's struggling a little."

"With you having feelings for her?"

"I think it's more that she's struggling with accepting that she has feelings for me. I know she's worried it'll ruin our friendship if things don't work out, but I think she knows I'm her future even though she hasn't fallen in love with me, and that's freaking her out. I just don't know how to help her get to the point where that's what she wants. How do I do that?"

"Are you asking how you make her fall in love with you?"

"No…"

She gave him that *I'm your mom so stop bullshitting me* look.

"Maybe. Not *make* her but…encourage it?"

"You can't, Nick."

His shoulders slumped. He let go of his spoon, his appetite ruined. "What am I going to do if she doesn't? I want her to be crazy about me like I am about her."

"Stop trying to force things to happen. Let what's meant to be, be."

"Do you think we're meant to be?"

She smiled and gave a little shrug.

"Mom."

"No one could love her more than you already do, but you're getting in your own way. I don't think it's a big jump from how she feels about you now to her falling for you if you let her get there on her own."

"I don't know what that means. I'm supposed to stand back and do nothing, and hope that she returns my feelings?"

"Nick, listen to me. Taylor loves the version of you she grew up with. But you're a man now, and I don't think she's opened her eyes to that version of you yet."

"Are you telling me to be myself?" He crossed his arms and frowned.

Laughter bubbled out of her. "I guess so."

"I am myself with Taylor."

"Then, be patient. Let her figure it out on her own. I know that's not what you want to hear, but I've never sugar-coated things for you and I'm not going to now. It's about time something you want didn't land in your lap."

He scowled, seriously tempted to stomp out of the kitchen and probably would have but stomping wasn't something his knee allowed. "What are you talking about? I worked my ass off to get where I am."

"I'm not discounting that. I'm your mother, I've witnessed your drive to accomplish your goals. But those things have been within reach. You've faced difficult challenges, but never impossible ones. You've never had to accept that no amount of hard work is going to get you the thing you want."

"Jeez. Thanks, Mom. So, I'm doomed?"

She shrugged. "I don't know about doomed, but you are at the mercy of Taylor's feelings. Having someone fall in love with you isn't a challenge. It's not a series of smaller goals that lead you closer to the big goal. Take it slow, and soak in what it's like to fall in love."

"I'm already in love with her. The falling part is over."

She shook her head. "No, it's not. You've decided that you're compatible, but that's not the same as you getting to know who Taylor is as a woman, or learning how that changes you into the man you're going to be."

His mouth opened but he didn't have a rebuttal.

"Don't rush this. She deserves to have a beautiful love story unfold for her."

"I want her to have that too. I want to be the one to give it to her."

"Then, chill."

23
Big Brother Bullshit
Nick

"WE NEED TO FIRE Josh."

Nick glanced up from his phone as Hope came into the living room, her face red.

"Josh technically works for Brody, not us. What did he do?"

"He told me to shut up."

That didn't sound like Josh. "In what context?"

"There's a context where it's acceptable for a boy to tell me to shut up?"

He held back his smile, not wanting to set her temper off more than it already was. She was too damn smart for her own good. Of course, it was never acceptable for a boy to be rude to his sister, and he didn't want to give her the impression that he didn't take her problems seriously, but he'd told Taylor to shut up countless times. It didn't mean he didn't respect her. The only time he did it was when she was talking foolish, either accusing him of shit she knew wasn't true, or talking poorly about herself.

"Are you going to give me the whole story or should I go ask him?"

"I live here. This is my farm too." She jabbed her thumb toward her chest. "I shouldn't have to put up with someone I can't stand."

"Brody's not going to fire him just because you don't get along with him. He's worked on the farm for almost a year, and he's never once been late, never called out sick. He's a good ass mechanic and a hard worker."

"He's also rude, arrogant, and I don't trust him."

"It's not really my place to get in it. You need to talk to Brody." He went back to his phone, checking his e-mail for the paperwork management was sending over for him to sign.

"Brody and Morgan love Josh. They think he's perfect."

"Oh, I see. You already went to Brody about this and didn't get your way."

She put her hands on her hips and wrinkled her nose. "Because he's biased."

"You're his little sister. If there's a bias, it's going to be toward you."

"You'd think so, but Josh is still working here. Please, Nick? Help me get Brody to see how unfair it is that the one person in this world I can't stand is working here."

"You're working for Taylor this summer. Your paths won't even cross that much. Just ignore him when they do."

She stomped her foot so hard the knickknacks on the shelves rattled, then stormed off.

Nick sighed and stood from the couch. He'd talk to Josh, since he doubted he'd come to any resolution with Brody regarding his most valued employee. Hope thinking she couldn't come to him for help wouldn't be cool.

He found Josh in Brody's new barn listening to music and working on a tractor engine. "Did you tell my sister to shut up?"

Josh froze. "I might have."

"Do you have a good reason for why you did that?"

"Not one where you'll take my side over hers." He put his head back down, focused on his work.

Nick bit the inside of his cheek to keep from laughing. This kid knew what was up. "Start talking."

"Hope was supposed to clear out the blue haybarn before we start using it again, but I've seen her use the leaf blower and I knew I could do it in half the time it'd take her, so I did it first thing this morning. When she found out, she was pissed. She followed me around while I was trying to get shit done, yelling at me, so I told her to shut up."

"Wow," Nick drawled out. "You're stupid."

"Yeah, I guess so."

Nick laughed. "Don't do her chores, man. All that's gonna do is tell her you don't think she's as capable as you. Just stay out of her way as much as possible, okay?"

He nodded. "Yeah, sure."

"Do you know where Brody's at?"

"Fussing over Morgan, probably."

Nick shook his head the entire walk from the barn to Brody's house, grinning. Josh had a lot to learn about women, but at least he hadn't done anything to deliberately hurt Hope.

In their kitchen, Morgan stood with one hand gripping the counter and the other on her lower back.

Brody sat at the kitchen table, arms folded, leaned back, looking pissed.

"You okay?" Nick asked.

She nodded, but her eyes were squeezed shut.

"Fuck, baby," Brody muttered. "Can we please just go to the hospital?"

"Is she in labor?" he asked.

"No." She straightened up. "I'm having contractions, but they're not close enough together. Babysit your brother. I'm going to go play cards with your dad."

Nick saluted and held the door open for her.

"You better drive," Brody called after her.

"I'm walking," she called back.

Brody scrubbed his face with his hands.

Nick sat across from him at the table. "Hope asked me to talk you into firing Josh."

"Don't waste your breath."

"I'm not going to. She's pissed because he did the chore you assigned her before she had the chance. She'll get over it."

"She stays mad. That's just an excuse for her to yell at him without admitting the real reason she's frustrated."

"And that is?"

"Because Josh has a girlfriend."

"So, what? Hope can't stand Josh."

Brody leveled him with a stare. "She works very hard to make it seem like she doesn't want him around, so no one notices that she goes out of her way to get his attention."

Hope having some type of hate-crush on Josh totally tracked. It wasn't a secret that before he'd started working at the farm, he'd had feelings for her but was being respectful of the Lewis family rule of no dating until sixteen years old—even though Hope had played fast and loose with that rule. Now that she'd turned sixteen, Josh had moved on. That's exactly the "don't want it until she can't have it" mindset that Hope lived with.

He doubted it was voluntary, though. Acknowledging his feelings for Taylor had taken him a painfully long time, and even once he'd accepted that he wanted her to be his, he'd still struggled with it. "Have Morgan talk to her."

"And do what, exactly?" Brody asked. "Get Hope to accept that she has feelings for Josh while he's involved with another girl?"

"I can see how that would be problematic. So, what's the plan?"

Brody shrugged and ran a hand through his hair. "Try to survive the next two years until she goes off to college."

"You think Josh will still be working here?"

"I hope so. Losing him would cripple us. It'd take two or three guys to get done what he gets done around here."

"He's only sixteen." And now that Nick's mobility was an issue, this sixteen-year-old could work circles around him, which fucking sucked balls.

"Exactly. So, Hope can have the biggest tantrum she's capable of. Unless he hurts her in some way, I'm not firing him."

Nick stretched his neck. "Can you tell him to stay out of sight of Mom and Dad's house as much as possible? And if he knows she's assigned a chore, to just let her do it—even if he thinks he can do it better and faster?"

"I'll talk to him about the last part, but he's not even over there that much. She comes over here. Mostly, to see Morgan, but she doesn't usually leave without butting heads with Josh. I hate to say it, but Hope is the problem."

"Damn it," he muttered. "Maybe working with Taylor will mellow her out."

"If anyone is a shining example of mellow, it's Taylor, but Hope has known her her entire life and she hasn't rubbed off on her yet."

"True."

"How's it going with Taylor?"

He thought about how he'd woken her up this morning and couldn't fight his grin.

"You already slept with her?" Brody shouted.

"What? I didn't say that." His brother couldn't possibly figure that out from a two-second facial expression.

"Why'd you get that look on your face, then?"

"I didn't have any look on my face."

Brody angled his head to the side and narrowed his eyes, like instead of a kitchen, this was an interrogation room and Nick was a suspect. "So, you didn't have sex with her?"

He froze. He was a terrible liar, but he didn't want to kiss and tell, especially not when it came to Taylor.

"Holy hell, Nick. Already?"

"I'm not saying that I did, but if I did, what would be so terrible about that?"

"Nothing." Brody shrugged. "If she was into it, that's cool. I'm just surprised it happened so quickly."

"*If* she was into it?" He'd never wanted to punch his brother more. "I sure as shit didn't coerce her."

Brody put his hands up. "Calm down. That's not what I was implying."

"Then, what the hell were you implying?"

"That it happened fast, like I said. You told her how you felt two days ago. I thought she'd need more time to adjust to the idea."

He set his elbow on the table and leaned his forehead into his palm.

"I wasn't expecting it to happen. But it did and it was great, but then…"

Brody sighed, like he'd known there'd be a catch. "What happened?"

"She cried. She said I unraveled her soul, and she wasn't ready to face us being…I don't know, meant for each other, I guess."

Brody blinked for a good ten seconds, then a grin crept out. "The poor girl just wanted to get laid, and you acted like it was your wedding night."

"Shut the fuck up." He stood. "You're an asshole. I'm never gonna tell you anything again."

"Oh, come on. I'm just joking."

He kept heading toward the door. "I'm not laughing."

"It sucks that she cried, but it sounds like you ruined her for all other men, so you've got that going for you."

Nick stopped with his hand on the door and shrugged. "I guess."

Brody laughed. "Maybe you should dial it back a little until she comes to terms with everything."

He turned around and faced his brother. "I can't put the genie back in the lamp."

"True, but next time you could keep things on the lighter side. Corner her in one of the guest rooms and have a quickie."

"I don't want her to feel used."

"It's not using her. You love her. It's showing her that you want her so bad you can't keep your hands off her."

Maybe part of the problem was that he was being *too* respectful of

Taylor, in addition to being—he hated to admit it—vanilla. It's not like he'd never fantasized about making her scream his name.

His mom had told him to be patient and let things progress naturally. Brody was basically telling him to go feral on her.

Screw it. Neither of them were Taylor, and therefore, couldn't truly know what she wanted. He was just going to ask her.

24
Post-Pool Party Problems
Taylor

SABRINA LAUGHING UNTIL SHE had tears in her eyes was the highlight of Taylor's day. All in all, her day had been full of good memories. Waking up with Nick had been magic, even if she'd spiraled in the bathroom afterward. Saying he'd rather weather the storm with her, than have sunshine with someone else was exactly what she'd needed to hear, even if she'd already known it deep down.

She'd dragged Sabrina along when she'd gone out to lunch with Jaci and they'd gotten her mind off her woes with stories about the ridiculousness that ensued whenever they were together.

They'd come back to the inn to swim and lounge by the pool, then came in for drinks and dinner. Taylor loaded the dishwasher while Sabrina dabbed at her eyes and clutched her middle and Jaci tried unsuccessfully to stop her own fit of laughter when a loud knock came from the foyer. Her amusement ran out of steam and a chill ran down her spine as she walked to the door. A courier stood on the other side with a large envelope that required her signature. No return address.

She took it back into the kitchen and ripped it open. When she saw the contents, she glanced at Jaci. "Did you send this?"

"Send what?" Jaci left the dining table and walked over.

Taylor handed her the photographs and a piece of white paper fell to the floor.

"What the fuck?" Jaci said, flipping through the eight-and-a-half-by-ten boudoir photos of Taylor. "I did *not* send these. I only sent them to your e-mail."

After picking up the letter and reading the name at the bottom of the page, Taylor looked at Jaci. It was from Gavin. And the letter was a threat to send the photos to every community organization Taylor belonged to—all listed—as well as a copy of the hidden, password protected part of her website where couples could browse the spicy offerings she'd arrange for them. *But* if Taylor convinced Sabrina to forgive him *or* kicked her out of the inn so she'd have to come home, he'd leave her reputation untarnished.

She handed the letter to Jaci.

"That mother fucker." Jaci slapped the photos and letter on the counter. "This is extortion, and it's illegal. I'm calling the police."

"No. You can't do that," Taylor said. "If you do, we have to show them the letter and the photos and this is a small community. Word will get out."

"What's going on?" Sabrina asked, her forehead wrinkled as she came to stand closer.

"Your douchebag husband got a hold of Taylor's boudoir photos and is trying to use them to blackmail her to talk you into taking him back."

Sabrina's face fell. "Oh my god."

"It's not your fault, Sabrina," Taylor said. "Don't you dare think about going back to him. I'm a big girl. I can handle Gavin."

The front door creaked as it opened.

Cal rose from his bed and rushed to the foyer.

"That's Nick." She scrambled to get everything back into the envelope. "Don't say anything to him about this." She shoved the envelope between two cookbooks on the shelf under the island.

"Hey, ladies."

Taylor turned to face him. Every thought left her brain.

A crisp white T-shirt stretched across his chest and around his biceps. Those jeans he wore had to be specifically designed to turn on women. Not too loose, not too tight, and faded. And why did the blue of his eyes seem so much brighter?

There she stood in an oversized T-shirt with the sleeves cut off and the ripped collar exposing her bikini top ties.

Cal wagged his tail by Nick's side.

Nick rubbed his head while his gaze flicked up and down her body. "How come I didn't get an invite to the pool party?"

"We didn't think you could handle seeing Taylor in a bikini without drowning," Jaci said, dryly.

His lips twitched. "You're probably right about that."

Taylor rolled her eyes. "You've seen me in a bathing suit before."

He came closer and whispered in her ear, "I've seen you in less."

Her face heated and she throbbed in a place she wished she wasn't throbbing with Jaci and Sabrina present.

Nick's smile took that heat in her face and expanded it until her entire body felt like she was standing by a fire.

"Oh, my god. He made you blush. This is the best moment of my life," Jaci said.

She turned away, hoping to distract her racing heart.

"I think the sun got to me," Sabrina said. "I'm going to go lie down."

It wasn't the sun.

Taylor didn't want her to have any guilt for what Gavin had done. He'd already done enough harm. Her being alone in her room, left to her thoughts, might not be the best idea.

"I'll come with you," Jaci said. "You're probably dehydrated and should drink some water."

"I'll make a tray." Taylor opened an upper cabinet and took out a serving tray.

Sabrina disappeared without commenting.

Jaci kept her back to Nick and widened her eyes at Taylor, mirroring her worry.

She appreciated that she didn't voice her concern in front of Nick.

Sure, they could blame it all on Gavin's cheating, but until she came up with a solution to his blackmail stunt, she didn't want to talk about Sabrina's situation any more than she had to with Nick.

She put two empty glasses on the tray and filled a small pitcher with ice water.

Jaci slid it off the counter. "You two behave yourselves. I'll check on her, then I'll see myself out."

"Thanks, Jaci." Taylor grabbed her plate from the table. She'd lost her appetite.

"I shouldn't have flirted with you in front of Sabrina."

She pinched her eyebrows together. "That wasn't about that. She was upset before you got here." But him having the awareness to even consider that he might have impacted Sabrina's feelings made an undercurrent of appreciation flow through her.

"You swear?"

Taylor moved in front of him and stared up. "Yes, I swear."

He put his cane-free hand on her waist and brushed his mouth over hers, then lifted his head and locked gazes with her.

Cal pushed between them.

"Dude." Nick glanced at him and chuckled. "Let me give your mom some attention."

"He's been hanging out with the girls all day. Have boy time while I shower."

"Fine, but you're going to be getting all of my attention after that."

"Fine," she huffed, like it was the worst thing she'd ever heard, then smiled and scurried off.

While she showered, her mind went over the letter from Gavin. Maybe hitting him in the gut with a baseball bat wasn't the wisest move. Telling his wife that he was cheating on her and going out of her way to provide evidence probably didn't win her any points, either.

Nick would flip out if she told him about this. She didn't want to lie or keep secrets, but until she came up with a solid plan for how to deal with Gavin, telling him could be bad. Very bad. For Gavin. Not that she cared about that shoulda-been-a-cum-stain. She cared about Nick going off half-cocked and ruining any shot she had of protecting her business and keeping those photos private. She didn't even want *him* to see them. Maybe eventually. Not right now, though.

He'd seen her naked a total of once.

Jaci's photographs had turned out pretty good. Still, there was something vulnerable about showing them to someone. Especially when she wanted that someone to think her body was as sexy as she thought his was.

Out of the shower, she lathered herself in after-sun lotion, hemmed and hawed over her underwear and bra selection, and finally, chose a matching teal thong set and covered it with a soft black jersey midi dress. Her stomach knotted as she looked in the mirror, wanting to look good, but not wanting it to seem like she'd put much effort into it. She skipped makeup and let her hair air dry.

Nick sat on a bench on the back patio, the string lights glowing overhead. Spring, summer, and fall, she had the outside ambiance lights and music on a timer that powered them on at dusk. Watching the sunset from the dock was the top-mentioned highlight of most guests' stay, but lazing on the patio beforehand was frequently written into their reviews as well.

Nick launched a tennis ball far out into the yard, and Cal, who'd been hawk-eying the ball, took off after it.

Taylor came up behind him and put her hands on the back of the bench. "Have you two had enough boy time?"

He craned his head back and gazed at her. "Cal probably hasn't, but I'm ready for some Taylor-time. We should get Cal a girlfriend."

She rolled her eyes and walked around in front of him. "Don't even think about it."

He propped his elbows on the back of the bench and tilted his head, giving her a thorough appraisal. "I wanted to talk to you about something, but now, I don't remember what it was. That dress is hazardous to my brain cells."

Cal trotted up beside her and nosed his way between them, nearly knocking her off balance to present Nick with the ball he'd fetched.

He reached out, slipping his arm around her waist to steady her. He pried the ball from Cal's mouth. "You're going to be sharing your doghouse with me if you keep this up, bud."

Clueless, Cal anxiously danced in place until Nick tossed the ball back into the yard.

Except for him jumping on the furniture, Cal's behavior around Nick made her heart squeeze. It was always like that until he left, and then for a week after, the dog would take off for the door whenever it opened, just to go lie down and pout because it wasn't Nick. He got used to him being around—and so did she. No matter how much she tried not to.

Taylor shifted closer to the bench, intending to sit next to him.

"Nope." He grabbed her hips and pulled her onto his lap. He let go of her hand, moving to her lower back, keeping her close, his other hand cupping her jaw, bringing his mouth to hers.

This kiss didn't feel like the others. It was needy and impatient. He slid his palm from her back to her waist, then her thigh, where he grasped her dress and pushed the fabric up around her hip.

She pulled her mouth from his. "Nick," she said breathlessly, both surprised by his urgency and because they couldn't just go at it here on the patio.

His mouth pulled up on one side, the hint of a devilish grin making her body flush with heat. Nick always had something to say. Something that would steal a laugh from her. Something that would earn him a playful shove. Something that maintained his class-clown status.

But when they were close like this, when he had his hands on her, he hardly said a word, even when his mouth wasn't occupied with hers.

Under his stare, her pulse raced, and her nipples hardened. If he wanted her here and now—and she didn't have to ask to know he did—she'd give in to him.

Admitting that was a slap to her ego.

He twisted a piece of her hair around his finger.

"I know what you're thinking."

"I know you do," he said, grinning.

"Well, knock it off, then."

"Why? I thought we were done pretending we don't want each other."

"We are, but…" She sighed. "It feels like it should be…not this easy."

"Easy?"

"Yeah, between us. How did we transition to this so smoothly?" She gestured at herself sitting on his lap.

"Do we need to question it?"

"I do. I'm an overthinker."

"How about you knock *that* off?"

"I can't."

Cal trotted back to the patio and panted next to them.

Nick removed his hand from her hip and took the ball from him. "Last time."

Taylor leaned out of his way so he could launch the ball.

The second Cal took off, Nick said, "You smell like summer."

"You smell like baseball." Leather and sunflower seeds and fresh-cut grass. A smell she'd always love even if sometimes driving past a baseball field made her want to punch someone in the face. Well, not anyone. A specific someone. Her dad. But she didn't want to let that man continue to sour her bond with baseball. Or her bond with baseball as it pertained to Nick.

Maybe their relationship evolving would buff out the scratches left by that resentment.

"I'm going to fix that overthinking problem you have."

"How?"

He pressed his lips to hers and laced his fingers through her hair. The sensation of his calloused hand landing back on her thigh and slowly skimming upward drew a moan from her throat. His technique was undoubtedly effective. Her mind hadn't let go of her anxiety, but it lost its death grip, allowing it to be pushed to the back.

He kissed her worries away until Cal barked. He scooted her off his lap, onto the bench next to him, then grabbed his cane and stood. "Come on, you're going in the house, so I can spend more than two minutes with her without you cockblocking."

Taylor pressed her lips together to keep a straight face. Her dress fell past her knees as she stood. "I'm going to call it an early night. I'll see you tomorrow?"

Nick's face fell.

She couldn't contain her laugh any longer.

He glared at her. "Oh, you think you're funny?"

She nodded and darted past him to the back steps.

"Taylor," he growled. "You're lucky I can't chase you."

25
The Closet of Sin
Nick

"TAYLOR, WE'RE GOING TO the dock to watch the sunset, not to board an ocean liner for a thirty-day voyage. We don't need all this stuff."

She glared at Nick and set a smaller cooler on the floor next to the fridge. "Go grab a quilt from the closet in the hall."

He groaned but let her boss him anyway. He wasn't going to be able to convince her that she didn't need to plan every small detail for every activity—even one as simple as watching the sun set.

He couldn't remember what half the doors in this place went to. He opened a door that went to a closet filled with board games, then shut it and moved to the next one. The keyhole had a key in it. He opened it and once he got a look at some of the contents, he froze. "Um, Taylor?"

She came around the corner with her eyebrows scrunched, then she gasped and put herself between him and the door and shut it. "What are you doing? There's no blankets in there."

"Yeah, no shit." He pointed at the lock. "Why do you have an adult novelty store in this closet?"

Her blush was so fucking cute. "It's for guests."

"That's taking hospitality to new levels."

"Shut up. Some couples come here to reignite their spark."

He moved her to the side and reopened the door. "Do you ever do quality testing?"

"Nick…"

He grabbed a box with a vibrator in it and turned it over in his hand, reading the packaging. "Come on, Taylor. How can you know what to recommend if you've never sampled the selection?" He set the box back on the shelf and snagged a bottle of lube. "Add this to your basket."

"Oh my god. Stop."

He shoved the bottle at her and grabbed another box. "What's this?"

This one said it was good for with a partner or solo time. *Bingo*.

"Put that back."

"Nope." He shut the door and locked it. He went to hand her the key, then thought better of it and wrapped his fist around it. "I'll hold onto this."

"No. Give it here, Nick."

"Make me, Taylor." He smirked, tucked the key in his pocket, and walked to the kitchen where he opened the box and pulled out the contents.

She set the bottle of lube on the counter. "Have fun with that stuff."

"Oh, I'm going to."

"Alone," she muttered, then went back to the hallway.

He set the box with the vibrator on the counter next to the lube, then waited for her to come back.

She returned with a quilt in her arms, avoiding his gaze.

He pulled it out of her grasp and set it on the counter, then nudged her chin up. "Don't be all pouty."

"I'm not." She turned and started rearranging the items she'd already carefully arranged in the basket. "If that's what you need to get the job done, bring it."

He brushed his mouth against her ear. "You know I can get the job done. If you don't want to have fun, just say so."

She shot him a dirty look. "Don't even try that."

"I kind of already did." He wrapped his arms around her and pulled her tightly to him. "It's the only surefire way I know to get you on board with my schemes."

"We better start saving up for couple's counseling."

He grinned. "You're not wrong about that."

"About that closet…"

"Yeah?"

She squirmed out of his hold and spun on him. Her next words tumbled out of her mouth in a rush. "There's a lot more to my business than most people know. I also arrange boudoir photo sessions and provide everything they need to act out a specific role play. And I've been renting out the cottages and rooms to content creators."

A slow smile spread on his face. "You're a sex worker."

She went to smack his chest, but he grabbed her wrist and brought it to his mouth for a kiss.

"No, I'm not."

"What you're describing is in the sex work industry, Tay. And you've been shaming me for my content? Hypocritical much?"

"I'm not taking my clothes off on camera or anything like that. I'm just the props department." She glanced up briefly. "You can't tell anyone, okay? I want to protect my guests' privacy. If they're out around town and someone asks where they're staying, I don't want people whispering behind their backs or judging them because they assume everyone who stays here is into kinky shit."

"Who would I tell?"

"I just want you to understand that I'm discreet when it comes to this."

"I respect that." He angled his head and tapped his chin. "How much does it cost if someone wants you to put together a roleplaying experience? Asking for a friend."

"Oh, your *friend* wants to role play?"

He moved his face in front of hers and tucked her hair behind her ear. He wanted to tell her that this is what he wanted for the rest of forever— the two of them antagonizing the shit out of each other in the kitchen for absolutely no good reason. His family was right about him. He was way ahead of himself and even further ahead of Taylor. Waiting for her to catch up was going to be agony.

"I think she might be into it."

"I have the perfect role for her."

Damn it, he did not like where this was going. "What's that?"

"The role where she never lets you see her naked again."

"Sounds like a challenge. One I've already overcome. Should be easy to do it a second time."

Her face fell. "My rejection isn't a challenge."

He shook his head very slowly. "You're right. It's an empty threat."

"Nick…" She grabbed a small first aid kit off the counter and put it in her basket.

He put his chest to her back, gripping the counter and resting his chin on her shoulder. "Why do we need a first aid kit?"

"Just in case."

He sighed. They were more likely to need the lube, but saying so was only going to get her more rattled. He brushed his lips to her ear, then whispered, "Still standing by that never gonna let me see you naked again bullshit?"

"Yes."

"You know…I don't need you naked to get you off." He kissed her neck, moving his hand to her throat, skimming his fingers over her smooth skin.

She sucked in a breath.

He gave her neck a gentle suck.

"This isn't going to work."

"It's not? Tell me to stop, then," he said, his voice rough. He applied gentle pressure to her chest with his forearm, keeping his hand against her throat, pulling her back against his chest.

Taylor melted into him and tilted her head, giving him better access to her neck.

"I'm getting mixed signals." He moved his hand up her throat, gently pressing under her jaw with his thumb while he kissed, licked, and sucked her neck teasingly. He took his other hand off the counter and placed it on her waist. "Tell me you don't want me to touch you."

The restless movements of her body against his and the little noises slipping from her lips drove him on. He moved his hand under her dress and trailed his fingertips up the inside of her thigh.

He nudged her chin higher and stared down at her face. He brushed the lace covering her pussy. "Say, 'Nick, I don't want you to touch me.'"

Her eyes flared, her gaze holding his.

"I'm listening," he said, tracing the edge of her panties. "Tell me or push me away, or I'm going to push your panties to the side and make you come."

"Oh my god." She rubbed her ass against him. "Nick."

He groaned, then worked his fingers under the panties, sliding his index finger over her bare, slick pussy. "Sorry. Got impatient hearing you say my name like that."

She moaned and dropped her head back, her chest lifting.

"But for real, Taylor," he whispered, stilling his fingers. "Tell me if you don't want to do this."

She moved her hips restlessly. "Thank you for checking but I really need you to keep going."

His grin stretched so wide it hurt. If he'd had any idea how sexy her reaction to his touch was, he'd have touched her a long time ago. He'd been anxious to cross this hurdle with Taylor, and now that he had, he was going to savor the fuck out of the early days.

He trailed his fingers across the silky-smooth skin hidden by her panties and continued his exploration of her neck and ear with his mouth.

Taylor trembled against his touch, her lips parting as she moaned.

Nick trailed his fingers from her panties to her lips and put his hand across her mouth to remind her she had a guest, and they were out in the open in her kitchen. "Be quiet, or I'll stop."

She closed her eyes and nodded.

"Can you taste yourself?" He rubbed his thumb across her bottom lip. Taylor moaned.

"I'm jealous." Right now, the only thing keeping him from tasting her was her panties. Once he saw her pussy, he wasn't going to be able to keep his mouth off it.

She rubbed her ass against his dick again.

His answer was to ease his finger inside her, rubbing against her clit with the heel of his palm.

Whatever word she tried to form was incoherent, but he was pretty sure it was supposed to be his name.

He kept her anchored to his chest, his hand still on her throat, stretching her upper body so her head rested back on his shoulder and left her neck exposed to his mouth. He loved the way she squirmed against him and all the noises she made. Loved how quickly she gave in to him even when he knew she was determined to be defiant.

Her muscles tremored around his finger as he slid his finger in and out of her slowly until she'd stopped coming and wilted in his arms.

"Go to your bedroom."

He took a step back but kept a hold of her waist until she seemed to have her balance.

"Why?"

He looked her up and down. "Because I want to put my mouth on you."

"We're going to miss the sunset," she said in a breathy voice, her chest rising and falling, her face flushed.

"Maybe. But you'll see stars if I do it right." He winked.

She shook her head. "You're ridiculous."

"Yeah, but you like it." He grabbed his cane and took a few steps backward. "If you didn't, you wouldn't be about to follow me."

26
Not a Thankless Job
Taylor

"COME OVER HERE AND take those panties off. They're already ruined."

Taylor's eyes widened and her jaw dropped. "What do you enjoy more, provoking me or touching me?"

"That's a tough one." He crooked his finger as he backed closer to her bedroom. "I'm going to need to do further research before I can make an informed choice."

Out of pettiness, she wanted to stay planted where she was, but the farther away he got, the stronger the pull to him grew. "It's not my job to educate you."

"Yes, it is." He crooked his finger again. "But it's not a thankless job. There are many benefits."

She rolled her eyes and walked to him. "Why am I so easily swayed by you?"

"Because you know I'd never let anything bad happen to you and all I want is to make you happy."

That probably was why. Well, that was one mystery solved.

He tugged her into the bedroom, then turned to shut the door.

Cal tried to follow, but Nick blocked him and whistled, then pointed to his bed in the living room. He hung his head and laid down.

Nick closed the door, then turned to her.

She raised an eyebrow. "That was kind of hot."

"He's going to have to get used to not sleeping in here. No sense dragging it out." He grabbed the skirt of her dress and hiked it up, tugging until it was over her head. He ran his hand along the curve of her lace-covered breast. "I guess you do have a lingerie drawer."

She angled her head and stared at where his fingers touched her.

"Do you like the way my hands look on you as much as I do?" he asked.

The tightness in her throat only allowed her to nod.

He tipped her chin up and kissed her, ushering her backward until her thighs hit her mattress, then scooped her up and laid her down. After covering her body with his own, he shifted so he could work her panties down and off her legs. He ghosted his fingertips over her, his teasing touch making her shift, chasing it. With his hands on her inner thighs, he spread them wider, his thumbs massaging the inside of her thighs close to her pussy.

Taylor moaned and bumped her hips upward.

He kept his touches slow and deliberate, getting close but never touching her right where she wanted him to.

"Nick," she whimpered.

He lowered his mouth, brushing his lips over the sweet skin a couple of inches above her clit.

"*Nick.*"

He flattened his tongue and ran it over the spot he'd kissed.

Eyes closed, she said, "I hate you so much."

He chuckled, but then kissed the inside of her thigh, then moved closer to her center. He sucked on the space where her thigh creased.

She arched her back. "You're an evil person."

He circled his tongue in a wide path with her clit in the center.

She bucked and moaned.

He licked up her slit, his tongue barely making contact.

The action drove her mad. Feeling this desperate and not having control was not something she knew how to handle. "Is it too late to tell you to stop?"

He froze. "Not if you mean it."

She groaned and pushed up on her elbows. "Could you just stop torturing me?"

"You mean, like this?" He suctioned a kiss an inch to the left of her clit.

"Yes," she whined, raising her pelvis.

"I'll give you what you want, but I want something too."

She nodded and wet her lips. "Yes. Deal."

"You don't even know what I want."

"I assumed you meant for me to return the favor."

He pressed a kiss to the inside of her knee. "That's not what I want."

"This feels like extortion."

He chuckled. "It most definitely is. Make a video with me."

She sat up, pushed him out of the way, and waved her arms like a traffic guard. "No way. Just because I let people do that here, doesn't mean I'm going to do it myself."

"No, not like that. Just a thirty second clip of us together."

"Why?"

"Because I need to let my followers know I'm not going to be posting anymore—or at least not posting the same type of content and not as often—and this is how I want to do it. I want them to know the reason isn't because my baseball career is over, but because I've got something better now and I want to focus my attention on that."

Something better. Her. Every woman wanted to be put first, to be told she was more important than anything else. Knowing that he felt that way was enough. She didn't expect or want him to sacrifice things he enjoyed because he thought she wanted him to.

"You don't have to give up posting for me."

"I've already made up my mind."

"It makes you money."

He moved his face closer to hers, his gaze intense. "Money isn't more important than you, Taylor. Besides, I don't want to be recognized constantly or have girls run up and feel my abs."

If she was with him and that happened, she'd probably lose her shit. "But can I touch your abs?"

"Anytime you want, baby."

"Even if I don't make a video with you?"

He frowned. "Why are you so against it?"

"Remember when I said every woman on the internet was going to hate me?"

"It doesn't have to show your face. It can be a cropped shot of you touching my abs, since you like them so much."

"They'll find out. With the number of followers you have, you don't think one of them is crazy enough to figure out who I am?"

"Fine. Forget that. For the next week, I want you to give yourself to me whenever I say so. No hesitating. I don't want you in your head."

"But not on video."

"No, not on video."

"Do I get a safe word?"

"Yeah, Taylor, it's stop. Don't ever use that word with me unless you mean it."

"Fine. Now, please, go back to what you were doing but minus the teasing."

He smirked, laid on his back, and motioned for her to come closer. "Bring that pussy up here."

She swallowed. She wanted his mouth on her so bad, but sitting on his face? Awkward.

Before she'd finished mulling it over, he raised up, grabbed her, and forced her to straddle his face.

He turned his head and kissed the inside of her knee. He ran his hand up her thigh and explored with his fingers, stroking and rubbing, then dipped his thumb inside her. The flick of his tongue against her clit made her gasp.

The teasing was over. He licked and sucked and fucked her with his fingers until her knees shook.

"Nick," she said, her voice unsteady.

He made a muffled noise, then alternated between sucking and swirling his tongue.

Taylor rocked against him.

He moaned and grabbed her ass with his free hand, squeezing, keeping her there grinding against his mouth while he pumped his fingers in and out of her.

She cried out, ripples of ecstasy moving through her body.

Nick kept going, prolonging her orgasm.

When the intense rush of sensation subsided, she pushed away, moving off him. It took forever to catch her breath as stared up at the ceiling.

He rolled onto his side and squeezed her breast. "I need you and I'm not sure I can be gentle—or anything close to it."

"Why do you think you need to be gentle?" She put her hand on the back of his head and lightly ran her nails to his neck, continuing down between his shoulder blades.

He shivered. "I don't want you to ever feel like I'm using your body."

She bit her lip to hold in her smile. "Nick, I want you to be rough sometimes. I want to know that I can make your control slip."

"Yeah?"

She put her hand on his cheek. "Don't hold back with me."

He sat up and pulled his shirt over his head, then stood and shed his pants. He made a spinning motion with his finger. "Flip over."

She rolled onto her stomach.

Nick grabbed her hips and lifted, guiding her onto her hands and knees. Her bed was low to the ground, the perfect height for him to fuck her from behind while standing. He thrust inside her, groaning as her heat surrounded him.

She gasped, then pushed her ass back, taking him deeper.

He didn't hold back. He increased the pace, fucking her hard and fast. "This feels too good for it to be over so fast."

27
Priorities and Peaches

Taylor

TAYLOR RUBBED HER EYES and yawned as she pulled a coffee cup from a cabinet. She'd woken up alone, and judging by the temperature of the coffee, it'd been a good while since Nick had left.

She went to feed Cal, but he'd already been fed and had a fresh bowl of water.

"He probably let you out already too, didn't he?" she asked the dog.

Instead of trotting to the door like he did every morning, he stayed put and stared at her.

Taylor took her cup of coffee to the bathroom so she could soak in the bath while she drank it. She didn't even care that Hope would be here in forty minutes. If she didn't sit in some warm water, the soreness between her thighs was going to irritate her all day, and at some point, Nick was going to demand to have her again and she was supposed to do whatever he wanted.

Instead of relaxing her, sitting in the tub gave her time to get properly anxious about Gavin's letter. She called Jaci while she soaked, and they'd worked it out that the *only* place he could've gotten a hold of those photos was through Taylor's or Jaci's e-mails.

She was dressed and halfway through making peach pies when Hope showed up.

Nick followed her in. He had on a faded, tattered ballcap, and his face was red and sweaty from being out in the sun for hours already. His jeans and shirt had a layer of dust on them. He grinned at Taylor from across the island.

Her entire body blushed.

"Oh no," Hope said. "Why are you looking at each other like that? Ew."

Nick rubbed the top of Hope's head, messing up her headband and the top of her hair. "You might want to rethink your choice of summer job because I'm going to be looking at her like that a lot."

"No. That's not fair."

Taylor put her fist to her mouth to hold back her laugh.

"Not fair?" Nick asked. "You could work at the farm. *With Josh.*"

"How do you stand him?" Hope asked Taylor.

"He's not that bad," she said. "Aside from the whole mama's boy thing. That's pretty unfortunate."

"Not unfortunate enough for you to keep your hands to yourself, though." Nick smirked.

"TMI." Hope put her hands to her ears briefly. "Can I have coffee?"

Taylor's gaze darted to Nick. "Sure, but don't tell your parents I gave it to you. If they find out, say it was Nick."

He mouthed, "Bad."

"Fix yourself a cup and then, I want you to stock the cottages with clean towels and toiletries. Everything you need is on a list hanging in the storeroom. Load it all into baskets and drive it down there on the golf cart."

Once Hope had fixed herself a travel mug, she disappeared into the storeroom.

"Brody is all fucked up because Morgan has been having false labor, so I'm in charge of the farm," Nick said, adjusting his hat. "I'll be tied up until five at the earliest."

"I have a beer league game at five-thirty, if it doesn't get rained out."

"Sweet. I'm going to heckle the shit out of you."

"Don't matter. I'll be in the zone."

He laughed and popped a peach slice into his mouth.

"My dad will be there." She mostly avoided him, but he still came to all her games. If she told him she didn't want him there, he'd insist on knowing why and she'd promised her mom she wouldn't tell him what she knew.

Nick froze. "I haven't seen him since I've been home. We need to tell him about us."

"Why?" Her dad didn't deserve to know the details of her private life. Nor did he deserve to have Nick's adoration, but again, she'd made a promise.

"What do you mean, why? I don't want him to find out from someone else. He's probably going to kill me either way, but I'd rather see it coming."

"It's none of his business."

"Taylor, why do you have an attitude about this?"

"He doesn't get a say in my love life."

"Did something happen that I don't know about?"

"I'm not ready for everyone to know about us." It wasn't untrue. She wasn't ready to be asked questions and small-town folks didn't hold back from being nosy.

"Hope knows. Jaci knows. Sabrina knows. Brody might know. .."

"Might know?" Nick and Brody were close, so it wouldn't at all be a shock if he'd told him.

He shrugged. "He guessed."

"So, it's safe to say Morgan knows."

"Probably. And your dad is going to find out eventually, so let's just get it over with."

Her stomach twisted. "If it's so important to you, you tell him. On your own. I don't need his permission and I don't want his blessing."

"Taylor, what the hell?"

"What does it matter if he approves or not? If he says he's not okay with you dating me, are you going to stop?" Her dad would come to terms with it eventually, but knowing him, his initial reaction would be that Nick should have asked his permission first.

"No. I don't actually think he's going to have a problem with it. Letting him know is a respect thing."

"If you feel compelled to tell him that you've had your dick in his daughter out of respect, go for it. Now, I need to finish these pies and get eighteen rooms and three cottages ready for guests."

"Fine. I'll leave you alone." He walked around the island and stood behind her. He covered her fist, being careful of the knife, and pressed it down to the cutting board. Once she'd released it from her clutch, he lifted her wrist to his mouth and ran his tongue across the sticky peach juice dripping down her arm.

"This is what you call leaving me alone?"

"No. This is what I call getting you all worked up and *then,* leaving you alone, so you think twice next time about this little attitude you seem to have caught." His lips brushed under her ear.

"Don't." She tried to pull away, but he tightened his arm across her middle.

"Hopefully, this is the only time I'll have to do it in order to teach you your lesson."

She snorted and giggled. "Go away."

He ran his hand up her side, moving around to cup her breast. "Remember our deal?"

"The same rules don't apply if you're messing with me."

"I don't remember discussing those terms."

"Let's discuss them now. We can negotiate."

He laughed. "Fine. I'll let you off easy this time."

He let her go, turned her, and kissed her until she almost couldn't stand. Then, he smirked and left.

28
He cares
Taylor

"WHAT IS YOUR MAN posting?" Jaci turned her phone screen toward Taylor.

It was a video taken from Nick's viewpoint as he cut a piece of brown paper and laid it flat on a table. He put a box of LEGO flowers in the center and started folding over the paper to cover the box. Once it was all taped up, he tied a piece of lace ribbon around it and drew on the paper with a pen. No names. Just kissing stick figures with hearts above their heads. Not so much as a glimpse of anything more than his hands and wrists.

"I don't know. Looks like he's wrapping a present." Taylor went back to kneading bread dough.

"The caption is: 'When she's surrounded by fields of flowers, but you want to show her you care.'"z

She snorted. "He's so stupid."

"He's sending his followers the message that he's taken." Jaci played the video again, sighing at the end.

"I told him not to do that. One enemy is enough for this week." Nick's romantic gestures were new and while she appreciated them, she really wished it was something he'd do privately.

"I'm not sure anyone could figure out who you are from this."

"Regardless, I have enough problems without adding another to the list." Taylor arranged the dough into a loaf pan and covered it with plastic wrap so it could rise.

"And yet you seem more relaxed than in the entire time I've known you."

She groaned. "Can you stop analyzing my behavior?"

"I'm not trying to. The difference is obvious. Look at you."

Taylor crossed her arms. She appreciated having a friend who didn't know her entire history with Nick. Having this same discussion with Morgan or Bree wouldn't be the same. She couldn't be as blunt with them. "I just haven't had time to dwell on everything that's wrong."

"Why not? Because...*oh*." Jaci's eyes went wide. "How many times has Nick distracted you?"

Taylor blushed. "Can you stop?"

"More than once?"

"Jaci."

"So, you guys went from strictly friends to humping like rabbits? Wow."

Her face grew hot. It was shocking to her as well. She'd never had this type of relationship before and having it with Nick was hard to wrap her head around.

"Are you going to tell him about Gavin's threat?"

"Yes," Taylor said. "But I want to have a plan first, and I need to stop freaking out about him seeing the photos."

Jaci's shoulders slumped. "It should have been your choice when, and if, to show them to anyone. I'm never sending anything by email again. I am so sorry."

"It's not your fault. Gavin is a dick."

"When are you going to tell Nick?" Jaci drummed her fingers against the counter and pursed her lips as though asking a question she shouldn't have to be asking.

"After I talk to Nova." The cyber expert should be arriving soon, and hopefully, she'd have insight into a plan to protect herself from Gavin.

The doorbell chimed. Cal jumped up from his bed, on high alert. He followed Taylor to the front door. The person on the other side of the door instantly charmed her. She was tall and slender, with short black hair that framed her face and accentuated her beautiful almond shaped eyes. She had on black biker shorts and a dark gray cropped T-shirt. A laptop bag hung from her shoulder.

"You must be Nova. I'm Taylor. Come in."

She led her into the kitchen. "Would you like coffee? Iced coffee? I have tea, hot and cold, fresh squeezed lemonade, and fresh squeezed orange juice."

"Dang," Nova said, taking everything in. "This place is magic. Um, I'll take orange juice."

"This is my friend, Jaci," Taylor said while pouring a glass of juice. "She's the photographer who took the photos and e-mailed them to me."

"We need to talk about your protocols for sharing sensitive photos with clients."

Jaci frowned like a child who'd been scolded. "I know."

"I've checked and the whole network here, everything you have, is not secure. It's going to require a massive rebuild."

"Rebuild of what?" Taylor asked.

"Your cyber security. I know it sounds intense, but don't worry, I've got it handled. Within two hours, I can have you buttoned up pretty tight, but it's going to take longer to put in place the digital infrastructure you need to protect your information."

"What about the photos that have already been compromised?"

"That's going to take longer than two hours, and it's going to take more than a few people to even have a shot at pulling it off."

"What will we have to do?" Taylor asked.

Nova took a sip of juice. "Lie with a straight face."

29
The Plan

Taylor

TAYLOR HAD REACHED NEW lows.

Here she was, in her living room with three other women, plotting a scheme to erase her boudoir photos from Gavin's digital possession.

"Once their devices are locked down, how are we going to deal with retrieving the copies of the photos that Gavin has," Morgan asked. "How do we even know how many copies exist, whether print or on a flash drive?"

"I can't do anything about the print copies." Nova leaned forward from her spot on the couch, her forearms braced across her thighs. "But I've been in his computer, and if I can go back and find the files, I should be able to get a history of if he saved them to other devices. Then, we'll have to make sure to locate all those devices and wipe them."

"How are we going to locate them?" Taylor handed Sabrina a fresh box of tissues and flashed her a smile she hoped would reassure her that everything would be okay—even though she wasn't positive it would be.

"Good question. Morgan is in no condition to be doing anything like that. I'm not as stealthy as her, but if he's distracted, maybe—"

"How are you going to get in?" Morgan asked. "You can't pick a lock, last I checked."

"That is kind of a snag."

"I'm going to call in reinforcements—Logan and Brody's cousin. Brody isn't going to like me getting involved in this even at the planning level. I'm going to have to tell him about the photos or he's not going to understand what's at stake."

"I haven't told Nick yet," Taylor said.

Morgan sighed and stacked her hands on her belly. "Just tell him. You don't have to show them to him if you're not ready."

"It's not just showing him. It's that the photos even exist. It's embarrassing."

"No, it's not. I wish I'd had them done before this." She did a swirly motion over her belly.

"I think you're a badass for posing for them," Nova said.

Jaci smirked and shrugged. "I think you're a hot damn mess, but those photos are the furthest thing from embarrassing. Nova is right. It takes guts."

"I'll just go back to him. You don't deserve to go through this," Sabrina said.

"No," Taylor, Jaci, Morgan, and Nova said at the same time.

"Not for real. Just until he gives the photos to you."

"It's easy to make digital copies," Nova said. "We can't just take him at his word that he's deleted them. He could have them saved externally."

"He also might not let you go again. He's starting to show his desperation and his true colors are coming out," Morgan said. "But, until we have a plan, we need him to think that his plan is working and that he's going to get his way. Taylor, you have to tell him you're going to try to talk Sabrina into going back to him."

"What if he doesn't believe me?"

"If you say what he wants to hear, he'll buy it."

"Okay, fine. We know how we're going to stall him." Jaci paced in front of the television. "But how do we get the photos back and know for sure that there aren't still copies stashed somewhere?"

"Taylor can meet with him, get him to sign a gag order about the photos. While she's doing that, our team will go into his residence, office, wherever and comb through it. We'll run any drives we find, do a sweep to find the photos. If they're there, we'll delete them. It'll be like they never existed."

"What if he has a drive in a security deposit box somewhere?" Taylor asked.

"I've been monitoring him. He's never rented one before. Still hasn't."

"This just seems like…we could go to all this trouble, and then, he could have a flash drive saved in an airport locker," Jaci said.

"You're right." Morgan winced. "There are a lot of holes in this plan, but we're five intelligent women. He's one limp dick man. This is why we need to stall him a little bit, so we can tighten up our strategy."

30

Beer Leagues and Bullshit

Nick

THE HOTTEST THING NICK had ever seen, bar none, was Taylor in cut-off jean shorts and a blue T-shirt she'd tucked the sleeves inside of, baring her shoulders, getting her feet positioned in her little canvas sneakers as she prepared to pitch.

He stood in the shade of a tree behind the backstop and watched for a minute. As soon as someone spotted him, it'd be hard to focus on Taylor. And that's all he wanted to do. He hadn't even gotten out of his car until the game had started. He'd called her instead to wish her good luck and tell her he'd be watching.

She struck out her first batter of the inning.

Nick came out of the shadows, close enough to the fence that she could see him if she looked his way. She didn't, though, so maybe she *was* in the zone.

Her team was mostly men in their 20s and 30s, but there were a few women.

She struck out the second batter.

Nick cupped his hands around his mouth. "You throw like a girl."

She glanced his way, grinning. "Thank you," she shouted back, then lowered her head and got positioned on the mound.

The spectators and some of the players laughed. But he'd drawn attention to himself, so now it began. He put up with the impromptu meet-and-greet for a few minutes, then excused himself.

Nick glanced around, looking for Coach. After the game, he was going to lay everything on him. He needed to get this all out in the open. Just get it over with. No, it didn't matter what her dad said. No one was going to tell him to leave Taylor alone. He'd done that for long enough.

Ollie sat next to the bleachers in a camping chair with his arms folded across his chest, his gaze locked on Nick. That was *not* a happy-to-see-you expression.

Shit.

Nick hadn't done anything wrong, but he suddenly felt guilty as hell. "Hey, Coach."

He nodded to him before he turned his attention back at the field.

Nick did the same.

Taylor didn't strike out the next player, but he barely made it on base. He looked back at Ollie.

"We'll talk after the game." Despite him not saying what they were going to talk about, the vibe coming off Ollie said he wasn't happy about it. That could just be the news about his knee. It's not like he could know about him and Taylor. Unless she'd told him.

Doubtful.

Probably more likely about how crushed he was that Nick's career was over.

He walked to the bleachers, trying not to be awkward about his cane, and sat beside Ollie.

"Her pitch is looking good."

"Real good. Too good for a beer league."

Nick shrugged. "I don't know, Coach. She's got a pretty sweet life, and she seems happy. Isn't that the point?"

Overall, Taylor was probably a more talented athlete than he was. He'd only been able to play one sport because his family needed him at the farm. Taylor had been a triple threat—playing not just softball, but volleyball and swimming. She'd gotten athletic scholarships to four different colleges. He'd only gotten one full-ride and the others were partial—except for the full academic scholarship he'd been offered by one of the schools that had offered Taylor a full-ride.

Her dad didn't like that Nick had accepted a partial athletic scholarship and had tried to talk him into going to one of the other schools because he'd be more likely to be seen by an MLB scout.

Ollie'd had bigger plans for him and Taylor—separately—and they'd let him down.

Taylor struck out the fifth batter, and jogged in from the field, ponytail bouncing. Inside the dugout, she set down her mitt and took a red cup a teammate handed her. She grinned at Nick just before taking a long swig, her gaze never leaving his until she'd lowered the cup.

She grabbed a batting helmet and a bat and went to home plate.

Her first swing, she hit a foul.

He was about to yell at her about her swing, but Ollie said, "After the game, you're coming by the house so we can have a talk in private about why Taylor was looking at you like that."

"I think we should have that conversation in front of witnesses, Coach."

Ollie shot him a look—the same one he gave Nick whenever he'd been clowning around on the field instead of being focused on the game.

Taylor cracked the ball and ran to second base.

"It doesn't matter how much I like you," Ollie said. "That's my daughter."

"I get it. We'll talk after the game." There was no way he was going to Ollie's house after this game, though. The only place he wanted to be after this game was between Taylor's thighs. Who knew watching her play was going to turn him on?

The game wasn't even close. Taylor's team may have drank more beer than the other team, but they had her. She'd had her own share but stayed sober enough to slaughter the other team with strikeouts, and it seemed like she was taking it easy on them after the second inning.

With Taylor's team having won, they had a little celebration by the keg afterward, so Nick gestured for Ollie to go stand under the tree with him, away from everyone else.

Nick leaned on his cane.

Ollie's gaze lowered to Nick's knee, then back to his face. "How bad?"

"It's not the kind of knee an MLB player wants to have."

"So, you're done?"

"Done playing ball. I'm not being put out to pasture."

"Just because you can't play doesn't mean you can't be a part of the game. You can still have a hell of a career."

"There's other things I want more."

"Taylor's not going anywhere. Get your career nailed down first."

Nick's jaw ticked. It sounded like he was implying that a career in sports was more important than Taylor, his own daughter. But that tracked. It wasn't the first time Ollie had taken him to the side to tell him to stop "goofing off" with Taylor and get serious about whatever thing at the time he thought Nick should be focused on. This was different, though. This wasn't goofing off.

"What exactly are you suggesting he do?" Taylor asked loudly.

Ollie half-turned, revealing Taylor standing behind him in a battle-ready stance.

"Even if Nick can't play, he's worked his whole life to build a future in this sport," Ollie said. "This could be his last chance to find a place in the industry."

She moved to stand by Nick. "And a career in baseball is a better opportunity than…me?"

A life with Taylor was the only opportunity he gave a damn about.

"You're not going to play the supportive girlfriend and make time to go visit him, so maybe this isn't the best time for whatever is happening between you two."

Nick leaned against the tree, keeping his hand on Taylor's hip. This conversation was headed south fast. Rage radiated off her body so strong seeped into his own body, but it never worked out well if he got between these two.

"You think I didn't go see him because I didn't care about being supportive? Do you have any fucking idea what you're saying to me right now? Tell me, how supportive is it to use your daughter's business while she's out of town to cheat on her mother?"

Nick knew from her tone he needed to keep her from letting her temper drive her to do something she'd either regret or get charged for. Once he had his arm looped around her waist, he processed her words. Her dad had cheated. That was a serious accusation and for her to make it against her father, who she'd idolized, she must have hard evidence.

Ollie narrowed his eyes.

"My security cameras caught it. You undressed one of them right in my foyer. Grabbed another one's ass as you whispered something in her ear to make her giggle. You're disgusting."

Nick moved his hand up her body, cupping her biceps and keeping her tight against him. "You did that?" he asked Ollie.

He rolled his eyes, like that action would somehow discredit Taylor. "She doesn't know what she's talking about."

He squeezed his cane so hard it hurt his knuckles. There were certain things people shouldn't do around Nick, and one of them was hinting, even slightly, that Taylor wasn't perfect. He didn't give a shit if it was her father. "You're calling her a liar?"

"No, she's confused."

"Confused about what were you doing with the women you brought to the inn that she saw you on camera with?"

Her dad looked around. "You could really hurt someone throwing around a rumor like that."

"Like Mom?" Taylor asked.

"Of course, it would hurt her. And it has nothing to do with this. This is about you not understanding how pivotal Nick's career choices are right now. Or maybe you don't care. You didn't care about your scholarship. You gave it up to bake pies and arrange bouquets, and now you want Nick to stick around here with you."

He adjusted his hold just before she lunged forward, pulling her tightly against his chest. "She's not holding me back." He was *literally* holding her back, but that was beside the point.

She tried to wrestle away, but he held her tighter.

The sky rumbled and darkened.

"I'm leaving before the sky opens up, but we need to finish this conversation."

"Not tonight," Nick said. "Taylor and I need to talk first."

He shook his head. "Forget it then. I don't stand a chance in hell against you two. Do what you want and fuck what I have to say, like always."

"Gladly," Taylor said.

Ollie walked off in a huff. He yanked his truck door open, and once inside, slammed it shut.

Nick stared at his taillights until they disappeared, his mind a whirl of questions and his heart feeling like it'd gotten slammed into by a bulldozer. "Taylor? How long have you kept this a secret?"

She turned to face him. "I found out when I came to see you when you first started college. Remember, you helped me install those security cameras? I hadn't told him about them yet, and after that I decided not to."

"Why didn't you tell me?"

"Because it flipped my world upside down. I truly believed he was the best father, husband, and coach to ever exist. I had to grieve the loss of that reality. I didn't want you to have to go through that too."

That made it worse. Instead of his heart feeling bruised, it burned like it'd been pierced with a thousand needles. She'd suffered alone. To spare him. He didn't want that. He'd never want that.

"I could have handled it, and I could have been there for you. We could've gone through it together." Just like every other thing they'd gone through together in their lives. But Ollie's betrayal had severed that attachment. He'd lost her and he hadn't even realized it. Not that he was completely oblivious that something was missing between them. He'd just blamed it on distance and getting older.

She gave him a weak smile. "Making logical choices isn't my strongest skill."

"Stop making them without me, then." He kissed her forehead. "I'm going to go for a drive and clear my head. We'll celebrate your win after, okay?"

She nodded. "Okay, Nick."

31

Getting Dirty in the Dugout

Taylor

TAYLOR COULD HAVE DONE the well-adjusted, emotionally mature thing and gone home and waited for Nick to process his thoughts and feelings. Instead, she drove around trying to cross his path. She wasn't going to be able to sit at home and be calm. She wasn't calm. And Nick was the person who made her calm. Without him, she had no chance at calm.

Rain pelted against her windshield as she drove around town, down backroads, looking for his car. She spotted it at the baseball diamond they'd played little league on. She parked and sprinted toward the closest dugout.

The infield had bare spots, courtesy of kids still using it for drop-in games, but the outfield needed a good mowing. They didn't have any league games on this field anymore, now that they had newer, shiner fields.

She jogged out by third base, then back inside the field, up next to the dugout, and slipped inside.

Nick straightened from where he'd been leaned back against the cinderblock wall, his hands curling around the bench's edge. "What's wrong?"

"You tell me." She brushed away the wet hair sticking to her face. "You're the one sitting in a dugout during a thunderstorm."

He grabbed her hand and pulled her closer. "I can't stop thinking about all the times I sat right here," he rapped the bench with his knuckles, "and listened to him preach honesty, and loyalty. *Integrity.*"

Taylor straddled him. "Forget what he said about that. Let me show you what those things look like instead."

He gripped her waist. "How?"

"Next time you think about this dugout, the only thing you're going to be able to remember is what we did here."

She stood, dropped to her knees, and put her hands on his thighs.

"What are you doing?"

Something that would take his mind off the bullshit circling around in it. She unhooked his belt.

"Taylor, I will literally never be the same if you give me head in this dugout."

She wet her lips.

He grabbed her ponytail and pulled her head back. "You've been warned. You're probably going to tear the fabric of my reality."

Taylor rolled her eyes, then finished undoing his pants.

She removed her wet T-shirt, leaving her in a sports bra.

"That's not helping."

One of the best parts of being with Nick was that she knew exactly where her power laid. Because he let her know. And that made her feeling something better than powerful. No one could so much as scratch or dent what they had. Tonight had proven that, or at least how she factored into the strength of their bond because she'd do anything to make him feel better. Although, there were worse places than on her knees in the dugout with Nick.

"Are we really doing this here?" he asked.

"Since when are you shy?"

"I'm not, I just don't appreciate interruptions."

"It's a freaking monsoon. No one is getting out of their car to come look what's going on in here. Get out of your head, Nick. Unless you don't want to have fun…"

"Hey, that's what I'm supposed to say to you."

"Well, apparently you need me to say it *to you* because I don't give a fuck, just like you wanted, but you're being lame."

He grabbed her chin and rubbed his thumb over her bottom lip. "I'm not lame. You're just a bad girl."

"So, treat me like one." She wiggled her eyebrows.

His mouth fell open, and if he'd started sputtering, she wouldn't have been surprised. She would have laughed, though. "By making you go down on me in the dugout?"

"No, by pulling my hair while I go down on you in the dugout."

Nick's jaw twitched. "You're killing me."

She tugged at his waistband, and he lifted his hips to help her work his jeans and boxer briefs to his ankles.

Her breasts brushed the tops of her thighs as she kissed a path toward his dick. She wrapped her fist around him and swiped her tongue across the tip.

He groaned and gripped the edges of the bench.

She stared up at him as she slid him past her lips, taking him into her mouth.

He hissed and tugged her ponytail. "Fuck, Taylor."

She worked her tongue around him as she slid him in and out of her mouth.

The groan that fell from his lips empowered her. She fought back her smile and continued to suck and lick his cock.

He yanked her ponytail, shifting to stare at her, then pushed her sports bra strap off her shoulder. After he traced his fingertips along the edge of fabric, he tugged it down until her breast popped free. "You look so good when you're being bad."

He rubbed his thumb over her nipple.

Taylor moaned, nearly gagging on him.

Nick's hips jerked. "Unless you want me to come down your throat, you better stop."

She didn't stop.

He groaned and warmth coated the back of her throat. For a few moments, he gazed at her, his eyes hooded, his chest rising and falling.

On her knees, waiting for his next move, she rubbed her tingling lips together. Sexy didn't even touch how she felt. How he made her feel by looking at her the way he was.

He pulled her up from her knees and skimmed his palms from her ribs to her hips. "These jeans."

"Yes? What about them?"

"They're hot. You're hot." He flipped open the button.

"What are you doing?" she asked.

"I need to know how wet sucking me off got you."

She gasped.

He slid his hand inside her jeans and underwear, right to her pussy, which was hot and slick. "Fuck, Tay. You must have really liked having my cock in your mouth."

"Obviously," she huffed.

"If you get sassy, I'm not going to finger you."

Taylor arched her back and groaned. "I'll probably feel a lot less sassy after you finger me."

32
Troublefaker
Nick

Nick's shirt was sticking to him by the time they got back to the inn. He couldn't believe she'd given him a blowjob in the dugout. Taylor was perfect. He'd never thought sex between them would be bad, but he hadn't imagined it'd be this good. They weren't taking things slow. He could admit that. But it wasn't just him in control of the pace. There was so much momentum behind this thing, he couldn't slow it down.

He peeled his shirt off and hung it over the shower curtain rod in her bathroom to dry, then went back into the bedroom.

She'd changed into sweats and a hoodie. The baggy clothes probably should've dampened how much he wanted her, but all it did was push that want from lust to contentment. Seeing her in an outfit she'd never let most people see her in built up that part of him that believed she belonged to him. *His* Taylor.

He walked up to her and kissed her forehead. "Thank you for finding me."

"My temper got control of my mouth. I'm sorry that you found out like that. I should have told you in private, gently."

"I mean, it sucks and all, but I'm more fucked up that he thinks I should prioritize my career over you."

"That's really a surprise?"

"I thought he'd be happy about us." Ollie had always treated him like a son. Son-in-law was the next best thing. Besides, unless he wanted

Taylor to be alone, who would he trust more than Nick with his daughter?

"He lost all hope for my athletic future when I dropped out before freshman year even started. You're all he had left. But he's wrong, Nick. If you want to accept the offer, we can figure out how to make it work."

She had to be crazy to think he'd want to be anywhere other than with her. "I don't want it. Especially now."

"I'm sorry he tainted something you love."

He wrinkled his brow. "You think what he did is putting a bitter taste in my mouth for baseball?"

"It did for me."

"When I think about baseball, I don't think about him. I think about you."

"Me?"

He sat on the bed and pulled her to stand between his legs. "You're the only person who I ever had a catch with who didn't want to stop before I did. Your idea of fun is going to the batting cages. You made me run with you and made fun of me for being slow. Just like you'd make fun of me for striking out or not being able to slide into home without getting out."

"I was just trying to get you fired up, so you'd work harder."

"And it worked. See what I'm saying? You made me into the player I became. I love baseball because it was our thing."

"Oh."

"It'll always be our thing, Tay. Fuck him."

She twisted the drawstring from her hood around her finger. "I'm in trouble."

Nick cringed. He didn't like the sound of that.

Taylor grabbed a large white envelope from the top of her dresser and handed it to him.

He slid out the contents and immediately froze. As soon as he could tear his eyes away from the large photo of her stretched over her bed, back arched, he slowly moved his gaze to hers.

She crossed her arms. "Keep going."

He had to turn the next photo to the correct orientation. She had on different lingerie in this one. That lingerie drawer definitely existed. This pose was less erotic than the previous one, but fuck, she looked hot. "Holy hell, Taylor."

There were six photos in all—one of them where she appeared to be fully naked, with a sheet placed strategically to hide her breasts and pussy. The last item was a letter.

After reading it, he jabbed his finger onto the center of the paper. "He has these photos of you?"

That asshole was going to be sorry he ever fucked with Taylor. He'd gone beyond just being a regular asshole. He was a mega asshole. This was twisted. Nick felt positively sick that Gavin had seen these photos.

But that wasn't enough. He was blackmailing her with them.

"I'm handling it," Taylor said.

"The way I'm going to handle it is more effective."

"Nick," she said slowly, warningly. "You'll get arrested."

"It'll be worth it."

"No, it won't."

He scoffed and crossed his arms. "Agree to disagree. Give me his address."

"No. It's my problem."

"Your problems are my problems."

"It affects me—my body, my business, so I get to say how it's handled, okay? If you go kick his ass, Mr. Tough Guy, he might back off, but he'll still have those photos of me."

"What's your plan?"

"Morgan's friend, Nova, is going to wipe it from his hard drive."

"How?"

She crawled to the center of the bed and hugged her knees. "We have a plan."

"And I'm asking what it is."

"I'm going to meet with him and while I'm doing—"

"No." He stood and dug his fingers into his wet hair. "That's a terrible plan. Absolutely not."

"Nick, you don't get to tell me what to do."

"The fuck I don't. I'm not going to let you put yourself in danger."

"We'll be in public."

"No," he stressed.

She pulled a face, like she'd gotten a whiff of something stinky. "I don't need your permission."

"You should want my input. I'd want yours, and I'd take it into genuine consideration. Not just say I'm gonna do whatever the hell I feel like, regardless of how you feel."

He would too. She knew it. He knew it. And her first instinct might not be to come to him for help—which fucking sucked—but that was something she was going to have to get comfortable with immediately.

"I can't abandon this plan without a better one."

"Then, I'll come up with a better one because you're not getting within a hundred feet of this guy." Man, this really had him pissed off. All of it. The threat. Her not coming to him right away. Her stupid idea that would put her within that asshole's grasp.

"I can handle myself," she said, her voice brimming with irritation.

"I. Don't. Want. You. Around. Him."

"Too. Bad."

He waved the photos and letter. "Why'd you tell me about this if you're not going to let me be a part of the solution?"

She covered her eyes. "I'm bad at this. My kneejerk reaction is to get defensive when someone thinks they get a say in my plans. But you do, Nick. I'm just not used to it."

"Does that mean if I come up with a better plan, you'll hear me out?"

She nodded. "But we don't have a lot of time. He wants Sabrina back before anyone notices something is up."

He glanced at the photos again. "What's up with you having these photos taken, Taylor?"

"Jaci took them the other day. She was scheduled to do a shoot with Sabrina, but she got here early and…" Taylor blushed.

"And?"

"Morgan and Drew were talking about the possibility of you and me, and it was awkward, so I used the photoshoot as an excuse to escape. I didn't really plan on having the photos taken, but Jaci tricked me into it."

He shuffled back through them. "I no longer have doubts about the existence of the lingerie drawer."

"Shut up."

He flashed her a grin. "Lingerie. Racy photos. An entire closet full of sex toys. A blowjob in the dugout. It's hard to believe I've known you all this time and had no idea what a freak you are."

33
Clingy as Shit
Nick

"I HAVE TO GO," Nick whispered against Taylor's head. "My mom is going to the hospital with Morgan and Brody, and I need to be at the house with my dad."

She stretched. "I don't want you to go."

"Come with me," he whispered.

She pushed up on her elbow. "Shouldn't we be able to spend a night away from each other?"

"Maybe we should, but we can't. Let's go."

On the way to his parents' house, Taylor texted Sabrina letting her know where they were going and that she'd be back in the morning to let Cal out.

The kitchen was lit up when they got there. Gia was organizing her purse at the counter and drinking a cup of coffee. She smirked at Taylor in a way that made her feel like she was a teenager who thought she was sneaky when it was obvious what she'd been up to. "It's nice to see you, Taylor."

She glanced at Nick. "Hope and your dad are asleep. I'll text you an update on Morgan and the baby when I get there."

Once the back door had shut, he grabbed a wrapped package off the kitchen island and linked fingers with Taylor. He led her through the dining room to the living room. After sitting on the couch, he pulled her into his lap and handed her the package.

The flower LEGO wasn't a surprise, but Taylor got excited after opening it anyway.

"It's a bribe," he said and stacked his hands behind his head, leaning back into the cushions of the couch. "I have to give a statement at a press conference that I'm retiring because of my injury."

"That doesn't sound fun." She set the box with the LEGO on the cushion next to them.

"No, it doesn't. I asked for it to be early in the week because I want you to come with me. I need you to cheer me up afterward."

Her chest got tight. "I don't have to be on camera, do I?"

"No."

"Okay."

"Yeah?"

"Yeah. Does this mean you're officially moving home for good?"

He walked his fingers up her bare thigh, sending shivers through her. "Someone has to help you run your den of sin."

Her mouth fell open. She pushed at his shoulder.

He grunted. "Kidding. I'll be helping Brody with the farm."

"Is that really what you want to do? Are you sure you don't want that marketing position?"

"I want to spend my dad's last years with him, and I want to lighten my brother's load while he's taking care of his family. I want to spend more time with my mom and glare at boys who come to pick up my sister for dates. And I want to see you every day."

34
VIP of Taste Testing and Company Keeping
Nick

TAYLOR WASN'T THE ONLY one receiving threatening letters.

Nick stared at the letter with his college's letterhead before him on the counter in his mom's kitchen. He'd been able to balance playing in the minors and taking classes. But he'd had one semester left when he got offered a contract for the major leagues. He'd hoped to be able to finish his degree, thinking maybe he'd find a way to take classes in the offseason. But now, this letter said he was in danger of losing credits if he didn't resume his course load this coming semester.

The coffee pot finished brewing and he took the letter and two steaming cups to the living room and set them on the coffee table. Look at him using the furniture for its intended purpose and shit.

He bent down and kissed her forehead. "Taylor."

"Hmm?"

"Morgan had the baby."

She struggled to sit up. "Really? Is everything good?"

"Yep. I have photos." He dug his phone out of his wallet and pulled up the message from his mom with all the photos. She'd gotten home a little before sunup, but after she'd given him a briefing about Morgan and the baby, he'd insisted she go get some rest.

She awed at the photos. "What's her name?"

"Demi."

"I'm so happy for them."

He wanted that with her. And he'd already made an ass of himself and admitted it to her. Fuck. Why couldn't his emotions work at a normal pace or why couldn't he just say how he felt without spiking her anxiety?

None of it even mattered right now. The more pressing issue was how he'd logistically do all the things he needed to do today in not just Brody's absence, but his mom's as well. His dad couldn't be left alone, and Hope couldn't handle the stress of being a caretaker for him. Besides, Hope was supposed to work at the inn. He couldn't expect Josh to handle the farm all by himself, so now Nick had to come up with a solution for how to work on the farm without leaving his dad unattended.

"I made you coffee," he said.

"Thanks." She took the mug he handed her, tucking the blankets around her legs. "Did your mom make it back home?"

"Yeah, but I sent her to bed. I expect when she wakes up, she's going to be anxious to go back to the hospital. They're not going to discharge Morgan and the baby until tomorrow."

"Hope's probably going to be chomping at the bit to see the baby too. She can have the day off if she wants."

He shook his head. "I can't leave my dad to take you back to the inn, so you can take my car, but it's going to be a while until anyone can visit, so Hope might as well work. Can you wait until she's ready and take her with you? She's in the shower now."

"Sure, but you know your dad could come to the inn too. I'll mostly be baking, so he can keep me company in the kitchen and be my taste tester. That way Gia can sleep in a quiet house, he'll be entertained, and you can do what you need to do on the farm."

"Fuck that. I want to be your company and your taste tester."

She angled her head. "You licked peach juice off me yesterday. That's a privilege reserved for the VIP of taste testing and company keeping."

"As long as I'm higher ranking."

She rolled her eyes. "So, can he come with us? Assuming he wants to?"

He kissed her. "Yeah, I'll drop the three of you off at the inn and take Cal with me."

"Can I pick strawberries while I wait for Hope? I was going to order them from Brody, but I'm guessing there will be a delay."

"I'll get Josh to pick a flat and deliver them." Which Hope wasn't going to like, but that was the kid's job and he'd get it done a lot smoother and faster than Nick could considering he couldn't carry a flat of strawberries and use his cane at the same time.

"I like picking them. I'm sure Josh has plenty of better stuff to do."

"Maybe I can convince all our customers to pick their own produce before Brody returns to work and he'll think I'm a genius."

She shrugged. "I'm sure those with bigger orders wouldn't be into that, but the smaller businesses and people with kids might be."

"Changing our whole business model while Brody takes a few days off probably isn't a wise move."

"It's as much your farm as it is his. If you have ideas for how to improve it, you shouldn't keep them to yourself."

He brushed his lips against her neck. "The only ideas I have involve you and me and no clothes."

She wriggled on his lap. "Don't start things you can't finish, Nick."

"Oh, I'll finish it. It's just a matter of when."

She groaned and pushed off his lap, bringing him nearly eye-level with her ass. He ran his hand over the curve of it. How'd he gone so long keeping his hands off her boggled his mind. Especially, since he no longer seemed to possess that ability whatsoever.

She turned and put her hands on his shoulders.

He moved his other hand to her ass and pressed his lips to the little strip of skin exposed between her shorts and her shirt, then tipped his head back and looked up at her. "If Morgan and Brody are up to it, you want to go see the baby this evening?"

A slow grin spread on her face. "You're dying to hold that baby, aren't you?"

"It's my brother's baby. Am I not supposed to be excited?"

"No, you are." She set down her coffee and moved into his lap. "But I'm still going to give you shit about it."

35
Lewis Luck
Nick

IF ANYONE EVER WANTED to know why Taylor was his favorite person in the world, this was the perfect example.

Here she was, hair up in a messy bun with pieces falling all around her face, her tongue stuck out of the side of her mouth while she assembled LEGOs with her crew. That's right. Her crew. His dad. Hope. Sabrina. She had them all working on their own kits and eating cookies. Homemade cookies evidenced by the entire house smelling of vanilla and sugar.

Cal bounded into the room, right over to her, his tail wagging.

"Did you miss me?" she asked as she rubbed his ears.

"Not as much as I did." He walked closer and leaned down to kiss her. Because he didn't give a fuck. This is what he did when he saw her now. Because she was his girlfriend. And if it was awkward for everyone else, oh-the-fuck-well.

No one said a word. Hope didn't even make gagging noises.

"LEGOs, cookies, beautiful women," he said to his dad. "Do you ever not fall up?"

He shrugged. "It's that Lewis Luck. Don't act like you don't have it."

Nick frowned and pointed at his knee.

His dad pointed at Taylor.

He shrugged and snagged a cookie from the plate. "Can't argue with that." He looked at Hope. "Getting paid to eat cookies and put together LEGOs? Now, *that's* luck."

"This is a team building exercise," Taylor said.

"But you're all doing individual kits."

"Shut up. There's a reason for that. I'm not going to explain it to you, though." Not to mention Sabrina and his dad weren't her employees. Not that he knew of anyway. Taylor's magnetism could have easily helped her convince them to work for her in exchange for LEGO.

"Mom is on her way. She's going to take Hope and Dad to see the baby. You wanna get some dinner and then we'll go visit after?" he asked.

Taylor stood from the table. "Let's just order pizza. Morgan's family made last-minute reservations. They'll be here late tonight and early tomorrow. Hope helped me accomplish a lot, but I have a few things left to do and I'd rather have time to see Morgan and the baby than go to a restaurant."

"Pizza it is. And I'm going to help you prep for the guests."

"I will too," Sabrina said.

Taylor opened her mouth, but Nick covered it with his hand.

"Don't say it." He didn't take his hand away, staring at her big eyes for a moment. "I'm going to help you and I'm not going to waste time arguing about it. Got it?"

She nodded.

He removed his hand from her mouth.

She licked her lips and kept her gaze on him like he was the only person in the room.

Nick grinned. Fine. If that turned her on, that didn't bother him any. All he had to do now was get rid of his family and Sabrina.

36
Darling Demi

Taylor

NICK HOLDING A BABY probably should have gotten some type of reaction out of Taylor's biological clock or whatever people called it. Her maternal instincts? Did she have those? Was it something that girls were born standard with but lied dormant until triggered?

Emotionally, it did do something to her, but it had nothing to do with wanting to have a baby with him. She couldn't even think about that. Well, maybe a little bit. Out of sheer curiosity she'd wondered what they'd be like as parents. Seeing him as an uncle and witnessing how happy he was for his brother was what got her in the feels.

"She's so little and perfect." With the tiny baby cradled in his arms like the precious thing she was, he glanced at Morgan. "You got mad skills."

She laughed. "Thanks, Nick. I try."

"I had a hand in that, you know," Brody said.

"If you did it with your hand, I have some bad news for you,' Nick said.

Brody rolled his eyes. "Smart ass."

"Do you want to hold her?" Morgan asked Taylor.

"Whenever Nick is done falling in love with her."

"That's right," he said to the baby. "You and me are besties now. Taylor who?"

She shook her head and lifted the two gift bags she'd carried in. "I brought you a few things."

"Thank you." Morgan went through the bags. One was food—cookies, banana bread, a raw veggie cup with hummus, and the other contained a dusty pink muslin baby blanket. "It's so soft."

"I can take it back with us and drop it off at your house so it's not one more thing to bring home. I'm sure you brought a blanket to use."

"Yeah, but I like this one better."

"Want me to take the other one back to the house?"

"That's okay. I think we can handle one extra blanket," Brody said.

"How is everything going with that thing that broke at the inn?" Morgan asked.

It took her a minute to catch on. "Oh. It's…still broke. Nick knows and he wants to help fix it."

Morgan seemed to relax a bit. "Good." She glanced at Brody. "Taylor is being blackmailed."

Brody straightened his posture. Through a clenched jaw, he asked, "How?"

Her face heated. She sat next to Nick on the small loveseat in the hospital room.

"We don't need to get into the details," Nick said.

"What's going on?" Brody demanded.

"I had my friend take some photos of me in lingerie, and a disgruntled guest hacked into my computer and is using me to help him get his wife back after cheating on her."

"That's…complicated. How are you supposed to help him?"

Taylor spent the next few minutes bringing Brody up to speed.

When she finished, Nick placed the baby in her arms and rested his head back. "You two don't need to get involved. You just had a baby. We've got this."

"I've already filled my brother in on the situation," Morgan said. "He'll be here tomorrow and I'm sure he has some ideas for how to deal with Gavin. If he and Nova collaborate, this problem is as good as gone."

"I don't want to hear any plan that puts Taylor in the vicinity of that asshole."

"Taylor knows how to take care of herself," Morgan said.

"Yeah, her and her Louisville Slugger." Brody chuckled. He'd stopped her after she'd recounted hitting Gavin in the gut and made her tell it a second time so he could laugh all over again.

"I know Taylor can take care of herself. But I don't want her to be in the position where she has to."

"Lucy and John are coming into town too. We could get their input," Brody said.

Taylor sat there with Demi in her arms, feeling like everything and everyone was moving around them at warp speed. She wasn't sure how to solve the problem with Gavin, or if it was even solvable. Nova's concern that there was no guaranteed way to ensure he had no remaining copies in his possession had given her major doubts.

"I don't want too many people getting involved in this," Nick said. "The whole thing needs to be handled discreetly."

She continued to stare at Demi and run her finger over the top of her little fist. This was the newest baby she'd ever seen or held. Taylor couldn't imagine being responsible for something so precious. Maybe she'd be better off staying a dog mom.

That would break Nick's heart. He wanted kids. No question. Not just since his sister-in-law's pregnancy, but he'd always loved little kids. She could fill her own photo album with the shots she had of Nick with Hope from when she was first born until now.

She didn't want to deprive him of this. Maybe it wouldn't be so scary if he was doing it with her. Aside from the part where it'd be her body going through all those changes, and her being the one to push the baby out of said body.

Yep. She was not there yet. Not even close. How could she be when she and Nick only became a reality four days ago? Parts of their connection weren't four days old, though, they were much older and deeper.

"We don't have to bring in Uncle John and Lucy," Morgan said. "We can if we aren't getting anywhere, or feel like we need backup, but for right now, we'll keep it to those who already know."

Nick ran his hand up her back. "You're quiet."

"We shouldn't be talking about this right now."

"You're one of the first people to see Demi because you're family," Brody said. "If you're in trouble, we want to help. We wouldn't like it if we found out you didn't tell us about this."

Taylor glanced at Nick, got choked up, and looked away. She didn't have the type of family she'd once believed she had. It'd all been fake. Lies. Her father pretending to be a good man and her mother supporting that bullshit lie.

"Let's table discussing it for tonight," Nick said. "Thank you for my beautiful niece. We'll be giving her back now so you can do all the unpleasant stuff."

Taylor gestured for Brody to take the baby from her. Once she'd successfully transferred Demi to his arms, she got up and hugged Morgan. "She's beautiful. Let me know if you need anything, okay?"

37

Flashlight Tag: Adult Edition

Nick

NICK RACKED THE BALLS on the pool table in the inn's billiards room. Neither he, nor Taylor, had time to send a text to the other throughout the day. She'd had a slew of guests to check-in, and he'd had six produce orders to fill, plus all the other regular farm bullshit.

A lot of people probably assumed that Nick didn't like farm work or wasn't interested in carrying on the family legacy like his brother was, but that wasn't true. Playing ball was fun, but he belonged on the farm. Nothing reset his mood like getting up early and seeing the sunrise and the fog lift off the fields.

"What's going on with the Gavin situation?" The more he thought about it, the more pissed off he became. He'd put a lot of thought into how to get Taylor out of this, but so far, he hadn't had any ideas that stood a chance against Gavin's scheme.

"Sabrina answered one of his texts. She said she was really hurt and needed more time to think about their situation." At the pub table in the corner, Taylor took a bite of her brisket nachos, then washed it down with beer.

He'd planned to call for takeout, but then he saw a BBQ food truck. After ordering way too much food because everything sounded good, he grabbed a few six-packs because she liked trying different craft beers. She'd acted like he'd bought her everything off her online shopping wish list when he'd showed up at the inn with dinner.

"Did he believe her?"

"I think so. I haven't seen my photos posted on a billboard in the center of town."

"I'd nail him to a fucking billboard if he did that."

She sighed and wiped her fingers on a napkin. "Logan said that since we'll never be able to know for sure that he's not holding onto those photos, we need something to hold over him."

"Did you ask Sabrina? Does she have any dirt on him?"

"Other than he's a cheating asshole? No."

"Can't she use that, though? He doesn't want anyone to know they're split up, what if she agrees to stay quiet for however long they agree to, but if those photos of you surface, she'll tell everyone he cheated on her."

Taylor slid off the stool and grabbed a pool cue. "I don't want her to have to be quiet about her breakup with him for that long. His book doesn't even come out for another six months. They're not going to announce their divorce during his book tour."

She broke and sank three balls.

"Okay. You're right. I don't want her to do that, either."

She took her next shot, getting the two in the corner pocket. "So, what do we do?"

Nick came up to her and took the pool cue. He rested it against the table next to his cane. "You know there's nothing wrong with those photos, right? It doesn't make you dirty or a freak for having them taken—despite my teasing you."

"Remember when you said I play a part? Little Miss Innkeeper? You're right. I do, and those photos are not part of that. Not to mention, if I can't protect my own privacy, how are guests going to trust me with theirs?"

Thunder boomed outside. The lights flickered. Taylor moved closer to Nick, pressing into him. He used his hand on her lower back to keep her close. The lights flickered again, then went out.

Taylor gasped, then tensed.

"Breathe. It's just a power outage."

"I have guests sitting in the dark."

"They have phones with flashlights. They'll survive."

"Can I just freak out, please?"

He laughed. "No."

"Why not?" she whined.

He lifted her to sit on the edge of the pool table. "Taylor, you prepare for every eventuality so that you don't freak out when something unexpected happens. What's the point if you're going to lose your shit either way?"

"Dramatic effect?"

He groaned. "Where's your candle stash?"

"Why do you assume I have a candle stash?"

"Because you're you. Where are they?"

"In the supply closet," she mumbled.

"Mmhmm." He nuzzled her neck. "Matches?"

"In the box with the candles."

"Flashlights?"

"In a compartment in the same box as the candles. There are more in a bin on the shelf in the storeroom."

"Your organization skills are so hot, Tay."

She smacked his shoulder.

"I mean it." He pulled his phone from his pocket and turned on the flashlight. It was still early, and not completely dark yet, but this room had windows, the hall didn't. He didn't need to bang his knee on anything. He lifted her down from the table, then grabbed his cane. "If there's ever a zombie apocalypse, it's you and me, okay?"

No need to talk about the part where he'd never survive zombies because he couldn't run.

"If there's any kind of apocalypse, it's you and me."

He grinned, then kissed her. "And Cal."

At the mention of his name, the dog crawled out from under the pool table and positioned himself right between Nick and Taylor.

"See?" He laughed. "He's ready to take on the zombies."

He gave her his phone to guide them, then intertwined his fingers with hers as they made their way down the hall and into the kitchen.

She set his phone face up on the counter, the flashlight reflecting off the ceiling.

"I need to find out how long the power is expected to be out, and when this storm is going to be over so I can let the guests know."

"I'll get the candles and flashlights."

While he explored the storeroom, Cal used his psychic abilities to determine where Nick would move next and place himself there a second before. Using his phone flashlight to find the tub that was one thousand percent labeled, knowing Taylor, he came across a small bin filled with glow bracelets and necklaces and pulled it out. He cracked a few sticks and took them out to the kitchen. He came up behind Taylor and slipped a glow necklace over her head as she listened with the phone held to her ear. She fingered the necklace, then glanced at him with her signature "are you ever going to grow up?" look.

He pecked her on the cheek, then went back to the closet. This time he found the candles and flashlights. It was a mix of candles with real wicks and battery-operated ones. He turned on several of the battery-operated ones and whistled for Cal to follow him, but the damn dog parked his ass on the floor next to the stool Taylor sat on.

"The lights are out. It's not an actual zombie apocalypse. She doesn't need you to protect her."

Cal turned his head, ignoring Nick.

He snorted and took an armload of the candles to the foyer, placing them on the table in the entryway around the giant vase Taylor kept filled with sunflowers.

He went back for another load and placed one on every table or stable surface he walked by as he made his way through the inn. He made several trips, placing candles throughout the common rooms while she checked the weather and outage alerts for the area.

When he ran out of candles, he returned to the kitchen.

Taylor was missing.

There was a flashlight on the counter, turned on, resting on its side. Its light cast a glow on an index card propped up against a fruit bowl.

Flashlight Tag: Adult Edition

If you win, I'll show you my lingerie drawer and let you pick what I wear.

But what if she won? Eh, whatever. He'd do anything she wanted whether he won or not.

He grabbed the flashlight and smacked it against his palm. They'd played flashlight tag here as kids on countless occasions. Aunt Penny had let them run all around the house. Of course, she wouldn't have if he'd attempted to play this version of flashlight tag with her favorite niece. At least, not at that age. But Penny had a soft spot for him, and he liked to think that she'd be happy to see him and Taylor together as adults.

He shone the flashlight around the kitchen, even though he didn't think it'd be that easy. "Taylor," he drawled out. "Come out, come out, wherever you are."

Cal was gone too. Probably following her around. Which meant ..

He whistled. "Cal, give up your mom and I'll give you a piece of bacon."

He listened, but the only sounds were the rain pelting the roof and a boom of thunder. A flicker of light in the foyer caught his attention. Shit. He was just standing here with a target on his head, he turned off the flashlight and flattened himself against the wall next to the doorway to the kitchen, glancing around the frame, looking for flashlight beams.

Not seeing any, he crept into the foyer, trying not to let his cane make noise as the end connected with the floor. He kept his trigger finger on the torch's power switch. Down the end of the hall where the billiard's room was located, a beam of light bounced off the walls. He inched toward it. The light bounced into the hallway, down near where she'd turned a room into a small gym. The light disappeared and he made his way toward where it had been, careful not to leave himself exposed.

Once he got to the gym, he pressed himself against the wall next to the doorway and listened. Faint rustling had him confident he'd located her. Now, just to shine her before she shined him.

A sharp beam of light from other hallway off the foyer caught his attention.

In the brief time his head was turned, something breezed by him, out of the gym and across the hall.

Cal's nails clicked against the floor as he walked into the *creepy room*. He groaned. "Really, Taylor?"

"Don't be a pussy, Nick," she taunted back.

He grinned and rolled his eyes. This woman was the only woman for him.

He sucked in a deep breath and snuck across the hallway, trying not to make a sound as he slipped into the room and used his cane to keep his balance as he knelt behind an armchair just inside the door. He leaned around the side of his chair and did a quick sweep around the room with the flashlight but came up empty. He shifted to the other side of the chair.

Thump.

The noise can come from the bed. Nick flicked on his light in time to see Taylor on her hands and knees, crawling out of the room. He lunged toward her and grabbed her ankle, pulling her backward, then flipping her onto her back as he covered her body with his, half-in-half-out of the doorway.

She squealed and tried to squirm out from under him, but he pinned her wrists to the floor. "I win."

"That's not how it works," she said, heaving for air between speech and laughter. "You didn't shine the light on me."

His flashlight was still behind the chair with his cane. But hers was within reach. She'd tucked it inside her shirt, between her tits. He let go of one wrist, pulled the flight light out slowly, making sure his fingers skimmed along as much of her skin as possible.

"Nick," she said on a shaky breath.

"You instigated this. I don't wanna hear your pleas. This was the risk you decided to take, babe." He flicked the light on, directing it at her cleavage.

"Is everything okay?"

Nick glanced up, moving his flashlight beam.

Lucy stood over them with her phone light directed at the ground next to her feet.

"Yes," Taylor squeaked out and tried pushing Nick off her.

"We were playing flashlight tag. Taylor lost." He let go of her other wrist and slowly got to his feet, then reached his hand out to her.

Lucy smiled, but it was restrained, like she wasn't supposed to think the situation was as funny as she did. "I heard the commotion and thought someone fell or ran into a piece of furniture."

"No," Taylor said as she gained her footing. She grabbed Nick s cane and subtly, placed it in his hand. "Just us goofing off. What can I do for you?"

"Do you have liquor?"

Yikes. That type of request never came from a good place.

But the hostess with the mostess knew exactly how to respond.

"Lots of it."

38

Lucy's Liquid Therapy

Taylor

"WHAT'S YOUR PREFERRED POISON?" Taylor asked Lucy as she opened the bar cabinet in the billiards room.

"Whatever has the highest proof."

"Well, alright, then."

"Kidding. Although, twenty-five years ago that would have been my answer."

She'd whispered in Nick's ear which drawer was her lingerie drawer and sent him to her room so she and Lucy could have privacy, because she sensed she needed it.

"How about some really expensive vodka I got as a white elephant gift?"

"That'll work."

While Taylor opened the bottle and pulled out glasses, Lucy asked, "Did you overcome your hang-ups about Nick?"

She smiled and nodded. "It's different than I'd thought it would be."

"How so?"

"We fit. I don't know. I guess it's always been there, but now, it's super hard to ignore. I know that Nick is the one, but the idea of that.. I can't even conceive of what it means."

"Sounds like your head needs a little time to catch up to your heart."

They both shot back the vodka and Taylor poured two more. "Are we celebrating Demi or numbing the pain?"

"Why not both?"

"That's fair." She walked to the pool table and started gathering the balls from the game she and Nick had started before the power went out. She couldn't believe it hadn't come back on yet, but it was kind of neat hanging out in the candlelight. "What pain are you numbing?"

"John and I...we *don't* fit. We're like people who keep trying to put pieces of two different puzzles together, turning them around all which ways trying to get them to snap in place, but they're never going to, and I've finally accepted that, but he won't let go."

"Oh, man. That's heavy. I'm sorry."

"We share Logan and Morgan, and now Demi, and a ton of friends. He's impossible to avoid for very long. So, I heal a little, until the next time we're thrust together again, and I get swallowed whole by this pull we have to each other, but I know it'll lead nowhere good. I've seen it play out over and over. The ending is never the one we're hoping for."

"That sounds devastating."

Lucy nodded. "It is. And now that we're here and everything is all emotional because of the baby, he wants...us. And I get it. I just can't do it. I'm not signing up for guaranteed heartbreak."

Taylor bit her tongue to resist encouraging Lucy to give John a chance. She liked them both, but it was mostly the oxytocin coursing through her, making her all fuzzy inside and wanting everyone else to be just as happy.

Her phone buzzed with a message from Jaci.

What are you doing to that man?

She texted back. *What are you talking about?*

Look what he just posted.

The message was followed by a link to a video. She tapped it and watched, then handed her phone to Lucy. The video was a short clip of one of the tractors at the farm, the tires on one side stuck in a ditch, with the caption "when you end up here," followed by another clip of her bed, with all the hanging plants around it and the boho quilt on it that did not take a genius to figure out it was a woman's bedroom, and the caption, "because you can't stop thinking about being here."

Lucy grinned and handed her the phone back. "He's smitten with you, and utterly unashamed of it."

"I doubt this is the content his followers are interested in."

"Sweetie, why are you worried about what his followers want?" Lucy poured more vodka into their glasses. "That's your man, not theirs."

"It doesn't feel like that to me. It feels like this part of Nick belongs to them and that I'm an interloper." She threw back her shot.

"Watch that video again." She nudged the phone across the table. "That's not a video he posted to appease his followers—just like you said, they're not there for that type of video. That's a love letter. To you."

She wrinkled her forehead. "If that were true, he could have sent me a text instead."

"You're right. He could have. And he didn't. He told you he loved you loud enough for the entire world to hear because he doesn't see any reason to hide it. I don't know Nick like I know his brother, but I don't think anyone in that family is shy about their feelings."

True. Theo and Gia Lewis were the most direct people she'd ever met. No passive aggressive behavior in that household. Hope had zilch as far as a filter.

"That's part of how I knew Brody would be good for Morgan. She needed someone who didn't leave any guessing about how he felt."

Taylor was fifty-percent appreciative that Nick shared that trait with his brother, but the other fifty percent of her was all twisted up inside over the intensity and pace at which he'd made his feelings known.

39
Her Harlot
Nick

FROM THE SEVERITY OF the storm, Nick knew before he ever stepped outside cleaning up fallen limbs and debris would dominate his workday. Untangling himself from Taylor's warm body—she was such a snuggler that if he moved an inch away, she swallowed up that inch and tried to fossilize herself onto his body—he'd snuck out of bed and gone to the farm.

After a few hours, everything had been cleaned up, but it was too wet to do much else, so he gave Josh the rest of the day off and returned to the inn to help Taylor. He could tell from a hundred yards off that she was in a mood as she straightened up chairs around the pool deck. He approached slowly, with a smile, so he wouldn't get bitten.

She stopped shoving around the chairs like they'd done something to personally offend her and turned in his direction. Momentarily, she froze. Then, she was moving, her face lit up as she made her way to him as he entered the gate.

She wound her arms around his neck. "Are you here to rescue me while woodland creatures do my chores?"

"Sorry. I haven't mastered the spell for getting woodland creatures to follow directions."

Her lips formed a pout.

"I'll keep practicing, but for now, I'll help you myself."

"What time did you leave this morning?"

Guilt crashed into him. Which didn't make a lick of sense because as much as he hated doing it, leaving her bed was not a crime. It was, unfortunately, going to be a routine occurrence.

He shrugged.

She glared. "Don't even try that, mister. You know what time it was."

"Five."

"You've already worked how many hours, and now, you're going to help me do my work?"

"Are you questioning my stamina?"

She snorted. "No."

"Alright, put me to work, then." He pecked her on the lips.

She pointed at the net for skimming leaves out of the pool that was in a holder along the fence.

It was like every damn leaf from every tree on the property had ended up in the pool. As long as he didn't try to move to fast, or take too many steps in a row, he managed to use the net without having to use his cane for support. He was about two-thirds of the way finished when Sabina came through the gate.

"Hey, Sabrina," he said.

"Hi." She waved at him and walked over to Taylor, who stopped spraying the debris off the deck. "Gavin won't leave me alone. He said people are going to get suspicious if I'm not in any of his videos."

"He gives relationship advice, right? So, he should just tell everyone you're having a fight. That's relatable."

"No." Nick set down the net and took a seat on the side of a lounge chair near Taylor to stretch out his leg. "We have to stay in control of the narrative. If his followers think they're having a fight, some are going to assume it's Sabrina's fault, and be sympathetic toward Gavin. Him not wanting his reputation as a model husband ruined is our only leverage. We need Sabrina to remain innocent in the eyes of his followers so that he doesn't have the chance to play the victim."

"But how do we use that?" Taylor asked.

"I don't know yet."

She huffed.

"I checked out his content. It's pretty…"

"Square?" Sabrina supplied.

He laughed. "PG. And there's nothing wrong with that."

"Yeah, I mean, imagine if we were all harlots like Nick."

In a flash, he reached out and pushed Taylor, not even looking her way as she fell into the pool.

Sabrina gasped and covered her mouth.

Taylor came up and screamed his name as she climbed out the pool. She toed off her wet canvas sneakers, grabbed a bucket, dipped it into the pool, then tossed water at him.

Nick stood, removed his hat, stripped out of his wet shirt, set his phone on the chair, kicked out of his flipflops, then stalked toward her, leaving his cane behind.

She stepped back, eyes wide, a smile tugging at her lips.

"Bold move, Taylor."

Her eyes got even wider. She turned, but he lunged for her, scooped her up, then jumped into the pool, turning mid-air so his body would break the water's surface.

She pushed away from him under the water and when they came out, she splashed him in the face.

He put his palm on top of her head and gently pushed her under, letting go as soon as she was submerged. It was unclear what her plan was when she came up and came at him, but it didn't matter. Nick backstroked until he could stand waist-deep in the shallow end, Taylor following. He grabbed her, lifted her high, then tossed her into the deeper water.

Every time she emerged, she looked more determined to destroy him. Feisty, just how he liked her.

This time, when she was within reach, she locked her legs around his waist. Honestly, he could have gotten out of her hold *if he'd wanted to*. But god, why would he ever not want to be between her thighs? He cupped her ass and squeezed.

Her nostrils flared.

He snickered and used his hand on the back of her neck to bring her in for a kiss before falling backward, taking her underwater with him.

She pushed at his chest as they went under, escaping his hold.

This time when he came up, she was scrambling to get out of the pool by the way of the steps in the shallow end. He grabbed her and flipped her so that her ass landed on the second step from the top.

He hovered over her, caging her in. "Where do you think you're going?"

"Let me go." She wriggled under him, laughing.

"Nope." He dipped his head and kissed her neck.

She gasped between laughing, trying to close the gap between her ear and shoulder so he couldn't access her neck.

He let her and redirected his efforts at the other side of her neck, perfectly exposed.

"Nick!" She pushed and bucked against him.

He snickered. "What do you expect from a harlot like me?"

Her laughter peeled. "Hey," she said breathlessly. "There's nothing wrong with being a harlot. It hasn't scared me off yet."

"Glad to know you're not turned off by my sluttiness."

"You're not slutty. You're just…using what your mama gave ya."

He laughed and kissed her.

Cal's bark reached them about two seconds before he jumped off the golf cart Hope drove. He barreled through the open gate and jumped into the pool, splashing them.

Hope walked through the gate. "Ew. What are you doing?"

Nick rolled his eyes and moved to sit next to Taylor on the step.

"Sorry, Sabrina," Hope said. "It's like they forget everyone else exists when they're together."

"Maybe we like having an audience."

Taylor splashed him and muttered, "That's your little sister."

"It slipped out."

"I prefer when it slips *in*," she whispered.

He glanced at Taylor and raised an eyebrow. "Your mind is so much dirtier than mine."

40

Lights, Camera, Action

Taylor

TAYLOR PLACED AN ICE pack on Nick's knee and handed him the remote. It kind of broke her heart that Nick—who had double the energy of the average person—had new limits that he couldn't seem to get onboard with.

"You need to stop overdoing it." She lifted his leg and stuck a throw pillow under his knee and readjusted the ice pack.

"New ice pack?" He raised an eyebrow.

She held her hands up. "Putting ice cubes in a plastic baggy is messy. It melts and gets things wet."

"Right. Not because you want to take care of me or anything."

Little did he know she'd had a bit of trouble choosing between types of ice packs. She now had a selection in her freezer that could rival the hall closet. This one was flexible, made of gel, and the size of a tea towel. A top choice among athletes according to the reviews.

"I'm taking care of you right now, asshole."

He laughed.

All jokes aside, she really was worried he was going to drag out his recovery by trying to do too much. But she couldn't stop him. The only thing she could do was prepare for when he needed to recuperate. Which is why she'd come up with a secret little project. What she planned to do might be a little extra, but she didn't care.

The project was going to require her to enlist help. Pace was her go-to handy man. She wasn't sure how Nick would react to her asking him for a favor. Whenever Pace replaced a fuse or replaced a splintering board on the dock, he never let her pay him. Her dad was also out. She'd stopped asking him for anything a long time ago.

She didn't mind hiring someone, but it was an odd job. Perfect for a teenager who wasn't afraid to get his hands dirty. Maybe she could ask that kid who worked on the farm. He could do it in the evenings so it wouldn't interfere with his farm work.

Although, it'd be hard to keep it a surprise form Nick if he saw him at the inn. He'd want to know what he was doing there. She'd work out all those details, but she had to make sure he didn't worsen his injury in the meantime.

"Seriously, Nick, you're still recovering. You need to take it easy."

"Yes, ma'am."

She huffed. "Stop."

"What?" His voice came out uneven and his shoulders raised in a pathetic attempt at acting innocent.

"You're being all flirty and cute while I'm trying to lecture you and it's…confusing me."

He wet his lips. "Come here."

"No." She backed away. "You've had your fun. Now, rest."

He whined and pouted.

"I have a lot to do, and no, you're not helping. Can't you do stuff on your phone? Edit your videos or something? But no more videos about me, okay? Go back to posting thirst traps like your fans want."

"Actually, I've been getting significantly more views since I started posting this new type of content, and I've been gaining hundreds of new followers each day."

She groaned.

"I said I'd shut it down. And I'm going to. But I don't think I should just yet because I have an idea."

"What?"

"Everyone on the internet is wondering who my posts are about—what if the big reveal is that it's Sabrina?"

"I'm sorry?" Taylor squeaked out.

"Not for real. We make a draft video of me revealing who the woman I've been doing all of this for is, and we show it to Gavin. It would obliterate his standing on social media if I posted it. Especially, if I post a few more things that make it seem like I'm the one helping her heal from a bad relationship. If Gavin gives us all the traces of the photos, and swears he'll never try to use them against you, I won't post the video. He can write his own narrative for how he and Sabrina split up, as long as he doesn't place the blame on her and paint himself to be the victim."

"What kind of a video?"

"The kind of video I wanted to make with you. It'd be sexy. If there's no shock factor, it's not going to go viral. This needs to be the type of video that not only would ruin Gavin in the eyes of his followers but would bring even more attention from people who've never heard of him." People who would instantly hate him. Especially, if they dove a little into Sabrina's story, and then, found out Gavin cheated on her."

"I don't know."

"If you don't want me to touch Sabrina—"

"I trust you. But the idea of her touching you the way I touch you—it pisses me off."

He grinned. "I like you territorial."

Taylor rolled her eyes and sat on the end of the couch. "We should talk to Sabrina. See if she's even comfortable with it."

"You tell her. See what she says. Discuss it and find out if you're both comfortable with it. If not, we'll figure something else out."

"You're comfortable with it?"

"Not really, no. It's going to be weird, but I think it's what we have to do to get Gavin off your back."

Sabrina was willing to do whatever Taylor wanted her to do. She wanted the ordeal to be over so she could concentrate on her next steps.

"Nick is okay with it?"

"It was his idea."

She nodded. "He'd do anything for you."

"He's getting his abs stroked by a beautiful woman. Don't make it sound like he's going to war." Taylor squeezed her shoulder. "Do you think it'll work?"

"Are you kidding? Gavin would die if a video like that got leaked. Nick was right about his content being PG. But it's not just his content. It's *him*. When you and Nick were playing in the pool earlier, it dawned on me that Gavin would have never done anything like that."

Getting pushed in the pool wasn't most women's idea of romance. It wasn't Taylor's, either. But it did do something for her. Laughing until she couldn't breathe on a regular basis with Nick was the best therapy.

"I keep asking myself what I saw in him. Why did I marry him? Why did I choose a life of dullness? Why did I sacrifice my privacy? I hated how we couldn't go anywhere without being recognized. And at first, if he were recognized, he'd explain that he was out with his wife, and ask for privacy, but then after a while that stopped. He was more than happy to pose for photos and there were so many times I felt invisible. Now, I can see how much he liked the attention he got from women."

"I'm sorry, Sabrina. You didn't deserve that."

"Nick has twice as many followers as Gavin, plus he's a professional athlete. He must get recognized everywhere when you go out."

She and Nick had yet to go on a true date. His plan to take her out after the press conference would have to be on raincheck. If Nick got recognized, she couldn't be recognized with him if they were going to be able to use the angle that he was seeing Sabrina. No reason to make it more of a soap opera than it already was.

"I've only been out with him around here and he grew up here, so people recognize him because they know him."

"It wouldn't matter. I've seen how he looks at you. No one else exists when you're near him."

41

Let's Make a Sex Tape

Taylor

"You want me to help you make a sex tape?"

"No," Nick and Sabrina shouted at Jaci simultaneously.

"Who is making a sex tape?" Drew swung into the billiards room and plopped down on the leather tufted sofa. She crossed her legs and tucked her fist under her chin.

Logan followed her into the room and surveyed it, hands in his pockets.

"No one," Taylor said, and swallowed. "Nick and Sabrina are going to make a short, suggestive video. Nick will post it, *unless* Gavin gives up the photos and lets Nova check his computer and devices for copies."

"That's brilliant," Drew said.

"A video of his wife with Nick that makes it look like he rescued her from an emotionally abusive relationship and now, they're blissfully happy?" Logan leaned against the pool table and whistled. "Brilliant might not be a strong enough word."

Taylor's shoulders slumped. Part of her was holding out hope that someone would point out a major flaw in Nick's plan and they wouldn't be able to go through with it.

"Will you be okay with the video going live if Gavin doesn't uphold his end of the deal?" Nova asked. "All of you?"

Nick looked at Taylor for a few beats. "Our lives probably won't be quiet for a while if that happens, but I don't think it's going to. I think we've got Gavin right where we want him, but I'm not doing anything you're not comfortable with."

"It's not that big of a deal," Taylor said and shrugged. "It's a thirty-second video."

"If they post it, they'll have to keep up the charade, at least for a while, or there's no point. Will it bother you for everyone to think Nick is with Sabrina?" Logan asked.

Yes. That would bother her. But she was a big girl. She'd get over it. "I don't care what a bunch of strangers believe. I'll know it's pretend."

"Do you think they should consult John and Lucy?" Drew asked Logan. "Maybe they'll think of something we haven't."

Logan rubbed his thumb across his bottom lip and shook his head. "Nah. They've got enough of their own problems."

"They're fighting again?" Drew asked. "I thought the baby would help bring them back together."

"Yeah, I think that's what Uncle John thought too, and that's what Lucy is pissed about."

Taylor was not typically a jealous person. Seeing Morgan's entire family show up to meet Demi and how close they all were, even when things weren't perfect, hurt her heart. Because she didn't have that. Not anymore.

42

Stress Making Out

Nick

CANISTERS OF FLOUR AND sugar on the kitchen counter and the silky scarf tied in a knot on top of Taylor's head waved at Nick like ten-foot red flags flapping in the breeze. Well, that and it was two a.m., and she had an apron tied over her nightgown.

A nightgown he'd never seen because he'd taken off the jeans and T-shirt she'd been wearing hours ago before they'd fallen asleep naked.

"Taylor," Nick blocked her by the dishwasher and wiped the flour from her cheek, "Stop stress baking."

"No." She tried to duck under his arm, but he pressed his pelvis to hers, keeping her trapped. "It helps me."

He believed that, but he wasn't interested in encouraging her coping mechanisms right now. He was interested in Taylor getting a full night of sleep. He was interested in her not having to worry at all. He was interested in her believing him when he said everything was going to be alright.

"We could stress make out instead." He grinned, amused at how fast that had become his go-to way to distract her. It sure was more fun than what he'd had to resort to before kissing and touching were options.

Taylor's lips twitched and she wouldn't meet his gaze. "That's not a thing."

"It is a thing. Let me show you." He squeezed her waist.

She laughed and pushed at his bare chest. "My cookies will burn."

He picked up a jar of thick, dark syrup from the counter. "What kind of cookies?"

"Molasses."

Really? "You made my favorite cookies? Is that a bribe?"

"It's a reminder that you'll never taste them again if you get turned on when you're touching Sabrina."

Nick cupped the back of her neck and pulled her forehead to his. "I'm yours, Taylor. I'm only doing this to get Gavin to leave you alone."

"I know, but how would you feel if it was the other way around? What if I was going to be sitting in some half-naked man's lap for a video?"

"Honestly, I'd fucking hate it and I'd probably hurt the guy, if I even let it get that far."

"See?"

"I won't do it if it's going to hurt you, but I don't know how else to fix this."

"I trust you, Nick. I know this is our best shot."

"What if I'm fully clothed?"

She huffed and pushed away from him. "That's not going to be as effective on Gavin. You said it yourself."

She slipped oven mitts on, pulled out a sheet of cookies from the wall oven, set them on a cooling rack she'd set up on the counter, then turned off the oven.

"Hey." He came up behind her, wrapped his arms around her, and kissed her temple. "Everything is crazy right now, but we're going to get through it."

She set down the mitts and turned to face him.

He untied the knot she'd tied over her stomach, then slipped the apron over her head and tossed it on the counter. The silky nightgown she wore stirred something in him. Something that made him want to scoop her up and carry her to bed and worship her for hours. It pissed him off that he couldn't do the scooping or carrying parts. "I didn't see that one in your lingerie drawer.”

“It’s new.”

“For me?”

She gave him a long stare. “Well, I didn’t buy it to wear it to the next meeting with the Historical Society.”

He rubbed his jaw. This woman baked cookies while wearing lingerie, and she was worried about his gaze wandering. Insane. “I’m afraid if I touch you, I’ll be too rough and rip it.”

“I’m willing to take the risk.”

He pulled her close and ran his hand from her waist to her neck. “What if I’m too rough with you?”

Her throat bobbed against his palm. She wet her lips. “Also, worth the risk.”

He slid the hand on her waist down her thigh and lifted the hem of her nightgown. The silk loosely covering her pussy was damp and as he stroked her through the thin fabric, he got harder at how quickly it became soaked.

Taylor squirmed.

“Grab some cookies,” he said, removing his hand.

Her eyebrows pinched together, but she grabbed a plate and put four cookies on it and followed him to the bedroom.

Nick took off his pants and sat naked in the armchair in the corner. He stretched his legs out across the ottoman and crooked his finger at her.

The second she set the plate of cookies on the side table, he grabbed her hips and pulled her to straddle him on the chair.

He sucked on her breasts through her nightgown until the silk was sticking to her skin and she was grinding against him, the fabric of her panties equally wet.

Something about feeling her pussy through her panties but not being able to sink inside her got him so turned on, he could have gotten off just from her rubbing against his dick.

"Nick, please."

"Please, what?"

"Let me take off these panties. Fuck me."

He groaned and shoved her nightgown up and over her head. "Not yet."

"Please." She arched her back, her hands behind her on the ottoman, bringing her tits right to his face.

He grabbed her hips and grinded against her, rubbing the head of his cock up and down her soaked panties, over her swollen pussy. "I like it when you beg."

She tossed her head back and rolled her hips.

Nick flicked his tongue across her nipple, then closed his mouth around it, sucking and licking.

He reached for her panties and pushed them aside. Nick hissed and gripped himself at the base, angling his hips to press his cock against her opening, but keeping control so that he barely entered her.

Taylor leaned her upper body away from his begging for more.

He pressed the head in and out, biting his lip against his frustration over how much he wanted to turn her over the chair and slam into her until she begged him to stop.

"No more panties," she said, voice shaky as she rose to her knees and pushed them down.

Nick waited until she'd gotten them off, then flipped her over.

She went to push up onto her hands and knees, but he used his hips to press her forward, forcing her to either grab the back of the chair or faceplant into the cushion. He rubbed his cock against her ass cheek as he rummaged for the item he'd hidden in the drawer of the side table, then slipped it beneath her body, running the vibrating toy down her belly, dipping it between her legs.

She bucked against him.

He leaned close to whisper, "Keep this here until I tell you."

He waited until she'd gotten hold of the vibrator, then trailed his hand up her stomach and chest, squeezing her breast while rubbing his cock between her thighs.

"Fuck, baby," he muttered, his cock nearly sliding inside her, but she was so damn wet he slipped past instead. He squeezed her thigh and rubbed his thumb over the opening of her pussy.

He pushed his thumb inside her. In and out. The view incited a craving to taste her. He shifted back, brought his face closer to her pussy, and rubbed her clit with the pad of his index finger. Then, he gave into his craving and swiped his tongue over her. Her taste depleted any stores of patience he may have had.

"Nick, I need you so bad. Please," she said, nearly sobbing.

At least he wasn't the only one who lacked patience. He gripped himself and eased inside her, gritting his teeth against how damn good it felt as he went deeper.

She gasped, moving restlessly beneath him, barely able to lift her hips off the chair.

Nick shifted his hips, sliding in and out of her slippery heat. "Is this what you wanted?"

She moaned. "Yes."

"Does that toy feel good?"

"Yes," she panted.

He squeezed her ass. "Turn it up."

She whimpered.

Stilling his movements nearly pushed him toward the brink of his sanity. "Do it."

The toy got louder.

He continued rocking his hips into her. Pleasure rippled through him. "So wet."

Taylor moaned and pulsed around him.

Nick groaned and thrust harder, digging his fingers into her hip.

Coming inside her was a high he'd never top. The shaking of his legs from the intensity of his orgasm was the only reason he didn't stay inside her longer, savoring the feel of her. He rolled to the side, so he didn't collapse and crush her.

Hopefully, that'd keep her mind off her worries for a bit.

43
Taking One for the Team

Taylor

THE COTTAGE LOOKED LIKE they were about to shoot an interview with a celebrity, not film a video that would be less than a minute long.

Jaci shifted her gaze to Taylor and flashed a little smile.

Petulance had such a grip on her, she couldn't even return a fake smile. Jaci would have known it was fake anyway, so making the effort seemed a waste. Taylor leaned against the windowsill and crossed her arms.

Jaci was there to help Sabrina pose and to find the perfect angle.

Taylor didn't know why she was there. Torture, maybe.

Nick whistled to get her attention, then tossed her a baseball.

Out of reflex, she caught it, but she was in no mood to have a damn catch. Squeezing the ball until her knuckles ached didn't alleviate any stress. Pitching it at seventy miles per hour right at Gavin's face might, though.

Nick walked over to her and tapped her arm. "Let's go outside for a minute."

Jaci was moving around the room, adjusting lighting and whatever else.

Sabrina was in a robe, sitting on a chair in the corner, biting her nails. "I'm fine, Nick."

"I didn't say you weren't. Can you just come outside?"

She stood and walked out of the cottage. On the small wooden deck, she leaned against the railing and tossed the ball to him.

He caught it, then rolled it around in his palm, studying it. "You know that photo my mom has of us where it was our first tee ball game, and we were sitting on the bench, but our feet couldn't even touch the ground?"

"The one where I'm teaching you to spit out sunflower seed shells?"

"Yeah, that one. I can vividly remember sitting there next to you and you saying, 'Don't you know how to do anything?'"

She tried to stifle her laughter, but it seeped out. "I don't remember that. How do I know you're not making this up?"

"You said, 'We're a team now. That means when you don't know how to do something, I'll show you. And you can show me when I don't know. But that probably won't happen.'"

"You're making this up!"

He laughed. "It's all true except for the 'probably won't happen' part. You weren't as snarky back then."

Her mouth pulled up at the corner. "Why haven't you ever told me about this memory if it's so vivid?"

"You'll know why when I finish the story."

Her chest tightened. She didn't even have a guess as to what he was about to reveal, but she couldn't handle having her life shaken up more than it already had been lately.

Nick wouldn't do that to her, though. He'd brought her out here to make her feel better, and she trusted that he would succeed.

"I pretended that I didn't know how to do things so I could have more of your attention."

She scrunched her eyebrows together. That was some damn fine self-awareness for someone who hadn't even started kindergarten. "When we were four."

He slowly shook his head. "The entire time we've been friends. I mean, in high school it was just saying I wanted to get more practice, so you'd train with me. In middle school, it was dumb stuff like pretending to be frustrated in art class, so you'd help me, and telling you I needed to study during lunch, so you'd eat with me in the hallway while I studied for a test I'd already studied for.

"Trust me when I say I learned plenty of stuff from you, but I just wanted to be near you and have you to myself. And I know that sounds like I've been hiding deeper feelings, but it wasn't like that. It wasn't the same kind of feelings I have for you now."

"I get it." She really did. Whenever it was only the two of them, she savored it. Like eating her favorite dessert slowly, or lying in bed for five extra minutes, indulging in the warmth and quiet before a busy day. "You could have just asked me to spend time with you, dumbass."

He tilted his head and wrinkled his nose. "Listen, you don't start a habit that young and then kick it when you realize it's an unhealthy behavior."

"It's not unhealthy. It's silly, but it's not toxic. Why tell me now?"

"Because you've always been my team. That's how I see us. That's how I've seen us since we were on that bench. And this is just me taking one for the team so that we can win."

"Nick." Her shoulders fell. "I said I'm okay with it. You don't have to pacify me. Just go get it over with."

He walked closer and pressed his forehead to hers. "You're not okay with it. I don't know why you think I can't read your mood with one look at you."

"You're right. I'm not okay, but I'm going to work through it. I guess we're both taking one for the team."

44
Taylor was a Good Girl
Nick

"ALRIGHT, CAL." STANDING ON the back steps, Nick swept his gaze over the backyard. "Where's Taylor?"

Cal trotted to the edge of the lavender field and sat next to a beaten path that disappeared into the lavender in the direction of the creek.

The path led to the water's edge where a tree grew out across the water a bit, creating a perfect little bench where Taylor had perched. The sun had just started to near the horizon, but the clouds rolling over the creek warned of another summer storm.

"Don't push me in," she said without turning around, her words slurred.

He snorted and leaned against the tree, angling his head to stare at her. "Drunk?"

She held up an excessively large, insulated cup with a straw. "I will be when I'm finished with this." Her voice didn't sound right. It was both sassy and sad.

"It's over. I'm going to edit the footage and we can show it to Gavin and be done with him."

Her head bobbed up and down.

"I did this because I didn't see another option. I didn't enjoy it." He grabbed her chin and turned her face until he could see into her eyes. Her tear-filled eyes.

She yanked her chin from his grasp, turning back to stare out at the water.

"Don't hide from me," he said, his voice low, his mouth next to her ear. "You don't get to go through shit alone anymore."

She sniffled. "It's not just the video. I miss my family."

Nick froze, his chest locking up. "Taylor..."

"And don't tell me that your family is my family. It's nice that they feel that way about me and I love them too, but I was close with my parents, and losing that still sucks. I'm not okay." She covered her eyes and sobbed.

"Get off the fucking branch, Taylor."

She glanced over her shoulder at him, tears streaking her face, looking him over like his mind had fallen out of his head and stuck to his shirt.

"I can't stand here and talk to your back. I need you in my arms."

A beat passed before she set down her cup, swung her leg over the branch, and stood.

Once she was clear of tripping, he pulled her close and kissed the top of her head. "I know everything sucks right now. We're going to get through it, though, and then we're going to make up for how sucky everything has been."

She wrapped her arms around him. "How?"

"I'm going to take you to that drive-in movie place you want to go to. And we're gonna go to all the mini golf courses in the state and I'm going to annihilate you at every one of them." Probably make his knee swell but fuck it. "We're gonna go to a resort that has a lazy river that passes by a swim up bar and float all day until they kick us out. Hang out with Colby and Bree. Babysit Demi so Morgan and Brody can have a date night."

"And play cards with your dad." She kept her cheek pressed to his chest.

He grinned and rubbed her back. "At least once a week. Monthly LEGO parties sound good too. You think your calendar is full now? Ha."

"You're not going to beat me at mini golf."

"I want a life with you, Taylor." He only felt safe verbalizing that because she'd been drinking. Hopefully, she'd be a little less skittish about the depth of his feelings for her and him being seventy-one steps ahead of her. But before things got too serious... "I'll let you win at mini golf if you change the diapers when we babysit."

She took a step back and wiped at her eyes. "Maybe he's not wrong."

"Who?"

"My dad."

Nothing that man had said had been worth a damn. But how'd they go from mini golf and diapers to Coach? "What the hell are you talking about?"

She took a deep breath. "I do hold you back."

"There's nothing to hold me back *from*."

"Now, but what if you'd taken that athletic scholarship instead? That college was an MLB pipeline. And if you'd gone there," her lip trembled and she hiccupped, "then everything would have worked out differently. You wouldn't have hurt your knee."

"Maybe not, but I could have gotten injured another way, on or off the field, and it could have been worse. But it doesn't matter. We can't change the past, and even if we could, I have no regrets."

"What if choosing a life with me is the same thing?"

She was drunk, so he shouldn't be surprised she wasn't making much sense, but she was making just enough to get him all worked up.

"I don't know what you mean."

"You're choosing this when there's a better opportunity waiting for you."

"Even knowing what I know, I wouldn't go back and do it differently. I don't care if your dad doesn't think my life is good enough. It's *mine*." He jabbed his chest. "You're stupid if you think a career in baseball, whether it be on the field or off, is the better deal. I envy your life, Taylor. I want to join the cornhole league—quite honestly, I think you should ditch Jaci and partner with me—and I want to sit around eating cookies and building LEGOs with my family. I want to watch the sunset every night, right here." He waved his arm around. "I don't want to eat dinner alone or have to drive two hours just to have coffee with my mom."

"Oh," she drawled out. "It's because you don't want to be away from your mommy."

He squeezed her. "I'd have my second cup of coffee with her every day if I could." Since he'd been home, some days, it just didn't work out, but he looked forward to getting to see his mom in the morning. Taylor could make fun of him all she wanted for that.

"Why your second?"

"Because I like having my first cup with you."

"Who is going to walk me down the aisle?"

Nick flinched. Where the hell had that come from? It was like alcohol turned her into a squirrel. "Let's start walking back to the house. I'm not gonna be able to carry you if you start stumbling, Drunky Pants."

He'd carried her a lot over the years when she'd had too many. Kinda sucked that he'd probably never get to do that again.

"It can't be him, Nick."

He thought about grabbing her drink, but he didn't think she needed whatever was left in it. He put his hand on her lower back. "Come on." Once they'd started in the right direction, he whistled for Cal, who quit nosing around in the weeds and rushed to Taylor's side, tail wagging. "If anyone has the right to give you away, it'd be me, but I'm not a fool. I'm keeping you."

"Someone has to walk me down the aisle."

He could not believe they were talking about getting married. Were they, though? She hadn't mentioned him as the groom.

"Says who? Let's be honest, *giving* a bride away is treating women like property and shouldn't even be a thing. Walk down the aisle on your own like the bad ass you are."

"This is why, Nick. This is why I can't see my future. This is why, subconsciously, I haven't *wanted* to see my future. There's always going to be those holes where my dad should have been."

He tucked her hair behind her ear. "Your family probably won't ever be what it was, but right now, it's still broken with crime scene tape around it. You're dealing with a lot, and I don't know, but maybe you'll find a way to make peace with what your dad did. Not because he deserves it. Because you do."

45
Nick the Innkeeper
Nick

When you force yourself to stop watching her sleep because it's been an hour and you're starting to feel creepy.

NICK FINISHED PUTTING THE caption on a video of him making coffee with the phone against the backsplash so all that was visible were his abs and his hands making coffee. He hit post as Sabrina came into the kitchen.

She swiftly turned around. "I'm sorry."

Nick chuckled and grabbed his shirt out of the laundry basket on the counter and slipped into it. "I'm decent now, you can turn around."

She did so, her face red.

"Not as good as what Taylor makes, but there's fresh coffee.'

"Where is Taylor?" she asked.

"In bed, dead to the world. I turned off her alarm." He'd woken up to another rainy day and a text from Brody to him and Josh telling them to take the day off. The freedom to do whatever would have been nice if Taylor had that same freedom. Since she didn't, and he was wide awake, he'd chosen to beat her to her chores.

"And you're doing her laundry and made coffee. Are you real?"

"I'm going to make breakfast for the guests too as long as she doesn't wake up first."

"I can help."

"Thanks. My sister will be here soon too. Between the three of us we can probably almost handle what Taylor does."

"She's an impressive woman. But I'm sure she appreciates having someone to shoulder the load without having to ask," Sabrina said.

"Are you kidding? She's going to be so pissed." Nick opened the fridge and started pulling out ingredients. Not that he had an idea of what to make, but hopefully, taking inventory would strike inspiration.

"But you're doing it anyway?"

"I care more about her wellbeing than whether she's mad at me or not."

She'd kick and scream when she found out he'd let her sleep in, but oh well. Taylor tended to go off the deep end before realizing whatever he'd done was his way of taking care of her. That was fine. He liked her fiery. It was fun playing with the flames.

Thinking he'd be able to figure breakfast out, he asked Sabrina to set the table, giving her very explicit instructions on exactly how Taylor did it. He'd pulled out a few cookbooks, got overwhelmed by all the choices, and called his mom.

She'd talked him through putting together two egg casseroles—one with meat and one without. He had no intentions of telling Taylor he'd asked her for help, though. He got enough flak from her for being a mama's boy.

It took barely any time for Nick, Sabrina, and Hope to clean up after breakfast. The guests scattered, going into town to browse the shops and small museums since the rain hit the kill switch on outdoor activities. Sabrina went to make calls to family and friends, trying to figure out where she'd go next, while he and Hope checked to see which rooms requested service.

"Do you really think Taylor is going to be mad that you let her sleep in?" Hope asked from the other side of one of the upstairs beds.

Nick tucked the sheet under the bottom corner. "Yep. I took her control away and she's going to freak out about it until I get her to see nothing bad happened."

"Why'd you do it then? Don't you want her to like you?"

He almost laughed, but he didn't want Hope to think they couldn't have these conversations. It was important that she feel comfortable coming to him with whatever questions she had. "My first priority is to take care of her. To make life easier."

"Even if she yells at you for it?"

He nodded. "Even if she yells at me *or tries to get me fired.*"

Hope gasped and tossed the pillow she'd been putting a pillowcase on at him. "This isn't the same."

"It kind of is. I mean, Taylor and I generally do enjoy each other's company, unlike you and Josh, but he does look out for you for some reason."

"Oh, so, you talked to him, and he said he was looking out for me?"

Nick rolled his eyes. "He was trying to help. He promised he'll stay out of your way from now on, though. Are you going to stay out of his?"

She stared at him, blinking a few times.

He grinned because Christ on a bike she was going to drive some man crazy one day. Maybe Josh. Who the hell knew? "No?"

Hope shrugged. "Do I have to?"

He shook his head. "No. But if you're going to keep torturing the boy, you're going to have to suck it up when he tortures you back. No more running to your big brothers because you swatted the bee and got stung."

46
Passing Up the Day
Taylor

TAYLOR ROLLED OVER AND grabbed her phone off the nightstand, knowing she'd overslept. It was ten-thirty and she had twenty-six notifications. Fifteen of them were from Jaci.

CHECK HIS LAST POST. PLS MARRY HIM.

Even Drew texted to squeal over what he'd posted.

Her heart flew out of her chest. She rushed to open the app to see Nick's most recent post. She put her hair into a ponytail and brushed her teeth while she watched on repeat. Because she never commented on any of his videos and didn't want to leave any clues about her identity for his thirsty followers to uncover, she typed, "You're dead" into a message and sent it.

Once she had herself together enough to be seen by guests, she marched into the living room.

Nick sat on the sofa with his leg propped up on the coffee table. He looked up from his phone, then tossed it onto the couch next to him. "How're you gonna do it?"

She crossed her arms. "Strangulation."

"Sounds fun."

"It's not funny, Nick!"

He shrugged. "I'm not apologizing for taking care of you."

"I don't need you to take care of me."

"The fuck you don't," he said in a booming voice. "Taylor, I was just going to get coffee started. I figured you'd wake up on your own. You didn't, so I prepped breakfast. I checked on you after that and you were sound asleep, so I cooked breakfast, and served it. Hope, Sabrina, and I cleaned the kitchen, cleaned up after the guests finished eating, and you were still dead to the world. You needed sleep and I'm glad you got it. You're fucking welcome."

"You turned my alarm off. That's not fair."

"I'd do it again. I probably will, in fact."

She stomped into the kitchen. The spotless kitchen. "You can't interfere like that. This is my business. My livelihood."

He joined her in the kitchen and leaned his elbow on the counter. "Would I have done it if I didn't know I could pull it off to your standards?"

"It's more than just making a meal and serving it." She yanked a coffee mug from the cupboard and slammed the door shut.

He straightened up and took a step toward her. "I know! I cut flowers and put them on the tables. I put tiny sprigs of lavender in the napkin rings. There's cinnamon in the coffee, and I made sure the windows were cracked so the guests could hear the rain hitting all those tin music makers you have outside. I put those papers you printed out last night with the local calendar of events on each table."

She froze with the coffee pot in her hand. "How did you know to do all of that?"

"I love watching you do your thing and seeing how much thought you put into every little detail. Seeing how happy it makes you is what makes me happy."

Her mad started to slip. Damn him. She poured herself coffee and replaced the pot. "So, why didn't you let me do it, then?"

"One time, Taylor! But if you don't start taking care of yourself, I'll fucking do it again."

Never mind. She was still plenty pissed. "You're out of line."

"When did you get to be so uptight that you get mad when I help you?"

She narrowed her eyes. "I'm not uptight. You overstepped."

"You're so fucking uptight."

"Shut up."

Nick grinned and moved until his toes touched hers. "Make me."

She put her hands on his chest to hold him back, but he kept pressing closer. "If you take it upon yourself to do something that involves the inn again—"

"How about *you* shut up?" Nick smashed his mouth to hers. There was nothing gentle or sweet about the kiss. It was unapologetic and possessive.

She shouldn't have liked it.

She shouldn't have gripped his shirt and pulled him even closer.

She shouldn't have let him back her into the pantry and close the door or pull off her underwear.

Nick removed his shirt, then lifted her, pressing her into the wall. "You're mine, now, Taylor. If you wanna be mad, be mad, but I'm still going to fuck you."

Her nipples tightened. Her clit throbbed. And her resolve was toast.

She reached for his belt buckle and worked to undo it while he kissed her neck. Her body flashed hot and achy. "Nick," she breathed.

He held her up with one arm and shoved his pants and boxer briefs down, exposing his cock. Once he'd adjusted his hold, he eased inside her.

They both made their own noises of gratification, although his was louder, and turned her on even more.

He took a staggering breath, then sealed his mouth to hers as he withdrew and thrust back in.

Pinned against the wall as he had her, she was at his mercy.

But it didn't matter. Everything he did to her felt incredible. She clung onto his biceps, letting him use his mouth and his cock to push her to the brink.

His movements became intense, driven. All she could do was hold onto him as she came so hard, she bowed away from the wall.

He continued to thrust into her in a frenzied rhythm.

When she almost couldn't take anymore and was about to tell him so, he stiffened and shouted her name. He hid his face against her neck and sagged against her.

Taylor ran her fingers through his hair while she waited for him to collect himself.

After a bit, he pulled out of her and eased her to the floor.

She stared up at him, amazed that he could be so unbelievably sweet and gentle, while also being capable of fucking her that hard and fast.

"It's my fault you haven't been getting enough sleep," he said softly. "Let me take care of you."

"I don't know if I can."

He kissed her temple. "We'll keep practicing."

"Do you need to get off your knee?"

He nodded.

She trailed her fingers along his collar bone. "I have a surprise for you."

"Does it involve *you* getting on *your knees*?"

"No, but it does involve me wanting to make you feel good."

He squeezed her waist. "See, this is where I'm smarter than you because I'm not gonna argue with you about taking care of me."

47

Surviving a Semester

Taylor

"Where did this come from?"

Taylor shrugged and smiled. Her private patio had been transformed with string lights, a sun sail, wind chimes, a hammock swing, an outdoor sofa with throw pillows galore, a gas fire pit, and in the very center of the patio, an inflatable hot tub. It'd been a group project that she'd included both Josh and Hope on—separately because after she'd contacted Josh about helping with the heavy lifting, Hope had coincidentally mentioned Josh was her nemesis.

"No, but for real. This wasn't here a couple of days ago."

"I've been wanting to do something with this area and the other day when I came out here, I could see it perfectly in my head. And I figured, soaking in hot water with massage jets would be therapeutic for you, so it was a no brainer. I had Josh hang the lights and stuff and set up the hot tub. Hope helped me make it all look pretty."

"You're pretty." He grabbed her neck and kissed her hard. He kept kissing her while he unbuttoned her blouse, slipped it off her shoulders, then started on her skirt.

Taylor tore her mouth from his. "What are you doing?"

"Getting you naked. You think I'm getting in this hot tub without you?"

"No, but I'm putting on a bathing suit."

"Why? No one is gonna see you but me, and I've seen you naked."

Hard to argue with that, but she had no intentions of having sex in the hot tub. The whole point was to make his knee feel better because he'd strained it having sex. "You need to relax and rest. Are you going to be able to do that if we're naked?"

He scoffed. "I do have *some* self-control."

She narrowed her eyes. "Then how come you never use it?"

"I will throw your smart ass in that hot tub."

She laughed and pushed her skirt to the ground, taking her panties with it, then unhooked her bra. While he stripped, she got in and got comfortable.

He winced as he swung his legs over the side, then settled into the corner and stretched his bad leg across the bench seat. The tension in his face disappeared. He closed his eyes and tipped his head back.

She couldn't *not* stare. Goosebumps spread over her arms and chest, despite the warm water. This man had been inside her only minutes ago, yet the flutters in her stomach and throbbing between her legs was as intense as if she'd never seen him up close before now. Or naked. Very, very naked. Damn it. He was too hot. Too far out of her league.

Nick peeked one eye open and crooked his finger.

Taylor moved close and he tucked her under his arm, her back to his side.

She stretched her legs out across the adjacent bench.

"Done being mad at me?" he asked.

"For now."

He ran his fingers up and down her arm. "Tay, we need to talk about some stuff."

She tensed. "Like?"

"To start, one of the coaches has decided to throw me a farewell party at his house the day after the press conference."

"Oh."

"I know that sounds like your idea of hell, but I'm obligated to go.

Will you go with me?"

She scooched back until she was on his lap and put her arms around his neck. "Do you really think I'd say no?"

He shrugged. "You already said yes to the press conference, and now, I'm asking for more."

"Asking your girlfriend to be your date to a party thrown in your honor is not asking too much." She placed a soft kiss on his lips. "It's my fault you feel this way. I should have never let my issues with my dad keep me from coming to see you play college ball."

"Speaking of college…"

"Yes?"

"I got a letter from mine," he said. "Some of my credits will expire within the next year and I would have to take those classes over to get my degree."

"How long would it take you to finish?"

"One semester."

"Oh." It could have been more, and that would be worse, but imagining him being gone for months hurt. "Okay, so you're going to go back to college? That's what you're telling me?"

"I'm telling you it's something we need to talk about. If I go back and finish, I'd rather do it immediately. I don't want to move home and get comfortable and then leave again. Because I probably won't."

She turned slightly away from him, her eyes stinging. "It sounds like you already know what you want to do."

"I don't want to be away from you."

"When does the semester start?" she asked.

"In two weeks."

That was soon. Too soon. She'd only just accepted that he was home to stay. This shift in their relationship was so new. One semester was the best-case scenario as far as him getting his degree and them being together again. It would be okay. She could survive a few months. "You'd be home by Christmas?"

"Yeah, but I'd come home on the weekends."

"That's a lot of driving back and forth."

He put his finger on her chin and guided her to look at him. "I don't have to do this. I'm not actually going to use my degree, so it doesn't matter."

"It matters to you."

"You matter more."

A tear rolled down her cheek. Did she want to be without him for months? No. But what was important to him was important to her. "We've survived on texts and video calls this far. We can do it again."

"That was before I found out how much I like kissing you."

"It won't be that different."

"Because instead of regular texts and video calls, you'll send me dirty texts and take your clothes off when we video chat?"

"Nick, stop being a clown."

"I'm not joking. I want to see your tits at least once a day or I'm not going."

48

Gavin Gets Owned

Taylor

TAYLOR DIDN'T LIKE THE idea of Gavin coming to the inn, but Nick and Nova convinced her that this needed to happen on her turf.

She'd told him that Sabrina was ready to speak to him and wanted to do it face-to-face. All that was a bold-faced lie. He wouldn't be getting anywhere near Sabrina. She'd gone to stay at Jaci's house until he left.

Taylor hadn't even wanted to watch the video of Nick and Sabrina, but she didn't want the first time she saw it to be in front of Gavin. If she appeared upset, she worried he'd find a way to use that against her.

The video was short. She'd insisted on watching it alone, even though Nick had begged her to let him be there. Locked away in her bedroom, she'd watched—only once. One time was more than enough.

Nick had to be careful with what he posted on the platform he was on. Showing his bare chest was acceptable, but anything more than that would get his account flagged and potentially shut down. He did occasionally post videos of him in nothing but his underwear, but he'd been strategic about it, knowing just how much he could get away with. A baseball mitt or some type of gear or other object always hid his crotch.

The video wasn't the sensual, hands-stroking-each-other's-bodies type that he'd wanted to make with Taylor. Nick stood in front of the camera wearing his uniform and holding a baseball in one hand. He looked down at his jersey, pulled a face, and the caption "What're you gonna do now?" appeared overlaid. He shrugged, then bent over, filling the frame with the top of his hat. When he straightened back up, he had on a dirty, beat-up John Deere ball cap, and his uniform was gone, replaced by a pair of jeans. He was shirtless and grinning like the devil. He held up the baseball and glanced at it, then tossed the ball up in the air, out of the frame. What came back down wasn't a baseball. It was a tomato. He shrugged, then snapped the fingers of his other hand. A garden hoe appeared in his grip. He looked at both objects, then shook his head and tossed the tomato over his shoulder and dropped the hoe. He held up a finger in a "wait a minute" gesture, then covered the lens with his hand. When he removed his hand, Sabrina was tucked under his arm, staring up at him like she was the luckiest girl on earth, her fingers trailing over his abs. She was dressed like a sexy farm girl with a plaid shirt tied above her navel and a pair of cut off jean shorts.

He nodded like, "Oh yeah." Then, he leaned down to kiss her, but before his lips touched hers, the video went black.

She'd put the phone face down on her bed and sat there for a long time, trying to dissect her feelings. It wasn't real. Just an act. A performance. She knew that. And no one except for Gavin would probably ever see it. But damn. Nick was hers. Even Sabrina's clothes were on loan from Taylor. She'd gotten to press up against him and touch his bare abs. Taylor really liked Sabrina and had come to think of her as a friend. She'd even suggested that Sabrina stay at the inn indefinitely and work for her. But none of that logical stuff would get through the block in her brain that kept rational thought away from the irrational thought of bitch slapping her.

It took a long time for her to cool off, but once she did, Nick had been waiting for her. Coaxing her out of her bad mood had been a task. He'd done it, though. His goofy, sexy ass had made her laugh and come in a matter of minutes.

Now, it was time to use the video that made her so jealous she couldn't see straight to bring Gavin to his knees.

While Nick messed with getting the video to cast from his phone to her television, she chopped vegetables for a salad to go with dinner. She didn't care if it was only eleven o'clock, she needed to work out her aggression on something besides a person, so cucumbers and carrots it was.

He came up behind her and kissed her shoulder. "It's going to work out."

"Stop saying that. You don't know."

"If the video doesn't work, I'm going to beat his ass, so yeah, I do know that one way or another this asshole is not going to release your photos."

She set down her knife and turned, holding onto the edges of the counter. "Promise me you're not going to lose your temper."

He made a face that expressed it was a silly request. "Tay, that shit has been lost since I saw those photos and that letter. Besides, you got to take a bat to him. It's only fair I get to beat his face in."

She huffed.

He grinned, put his hands next to hers on the counter's edge, and leaned in until they were face to face. "You want me to turn that frown upside down?"

She rolled her eyes. "Go away. I'm not in the mood for your jokes."

"Who's joking?" He lowered himself until his shoulder was level with her stomach, then grabbed the back of her thighs and tossed her over his shoulder.

"Nick!"

"It's upside down. How's my ass look from back there?"

She smacked it. "You stupid clown, you're going to fuck up your knee."

He eased her down until her feet touched the floor, then cupped her face and kissed her forehead. "That's my plan, so that you'll have to give me some hot tub therapy." He winked.

She fought her smile. "I don't have time for that. I have to pack."

He made another face. "It can't take that long. You're gonna spend most of the trip naked. Just pack something for the press conference and something for the party. And I guess if you want to bring some lingerie, I can live with that."

"Oh? You can live with that, huh?"

"Just goin' with the flow, baby."

"Mmhmm." She wrapped her arms around his neck, but as she pressed up on her toes to kiss him, the doorbell chimed. "That's probably him."

"Ready to wreck his day?"

She nodded. "Looking forward to it."

Nick squeezed her hand and didn't let go as they walked to the foyer. He'd left his cane behind, and even though he hadn't mentioned it, she knew he didn't want Gavin to see it as a weakness.

She opened the door, Nick standing beside her.

Gavin looked at her, then his gaze shifted to Nick.

"Who is—Aren't you that baseball player who takes his shirt off for views?"

"Yeah," he said, taking a step closer. "Aren't you the piece of shit blackmailing my girlfriend because you couldn't keep it in your pants?"

Gavin's face turned to stone. "Where's Sabrina?"

"She's not here." Taylor gestured in the direction of her living quarters. "You decided to bring me into this, so we're going to come to an understanding before you get anywhere near Sabrina."

"What's there to understand? I came here to talk to my wife, not you."

"Listen, motherfucker, I am barely keeping a lid on the urge to put my fist through your face. You're going to go into that room and sit down and hear her out."

Gavin looked between them, rolled his eyes, then held his hand out in the direction of the archway to the kitchen. "After you, Taylor."

She turned on her heel and walked back into her living room.

Gavin came in and crossed his arms.

"Have a seat." She gestured at the couch.

He huffed and sat on the end.

"You obviously know who I am." Nick made his way around the couch and grabbed the remote off the coffee table. "So, you must also know I have about five million followers."

"We all know sex sells. There's no substance to your content."

"What about yours?" Taylor asked. "It's all lies. You're a trash husband."

Nick turned on the TV, then pulled his phone from his pocket and cast the video he'd recorded with Sabrina on the screen. He hit play.

Gavin looked bored as he watched…until Sabrina appeared. His expression went from blasé to livid.

"This video is going to get posted unless you sign a gag order that you'll never say a word about my business, and you hand over all your devices so that my cyber expert can wipe my photos off them."

"I don't understand your ultimatum. You're going to convince the internet that my wife is cheating on me?"

"Glad you asked that question," Nick said in a voice that made him seem like a sexy professor. He used his phone to show the videos he'd been posting—the ones he'd made about her. "People are very interested in who I'm seeing. And it is not going to be hard to spin this into a story where I picked Sabrina up after you knocked her down. I'll be the knight in shining armor, and you'll be the villain. Your followers are going to drop you so fast, and my followers are going to learn who you are, and I won't be surprised if they drag your ass."

"Don't forget, we have timestamped screenshots of your convos with your mistress," Taylor added.

"I need time to think this over."

"The hell you do. It doesn't work like that. We're not here to negotiate," Nick said. "Either you agree, or I'll post this video right now."

"How do I know you're not going to post it after you get your way?"

"Gavin, you started this. Maybe you shoulda done some more research on who you were messing with." Taylor gave him a fake smile.

"I came here to talk to my wife and I'm not leaving until I see her."

"She doesn't want to see you. What are you going to do? Hold her hostage because you don't want to lose your platform?"

"No. I deserve a second chance."

Nick snorted. "Cheating bastards don't deserve second chances. Not only that, but this isn't about you wanting her back because you love her. You want to use her to protect your reputation and that's not cool."

"I broke it off with Danya. I want to save my marriage because I love Sabrina."

Nick groaned. "No one fucking cares, asshole. Your marriage is over. Your wife is divorcing you and *that's* what you deserve. Sabrina made that decision on her own, so leave Taylor the fuck out of it."

"If she's going to divorce me no matter what, then why should I care about that video?"

"Because she's willing to let everyone think it was amicable and sign a gag order that says she won't ever mention your infidelity. No matter what, you're going to lose followers, but at least you won't be labeled a cheater."

"I want to hear her say that."

"You're not getting near her," Taylor shouted. "This is called suffering the consequences of your actions. Your only option is to minimize the damage."

"So, Gavin," Nick said, "shall I post this video?"

"No," he muttered and pushed himself to standing.

"Alright, then, my cyber person will be coming to see you very soon. And if you think you can save my photos on an external hard drive— she'll able to find out how many times you downloaded or moved those files to other devices."

"Whatever." He stormed off toward the foyer.

Nick moved closer to her and pulled her tight against his chest.

The door slammed.

"It worked," she whispered.

He kissed the top of her head and rubbed her back. "Grab a bottle of bubbly and let's take Cal to the farm to run around while we drink it."

She liked that idea so much she teared up.

49

Daddy Saves the Day

Taylor

THE LIST OF THINGS Taylor had to get done before she and Nick could go away was daunting. One of the big-ticket items: mow the lawn. The property was twenty-two acres, and more than half was woods or fields, but there was still plenty of grass to maintain.

The hum of the lawn mower made her freeze with her hands on a bottle of wine she'd pulled from a box the local liquor store had delivered. No doubt Nick had noticed the grass was getting high and busted ass to finish his own chores so he could help with hers.

She walked out the back door and waited for the mower to come around the house.

It wasn't Nick driving the mower.

It was her dad.

Her stomach twisted and her throat got tight. She didn't need this right now. She didn't want his help, nor did she want an argument about it. At the edge of the patio, she waited with her arms crossed for him to glance her way.

When he did, he maneuvered the zero-turn in her direction, then cut the engine.

"I can cut my own grass."

"I know that. I taught you how."

"Right. So, I don't need you."

"Taylor, I know you don't need me. But you're my daughter and I love you, and I'm never going to give up trying to fix things so that I can be a part of your life."

"You can't fix it."

"I'm sorry for how I reacted to finding out about you and Nick. I thought maybe y'all would end up together, and I wanted to do everything I could to keep that from happening until *after* you pursued your careers. That's why I discouraged you from going to college together."

"I don't need you to cut my grass." It hurt her heart that he thought she and Nick would end up together but wanted to delay it. Who does that?

"I'm sure you have plenty of other things to do before you can leave. I want to help you." He took off his baseball hat and wiped his forehead, then put it back on. "Nick said you're happy and that's all that should matter to me. He was right. I'm sorry. My disappointment got in the way of what really matters—your happiness."

"Even if I could forgive you for that, I'm never going to forgive you for cheating on Mom."

"I wish you had talked to me about it when you found out. Why didn't you ever say anything?"

"She didn't want me to."

He flinched. "Vi?"

"Is that what you came here for? To find out if I'd told Mom, or if I hadn't told her, to try to convince me to keep your sick little secret?"

"No. She's been acting normal. I assumed she didn't know, but I wasn't going to ask you to keep it from her." He shook his head. "She's known this whole time?"

"I don't know what the hell is wrong with her that she lets you get away with it."

"Love can be complicated."

"Yeah, if you cheat on your partner."

"I'm sorry you had to learn what a fuck-up I am. Aunt Penny knew it. That's why she left her house to you instead of me."

"I'll cut my own grass." She wasn't going to play into his *pity me* act. Aunt Penny was very specific about why she'd chosen to leave her mansion to Taylor.

Aunt Penny said it was because Taylor loved the house, and the house loved her back. She said her voice echoed in the halls when she wasn't there. She'd left her the house because Taylor brought in wild lavender she'd found growing in the field and asked her what it was, and they'd spent every rainy day that summer in the library looking at books about plants with healing properties and because after that, the house always, always smelled like lavender. She had left Taylor her house because she'd made snow angels on the front lawn and hit Nick so hard with a snowball that he'd stomped inside the house and pouted while Aunt Penny made him hot cocoa, one of her favorite memories of all time.

It was because she'd been the little girl Penny wanted but never had.

"God, you're hardheaded." her dad muttered. "Let me cut your damn grass so you can go have a nice time with Nick."

"He's retiring. He's not taking another position with the team."

"I'm sure that's going to be a hard announcement for him to make. I'm glad you'll be there with him. He's going to need you."

"I didn't ask for your approval."

"Is the attitude necessary?"

She wet her lips. "It is if you're going to sit here and lie to my face."

"What lie?"

"You don't approve. You think he's making a mistake. And you think it's my fault."

"No, I don't. It's hard seeing his career end before he even played out a single season. I was his coach since he was this high." He held his hand out to the side of the mower about three feet off the ground. "Just like it was hard for me to accept that you weren't going to go to college. We spent your whole life working toward that. I didn't have parents that did that for me. But I thought you wanted it. I thought you loved playing as much as I did."

"I do."

"But you love this more." He gestured toward the house with a flick of his chin.

"Not more. Just differently. Softball would have been a few years of my life. This place had the potential to be a part of the rest of my life."

"You've done a great job. I'm proud of you."

She didn't want to feel any kind of way about his praise. Why should she care if a man as low as a snake was proud of her? She shouldn't. Even though they'd had countless arguments about her not taking that athletic scholarship, he'd helped her with all the renovations she'd needed to do before opening the inn. Those had been good times. Memories that still made her heart lift, even if she tried to forget them.

Hope burst out the back door. "Taylor! Come quick."

She turned and rushed toward the house. "What's wrong?"

"I don't know. There's water everywhere."

Her heart raced. Not good. Hopefully, it was something like the washing machine leaking.

She went in through the back door and followed Hope through her living quarters to the foyer.

Water sprayed from the wall that separated the kitchen and the staircase. It was flowing down the steps.

Cal barked at the water gushing out, like it was an intruder. It was definitely uninvited.

"Damn it!" She shoved her fingers into her hair. "Stupid old fucking pipes."

"I'll shut off the water," her dad said as he entered the foyer. He rushed out, heading toward the laundry room.

"Get all the towels you can find," Taylor said to Hope.

While she tried not to have a panic attack so she could think clearly about what she needed to do, the water slowed to a trickle and then stopped.

She went to her bedroom and to her bathroom. She grabbed every last towel from the storeroom and carried them back to the foyer where she tossed them down and got on her hands and knees to sop up the water.

Her dad came back into the foyer. "I'll call Terrance and get him over here."

Terrance was a friend of her dad's and a plumber. He'd done all the work on the inn over the years.

She didn't say anything. As angry as she was, she needed help. She needed to get this cleaned up before the floors got ruined. And she needed to know how bad the damage was. The pipes and drywall would need to be replaced, but this house was full of old metal pipes. This could happen again at any time.

Hope came back and dried off each step as she went up.

Sabrina appeared from the hall of the east wing and gasped. "What happened?"

"A pipe burst." She kept her head down, working to soak up the water with towels as fast as she could.

"What can I do?"

"Find more towels."

"Terrance is on the way," her dad said, wheeling in a mop bucket and mop. "Taylor, I've got this."

She wanted to tell him she didn't need his help, and maybe she didn't, but before she'd found out he was a cheater, this is exactly the kind of problem she'd have called him to help her with.

Without a word, she moved out of his way.

Her long skirt was soaked and clung to her legs as she stood. She gathered up the saturated towels. Once they were in a pile, she went to grab a laundry basket to haul them outside. She wouldn't be able to put them in the washer with the water off. They'd have to be wrung out and hung to dry until they could be washed properly.

It took over an hour with everyone pitching in to get the water cleaned

up and for Terrance and her dad to knock down the dry wall to see how
bad of shape the rest of the pipes were in. As it turned out, it all needed to
be gutted and replaced.

Taylor sat on the floor and hid her face with her hands and sobbed.

Sabrina sat next to her and patted her back.

"How am I going to tell Nick that I can't go with him?"

"He'll understand," she said.

"Yeah, he'll understand." She wiped at her face. "He'll be devastated,
but he'll understand, and he'll suck it up because that's what Nick does.
Like he hasn't had enough disappointment these past few months."

"You're going with him," her dad said. "There's no reason for you to
stay here. You're not a plumber or a carpenter. You can't hang drywall,
either. I'll oversee it and by the time you get back, all that's left to do will
be choose a paint color."

She glared up at him. "I'm not going away and leaving you here. I
learned that lesson the hard way."

"You think that lowly of me? You don't think you can trust me to fix
things when you're in crisis?"

She sniffled and was about to open her mouth to say something rather
mean when the front door opened.

Nick took a step inside and froze. "What the hell happened?"

"Pipe burst," her dad said.

He glanced her way.

She pushed up from the floor. "I can't leave." She had more to say, like
sorry, but she couldn't get it out and started blubbering.

He pulled her against his chest, his hand on the back of her head as she
laid it against his shoulder. "It's okay."

She cried harder.

"I've got this under control," her dad said to Nick. "She's going with
you. Get her into some dry clothes and head out."

"No," she said, clinging to Nick. "I need to be here and make sure

everything is fixed before guests arrive on Friday."

"Come on," Nick said, turning her around and ushering her toward her bedroom. Once they were alone, he pushed her wet skirt down to the floor and took her hand while she stepped out of it. "The press conference can be rescheduled, Taylor. It's not the end of the world."

"What about your going away party?"

"That can be postponed."

She got track shorts and a T-shirt and changed into them, then sat on the edge of the bed. "Why'd this have to happen today?"

"Shit happens, Taylor. There's no reason for it. Do you want me to tell your dad to leave?"

She shrugged. "He's not going to and you two getting into an argument is only going to make a bad situation worse."

"Fine, then I'm going to go make a call so they can reschedule the press conference. Just stay here and get yourself together."

50
Benched
Nick

Fuck.

Lewis Luck, his ass. The only luck he had—besides getting to be with Taylor—was the bad variety.

"Is she getting packed?" Ollie asked when Nick entered the kitchen.

"No. I told her I'd have the press conference rescheduled."

"That's not necessary. There's nothing she can do. I'll send her photos as the work is done so she can see the progress."

"Do you know your daughter at all? She's not going to leave."

"Convince her. If anyone can, it's you."

Nick squeezed his forehead. "There's no use in trying."

"The water is going to be shut off until the pipes are replaced, so she can't stay here, anyway."

"She can stay at my parents' or in one of the cottages."

"Why? Get her out of town. Take her mind off it. I'll take care of everything and when she gets home, it'll be done."

He glanced toward the bedroom, imagining her sitting on her bed with tears streaming down her face. He wasn't sure that would work. "She's gonna worry the whole time."

"Keep her busy. Distracted."

Nick rubbed the back of his neck. Maybe if she wasn't here, she'd be better off. Whatever work had to be done, it was out of her scope of abilities. Ollie would do whatever had to be done and bust his ass to make sure it all was fixed before she got back. The man had lost his trust in so many ways, but he didn't doubt that.

"What are you doing here, anyways?"

"Her mother told me you two were going away. I came by to mow the grass so it was one less thing she had to do before she left."

That was such an Ollie thing to do. Always showing up and lending a hand without being asked. The shitty thing was, for the most part, it was hard not to like Ollie. Yeah, as a coach, he'd been hard on him at times. But he'd also been there when he'd needed him.

Taylor came out of the bedroom. She had a garment bag draped over her arm and wheeled a carry-on suitcase along with her. "I'm ready."

Her face was red and splotchy, and she had on the equivalent of workout clothes, but he wasn't going to comment. "You sure?"

She nodded. "I promised you, I'd go. I'm not going to let you down."

He walked over and kissed her. He didn't give a shit if Ollie was watching. He did keep it short, though. "You're not letting me down. You can't help it that this happened."

"I can't do anything to fix it, either. I'm going to ask if Sabrina can stay with Jaci. I just have to figure out what to do about Cal, because Sabrina was going to take care of him here, and he'll eat Jaci's cats."

"Your mother and I can take care of Cal," her dad said.

Taylor kept her gaze on Nick. The pain in her eyes made his chest tight. She was probably conflicted between hating her dad and wanting to lean on him.

"I think that would be a good idea." Nick wished his building didn't have such a strict policy against pets. "Your mom will spoil him like she always does and that way he won't miss you so bad."

She nodded. "Cal."

The dog trotted over. She knelt and pressed her head to his. "You're a good boy. I'll see you in a few days."

Nick smiled, then scratched behind Cal's ears. "We'll be back soon."

They took Hope home and Nick grabbed his things, but he didn't really need to pack as they'd be staying at his place in the city, where most of his clothes were.

Taylor spent the first forty minutes of their trip on the phone with her insurance agency.

Once she'd hung up, he reached over and squeezed her leg. "I know it sucks, but it'll all get fixed, and you know your dad will make sure it's done right."

"I don't want to talk about it anymore or for the rest of this trip. These next few days are all about you."

"Nah, babe. It's gonna be all about us. Just like everything from here on out. We're a team, remember?"

She glanced at his hand on her leg. "I should have changed before we left."

He kept his eyes on the road, but moved his hand to her inner thigh and slowly slid it up. "No one is going to see you but me."

She spread her legs the tiniest bit.

Nick trailed his hand up and she spread them more. "You're gonna make me crash."

"You're the one who put your hands on me."

He groaned and kept running his hand back and forth across the inside of her thigh, teasing her by getting just close enough to drive her crazy. "Pull your shorts down. Panties too."

"Nick."

He worked his fingers inside the leg of her shorts and rubbed her pussy, pushing her panties out of his way. She was already wet. This was going to be the longest twenty minutes of his life.

She took a deep breath. "How long until we get there?"

He grinned. At least their minds were on the same track. "Twenty minutes. And I'm going to make you come at least twice before then. Take them off."

She did as told.

"Have I mentioned how much I like fingering you?" He dipped his finger into her wetness and trailed it up to her clit.

She angled her head back. "Whatever makes you happy."

He chuckled and glanced over at her.

Her eyes were closed and her jaw slack. She rolled her hips, lifting them off the seat.

"It's so hot when you move your body like that. It feels so fucking good when you do it when I'm inside you."

She moaned. "I want to make you feel good. Pull over somewhere."

"We're too close to my place to stop. Don't worry. I'll be fucking you soon."

The angle of her hips gave him prime access to dip his finger inside her. He pumped it in and out a few times, then focused back on her clit, rubbing and swirling until she was squirming.

It was hard as hell to keep his eyes on the road. Her lifting her hips, moving that incredible body of hers tempted him to pull over so he could watch her as she came.

"Oh, fuck." Her voice came out hoarse.

The tightening and pulsing of her pussy around his fingers had him so hard he lifted his own hips, wishing he could thrust into her. He was so overcome with lust, he could barely get out, "One more, Taylor."

Her ragged breathing and whimpers robbed him of his good sense. He wanted more. More of those noises. More of her wetness coating his fingers and palm. More of everything that made Taylor the enchanting goddess he wanted to pleasure until she was spent.

He lightened the pressure as he rubbed her swollen flesh. "I wish I could bury my face between your thighs and suck on your clit."

"*Nick.*"

Her saying his name like that was the hottest thing ever. If he'd been able to take his hand off the wheel, he'd have stroked himself, and probably come on the spot.

As he took the exit toward his townhouse, she cried out, then squeezed her thighs shut and pushed his hand away. She sagged against the seat, heaving for breath.

Nick took his fingers to his mouth and sucked them.

She reached across to his side and covered the very obvious bulge in his pants.

It took everything he had to focus on driving, especially in the city where there was so much more to pay attention to.

She went to work on his belt, but he stopped her.

"We're almost there."

She whined.

He grinned and kissed the back of her hand. "This is my street."

A minute later, he turned into his driveway and hit the button to open the garage. Once he'd parked inside, he took his time getting out, being mindful of how stiff his knee got after sitting for extended periods.

Taylor reached for her panties and shorts off the floor of the passenger side.

"Do not put those back on."

"But—"

"I'll just take them right back off."

"Aren't we going to go inside first?"

"Nope." He straightened to standing and closed his door, then walked to the weight bench that occupied the second car spot. He unfastened his belt and stripped, then straddled the bench and stroked himself. "Get over here."

As if she had reason to be shy, she shuffled over and stood next to the bench, tugging at the bottom of her shirt.

Nick put his hands on her ass and lifted her, settling her over his lap.

She gasped and held onto his shoulders. She sure as hell wasn't thinking about those burst pipes anymore. The only pipe she worried about this weekend was going to be his.

He grabbed the bottom of her shirt and tugged it over her head. The privilege of undressing her was like hearing the National Anthem prior to a game. It filled him with anticipation and reverence. He dragged her bra straps down her arms and pulled her tits out of the cups. "You have the best tits in the whole fucking world."

She snorted. "How do you know? Have you seen them all?"

He rolled his eyes as he rubbed his thumb over her nipple. "Nah, but I don't need to see any more after seeing yours. They're incredible."

Her cheeks turned pink. Taylor's bashfulness added to her appeal. There was no way she believed she was ugly, but it thrilled him that she was genuinely free from vanity. The job of proving to her she was the most beautiful woman he'd ever seen was like getting paid to do something he'd have done for free.

He grabbed her hips and raised her above his cock. Sliding inside her always felt like the first time. Memories couldn't quite capture the intensity of the pleasure. Holy fuck, being inside her was heaven.

She rolled her hips, just like she'd done in the car.

Needing to see his cock sliding in and out of her, he leaned back. Watching a few strokes nearly pushed him over the edge. He moved his gaze upward, taking in her amazing body as her tits bounced. Nick leaned in and took her nipple into his mouth and sucked.

"Oh, my god. It's too much. I can't." She pushed his head away and put her hands behind her on the bench, reclining, like she'd be able to escape him while his dick was still inside her. Maybe he really had fucked her brains out.

Nick gripped her hip as he thrust up. "You can. Let it happen, Taylor."

She tipped her head back and gasped. Despite her denial, she continued to roll her hips. "You first."

He put his palm on her lower abdomen and slid it up, squeezing her tit before traveling higher. Her pulse raced under his hand as he ran it up her throat, his thumb pressed under her jaw. "Not yet. This feels too good for it to be over so fast."

Her whimper pushed him so close to the edge, he gritted his teeth trying to make it through another minute or two. He couldn't take his eyes off her naked body, entranced by how incredible she looked arching backward while taking his dick.

She stared at him from under her lashes, her head still thrown back as her hips rose and fell.

He kept his grip on her throat light but used the tips of his fingers to apply pressure. "Come for me. *Now*."

Her mouth opened but no sound came out. A tear slipped from her eye, rolling over her temple as her pussy tightened and convulsed.

Every inch of his body tightened, threatening to erupt in his release. He removed his hand and leaned over her, sucking her neck, supporting her back with his palm splayed across it.

Taylor grinded against him and that was it.

He came hard, a deep growl escaping his throat.

She pushed herself up straighter. Her breath was hot and rapid as she dropped her cheek to his shoulder, clinging to him. "I've never come so hard that it made me cry."

He stroked her back, their pulses racing in tandem. "I hope that's the only way I ever make you cry."

51

Orgasms are okay and all...
Nick

NICK'S TOWNHOUSE WAS A two-bedroom with a small kitchen, a breakfast bar, and a cozy living room. It was furnished and somewhat decorated.

Taylor wandered around in a white T-shirt she'd borrowed from him, stopping to pick up a framed photo of the two of them sitting on the porch swing at his parents' house. They weren't paying attention to the camera. They'd been too busy laughing their asses off. "I don't remember this being taken. We look so young."

"We were." He flipped through a stack of mail with a towel tied around his waist. As soon as they'd come into the house, he'd dragged her to the shower and stood with her under the hot water, kissing her and soaping her up. Neither of them had recovered enough to go at it again, but damn, he couldn't keep his hands or mouth off her. "That's the summer before eighth grade."

She set down the frame. "Where did you get this?"

He glanced up.

She'd picked up a little teddy bear wearing a baseball jersey and hat. The fabric was faded, and the fur was matted, like it'd been washed and dried with too much heat. The black eyes had lost their glossy shine.

He walked over and picked up a tiny, old photo that had been tucked into the outside of another photo's frame. He handed it to her. The photo was professionally taken, of a very small baby with the bear propped up next to him. He handed it to her. "That's me when I was a baby before my biological parents died. Brody got more curious about them while Morgan was pregnant, and they tracked down my dad's best friend. After they died, he and his wife tried to get custody of us, but my parents had specific instructions in their will about our guardianship. Anyway, he played baseball in high school with my dad, and he gave me that bear when I was born. It was left behind when we were put into foster care, so he took it."

"And he saved it all these years?"

Nick nodded.

"That's pretty cool that your birth dad was a ball player."

"I guess." He didn't get into all this biological family crap. He could understand Brody wanting to know things. His brother had been old enough that he had a few memories of their birth parents, but Theo and Gia were the only parents Nick remembered.

"If this bear doesn't mean anything to you, you don't have to keep it." She put the bear and photo where she'd gotten them from. "If you aren't interested in learning about your biological family, you don't need to feel guilty. Just like Brody doesn't need to feel guilty for being curious."

She had a point. He'd kept it because the man had given it to him, and he'd felt guilty for not being excited about it after he had hung onto it for twenty-some years.

"Wanna see my bedroom?" Her bare thighs and the outline of her tits through the shirt she'd borrowed enticed him. He pulled her close, grabbing her ass and grinning.

"Will you break out in hives if you're serious for more than five minutes?"

"Probably not, but why risk it?"

She rolled her eyes. "Maybe you should show me to the guest room first, so I can put my things in there, since that's where I'll be sleeping."

"Your empty threats don't upset me. *You* wouldn't last five minutes sleeping in that room before crawling into my bed."

"Your arrogance is astounding."

"My arrogance is justified. If I was a loser, I wouldn't have a hot girlfriend who has her own business and a closet full of sex toys."

Her laughter made him feel so fucking good. Giving her an orgasm was nice for his ego and all, but it was nothing compared to this.

He pulled her close and wrapped his arms around her. "Thanks for being here, Tay," he whispered, then kissed her neck and smelled her hair.

Her phone chimed, and she pushed him back, then went to grab it from the arm of the couch. "It's Nova." She held the phone out so he could see the photo she'd received.

It was Nova sitting at a desk with a laptop, grinning and posing for the camera like a thirteen-year-old girl, throwing up some weird hand sign.

Gavin stood behind her, arms crossed in front of his chest.

Nick laughed. "Man, he does not look happy."

Taylor's phone rang. She tapped the screen, then held it out so they could both hear Nova on speaker. "Hey, Nova."

He walked around the couch, sat, and pulled her onto his lap.

"Ready for story time?"

"Uh, sure," Taylor said, her forehead wrinkled.

"I hacked into Gavin's e-mail and got his flight itinerary. When he got home, I was waiting for him on his front step. You know what's messed up? He didn't even offer me a drink." She sighed heavily. "But I guess he was a little miffed that he didn't have the chance to try something stupid like hiding a drive with the photos."

"So, you got them all? You're sure there's no way he has other copies saved anywhere else?"

"I was thorough. He's got nothing on you now. He didn't have time to bury the evidence—not that he'd know how, and even if he did, I'd still have dug it up. Rest easy. The only one who is going to see you in your lingerie is that dreamy baseball guy who's always hanging around."

Nick wiggled his eyebrows at her.

"Thanks, Nova."

"My pleasure. Fuck guys like that. I'm not going to charge you, and don't argue with me. You can return the favor someday, if I need it."

"Sure, if you ever need a wedding venue or a pie recipe or a field of lavender to bury a body in."

"Probably not the lavender field. Maybe the pie. You keep that wedding shit to yourself, though, alright?"

Taylor laughed. "Alright. Thanks, again."

He waited for her to end the call, then cupped her neck and pulled her in for a kiss. "It's over. How do you want to celebrate?"

"Greasy burgers, fries, and milkshakes here on the couch while we watch a movie."

"Did you know you're my favorite person in the whole world?"

52

Safe

Taylor

"You look like a sexy librarian. All you need are glasses." Nick came up behind her in the bathroom as Taylor pinned her hair into a twist and kissed her neck.

"How about a sexy innkeeper?" She wore a loose silk blouse and a pencil skirt, but she had doubts about whether it was right for the occasion. No one at the press conference was going to see her, but she'd meet his coaches, teammates, and other staff.

"Yeah, that'll work." He smirked at her in the mirror's reflection.

She turned and smoothed her hands down the lapels of his gray suit jacket. He'd worn jeans and a white shirt but no tie. "I'm going to change."

"Why? You look great."

She sighed and kept her gaze on his shirt button. "I don't want to be Taylor the innkeeper today. I want to be your Taylor."

He cupped her neck and looked deep into her eyes. "You're always my Taylor. Clothes don't change that. Wear whatever you're comfortable in. Leave your hair like this, though."

Clothes didn't change who she was, but dressing like a professional did change the way she carried herself. If she showed up for Nick, she wanted to show up as her true self. It was easier to do that when it was just the two of them. Today was about helping him get through a difficult but necessary task, and then helping him through the pain that was bound to come once it was done. She needed to be soft and familiar. She needed to be the girl he'd spent the better part of his life devoted to.

She wiggled away from him and went to the bedroom to dig through her suitcase. Her cream-colored cropped T-shirt and sage green hi-low skirt would be more appropriate.

While she unbuttoned her blouse and shimmied out of her pencil skirt, Nick laid on the bed on his side and propped his chin on his fist.

"Before you put on more clothes, can you do one of those poses Jaci taught you?"

"No." Her mind was too busy overthinking to be amused.

He stuck out his bottom lip. "Please?"

She sighed. "We have to leave soon."

"I'll behave. Please?"

She stepped into her other skirt and tugged it up over her ass and hips. "My anxiety is climbing."

He pushed off the bed and pulled her into his arms, then planted a kiss on her forehead and hugged her. "I can tell. That was a distraction technique—not a successful one, apparently."

"I don't need you to distract me." She moved away and traded her blouse for the more casual shirt.

"Tell me what you need, then."

"Therapy?" She plopped on the bed and put her head in her hands. "I want to be what *you* need."

He sat next to her and wrapped his arm around her shoulders. "You are. How could you doubt that?"

You're not going to play the supportive girlfriend, so maybe this isn't the best time for whatever is happening between you two.

Considering the source, those words shouldn't haven't carried any weight. They'd created an insecurity though—a subconscious fear that she couldn't be what he needed.

All the coping strategies in the world didn't stand a chance against that fear. Her only option was doing everything in her power to prove it wrong.

Because just the thought of the alternative made her chest feel like it was going to cave in.

If there was one thing Taylor was absolutely certain she couldn't survive, it was losing Nick.

Taylor couldn't sit still during the press conference. It was a good thing they'd put her in a skybox suite to watch it on a screen. She paced as the reporters asked Nick questions.

"What are you going to do now?" one asked.

"Finish my degree. Spend time with family. Eat cheeseburgers and fries whenever I want."

His audience laughed collectively.

"There are rumors floating around that you're seeing someone and are quite smitten."

Nick smirked. "I think I probably started those rumors."

"So, there's no truth to them?" the same reporter asked.

"Are you asking if I have an imaginary girlfriend?"

Taylor smacked her head. So dumb.

Again, the people in the room with him laughed.

"Yes, I am seeing someone," Nick said, still smiling but not his normal jokester smile. "But it's new and we'd like to maintain our privacy."

"Is she here?" someone had the audacity to ask.

"Does anyone have any questions that aren't about my love life?" he shot back.

Taylor watched him answer a couple more questions about how he felt about his injury. Once he'd gotten up and let one of his coaches take his spot, she shut the television off, went out to the balcony, and stared out at the field. Nick was leaving this behind for a far different life.

One with less excitement. Less opportunities.

She couldn't shake the fear that she was holding him back.

Nick had argued that wasn't true, but maybe he just didn't see it yet. Maybe the shine would wear off and that's when he'd realize how bored he was living in a small town with a girl he'd known his entire life.

A door shut and she whirled to see him walk into the suite. His gaze swept the room before landing on her. He came right to her, wrapped his arms around her and hid his face against her neck.

She stroked his back.

"I feel so damn spent. I wish we could go home now. Curling up on the couch to watch a movie with you while Cal tries to weasel his way between us is the only thing that'd make this hurt less."

She held him, speechless. Anxiety really sucked. All day, she'd been doubting whether she was enough for him, whether she had anything to offer that could hold a candle against what he'd had taken from him. But that wasn't how Nick saw it at all. He saw her as home. His comfort. His safe place.

53

Unsustainable or Unshakeable?

Taylor

TAYLOR WOKE UP WITH her stomach toasty warm, but her breasts getting a chill. Nick's face was pressed to her stomach and his breath blew across her hip. He held onto her like a kid with a stuffed animal, one arm under her, the opposite hand clutching her waist.

She ran her hand through his hair.

He was hers.

This wasn't the first time she'd felt that way, but it was the first time without also feeling she shouldn't. She ran her hand through his hair. Her pulse thumped. How long ago had she convinced herself that she couldn't have him? She searched her memory for the moment she'd turned the lights off on her imagination daring to show her a reality where she'd be enough for him.

She rolled her head to the side and studied the outlines of his back muscles, tracing them with her fingertips.

He rubbed his cheek against her stomach, his stubble tickling her.

She squirmed.

His groan vibrated through her body as he gripped her waist tighter.

Wetness spread to her thighs from her movements, and she bit her lip and squeezed her eyes shut. She couldn't make sense of why she got so turned on so fast with him. Or why he wanted her so often.

He placed a soft kiss on her belly and trailed his hand from her waist to breast. "Wake me up like this any day. God, you're so perfect."

Taylor shifted her pelvis, his sleep-raspy words making her ache. He always knew what to say to make her pussy clench. "Touch me."

She shoved aside how desperate she sounded. It didn't matter. She *was* desperate and Nick was pulling the strings. She'd beg him for what she wanted if that's what got him off.

"I am touching you," he whispered, his hand wrapped around her thigh, his thumb brushing back and forth along the edge of where her panties would have been had she been wearing any. He squeezed her breast with his other hand.

"But not where I want you to."

His lips moved against her skin, and she knew his cocky ass was grinning ear to ear. "Where do you want me to touch you, Taylor?" he asked in a low, predatory tone.

She covered his hand with hers and moved it between her thighs, guiding it up and down so they stroked her heat together. Her eyes fluttered shut, the pleasure too consuming to keep them open.

He untangled his hand from hers and pressed her thighs farther apart. "Fuck, it's hot how wet you get."

Heat spread through her as he rubbed his thumb up and down along her smooth, slick flesh. His tongue darted out and traced the same path.

Taylor's hips jerked off the mattress and she moaned.

He spread her open and delivered a long, slow lick.

"Nick," she said breathlessly and shoved her fingers into his hair.

His gaze traveled up, across her stomach and breasts, meeting her eyes. "You like that?"

"Yes. Do it again."

He did.

She moaned louder.

He rubbed his finger in a circular motion over her clit, then flicked his tongue across it.

Heat raced through her until she was pulsating with need. Desperation threatened to drown her restraint. She wanted all of the pleasure Nick normally gave her, but she wanted it *now*.

He covered her clit with his mouth and sucked.

She dug her heels into the mattress and lifted her hips off the bed, shoving her pussy into face.

He slowly worked his finger inside her, lazily sliding it in and out as he explored with his tongue. Ripples of pleasure coursed through her, but it wasn't enough. She wanted more.

"Nick, I can't—I need—"

As if she'd finished her sentence, telling him exactly what she needed, he moved up her body, lifted her hips, and slowly pushed his cock inside her.

Taylor gasped and hid her face against his throat. Damn it. How could they be this sexually compatible?

How could they be as emotionally compatible as they were?

Why couldn't she stop questioning it?

Nick lifted his upper body and stared down at her. Braced on one elbow, he placed his palm flat between her breasts and slid it up, circling her neck and applying gentle pressure with his thumb. "You're all I need. You're all I'm *ever* going to need."

Her lips parted but she had no words.

A faint grin lifted his lips before he lowered his mouth to hers.

She cupped the back of his neck and kissed him like she could somehow communicate everything she felt for him with her lips and tongue.

Without warning, Nick flipped her onto her stomach and thrust into her.

Taylor moaned and rocked against him.

Euphoria washed over her. The warmth of his palms against her hips as his fingers dug into them sent her spiraling. All she could do was gasp for air and moan, and if there'd been even a tiny bit of her that he hadn't already claimed, she'd have given it to him right then.

He took her over the edge and kept her there, prolonging her orgasm by popping the head of his cock in and out of her opening. Warmth hit her as his cum coated her pussy and thighs. He thrust back inside her and groaned.

After a moment, he pulled out and ran his hand over her ass and down her thigh. He swept his fingers across her overly sensitive swollen flesh. "Your pussy looks so good covered in my cum."

Taylor wet her lips and swallowed. "Does that mean you're going to leave me like this?"

He chuckled and pushed his thumb inside her. "It means I'm already getting hard again."

She gasped. "Nick, I need a minute."

"Sorry." He removed his hand and pressed his forehead to her shoulder. "I can't stop wanting you."

"I'm not asking you to."

He moved to lie on his side. "Leaving you every morning before dawn is going to be even more painful after this."

She laid on her stomach. "So, you *are* leaving me like this?"

He grinned and ran his knuckles down her spine. "Just for a little longer."

Morgan adjusted the camera to show Taylor the sleeping baby in the bassinet. "Watch this." She rubbed her finger against Demi's cheek, and the baby smiled in her sleep, revealing a dimple. "She's got Brody's dimple."

"How many hours a day do you spend staring at her?" Taylor tucked her legs under her on Nick's couch.

"All of them. How is Nick? We watched the press conference. He handled it well."

"He's doing alright. We're going to a farewell party one of his teammates is throwing. Can I ask you something completely inappropriate?"

Morgan wiggled her eyebrows and smiled. "Please do."

"When you and Brody first got together, how often did you...you know?"

She laughed. "I don't know. Why?"

"I talked to Jaci a little bit ago, and she made it seem like Nick and I are doing it excessively."

Morgan tilted her head to the side. "How often?"

"I don't know..."

"More than once a day?"

Taylor shifted nervously on Nick's couch. "Yes."

"Have you had sex with him today?"

She nodded.

"How many times?"

"Three." Taylor hid her face with her free hand. When Morgan didn't respond, she peeked between her fingers to see her reaction.

Her eyes and her grin were comically wide. "It's only ten-thirty."

"So, you do think that's too much."

"It sounds like you and Nick have high sex drives, which doesn't really surprise me. Nick is a ball of energy, and you've somehow managed to keep up with him for all these years. Plus, you're away and don't have any obligations, so it makes sense you'd have more time to spend in bed."

Bed. Right. Where people who weren't sex addicts generally did it. They'd gone from the bed to the dining table to the walk-in closet. "When we're home, he gets up early and usually lets me sleep, but he...makes up for it later."

"You and Nick not being able to keep your hands off each other is not a bad thing, Taylor. Remember when you were worried you weren't going to have chemistry? Seems like you've got plenty."

If chemistry was being super horny all the time, then sure.

"We shouldn't be like this, right? We've been friends forever. Things should be less…passionate."

"Maybe it's a once you start, you can't stop kind of thing." Morgan shrugged.

Or it was Nick's fault for flirting with her non-stop. Sometimes with his eyes alone. Which really twisted her up.

"I think it's great, Taylor. You have romantic chemistry with your best friend. That's what everybody wants."

They did? She'd never wanted that before recently. "I keep thinking… what if we're doing this wrong?"

"Wrong?"

"I know it sounds stupid, but sometimes things between us are so intense that it feels like they're not sustainable. Like they're going to burn out or combust."

"That's not stupid," Morgan said softly. "That's what being in love feels like."

"Really?"

"Don't you also have the opposite feeling sometimes? Like things are so unshakable that nothing could get between you?"

"Yes…and I wish to stop talking about this now." Because damn it, this was getting too deep. Had she fallen hard for Nick without even realizing it?

Morgan covered her mouth, her eyes glinting with withheld laughter.

"I've always loved Nick. It's not new."

"But the lust is." Morgan said. "There's nothing wrong with being obsessively attracted to your partner. That's one of those things you think is a problem, but everyone else would love to have."

"*Everyone* is obsessively attracted to my partner, not just me."

"Yeah, but he's obsessed with you and only you. Don't overthink it, Taylor. As long as you and Nick are both happy, that's all that matters."

"We're happy."

54
Out of Town Taylor
Nick

A HARD WORKOUT GAVE NICK a high. The only better high was Taylor. Not only was she addictive, she got him real fucked up.

He pulled his sweaty shirt over his head and wiped the sweat off his face and neck with it.

Working on the farm burnt calories, but it used different muscles. His body was used to both, but the intensity of doing 250 sit ups made him feel different.

Between physical therapy and him learning to accommodate his injury in day-to-day life, his knee felt a lot better.

He reached for the pull-up bar that he'd installed on the ceiling of the garage, adjusted his grip, and pulled up. He'd done five when the door opened.

Taylor stopped in her tracks. Her lips turned up and she shut the door behind her, then walked to the weight bench with a little spring in her step.

He hung, watching her, mesmerized. Good thing they didn't go to the gym together. He'd never get in a workout. Not this kind, anyway.

"Don't stop on my account." She settled in like she was about to watch a movie, minus the popcorn.

His lips twitched, trying to fight his smile. Man, he loved her. Funny, he'd gone from worrying Taylor wasn't attracted to him, to her looking at him like that—fully objectifying him.

He started to pull himself up but the hilarity of her sitting there like that got to him. He got half a pull up in and eased himself to his feet, putting the majority of his weight on his good leg.

"Listen, if I can't get an in-person performance, then we're going to have to talk about expectations for this relationship," Taylor said, arms crossed.

He rubbed his hands together and flexed his fingers. He did not care one bit if she wanted him for his body in this moment. Being friends for as long as they had, and as close as they'd been, didn't allow for him to have doubts about whether she liked him for his personality.

"No, you're right. In fact, you deserve more than just a performance. You can be a part of it." He crooked his finger at her.

"No, thanks. I'm camera shy."

"There is no camera. Get the fuck over here."

She kicked off her shoes and walked to where he was standing under the bar. "Okay, now what?"

"Now," he said as he lifted her chin. "I kiss you until you drop your sassy attitude."

 Although, he hoped she didn't drop it for too long because he liked her sass.

He lowered his mouth to hers.

She placed her hands on his chest and angled her face upward.

He cradled the back of her head as they sealed their lips together.

After he'd kissed her thoroughly, he asked, "You ready?"

"For what?"

"Wrap your legs around me." He reached down and put his hands on the backs of her thighs and lifted her.

She wrapped her arms around his neck. "What are you doing?"

"Showing off." He grabbed the bar and pulled up, taking her with him. "Watch your head."

She shrieked when his feet left the ground.

"Grab the bar."

She did and he pulled them both up. With her legs wrapped around him, her head rose above the bar.

"Come here often?" he asked, the bar between them.

She rolled her eyes.

He kissed her, then lowered them.

She started to unwrap her fingers from the bar, but he pulled up again.

"Nick!"

He kissed her, then repeated the action. After five pull ups, and five kisses, he lowered them. "Hop off. The ride's over."

She unwrapped her legs from around his waist, then let go of the bar, landing on her feet.

He took a slower, more gingerly approach.

"I'll have to tell Lucy I got to live out her fantasy."

"Huh?"

"She saw a video of you doing pushups and said she wanted to be the floor."

Nick's eyes widened. "She did not."

Taylor nodded.

"She's so classy. It's hard to believe she'd appreciate my content."

"Just because she's classy doesn't mean she doesn't have a libido. Besides, that video?" She fanned herself. "This was pretty hot, but now I'm wondering if being under you while you did push ups would be hotter."

"I suppose you want to find out?"

"I mean…if you're doing demonstrations, I won't turn one down."

He shook his head. "Fine, then. Go ahead and lie down."

She smirked and lowered herself onto the thick mat on the garage floor, then stretched out on her back.

Nick took a deep breath, then went down on his good knee and braced himself with his palms flat on the floor beside her shoulders, assuming a plank position, the ankle of his bad knee crossed over the other.

Taylor ran her hands down his chest. "Can we make this part of your regular workout routine?"

"No." He bent his arms and lowered his body. He brought his lips to hers, gave her a thorough kissing, then pushed back up. "Count for me?"

"Sure."

He lowered himself again, then back up.

"Two."

He used his arms to pump his body up and down fifteen times. He'd have done more if he was actually working out, but with Taylor this close, he wasn't thinking about exercise. Once he'd lowered himself, he rolled onto his back and laid next to her.

"Okay, maybe Lucy knows what's up. That was way hotter than the pull ups."

Nick rolled onto his side and ran his hand from her knee to her hip, sliding it under her dress. He gripped the side of her panties and tugged them down a little, then worked on the other side. He had them almost to her knees when he paused. "Want me to take a shower?"

"No." She took a long breath. "Do we have too much sex?"

"Is that a serious question?" He worked her panties the rest of the way down.

"Does that mean you don't think we do?"

"No. Do you?"

She shrugged. "Jaci does, and Morgan said she didn't think so, but I'm not sure I believe her."

"You talked about that with them?" He grinned all goofy-like. "I hope I got a glowing review."

"Five stars. One for each orgasm you're about to give me." She put her hand on the back of his head and pulled him toward her until their lips touched. They made out for several minutes before he lifted his head.

"I like Out of Town Taylor. She's fun."

She wrinkled her nose. "At Home Taylor isn't fun?"

"Of course, she is, but Out of Town Taylor is far more adventurous.

All I needed to do was get you away from the inn for a little."

"I'm boring when we're home?"

He groaned. "No. You're just more carefree right now. Probably because you live where you work and so you're never really off the clock."

"A boring workaholic."

He bit her shoulder.

"Nick!"

"Now that I have your attention: shut the fuck up."

Her mouth fell open.

"Hey, I have a quota to meet, and we have to leave for the party in two hours."

"Are you sure that no one there is going to take photos or post about us?"

"Mmm. I like being your dirty little secret, but…" He kissed her chest, pulling her dress straps down. "Head coach talked to everyone on the team and told them there couldn't be any photography, and that if they or their dates couldn't adhere to that, they'd be kicked out of the party."

"I'm just not ready for your fan club to know who I am."

"I know. It's going to be okay. I promise."

"But what if Gavin comes up with some other plan to get Sabrina back in his clutches?"

"Taylor." He'd dropped his voice, out of patience. He was hard and wanted to be inside her so bad he couldn't form a straight thought. "Stop talking."

55

Substitute Bestie

Taylor

TAYLOR'S NERVES ABOUT ATTENDING Nick's going away party frizzled out of control as he parked in the driveway of a waterfront home that had to be worth several million dollars.

Nick leaned over and grabbed the headrest of her seat. He came into her personal space, his left hand tracing the chain of her necklace to the star and moon pendant hanging from it. "Before we go in, we need to talk about something."

"Okay…" Her heart pounded and her mind darted around like a bouncy ball in a tight space, racing from one thought to the next. Maybe he was going to warn her about something with one of his teammates, or maybe he was going to tell her he didn't want her to mention certain details about life at home.

"If being here gets to be too much for you, tell me. We can have a code word or a signal or whatever, but I need to know."

Her heart stopped racing and filled with warmth instead. She touched the side of his face. "I'll be okay, Nick."

"Promise me. I'm not into having a good time while you're having a lousy one."

"Fine, I'll tell you."

"You promise?"

"I promise."

He kissed her palm, then got out of the car and walked around. He opened her door and put his hand out to her.

She took it and stepped out of the car.

Nick led her around the house.

She'd expected the party to be more country club and less…backyard barbecue.

Brown-paper covered picnic tables covered in steamed crabs ran in a row down the side of the lawn. A keg floated in a big tub of ice next to the table on the end.

A grill smoked and one of the men she recognized as a coach stood near it with a set of tongs while he talked to a small group of players.

She scanned the party for other women to see if she was overdressed. The men were dressed in an array of shorts, slacks, jeans, and every variety of shirt. There weren't even that many women unless they'd congregated inside. The ones she spotted wore dresses too. Although, theirs were slightly more casual. One woman had on wedges, but she didn't see anyone else wearing high heels.

"Did I overdress?" she asked quietly. Her coral dress wasn't overly short, but it hugged her body and had a deep V-cut into the neckline, revealing more than a hint of cleavage. Drew had told her if she wanted to look classy but sexy to show cleavage or leg, but not both.

He stopped, his grip on her hand tightening, causing her to stop as well. "Who'd you wear that dress for?"

Her mouth opened, then shut. This felt like a trick question.

He looked her up and down. "Well?"

"You."

"I like it and I think you look beautiful. So, does anything else matter? You're never going to see these people again."

"I really hate it when you talk me out of my anxiety."

He grinned. "No, you don't. You need me and you know it."

"You're so full of yourself."

He tugged her close. "You're gonna be full of me too when I get you home and out of that dress."

She slapped his shoulder. "Nick!"

"Where's the lie, Taylor?"

"How'd you talk this beautiful creature into being your date?" someone with a deep voice asked from behind her.

Taylor whirled around.

A man with dark hair and brown skin stood there. He had on black pants and a white shirt, open at the collar.

"This very unimpressive person is Tate Benson," Nick said. "You might have seen him standing on the pitcher's mound helping the other team score runs."

He clapped Nick on the back, then turned his attention to her, and extended his hand.

She shook it. "Hi, I'm Taylor."

"I figured. I'm glad you could come."

Her gaze slid to Nick. He'd talked to Tate about her? Her stomach did a swoopy thing. "Me too."

"Drinks?"

"Immediately," Nick said.

Tate gestured for them to follow.

Nick grabbed her hand and held as they walked across the massive patio area, weaving around other guests.

"This is my wife, Liz," Tate said to Taylor as he stopped at an umbrella-covered patio table. A woman wearing a short, light blue dress with a little flouncy ruffle at the bottom and a boat neckline stood from her chair. She must have known about the cleavage or leg rule.

She held out her hand. "You must be Taylor."

Taylor shook it and shot Nick another look, wondering what he'd told these people about her.

He winked.

"It's nice to meet you," Liz said, then pulled Nick into a hug. "Tate is heartbroken. He said you're the best catcher he's ever played with."

Tate rolled his eyes and positioned Liz in front of him, his arm across her chest. "This is my last season and since you've been gone, it's been shit."

"Hey, don't blame me. It's not my fault you're old."

Tate laughed. "My ego would rather blame it on you abandoning me."

"I didn't abandon you. Christ. You're more dramatic than my teenage sister."

"Is your girl too classy to drink beer from a keg?" Tate asked.

Nick laughed. "She's classy, but don't be fooled into thinking she's never done a keg stand."

She swatted his arm. "You made me do it."

"That's a bold-faced lie, Taylor Van Belle." He grinned. "All I said was that you wouldn't be cool unless you did it."

"No one is going to peer pressure you into doing a keg stand," Tate said. "Come on."

They all walked to the keg, and Tate pulled cups from a stack and filled them, handing Taylor one first, and then Liz.

"I heard you're a pitcher too, and that you've got one hell of an arm," Tate said.

"Is it possible the person who told you that is biased?" she asked.

Nick smiled and took a sip of his beer.

"You two played on the same team when you were younger, right?" Liz asked.

"Her dad was their little league coach," Tate said, clearly familiar with the story. "He coached Nick in high school too."

"Wait. Your girlfriend is your coach's daughter?" Liz's eyes widened. "I knew you had balls, but I had no idea they were that big."

Tate choked on his beer.

"Well, now you know," Nick said. "We better make the rounds."

"Fuck that. Let them come to you," Tate said. "Enjoy yourself."

Nick wrapped his arm around Taylor's waist and pulled her even closer. They really hadn't been anywhere as a couple before this. In private, he never held back from touching her whenever he wanted, and yet, they easily fluctuated between friends and lovers. But in this moment, his touch felt performative and possessive.

"I heard you're going to be keeping an eye on Mama B for a bit," Liz said to Nick.

Taylor's eyebrows pinched together.

He turned to her. "Tate grew up about fifteen minutes from my campus. He tore down his mom's house and built her a fancy one. I'm going to stay in the guest house while I'm finishing school."

"Oh."

"Tate offered yesterday. I forgot to mention it."

She nodded. She didn't care whether he stayed in Tate's guest house or the dorms or somewhere else. What upset her was that he was going to be away at all.

Nick squeezed her waist, then leaned in and whispered, "I'll come home every weekend."

Damn it. She hated when he did that. It wasn't fair that he could see into her mind so easily.

People came over to say hi to Nick and meet her. She'd started to get a bit overwhelmed when someone tapped on her shoulder.

"Nick, I'm stealing your girl," Tate said. He held out his arm.

"The fuck you are." Nick said as Taylor looped her arm through Tate's. "You have your own."

"Yeah, but Liz sucks at cornhole and I need a partner."

Nick blew out a breath. "Fine."

Taylor bit her lip to keep from laughing.

"Show 'em how it's done, Tay."

Tate led her closer to the water where a set of cornhole boards were on the lawn.

"You know, I'm sure there's a professional athlete or two around here you could ask to be your partner. Might be better odds for you."

"I heard you're in a cornhole league and pretty damn good."

"Nick has told you a lot about me, it seems."

"He wasn't into partying with the younger guys, and my idea of a good time is making pizza in my wood-fire oven and watching Good Girls, so we hit it off. After he got hurt, I stopped over to see him almost every day. Not one time did he fail to bring your name up."

She smiled. "Thanks for being his substitute bestie."

"You can return the favor by helping me kick these bozos asses."

She took off her high heels. "I'll try."

56
The Final Flex
Nick

NICK WATCHED FROM SEVERAL yards away as Taylor played cornhole with Tate and two other teammates. He had to keep asking people to repeat themselves because he was far more interested in her. She'd taken off her high heels and stood in the grass barefoot. He hadn't been paying close enough attention to the game itself to know who was winning, but she and Tate were all high-fives and smiles while the other team didn't look to be having nearly as much fun.

Once he found an out, he escaped and headed straight for her.

"What's wrong, Mears?" he asked the short stop standing near Taylor. "Don't like getting beaten by a girl?"

Taylor snorted and sunk a bag in the hole without it touching the sides.

"Ouch," Nick said. "What's the score?"

"Seventeen to nine," Taylor said.

Nick winced. "Better get this one in, Mears."

He got it on the board, but not in the hole.

"You tried your best and that's what counts."

"It's hard to focus with such nice scenery." Mears swept his gaze over Taylor.

He took a step toward him. "Watch yourself."

"I'd rather watch her."

He liked Mears and he trusted that he wasn't the type of guy that'd hit on another man's girlfriend, especially one of his teammates', but in that moment, he wanted to deck the bastard.

Taylor moved in front of him. She put her hand on his chest and pressed up onto her toes.

He glanced down at her.

She kissed him.

He placed his hand on her lower back and slanted his mouth across hers. Okay, fine. He wouldn't rearrange Mears's teeth.

He pulled his lips from hers. "Kick his ass for me."

"In the game, or…?"

"Either works. Want me to hold your earrings?"

She rolled her eyes, then picked up the last blue bag on the board and tossed it at the other board where Tate and Sills stood.

It slid up the board, teetered on the edge of the hole for a second and then fell in.

"Hell, yeah!" Tate fist pumped. "That's the game, losers! Who's next?"

"Hey, I only loaned her to you for one game," Nick said.

Tate walked over. "We have to defend our title."

"It's cornhole. Not the World Series."

Tate chuckled. "Fine. You can have her back. I'm gonna go find Liz."

Taylor poked Nick in the shoulder after Tate walked away. "Did you ask him to play cornhole with me to give me reprieve from peopling?"

"When would I have done that? He's a good man. He might've assumed you'd need a break from it all, but he probably just wanted to make sure you had fun." He brushed her hair over her shoulder and lowered his voice. "Are you having fun?"

She nodded. "Are you?"

He shrugged. "It's always good to see Tate, and I like the rest of the guys, but hanging out with them like this has never really thrilled me all that much."

"Oh." She glanced around. "What are we doing here, then? When they offered to throw you a party, why didn't you just say you wouldn't be able to make it?"

"I came here to show you off." Admitting it didn't bother him. Not with Taylor. She ribbed him enough about his ego that it'd be a waste of time trying to fool her into thinking he didn't care about other people's impression of him.

"What?" She looked at him like it was his head that was busted instead of his knee.

"It's a flex, okay? I have a hot girlfriend and I want them to see me with her and be jealous." Not just jealous. He also wanted to prove that even though he'd had his baseball career snatched away from him, he'd still landed on his feet.

"Why are you so crazy?"

He laughed. "I don't know. It's gotta be your fault in some way, though."

She elbow-jabbed him in the ribs.

He grunted, then slung his arm around her neck, and led her to get some food because he was starved.

Taylor refused to pick crabs in her pretty dress, so they filled their plates with the other food that'd been set out in the kitchen. After they'd eaten, Liz introduced her to the other wives and girlfriends while he laid on a lounge chair and rested his knee, keeping his eye on her to look for signs of discomfort.

As the sun went down, the party got louder and rowdier, with the younger set taking control of the music and turning it up. He'd about had enough and wanted nothing more than to take Taylor back to his apartment and have a quiet rest of the evening.

She pulled her phone from her purse and stared at the screen. "It's my mom. Looks like my dad has tried to call a couple of times. It's probably about the repairs. I'm going to go answer over there so I can hear."

He gave her a quick kiss, then watched her walk away. Hopefully, it was just Ollie wanting to give her an update, or maybe even tell her it was all finished in time for them to arrive home tomorrow.

Ten minutes after she'd disappeared around the side of the house and hadn't returned, he went after her.

She leaned against the railing inside a gazebo with a garden around it, no longer on the phone, just staring out into the dark.

He stepped into the gazebo. "Everything good?"

"Yeah." She nodded. "The repairs are done."

Deciding whether she looked upset or not proved impossible. She wasn't smiling, but she also didn't look like she was about to burst into tears. "What's up?" he asked.

"Nothing. I just got lost in thought."

"About?"

"About what it's going to be like when we get home. About what our future will be like."

As far as he was concerned, life was going to be fucking awesome. He and his dad had finally had that talk. The farm had been transferred out of his parents' names and into Nick's, Brody's, and Hope's. Profits would be split between the three of them, with Hope's going into a college savings account. While he finished his degree, his dad wanted him to consider what he saw in the farm's future. Nick already had a few ideas. If the farm was going to support him and his two siblings, they'd need to talk about ways to increase profits. The money from his contract with the Hustlers wasn't going to last forever.

He leaned his cane against the railing and brushed his mouth over hers. "It's gonna be beautiful, Taylor. I promise you."

She draped her arms over his shoulders and kissed him, at first sweetly, but it didn't take long until she was rubbing her tongue against his and pressing her tits against his chest.

With his hand on her back, he pulled her tighter to him and growled against her lips.

The restless movements of her body against his erased the little bit of restraint he'd been allotted in life. He grabbed a piece of the fabric covering her thigh and pulled, slowly working her dress up until he could get his hand under it. The instant he pushed aside her thong, needing to feel her slick pussy, he tore his mouth from hers and groaned.

She sought his mouth for another kiss, but he moved his head to avoid giving her what she wanted.

"How far will you let me go?" he whispered against her ear. "Hmm? Will you let me make you come on my fingers while there's all those people right around the corner?"

Her saying yes was the only thing he cared about right then. He stroked her clit, his touch teasing, ready to make her beg.

She moved against his hand, gasping, and arching toward him.

The more he explored, stroking up and down until his fingers were coated, the more she moaned. "Are you mine, Taylor?" he rasped against her ear.

"Yes. Now, please do your job. Make me come."

Nick scoffed. "My job? Is that all I'm good for?"

"Not all, but you are *really* good at it." She tried for his mouth again, but he ran his free hand up her back and twisted her hair in his fist, forcing her to look at him.

"Taylor…don't try to stroke my ego to get your way." God, he enjoyed dragging this out. Enjoyed how desperate she got for his touch. Enjoyed how she let go of her defenses because of her trust in him.

"Is there anything I can stroke to get my way?" She rolled her hips and bit her lip.

"Such a bad girl. Take your panties off."

She hooked her fingers in the sides, worked them down to her ankles, and kicked out of them.

Hand between her thighs, he stroked her, teasing at her opening, then dragging his middle and index fingers up, swirling her clit.

Her head fell back.

He bent his head and kissed her neck.

Her breathing grew heavier and when he ran his tongue around the rim of her ear, she bucked against his hand, whimpering.

Nick looped his arm behind her and held her steady. He loved that he could do this to her. Make her legs shake. Make her sweet pussy pulse around his fingers. Make her so mindless to anything but release that she didn't give a fuck he was fingering her in a gazebo at his going away party.

"Nick," she cried out, her voice as unsteady as her legs.

"Come, so I can drag you out of here and park down some back road while you ride my dick," he whispered.

"Oh, my god." She clung to him, moaning.

He waited for her orgasm to subside, slowing and lightening his touch until she pushed his hand away. Once she seemed steady enough, he let her go and took a step back. He smirked. "Pick up your panties and let's get out of here."

She stooped down and grabbed them.

Nick snatched them away from her and shoved them into his pocket.

"Do I look like we were just doing what we were just doing?"

"Yes."

She groaned. "Can I sneak out while you say goodbye to everyone? Tell them I wasn't feeling good."

"If I have to go out there like this"—he gestured at the bulge in his pants—"then you're going out there with a flushed face and a swollen pussy."

She sucked in a breath. "No one has come looking for us yet. Let's just wait until we're both presentable."

He adjusted himself. "After that, my dick isn't going down until I fuck you."

She did her own adjustments, pulling the bottom of her dress down and making sure her hair wasn't a disaster. "That'll make five times today alone."

"Why do you keep telling me what the count is, like I'm going to feel bad about it?"

"Because it's a lot."

"And *you* feel bad about it?"

"No, I just don't want us to be…abnormal or something. Morgan said we both probably just have high sex drives."

He laughed. "Ya think so, Taylor?"

"I'm afraid of losing you, Nick," she blurted out.

He sighed and shook his head. "That's not going to happen. We don't have to be perfect. Our relationship can have flaws—although I don't think having lots of sex is one—and still thrive."

57
A Dog Doing Dog Stuff
Nick

NICK STORMED INTO THE inn from the back door.

"I hate this weather," he muttered. Farmers were always thankful for rain, but this was excessive. It had been beautiful and sunny when they'd gotten on the road home this morning. He'd dropped Taylor at the inn and taken Cal with him to the farm, but he'd barely gotten in an hour of work before the sky opened up. It'd only been raining for a little over an hour and they'd already gotten two inches. Besides the crops getting drowned, the wind brought down limbs and leaves everywhere.

He held the door open for Cal, then told him to stay and went right to the laundry room. The dog was covered in mud, the little asshole.

"What's wrong?" Taylor asked, holding onto the doorframe to the laundry room where he stripped out of his jeans and T-shirt.

"Your dog is an asshole."

"Oh, *now*, he's my dog." She glanced over her shoulder at Cal. "What did my little angel do?"

"When I let him out of the car, he took off after a rabbit that was trying to keep dry under your Jeep. I went after him, but when I crouched down to grab his collar, my knee went out and I slipped in the fucking mud, which might not have been that bad, but then he ran through a big puddle, and when I finally got my ass off the ground and got him to come back, he shook all over me."

"Is your knee okay?"

"No, my knee isn't okay. It hurts like a motherfucker, and my damn pain pills are in the car."

"I'll go get them. Get off your feet."

"I can't because I have to give this dumbass a bath." He tossed his clothes into the washing machine, then looked at his boxer briefs.

"I can do that."

"No sense in you getting all wet and muddy trying to wrestle him. Anyone here?"

He might take his clothes off for the camera and post it for the entire world to see, but that was controlled. Right now, he was in a shit mood, and he didn't want her guests seeing him in his undies and disheveled.

"Just Sabrina, but she's upstairs."

"Cal," he called. "Get your ass in here."

"I've got it, Nick. I'm going to go grab your medicine, and then, I'll wash him up." She pointed a finger in his face. "When I come back inside, you better have that knee elevated."

Once she'd gone out of sight, Nick pressed his back against the wall inside the doggie shower in the laundry room and slid down until his butt touched the floor. He reached for the spray head and beckoned Cal closer.

He lathered him up, then sat on the shower floor with Cal standing over his outstretched legs while he rinsed the suds off. He might as well just hose himself off too. Maybe doggie shampoo was okay for humans. Probably. Soap was soap, right?

Cal nudged his muzzle under Nick's chin.

He hugged him, not caring one bit that he was all wet and soapy. "I'm not mad at you, buddy. I'm sorry. You were just being a dog, doing dog stuff." He took a deep breath. "I'm just bitter because I can't chase rabbits, or you know, slide into home, or give Taylor piggyback rides."

He felt like he was being watched and looked up.

Taylor stood there with a glass of water and his bottle of prescription pain killers.

"I don't want your pity."

She put the glass and medicine on the ledge, nudged Cal out of the way, and climbed into his lap, getting herself all wet. "I love you. Your pain is my pain."

He tucked her hair behind her ear. "It feels like I've been holding my breath forever, waiting to hear you say those words."

"It's not the first time I've said them."

"It's the first time you said them and meant them that way."

She frowned. "You haven't said them and meant them that way either. You still haven't."

"Did I need to, Tay? You didn't feel it in how I touched you? How I want to spend all my time with you? How proud I am to tell people you're mine?"

"No, you didn't need to, but it'd be nice to hear it now."

"Taylor, I love you and I'm never going to stop."

She leaned away from him and smiled. "Are you threatening me?"

"No. I'm just letting you know how it's going to be."

She slid off his lap and sat next to him on the wet floor. "I know right now having to watch others do what you can't is torture, but you don't have to completely walk away from baseball just because you can't play. Every team needs a coach."

"I'm not ready, but maybe one day. You know, like, tee ball or little league, though."

"I'm not letting you coach our kids," she said, a smile lining her voice.

Our kids. He didn't think either of them wanted to become parents tomorrow, or even in nine months, but witnessing her talk about it without having a panic attack was nice. "You're going to coach them?"

She flipped her palm up. "I'm clearly the more qualified person for the position."

"Oh, I see. So, I'll just sit the sidelines?"

"I think that'd be best."

He turned his head in her direction and guided her to look at him. His mood had been absolute trash a few minutes ago, but a moment with her turned it all around. He'd be so lost without her. She was his everything.

58
Loco Loophole
Taylor

"Those fucking sluts."

Jaci tugged her phone out of Taylor's grasp. "It's just for views because it's trending."

Taylor had scrolled through several videos of women sporting college sweatshirts and hats with Nick's school's logo on it. Some said they were transferring colleges. Alumni said they were going back to school. The comedic creators dressed up as professors and acted out what having Nick in their class would be like.

It'd been a week of this since a clip of his press conference where he mentioned going back to school circulated. It'd been a week of him getting tagged in post after post. It'd been a week of her being miserable because she couldn't resist watching other women's videos about *her* boyfriend.

Taylor huffed and slumped over onto the kitchen island. "I know but it still makes me crazy. Some of them don't even look eighteen."

"I shouldn't have shown you."

She squeezed her forehead. "No. I want to know what's going on with that part of his life."

The front door opened and a couple of seconds later, her mom walked into the kitchen. "Good morning, ladies."

"Hey, Mom."

"Hi, Miss Vi. How are you?" Jaci asked.

"I'm doing fine." She set a basket on the counter. "Why are you so down in the dumps, Taylor?"

"Just tired."

"That's a lie." She turned to Jaci. "What's wrong with my daughter?"

Jaci froze, her mouth half open.

"Mom, it's really nothing," Taylor said, saving Jaci from the awkwardness of being put on the spot. "Girls online are drooling over Nick, and it pisses me off, but it's not that big of a deal."

"You better get used to that," her mom said.

"He doesn't plan on posting for much longer."

"He's still going to be attractive, and he's a flirt. Trust me, your father never posted any videos of himself, and women always stared at him."

"He was probably staring at them first," she blurted out.

Jaci grabbed her purse. "I think I'm going to go."

"Call me later." Taylor gave her a wave. Once the front door had shut, she turned back to her mom. "Nick isn't like Dad."

If she ever implied that they had anything in common again, she'd probably start throwing and breaking stuff. Nick was *nothing* like him. He had all the traits she'd once believed her father had.

"And if he ever did what dad did," Taylor said, her voice catching, "I'd have enough respect for myself to leave him."

Her mom crossed her arms. "It's easy to say beforehand that you'd draw a hard line in the sand but sometimes it's not that cut and dry. You don't know what you'll do until it happens. I hope it doesn't."

She'd never forgive him if he did that to her. But he wouldn't. Never.

"Your father is my best friend, just like Nick is yours. We might not have started out that way, but we became that. When we found out I was pregnant with you, it was never a question of whether he'd still play ball. He wanted you from the second he found out, and no one could have changed his mind about dropping out of college and giving up his shot at a baseball career so I could finish high school and we could raise you together. He never made me feel like he resented me for it. He loved being

your dad, and we might have not had much, but he worked his ass off to give us everything we did have."

"That doesn't excuse what he did!"

"Okay, Taylor." Her mom huffed. "Keep living in your dreamworld where good people never make mistakes."

She stared at her mom with her jaw set, tears pricking her eyes.

"It might not be another woman, but one day Nick is going to let you down about something and you're going to have to decide whether or not to throw everything you have away." Her mom turned on her heel and stomped out of the house.

Three of Aunt Penny's five husbands had cheated on her. That's how she'd amassed her wealth—grounds for divorce and alimony. Her first husband had died in a freak accident and left her everything. The next three slept around. The fifth was faithful for the two months they'd been married. If he'd not had a fatal heart attack, maybe he'd have proved to be a cheater too.

Maybe her mom was right. Maybe all men had some degree of a breaking point if faced with enough temptation. Nick might be on the far end of the spectrum, strong enough to resist most women, and sure, not all men cheated, but all men also weren't faced with the level of attention he got. His chances of caving to temptation were greater than most men's.

Nick meant it when he said she was it for him. She believed him.

But just because he wasn't going to throw up a profile on a dating app, or DM one of the many, many women lusting after him online, didn't mean that women weren't going to do everything they could to tempt him.

Girls were already chomping at the bit to see him on campus. Even if someone hadn't seen his videos, Nick was hot. He had the best facial expressions and could melt panties with a wink or a hint of a grin.

Maybe they weren't ready for this. He was leaving and although he wouldn't be that far, there'd be plenty of opportunities for women to hit on him.

She would not survive him betraying her.

Unless...

He couldn't betray her if they didn't commit to being a couple. She'd only be able to get past it if they went back to just friends. Not forever. Just while he was away. A few months. It'd take the long-distance relationship pressure off.

They'd slept with other people before all this. It wouldn't be any different.

It might be a loophole, but it felt like her safety net.

59
Stop
Taylor

TAYLOR'S HEART POUNDED AS she met Nick in the foyer to say goodbye before he left for college. Despite the bile rising in her throat, she was determined to do this. It would hurt them both, but not as much as it'd hurt if they lost everything they'd ever had. This was temporary.

"What's wrong?" he asked immediately, making his way to her.

The words clogged her throat.

"Taylor."

She took a shaky breath. "I want to put things on hold until you finish your degree."

There. She'd said it.

"What?" His gaze searched hers, his brow furrowed. "Put what on hold? Tell me you don't mean our relationship. Tell me right now that you don't fucking mean that, and I've got it all wrong."

Her stomach clenched. "Nick, it's been a rough couple of weeks. A lot happened and my mind is still spinning from it all. The timing was bad, and now, you're leaving. I just think—"

"Then, I won't leave."

"Nick…" She fought against the pain flooding her. "Your degree is important to you."

"Jesus fucking Christ," he shouted. "It's not more important than you. Why are you doing this?"

"Because I need to be in therapy. I want to get over my issues with my family and get a handle on my anxiety. Give me this time to get my shit together. Besides, we both know what it's like being long-distance friends. It's only going to be harder being in a long-distance relationship. We can try again when you finish your degree, once you're home for good, if that's what you end up doing."

"There's no if. I'm moving home. We can make it work for a few months, Taylor. That's a blip in our lives."

"I don't want to. I'm not ready."

"Too bad," he said.

"It's not too bad. I have a say."

"So do I. And I say you're being stupid as hell right now."

"We have the rest of our lives to figure out how to make this work. December will be here before—"

"Figure out how to make it work?" he shouted. "It works. There's nothing to figure out."

It worked when they were together. When the odds of him crossing paths with some chick who drooled over his videos was less likely.

"You're going to go finish your degree, and then you're going to come back here, and we can try again."

"Trying again implies that we failed the first time."

"I wasn't ready for this. You rushed me into it."

"Don't say that." He glared at her. "I tried to take things slow. I only pressured you when it seemed like your anxiety was getting in the way of what you wanted."

"I need to take a step back. And you need to focus on school."

He white-knuckled his cane and his jaw twitched. "This doesn't make any sense. This morning everything was fine. Something is up. You could at least be honest with me and tell me what it is."

"I just don't think a long-distance relationship is for us."

"Why not?" he demanded. "What am I supposed to do without you?"

The way his voice cracked on that last part tore her up inside, but no matter how hard this was, finding out he'd been with someone else would be worse.

"You can do whatever you want. If you're out and there's someone—"

"That's what this is about?" he roared. "You think I'm going to cheat on you?"

"If my dad could do that to my mom—my dad, who I spent my entire life admiring and trusting and idolizing…"

His glare sliced her to the core. "I'm not going to do *that.*"

"I know you believe that, but until you're in that situation, you don't know what you'd do."

He put his hand to his forehead. "Are you gonna fuck someone else while I'm gone?"

She stared at the floor.

"Pace?"

With her gaze still lowered, she shook her head.

"You're acting like I'm not going to come home at all between now and December. I'm going to another state, not a different country."

Her shaky breath did nothing to soothe her aching chest.

"We can make it work," he said. "I'll come home every weekend."

"The weekends are my busy time. You know that."

"So, you're breaking up with me right before I leave? Even though we love each other?"

She stayed silent, unable to affirm that, even though that was exactly what she was doing.

"I refuse to accept that." He came toward her.

Taylor took a step back. She glanced up and said the only thing she knew that would get through to him. "Stop."

He froze in his tracks. His shoulders sagged.

"You promised me if I said that word that you would."

"That's really fucked up."

"You promised."

Cal was right next to him, and Nick stared at him for a couple of heavy seconds.

He patted the dog on the head. "Look after your mom. I'll see you soon."

Cal whimpered and rubbed his head against Nick's leg.

He glanced her way. "Bye, Taylor."

He was two steps from the door when he stopped, turned, and walked back over to her. He cupped the back of her neck and crushed his mouth to hers. He kissed her hard and fast.

"I'll be back this weekend. Maybe you'll be less stupid by then."

60
U-turn
Nick

ON HIS WAY OUT of town, Nick slammed on the brakes. He did a U-turn and headed back the way he'd come.

Dust flew up in his wake as he drove up Taylor's parents' driveway. He threw the car in park, got out, and slammed the door. He was halfway to the house when the door opened, and Ollie came out.

"Men like you give all of us a bad rap," he said, barely able to suppress the urge to spit in Taylor's dad's face once he was close enough.

He crossed his arms. "I can see you're mighty pissed off about something, but you better watch yourself, boy."

"I'm not a boy. I'm a man. A better one than you, not that you set the bar very high."

"You gonna come here and blame me every time you and Taylor have a fight?"

Nick swung. He didn't even think about it, just clocked the bastard right in the nose.

Ollie doubled over and covered his face with both hands.

"You're a selfish bastard. Do you even feel bad about what you did? Do you care how much you've hurt her? Does it bother you to know she's struggling to trust me because of the trauma you've caused?"

He took his hands off his face and glared. "I think you need to mind your own business."

"Taylor is my business. She's mine. She's always been mine. To keep safe. To show her what true loyalty is. To put before myself. The universe must have assigned me to her because it knew her father wouldn't do those things. Stay the fuck away from her unless you have permission from me."

"She's my daughter. You don't dictate when I see her."

"You know what? You're right. It's up to Taylor. If she wants you in our lives, I'll respect that, but you better watch yourself. If you upset her the tiniest bit, you'll get a lot more than my fist."

61
Boy's Mama
Taylor

TAYLOR HAD GONE THROUGH a box of tissues and all of her dignity, and she still couldn't stop crying.

Jaci and Sabrina had been doing their best to console her, but the pain was too much.

She couldn't even fully explain what had happened. She was that much of a wreck over what she'd said to Nick. All she could do was lie on her sofa with her head in Jaci's lap.

"He loves you," she said while stroking her hair. "You've been through so much lately. He'll understand and you'll work this out."

Taylor sobbed. Because Nick did love her. And she loved him But she was the one who'd hurt them both.

"What's wrong?" Hope asked as she came in.

Taylor had forgotten Nick's little sister was working at the inn today. She didn't want Hope to see her like this. She took the second box of tissues when Sabrina offered it to her.

"Taylor is having a rough time with your brother leaving," Jaci said.

God, how she appreciated her as a friend. She always knew when to step in and smooth things out until Taylor got herself together.

"He's coming home this weekend." That voice. It wasn't Hope's.

Taylor pushed herself up and swiveled her head. Sure enough, Nick's mom stood there, frowning. "Have you talked to him?"

"Not since earlier when he said goodbye to me and his dad before he left to see you."

"Wait. You're Nick's mom?" Jaci asked.

"Yes."

Jaci's mouth turned into a severe line, drawing more to one side in a *yikes, that's awkward* grimace.

Taylor sniffled and reached for a tissue, but before she raised it to her face to wipe her nose, another sob wracked her body. It felt like her chest was caving in.

"Did your goodbye not go well?" Gia asked.

She shook her head. "I told him I wanted to put things on hold until he moves back home for good, and that I wouldn't consider it him being disloyal to me if he was with other women."

"Nick's as loyal to you as can be. He always has been."

She took a shaky breath. "He's dated other girls."

"And they were all jealous of your bond with Nick. You'd have only had to say you didn't like the way she breathed, and he'd have ended it."

Taylor cast her gaze at the edge of the coffee table.

"Your reaction tells me you know that to be true, but it doesn't support your argument and that bothers you." Gia turned to the others. "Could I talk to Taylor alone?"

Once they were gone, Gia sat next to her on the couch. "What happened, Taylor?"

"I messed up. My mom said something, and it freaked me out. I wasn't thinking clearly."

"What did she say?"

"She was defending her choice to stay with my dad after finding out he cheated on her." She wasn't keeping secrets for them anymore. It cost her too much emotionally.

"Oh."

Taylor glanced at her, searching her face for a clue as to why she didn't have more to say. "You don't seem surprised. You knew about my dad cheating?"

"I suspected. I've seen how he behaves with women when your mother isn't around."

"Did he behave that way with you?"

Gia shook her head. "No. I wouldn't have stood for it, and Theo would have hurt him. I'm sure he knew that."

Her phone rang and she snatched it off the coffee table, holding her breath, hoping to see Nick's name on the screen. But no. It was her mom.

She'd love to silence the call and wait to speak to her mom when she'd gotten her emotions under control. But that's not how her mom operated. She'd call back again and again until she got an answer, and if she didn't get one as soon as she'd like, she'd come over.

"Hi," she answered.

"Would you like to tell me why Nick showed up here and decked your father?"

"He did what?" She pressed her fingertips to her lips.

"He punched him, Taylor. Your dad thinks something happened between you two and that he's taking it out on him."

Well, he was right. She wasn't gonna say that, though.

This news should feel like one more awful event in this whole fucked up situation. But it didn't. Nick had punched her dad, and she wasn't even mad about it. If anything, it helped to stop her tears from flowing.

"Did you hear what I said?" her mother asked.

She nodded, then remembered her mom couldn't see her. "I heard you."

"Care to explain why that might have happened?"

"Dad's an asshole?"

"Taylor!"

"I have to go, Mom." She hung up and turned to Gia. "Nick punched my dad."

Gia gasped.

"I need to fix this. I don't know what I was thinking."

"You should call him before he gets too far. He'll turn around if you ask him to."

That was true. But Nick had already pushed leaving until the last minute. His classes started tomorrow. She had to make this up to him and that meant meeting him more than halfway.

62

Course Correction

Nick

FOCUSING DURING HIS FIRST day of classes wasn't easy. All he could think about was Taylor.

She hadn't called. Not even a text.

He'd honestly expected her to realize her fears were unfounded and that she'd made a huge mistake by now. The only thing keeping him from reaching out to her was his own fear—that he'd make it worse.

By the time he got back to Tate's mom's guest house, he missed her so bad that he started to seriously consider driving back to Maryland and not leaving until they fixed this. But again, he worried he'd make it worse.

He walked inside the house and was nearly knocked to his ass by a giant dog. "What are you doing here?" he asked Cal as he petted him and scanned the room for Taylor. "Where's your mom?"

Cal pranced around, not being helpful at all in helping him figure out what the hell was happening. Was Taylor here? God, he hoped so. She wouldn't just drive Cal down here and dump him on Nick. Unless she'd gotten pissed at the dog too and wanted to punish them simultaneously.

Nah. Even though he hadn't seen her Jeep in the driveway, he could sense she was here.

He walked to the bedroom.

When he opened the door, he found everything he could have ever wanted.

Taylor knelt on his bed, wearing a baseball jersey of a very familiar team. He didn't know what she wore under the jersey, but it wasn't pants. Knee-high socks with stripes at the top covered her legs. Her hair was up in a ponytail.

"What's going on?" he asked, standing in the doorway.

"I'm course correcting…if you'll let me."

Nick sauntered closer and tilted his head to one side. "I'm hella confused right now, but fuck, you look so good on my bed, I'll let you do whatever you want."

Taylor reached out and draped her arms over his shoulders. "I changed my mind. I don't want to put things on hold. I don't want you to be free to hook up with other women."

He rolled his eyes. "I was never going to do that anyway."

"Well, it's no longer an option. I will throat punch any bitch who gets near you."

He grinned. "Change your mind about anything else?"

"Mmhmm. We're going to spend the weekdays here while you take classes, and weekends at the inn. I've hired Sabrina to help."

No way. He loved that idea, but he couldn't see Taylor loving it. "That's a lot of back and forth, and a lot of time away from the inn for you."

"It's not forever. But we are."

Nick cupped her face. "I love you, Taylor."

She smiled. "I love you too."

He kissed her, and although he had every intention of doing so much more, he needed to ask something. "Is my name on the back of this jersey?" It fit her well enough that he knew she didn't get it from his closet. Besides that, he hadn't brought one when he'd left Maryland.

"Would I wear anyone else's jersey?"

"Nah. You're smarter than that. You know I'd rip that shit right off you."

Taylor pushed at his shoulder.

He grabbed her around her middle, lifted her, then turned and fell backwards on the bed.

She wiggled away and loomed over him. "Wait," she said, laughing. "I'm not just wearing this because I was banking on you having a fantasy about it. I had an idea."

The joy drained from his face and heart. "Why do I not like the sound of that?"

"Remember you wanted to do a video with me as your way of signing off?" she asked.

"Yeah…"

"I want to do it."

He brushed his thumb over her bottom lip. "You do?"

She rose from the bed. "I have a tiny tweak to make, though."

He boosted himself up onto his elbows.

Taylor tugged on the jersey. "I'll be wearing this."

He laughed. "Stop fucking with me."

"I'm serious. Show everybody that I'm yours."

He sat the rest of the way up and shook his head. "I don't need to do that." Making Taylor uncomfortable just so he could fuel his ego was not it. It was never going to be it. She was always going to come first, just like she always had.

Taylor swayed on her feet. "But do you want to?"

"Well, yeah." He wasn't going to lie. Yes, he absolutely wanted the world to know she was his and he couldn't think of a better way than her wearing a jersey with his name on it.

"Everyone will be expecting something sexy from you, and I'm fine with that, but if you show them your abs, it's going to be with my hands on them."

"People at home are going to talk when they see it. You didn't want those boudoir—"

"Without my consent! Would I post daily videos of myself in lingerie? No. But just because I don't want some douche bag releasing my private photos against my wishes, doesn't mean I'm a prude. So, set up your camera and lights and whatever."

He'd only brought his equipment because he'd planned to post one last video while he was here, signing off. Not without his shirt. Just him, fully clothed, thanking his fans and asking for his privacy to be respected going forward. He'd planned to post it before he left for the weekend so that when he'd gotten home, it'd be one less thing causing trouble between him and Taylor.

While he set up, she gave Cal attention, and once he was ready, they shut him out of the room. He did not need to see what Nick was going to do to his mom. It was for his own good.

"You're the director, so how are we doing this?" he asked.

"Sit on the end of the bed."

He adjusted the tripod, so the camera was aimed at the bed, then sat.

"Take your shirt off."

"Yes, ma'am." He pulled it over his head and dropped it on the floor. "Now what?"

"Just stay there." She went over to a bag that was on top of his dresser and pulled out a baseball. Then she stood behind the camera and tossed it to him.

He caught it, glanced at it, then back at her.

Taylor unbuttoned the jersey and walked forward, putting her hands on his shoulders and straddling him.

Nick put his hands on her lower back and stared at her as she shrugged the jersey off her shoulders, revealing a lacy red bra. The camera only got a view of the top half of her back, as she kept the sleeves of the jersey bunched at her elbows. His view was far nicer. Her matching panties weren't going to last long.

She leaned in and pressed her mouth to his.

Nick cupped the back of her neck, keeping her close, kissing her with all the pent-up longing he'd acquired over the past twenty-four hours. He laid back, taking her with him.

He kissed her until she started to rub herself against him. "Let me turn the camera off."

She whined. "Can't you just edit this part out later?"

His eyes widened and all he could do was nod. He hoped she didn't think editing meant that he'd be deleting the parts they didn't want anyone else to see. At least not before he'd watched it a few times.

She grinned and smashed her mouth to his.

Before they got too far, he had a question. He broke their kiss and looked her in the eye. "You gonna marry me, or what?"

For a second, something flashed in her eyes that he prayed wasn't her shutting down. Then, she nodded, and his heart started beating again.

Taylor grinned. "We *do* have a standing invitation to visit Las Vegas."

Epilogue
Taylor

"Do not come at me with that 'we're not going on a thirty-day voyage' bullshit." Taylor glared and shook her finger at Nick. "It's a sixteen-day voyage, most of which will be spent in the middle of the ocean with no access to anything, so I'm going to prepare for every eventuality and you're not going to give me a hard time about it."

He continued his perusal of the numerous items she'd laid across her bed. "Babe. You don't think Drew and Logan have a first-aid kit?" He picked up a clear bag filled with various charging cords. "What are you bringing that you need to charge besides your phone? Does it go *buzz buzz*?"

She shrugged. As it turned out, they had a lot of fun testing out the various offerings she had in her special closet. They'd developed a ratings system, and if a sex-cessory earned four to five stars, she'd make sure to keep it in stock. "Maybe."

"What about the other cords? There's got to be at least ten in here."

Nick had finished school over a month ago but celebrating had to be postponed due to the busy holiday season. He'd insisted that his graduation present be, at minimum, a week with Out of Town Taylor.

Somehow, Drew had talked her into a trip to Antigua for a poker tournament Logan was in. But they weren't flying. They were going to sail on their luxury yacht. It'd be a six-day trip just to get there.

Before she had a chance to defend her need for so many cords, he set them down and picked up a container of antibacterial surface wipes.

"What are you going to do? Clean their boat for them?"

"No." She snatched the container from him and put it back where it had been. "I probably won't need them, but it's just in case."

"In case of what?"

She put her hands on her hips. "Will you leave me alone?"

He laughed. "Not a fucking chance."

"This is who I am, Nick. You either accept that, and love me anyway, or go on this trip by yourself." Was she strung out? Yes. No question. She'd be strung out until their plane landed in Savannah. Realistically, she'd be even more strung out while in the air because being tens of thousands of feet off the ground freaked her the fuck out. But once they got there safely, she was kicking herself into vacation mode.

His breath was warm against the back of her neck as he stood behind her and splayed his hand under her breasts. "You're doubting whether I love you or not?"

"No, but you're annoying me." She shrugged him off and went back to organizing toiletries. "Let me pack in peace, without judgment."

He grabbed the back of her sweater, fisting it as he pulled her away from the bed and turned her to face him. "Got five minutes? I want to show you something, and then I'll leave you alone."

While she was hyperfocused on packing? Her shoulders fell. "What do you want to show me?"

"I taught Cal a new trick."

"And you want to show it to me right now? Seriously?"

"Yep. Right now." He grabbed her hand and tugged her from the bedroom to the living room. He used his cane a little less these days, thanks to physical therapy and respecting his own limitations.

Standing behind her, with his hands on her shoulders, he positioned her to stand next to the couch, facing the kitchen. He whistled.

Cal appeared and parked himself several feet away, waiting, his tail wagging.

"Okay, watch this." Still behind her, he tossed a baseball to Cal.

He caught it in his mouth, then carried it over to Taylor.

She glanced over her shoulder. "Nick, that's not a new trick."

Cal bumped his head against her thigh.

She tugged the ball from his mouth, knowing he'd keep nudging her until she took it.

When she turned to Nick, he was down on his good knee, holding out a sparkly ring between his thumb and finger.

Her heart slammed in her chest. She'd agreed to marry him months ago, but he'd continued to refer to her as his girlfriend and there'd been no talk of a wedding. Which was fine with her because she didn't want to plan one. Coordinating weddings at the inn made dreaming about her own less appealing.

Nick's gaze dropped to her hand and then slowly lifted to her face.

She glanced at the ball, noticing embossed letters. She turned it around until she could read them. *You gonna marry me, or what?*

A laugh burst from her lips.

"More specifically, will you marry me in eight days?" he asked.

Her laughter stopped and she locked gazes with him, eyes wide. "What?"

"Let's elope. Logan said the captain can do it right there on the boat, and Drew said she can help with the dress. Food, flowers—it's all taken care of. All you gotta do is say yes."

Her throat was too tight to speak, so she stood there, blinking at him, then grabbed his biceps and tugged, urging him to stand.

He straightened until he was staring down at her. "If that's not what you want, it's okay. You can still have the ring and we'll have whatever kind of wedding you want. We can do Vegas, like we talked about. I just thought this would be more romantic. Or, if you want to take a year and plan a big wedding, I'm cool with that too."

Her gaze went to the ring still pinched between his fingers. She took it from him and studied it. It was freaking gorgeous. It was a round cut diamond in a rose gold setting with intricate details, like vines weaving around it, tiny diamonds inlaid in half of them.

She'd thought maybe Nick would give her a ring on the trip. The beach seemed one of the more popular places for a proposal, but she'd refused to have expectations. Setting herself up for disappointment if she came back from their trip without a ring on her finger would not be wise.

Finally, she found her voice. "I packed for a regular vacation, not a honeymoon. I'm going to have to start all over."

Nick wrapped his hand around the back of her neck and pressed his lips to hers. He kissed her until she put her hand under his T-shirt and stroked his abs. "Can I put that damn ring on your finger now?"

She nodded. Once it was on, she turned her hand, the diamond sparkling in the light. "You did good."

A strangled croak came from his throat. "My mom picked it out. She said the one I liked was too gaudy once the wedding band was next to it."

Her smile grew wider, and she pressed her lips together to keep from calling him a mama's boy. She loved him even more for taking his mom ring shopping. It'd probably meant the world to her.

"Did you get bands?" she asked, mentally going through the list of all the things they'd need for a wedding, even if it was an elopement.

"Yes. Also, you might not like this part, but it's not gonna be legal. I couldn't apply for a marriage license without you present, and it takes weeks, so we'll have to go through that process when we get back."

She smiled and leaned up on her toes to place a soft kiss on his lips. "I don't care when we get it rubberstamped. All that matters is us promising to belong to each other forever."

He cupped her jaw and brushed his mouth over hers. "We've always belonged to each other, Tay."

Aubrey

Aubrey carried a box with a cake in one hand and an enormous brown paper bag holding fresh cut flowers while Drew walked alongside him to the tenor boat, her arms filled with all kinds of crazy stuff she'd insisted on buying for her friends' wedding. He'd had no idea when he'd accepted her invitation to come on this trip that he'd be an assistant wedding planner and errand boy, but it was all good.

Spending time with his sister when she wasn't in work-obsessed mode was one of his favorite things to do, especially now that it happened less and less frequently. That was totally his fault, not hers. He got obsessive with his own work and spent more time away from home than she did. Fieldwork fascinated him enough that he could put up with the unstable nature of being an anthropological archaeologist. Discovering artifacts was cool and all, but using them to paint a picture of how the people they belonged to lived was riveting.

"You wanna go with me to Antigua's first sugar plantation tomorrow morning?" he asked as they got on the tenor boat and settled in. "I wanna see the windmill ruins and check out the museum."

"How early are we talking?" Drew put a hand on top of her big floppy sunhat to keep it from blowing off as the tenor captain steered the boat away from the pier. His sister would rather stay up past midnight working than drag her ass out of bed before eight.

"Not that early. Definitely not before your second cup of coffee." He smirked at her. Drew was sassy, and he loved that about her, but before her daily dose of caffeine, she was a big-time grouch.

She wore dark sunglasses, but he was sure she was giving him a death glare. "If Logan will let me out of bed, sure, I'll go." She returned his smirk.

He scrunched his face. For the next several minutes, he took in the beauty of the blue water surrounding them, trying to erase the ick of being reminded that his little sister had sex.

Once they were back on The Splurge, he helped with what he could to set up for the ceremony, then grabbed a book and found a comfortable spot on the flybridge.

Two chapters in, Logan joined him and flopped onto the captain's chair. "Your sister is fucked up."

Aubrey snorted. "She hurt your feelings again?"

"No." He pulled out a cigarette and held the pack out in Aubrey's direction.

He shook his head. Five whole weeks without a cigarette. He wasn't going to blow it now.

Logan lit up, then puffed out a cloud of smoke. "She won't set a fucking date to marry me, but she'll plan a destination wedding for another couple. What kind of fucked up shit is that?"

Lot of fucks to weed through in that...*accusation?* He didn't know what it was, but clearly, Logan needed to talk, and Aubrey was the only one available to play therapist. He set his book to the side and rubbed his cheek. "You live together. She wears your ring. There's no one else for her and you know it. What's the rush?"

Drew was as crazy about Logan as he was her. Their relationship was madness most of the time, not that he'd ever admit that out loud.

"I don't know," he muttered. "It just bothers me that she's this excited for someone else's wedding but if I bring up ours, she changes the subject."

"Tell her that, then."

He stared at the ash on his cigarette. "She'll be mean to me if I do."

Aubrey snorted.

Logan liked getting bullied by Drew. Which was whatever. As long as he treated her right, Aubrey stayed out of it.

"You'll probably get married before we do." Logan shot him a grin.

He held his hands out. "I'm not even seeing anyone."

And he damn sure wasn't going to start within the next year. When they got back from the trip, he was headed to Europe to prove the theory he'd based his doctoral thesis on. Modern archaeology widely accepted that in the 9th century, there had been a civilization south of the country of Alreyn, known as the Halori, but a century later, the people had assimilated into northern society. Aubrey's expertise in anthropology led him to the belief that the Halori had been allies with another society, but he hadn't been able to pinpoint their regionality. He couldn't ignore the evidence that prior to assimilation, the Halori had been adopting customs and technology from another culture, far different from that of the Alreynians, or even their own.

Now, he just had to prove that culture existed so everyone in his field didn't think he was a total idiot. He really didn't want to end up doing something mind-numbing like inventorying artifacts or even worse, giving lectures.

So, the single life it was. For the foreseeable future. He was fine with that. The last woman he'd gotten involved with was batshit crazy. It'd put such a bad taste in his mouth, if a woman showed interest in him, he immediately became suspicious.

"You know, I've heard they have women in Europe," Logan said.

He groaned and seriously reconsidered bumming a smoke. "I can't afford to get distracted."

"Drew said that same shit when we met." Logan stretched out his legs and waggled his eyebrows. "But I distracted the hell out of her."

"That's my fucking sister, dude. Cut that shit out, or I'll throw you off your own damn boat into the Caribbean Sea."

He chuckled. "Look, eventually, a woman is going to come into your life and regardless of where you're at with your career, you're going to get so twisted up over her, you'll do whatever you have to do to make it work. And I'll be honest, I hope she wrecks you."

SUPPORT AN INDIE AUTHOR

If you enjoyed this book, please review it and tell your friends about it. By doing so, you'll be helping me spread the word, which means I can spend less time marketing and more time writing.

Sign up for my mailing list:
https://www.marycainbooks.com